In the Language of Love

In the Language of Love

A Novel in 100 Chapters

Diane Schoemperlen

VIKING

VIKING
Published by the Penguin Group
Penguin Books USA Inc., 375 Hudson Street,
New York, New York 10014, U.S.A.
Penguin Books Ltd, 27 Wrights Lane,
London W8 5TZ, England
Penguin Books Australia Ltd, Ringwood,
Victoria, Australia
Penguin Books Canada Ltd, 10 Alcorn Avenue,
Toronto, Ontario, Canada M4V 3B2
Penguin Books (N.Z.) Ltd, 182–190 Wairau Road,
Auckland 10, New Zealand

Penguin Books Ltd, Registered Offices:
Harmondsworth, Middlesex, England

First American edition
Published in 1996 by Viking Penguin,
a division of Penguin Books USA Inc.

1 3 5 7 9 10 8 6 4 2

Pages 357–58 constitute an extension of this copyright page.

LIBRARY OF CONGRESS CATALOGING IN PUBLICATION DATA
Schoemperlen, Diane.
In the language of love: a novel in 100 chapters / Diane Schoemperlen.
p. cm.
ISBN 0-670-86517-6
I. Title.
PR9199.3.S267I5   1996
813'.54—dc20   95-35098

This book is printed on acid-free paper.
∞

Printed in the United States of America
Set in Garamond #3

For Carla Douglas, my friend

Contents

1. TABLE • 1
2. DARK • 11
3. MUSIC • 13
4. SICKNESS • 18
5. MAN • 25
6. DEEP • 26
7. SOFT • 35
8. EATING • 36
9. MOUNTAIN • 46
10. HOUSE • 53
11. BLACK • 65
12. MUTTON • 65
13. COMFORT • 67
14. HAND • 73
15. SHORT • 79
16. FRUIT • 83
17. BUTTERFLY • 89
18. SMOOTH • 91
19. COMMAND • 96
20. CHAIR • 98
21. SWEET • 101
22. WHISTLE • 103
23. WOMAN • 105
24. COLD • 106
25. SLOW • 118
26. WISH • 122
27. RIVER • 123
28. WHITE • 124
29. BEAUTIFUL • 126
30. WINDOW • 128
31. ROUGH • 136
32. CITIZEN • 139
33. FOOT • 147
34. SPIDER • 150
35. NEEDLE • 151
36. RED • 154
37. SLEEP • 155
38. ANGER • 161
39. CARPET • 163
40. GIRL • 164
41. HIGH • 165
42. WORKING • 167
43. SOUR • 169
44. EARTH • 171
45. TROUBLE • 172
46. SOLDIER • 181
47. CABBAGE • 186
48. HARD • 188
49. EAGLE • 189
50. STOMACH • 193
51. STEM • 202
52. LAMP • 204

53. DREAM • 207

54. YELLOW • 209

55. BREAD • 210

56. JUSTICE • 213

57. BOY • 214

58. LIGHT • 214

59. HEALTH • 217

60. BIBLE • 222

61. MEMORY • 225

62. SHEEP • 227

63. BATH • 230

64. COTTAGE • 234

65. SWIFT • 238

66. BLUE • 239

67. HUNGRY • 240

68. PRIEST • 241

69. OCEAN • 246

70. HEAD • 247

71. STOVE • 248

72. LONG • 254

73. RELIGION • 258

74. WHISKY • 270

75. CHILD • 272

76. BITTER • 272

77. HAMMER • 277

78. THIRSTY • 278

79. CITY • 280

80. SQUARE • 283

81. BUTTER • 287

82. DOCTOR • 289

83. LOUD • 293

84. THIEF • 301

85. LION • 305

86. JOY • 306

87. BED • 309

88. HEAVY • 312

89. TOBACCO • 316

90. BABY • 317

91. MOON • 321

92. SCISSORS • 324

93. QUIET • 330

94. GREEN • 337

95. SALT • 338

96. STREET • 341

97. KING • 343

98. CHEESE • 345

99. BLOSSOM • 349

100. AFRAID • 353

ACKNOWLEDGMENTS • 357

In the Language of Love

1. Table

THE MOTHER SLAPPED the plates down on the table in that way all angry mothers do. The father, folding up his newspaper, pretended not to notice. Or maybe he didn't notice. Maybe he was too busy thinking about other things. About a story he'd just read in the paper about a man who'd murdered his wife and her lover in Toronto (that evil city), and in the photograph the man was being led from the courtroom with a black coat over his head. About the pretty woman in the corner store who had flirted with him when he stopped to buy a treat for his daughter on the way home from work. Maybe he was thinking about fixing himself another whisky and Coke.

Or maybe he did notice and just thought all women were like that: furious. Maybe his friends' wives were like that too. Maybe that was what the men talked about in the lunchroom at the paper mill while eating the sandwiches their wives had slapped together the night before. Maybe that was what they laughed about while carefully smoothing and refolding the sheets of wax paper and the little brown bags, returning them to their black lunch pails because if they didn't, there'd be hell to pay at home.

The daughter picked at the foam rubber backing on the yellow plastic placemat and studied the plate plopped in front of her. It was plaid, of all things, brown-and-white plaid. The daughter was mortified. She thought she would die, just *die*, if she had to eat one more meal off these plates at this table with these people.

The table was blue arborite, speckled with white-and-gold flecks, and it had splayed chrome tubular legs and ridged silver edges. Crumbs and grease had collected between the arborite and the silver rim. The table pulled apart in the middle where an extension could be inserted for special occasions.

The father, Clarence, dished out the potatoes and the peas. The mother, Esther, slapped a pork chop on each plaid plate. The daughter, Joanna, clenched her teeth and looked at the pork chop on the plaid plate on the yellow placemat on the blue table and thought, as do all people past the age of twelve, how much happier she'd been when she was younger. It was 1967 and she had just turned thirteen three weeks before.

She remembered a rainy Saturday when she was six or seven and had spent the whole afternoon beneath this kitchen table, drawing on its underside with her new crayons. Her mother was cooking pork hocks in the big silver pot and she let Joanna colour to her heart's content and she wasn't even mad. Her father was building bookshelves in her bedroom and the circular saw was singing. The whole house was filled with the humid fragrances of boiling meat and cut wood. When Clarence came into the kitchen, there were curls of blond wood tangled in his dark hair like ringlets.

Before that she was even happier. There was the story her mother loved to tell of how Joanna would haul the cookbook drawer out from under her bed (no one ever questioned the rationale of keeping the cookbooks in an old dresser drawer under the little girl's bed) and make up wild and fantastic stories from them. She could not remember but could clearly imagine herself sitting cross-legged on the kitchen floor with a cookbook open in her lap and her mother at the table rolling sweet dough and stamping out cookies with the special silver cutters, and Joanna saying, "Once upon a time, there was a beautiful mommy," and Esther laughing and laughing with flour on her nose and white sugar in her wavy black hair. When she sat down on the floor and

TABLE 3

kissed the little girl's cheek, her hair fell around them like a fragrant curtain.

Joanna's favourite cookbook had been the one with the line drawings of different animals. They said: BEEF, VEAL, PORK. They did not say: COW, CALF, PIG. Only the LAMB was called by its real name. She knew about Mary and her little lamb, whose fleece was white as snow. She knew about March, which if it came in like a lion, would then go out like a lamb. She did not know yet about sacrifice.

Each drawing was carefully divided into sections labelled in capital letters: CHUCK, RIB, RUMP, LOIN, BRISKET, FATBACK, PICNIC SHOULDER. Only the PORK still had its head, tail, and feet on. The others had stumps instead.

Joanna carefully coloured these diagrams in startling Crayola colours: yellow, red, blue, purple, the LAMB with a turquoise leg, the BEEF with a kelly green rump. It never occurred to her that this was how the animals were butchered. She was so innocent, no wonder she was happier then.

This was like last summer when her father took her to the rodeo. The Nystrom twins, Penny and Pamela, from across the street came too. Penny and Pamela were a year older than Joanna but they walked to school (it was only three blocks) and played with her anyway. They all sat high up on the wooden bleachers, and when the broncos came out bucking Joanna leapt up and cheered, waving her pink cotton candy in the air. One after another, the wild horses flung the riders off their backs as if they were flicking off flies. Joanna cheered them on hysterically. She wanted the horses to win, to be free, to run right out of that dirty corral and be gone forever back to their sweet green fields far off in the hills.

"They're wonderful!" she cried. "Strong, brave, beautiful!" She was sure their spirits would never be broken by these silly men in cowboy hats and fringed pants. The rodeo cowboys looked no more dangerous than Penny and Pamela's little brother, Billy, dressed up last year for Hallowe'en in red-and-black chaps with a white vinyl fringe, a red bandanna over his mouth, and two silver pop guns jammed in his father's belt wrapped twice around his skinny waist.

Penny and Pamela hooted and slapped their scabby knees. Their cousin, Louvaine, was married to a real rodeo cowboy, so they knew better. They couldn't wait to set Joanna straight. They couldn't wait to tell her that the only reason the broncos bucked like that was because they were tied up.

"Their bums," Penny said. "Their bums are tied up."

"Not their bums, silly," Pamela said scornfully. "Their balls. Their balls are tied up with a leather strap. It's their balls. That's why they buck."

When they got home, Joanna threw away all the pictures of horses she'd been saving that summer in a scrapbook the size of the *Eaton's Catalogue*. She ripped them out and shoved them in the kitchen garbage pail where soggy lettuce, greasy bones and cold wet coffee grounds would get all over them and serve them right.

She spent the rest of the weekend filling up the scrapbook again. She went through every single catalogue and magazine in the foot-high pile in the bottom of her father's closet. She chose pictures of fine ladies in fancy clothes and sparkling jewellery, of elaborate rose gardens with fountains and fish ponds. To these gardens she added even more flowers, clipped from old seed catalogues. She did two whole pages of flowers, especially the blue ones because blue was her favourite colour.

She cut out pictures of elegant parlours filled with massive mahogany furniture and plush Persian carpets, glittering dinner tables set with acres of crystal, bone china, and pristine linen. These table settings fascinated her with their inexplicable silverware (what did these people eat that they needed so many forks?), fragile fluted glasses, linen napkins held in silver rings or folded into miraculous shapes like origami birds. Above these tables there were always chandeliers shedding splintered light from miniature prisms all around the room.

Penny and Pamela had scrapbooks too but theirs were all full of the Queen waving with white gloves from open black cars, sitting around in rooms like museums, looking bored or superior, patting her Corgi dogs. The twins were fascinated by all aspects of royalty and gossiped about them as if they were people they really knew, just the way Esther talked about the characters in her favourite soap opera.

Now Esther and Clarence were stuffing their mouths, making mean-

TABLE 5

ingless dinnertime talk, and Joanna was miserably chewing on a piece of pork chop, chewing and chewing until it was a pulpy chunk of dead white flesh in her throat.

Perhaps she had never been happy. Maybe she had been no happier when she was younger than she was now, no happier than she would ever be. She thought of how her mother always made her rip up the bread for the turkey dressing on Christmas, Easter, and Thanksgiving. Esther would cover the kitchen table with yesterday's newspaper and bring out the huge silver mixing bowl and bags half-full of stale white bread. Then Joanna would perch on the edge of the table and shred the bread into the bowl while Esther complained the whole time that the chunks were too big, the chunks were too small, she was getting crumbs all over the floor, she wasn't making enough, she was making too much, how big did she think that bird was anyway? Then Esther would whisk the full bowl away, sprinkle it with lukewarm water and poultry seasoning, shove whole handfuls into the naked white bird so that her arm disappeared into its bum nearly up to the elbow. By the time the turkey was cooked, Esther was slapping down those plaid plates again, Clarence was asleep or half-drunk, and Joanna thought she would die, just *die*, if she had to eat one more Christmas, Easter, or Thanksgiving dinner off these plates at this table with these people.

After the turkey there would be pumpkin pie for dessert, a frozen pie crust with canned filling, and Clarence never learned not to say that his mother's pumpkin pie was better than this. Esther, despite the cookbooks under the bed, was not much of a cook.

Tonight there would be vanilla ice cream and canned pears for dessert. Joanna remembered how she used to be allowed to pour a little hot tea over her ice cream and then muck around with it until her bowl was filled with a luscious sweet goop which she spooned carefully into her mouth, and sometimes they would even let her have a second bowl. Of course she was too old for such foolishness now.

Tonight her mother admitted that the pork chops were dry, the mashed potatoes were lumpy, the peas were mushy, and the cucumbers in vinegar and salt were already giving her gas. Clarence agreed with everything she said. He nodded and burped.

Esther leapt up and began slamming the dirty dishes into the sink while Clarence ambled towards the living room. (Esther and Clarence called the living room "the front room." They also said "chesterfield" instead of "couch." Joanna was embarrassed. They sounded like farmers or foreigners.) Clarence would sit in there all evening, doing the newspaper crossword puzzle and the cryptogram. Or else he would work on his paint-by-number sets. He did horse heads, seascapes, forest scenes, and gulls in flight. Once he did a pair of nudes: two brown-haired women with nipples the same colour as their hair, smiling lips the same colour as their toenails, each of them holding a blue towel draped carefully to cover their private parts. Esther made Clarence hang the nudes in the garage.

In the kitchen, Joanna dried the dishes and convinced herself that if she had to eat one more meal in this house at this table with these people, she would never grow up and get free. It never occurred to her to ask Esther what she was always so mad about.

After a while, of course, Joanna did grow up. She finished high school, went to university, and then moved to a larger city when she was twenty-two. This was not a common thing to do in their town, at least not in their neighbourhood. Even Penny and Pamela, who had always seemed likely to become renegades, had stayed, marrying young, having babies, coming to their parents' house for Sunday dinner every week with their arms full of diapers, baby bottles, and stuffed toys. Their husbands stood around in the driveway smoking and talking to their father-in-law, all of the men shuffling their feet in the gravel and pushing their baseball caps back in the sun. Penny and Pamela went to Tupperware parties, sold Avon, did their Christmas shopping early, and always saved the used wrapping paper from one year to the next. They named their children alliteratively.

In her house across the street, Joanna sat reading her university textbooks, envying or pitying them.

When she did move away from home, her reasons for leaving were flimsy enough, something about there being more opportunities for artists elsewhere. Joanna did not know this for sure, but she could not

TABLE 7

imagine being an artist in her hometown. She had expected indignant opposition, especially from her mother, but Esther only said, "I hope you know what you're doing." Joanna did not. Clarence said, "You can always come home again if it doesn't work out." Joanna agreed but knew she would not.

Once settled in her new apartment, Joanna worked at a variety of jobs to support her artistic habit. She worked briefly (always briefly) as a secretary, a convenience store clerk, a bank teller, a chambermaid, and assistant manager of a small art gallery which promptly went bankrupt. She also applied for grants and sometimes got them.

When she could afford it, she ate in restaurants and cafés. Mostly she ate alone, admiring the heavy white plates, the pastel linen napkins folded to fit inside the long-stemmed wineglasses, the freshly cut daisies or the flickering candle in the center of the table, the music, the waitress, the menu, the delicious unusual meals that appeared before her as if by magic, without effort, anxiety, or anger. Sipping her dry white wine slowly, she read or watched the other patrons eat, chat, hold hands, or argue. She lapped up the soup and the sounds around her which appeased her loneliness without intruding upon her life. Lingering over her coffee and Grand Marnier she dreamed of a perfect future life in which she would never have to cook or wash dishes again.

Later she learned to cook and loved it. She bought pots and pans, wire whisks and wooden spoons, many cookbooks and a special shelf to put them on. She bought a kitchen table at a garage sale just like the one they had at home except it was white and the extension was missing. She covered it with a peacock blue Indian cotton tablecloth and learned to ignore its tubular legs. She bought a copy of *Larousse Gastronomique*, which cost more than the table and cloth combined.

None of them liked to travel much so visits were infrequent. They were all still in Ontario, Esther and Clarence in the northwest corner of the province, Joanna now in the southeast, but they were fifteen hundred kilometres apart. Every couple of years her parents came down for two weeks in the summer or at Christmas. Joanna never went there and nobody ever suggested it. They stayed, the three of them, in Joanna's small basement apartment and worked hard at being pleasant and polite. But there was always something, and Esther always ended up angry and Clarence, watching TV half-asleep in the darkened living room, never seemed to notice until Esther went slamming out of the apartment and sat crying in the car in the driveway in the rain. Then Clarence would blink his bleary eyes and say, "Now what's the matter with *her*, do you think?" But it was a rhetorical question and still nobody ever asked Esther why she was always so mad. Maybe all mothers were like that—furious.

The summer Joanna first started seeing Henry, Esther hated him on sight and landed crying in the car on the second day of the visit. This despite the fact that Henry had put all his stuff in two green garbage bags and gone to stay at a friend's place to delay having to break the news that he and Joanna were living together. Esther and Clarence were supposed to be staying for two weeks but Esther insisted they leave after one. That morning, while Esther repacked their suitcases, Clarence held his hands out in the kitchen, helpless, and said, "I'm sorry, honey. I like him all right but what can I do? You know your mother when she gets mad."

The next time Clarence and Esther came to visit, it was Christmas. Joanna was seeing a man named Lewis, but he was married, gone away for the holidays with his wife. Nobody mentioned the hasty whispered calls at all hours, the way Joanna lunged at the telephone whenever it rang, the mysterious presents under the tree from this man who never materialized, three beribboned boxes which turned out to be a book, a tape, and a black lace camisole.

Shortly after this, Esther died, suddenly, of a heart attack.

After that, Clarence came to visit more often, arriving at least once a year, usually at Christmas, always looking surprised when he got off the plane and walked into the terminal where Joanna hugged him hard and he smelled like dry cleaning. Maybe he was surprised that he'd made it from his airport to hers. He still didn't like travelling, had no faith in flight, but he didn't want to drive all that way by himself, he got motion sickness on buses, and the train took too long. Or maybe he was still surprised that Esther had died on him. Just up and died

TABLE 9

on him, right when, as Esther had once told Joanna on the phone, they seemed to be falling in love all over again. Or maybe it was Joanna who surprised him by having grown up when he wasn't looking.

During these visits, Joanna realized that one of the great pleasures of living alone was being able to go into the kitchen at ten o'clock at night to make a salami-green-pepper-and-mozzarella sandwich without having to say, "I'm going to make myself a salami-green-pepper-and-mozzarella sandwich—would you like one?" Wanting the second night of her father's visit to fix herself a plate of cheese and crackers and garlic sausage, Joanna discovered that she was seething with resentment, thinking that she really *should* ask him if he wanted some too, wishing she was the kind of assertive independent person who could just get up and do it without either asking or feeling guilty about not asking. (Of course, she would be gracious enough to offer him some once she'd fixed it and gone back into the living room where he was watching *Miracle on 34th Street*, and he would see that there was really only enough on the plate for one and say, with just as much grace, "Oh, no thanks, I'm fine.") Feeling so invaded and defeated by the whole thing that she couldn't be bothered getting up to fix the snack anyway, she said instead, "I'm going to get a beer—would you like one?" and was just as angry when he said, "No thanks, dear," as she would have been if he'd said yes please.

Joanna no longer wondered what her mother had always been so mad about. Now she wondered why she'd never exploded. Just as she no longer asked her divorced friends why they'd left their husbands. Now, after listening to their stories, she asked, "Why did you stay so long?"

The next time Clarence comes to visit, Joanna is going out with Gordon. Clarence appears to like Gordon, although it's hard to tell. Clarence talks to him about baseball, cars, hunting, fishing, and poker. Gordon has no interest in any of these things. He thinks baseball is boring, cars are perhaps necessary but not worth worrying about until they break down, hunting and fishing are blood sports, and he is no good at cards. But Gordon is a good listener and Clarence doesn't seem to notice the one-sided nature of these manly conversations. Gordon comes over for supper nearly every night. He sits at the kitchen table peeling potatoes, chopping onions, or slicing mushrooms, nodding and smiling while Clarence chats on about calibres, carburetors, RBIs, and the astronomical odds against drawing four aces two hands in a row.

Joanna hopes her father will appreciate her new culinary skills. She tramps all over town in the heat, ferreting out the firmest vegetables, the prettiest fruit, the most tender cuts of meat, and the freshest home-made pasta. She feeds him cleverly constructed gourmet meals with carefully co-ordinated (occasionally flaming) desserts. She tries to explain that creating the perfect meal is like creating a work of art. He just looks at her. She changes tactics. She tries to explain that it is like doing a puzzle: if you put all the best ingredients together in the right proportions in the right order, if you follow the instructions to the letter, then what you end up with is truly an achievement, a masterpiece maybe, certainly a creation which is more than the sum of its parts, a domestic synergy. Clarence just looks down at his still-empty plate, as if wondering what the hell is taking so long. She does not explain to him that she has lately come to see all this cooking as a sensual and meaningful expression not only of her creativity but of her sexuality as well.

Clarence obligingly eats everything she puts in front of him (except for the Tofu Stroganoff—he has a peanut butter and jelly sandwich instead) and he never says a word either way. Joanna realizes that he would be just as happy with fried Spam and Minute Rice as he is with her Spinach and Feta Cheese Quiche with Veal Piccata and Cucumbers in Sour Cream. She refrains from pointing this out to him, but the next night they order pizza.

After the dishes are done and Clarence is settled on the couch with the newspaper crossword and the TV on, Joanna and Gordon often go out for the evening. Sometimes they go to a movie, sometimes downtown for drinks or dessert. Usually they go to Gordon's place and make love because Joanna has warned him long before Clarence's arrival that she will be completely incapable of having sex under the same roof as her father.

Afterwards they go walking through the hot streets, smelling of sex, nodding amiably at strolling strangers, stealing pansies from the beds in Patterson Park and giggling. One night they stop in the park and make love again in the cool grass beneath a large elm tree with the traffic noises all around them, and Joanna is so excited that she comes even before Gordon has pulled down her underwear.

Back at her apartment she finds her father at the kitchen table with the pieces of her broken fan spread all around, a screwdriver in one hand and the instructions in the other. He waves and says, "Just thought I'd make myself useful," as she backs down the hallway into her bedroom so he won't see the green and white stains all down the back of her dress.

After Gordon and Joanna are married and their son Samuel has been born, Clarence is more than happy to babysit when he comes to visit them in their big house on Laverty Street. Sometimes they go to a movie, sometimes downtown for drinks or dessert. Most often they just go walking through the quiet neighbourhood. One night they stop to pick pansies in the park and without a word Gordon leads Joanna to the big elm tree and they lie down on the cool grass. Joanna pulls her summer skirt up around her waist and her thighs are white in the darkness. Gordon comes when she puts her hand on his belt buckle.

When they get home, they find Clarence sitting in the kitchen in the dark with Samuel sleeping in his arms and the baby bottle empty on the table. It is an antique oak drop-leaf table with smooth curved corners, carved legs, and six matching chairs with needlepoint seat covers: pictures of red roses, green leaves, graceful stems, no thorns.

Clarence looks up at them, surprised and shiny-eyed, as if he'd been expecting someone else.

2. Dark

JOANNA HAS ALWAYS been afraid of the dark.

dark *adj.* 1. *a)* partially or entirely without light, *b)* neither reflecting nor transmitting light. 2. *a)* nearly black, *b)* not light in colour; of a deep shade.

Esther said she was just being a big silly baby and would not let her
come into their bed on scary nights. Clarence said he understood but
there was nothing he could do. The dark was just one of those things
she had to get used to and when she grew up it wouldn't worry her
any more.

dark *adj.* 3. difficult to understand; obscure. 4. dismal; gloomy; som-
bre; hopeless. 5. angry or sullen.

Even now with Gordon in bed beside her she is sometimes frightened.
All noises seem to be amplified by the dark, as if having the lights on
muffled everything, filled up all the spaces where scary sounds lurked.
She tries to look bravely into the darkness and then closes her eyes to
get away from it. Of course this doesn't work.

dark *adj.* 6. sinister; wicked; evil. 7. unenlightened; ignorant. 8. rich
and deep, with a melancholy sound.

By way of consolation, Gordon tells her that he used to be afraid of
the dark too but he got over it. This does not help.

dark. *n.* 1. the state of being in darkness; the absence of light.
2. nightfall; night. 3. a dark shade or colour.

All of them have dark hair, including Samuel who is born with a full
head of black curls. Joanna remembers Esther singing her the nursery
rhyme: *There was a little girl/Who had a little curl/Right in the middle of
her forehead,/ And when she was good/She was very very good,/And when she
was bad/She was horrid!*

For the first two months of his life Samuel is one of those upside-
down babies who think night is day and day is night. Joanna learns
why sleep deprivation is an efficient form of torture.

The first time Samuel sleeps through the night, Joanna wakes at
7:00 A.M. and panics. She leaps out of bed and grabs his white wicker
bassinet beside the dresser. She and Gordon have agreed that Samuel

will sleep in their room for the first six months. The bassinet has wheels, and when Samuel sleeps during the day Joanna drags him from room to room with her so he won't die when she's not looking. Now she shakes the bassinet so hard that Samuel wakes up wailing.

Gordon smiles sleepily as Joanna brings the baby into their bed and puts him to her breast. Her long dark hair, which is always wild and comical in the morning, floats all around him and they doze together till the alarm clock rings.

3. Music

"NOW YOU'LL HAVE to face the music," Esther always said after learning about yet another of Joanna's transgressions. Major or minor, all crimes and sins, it seemed, must eventually be confronted with musical accompaniment.

Joanna imagined musicians lined up like a firing squad against a black horizon and she, not being musically inclined, was helpless before them. While she stood naked and trembling in the white sunlight, they tuned and aimed their instruments, blasting her to bits with a trumpet, a tuba, a saxophone, and a trapezoidal electric guitar. The notes rained down upon her like bullets and then the violinist finished her off, wielding his bow like a bayonet. The strains of a harp accompanied her to the afterlife.

There would be, she imagined, a different kind of music for each category of sin. Country-and-western laments for crimes of the heart, unrequited love for thy neighbour's wife, horse, or four-by-four. The sultry smoky piano blues for crimes of passion, marital infidelity, and all other consummated lusts. Rabid rock-and-roll for rebelliousness, vandalism, drug use, and petty theft. Cool watery jazz for crimes of detachment, lack of compassion, errors of omission. Classical music for lofty intellectual crimes, failure of integrity, betrayal of ideology, plagiarism, and pettiness. Opera would be reserved for the most heinous crimes: terrorism, international drug trafficking, child abduction and abuse, rape, and murder. Esther always said all that caterwauling sounded like someone being tortured.

In those high school days, Joanna loved the Rolling Stones, Led Zeppelin, Carole King, Janis Joplin, Three Dog Night. In the grip of adolescent angst she was sure that this music was the closest she would ever come to passion and its incumbent exquisite imperative pain. She endured the inevitable skirmishes with Esther over volume and frequency of play. As in: "If you play that song one more time, I'm going to scream!" As in: "Turn that damn thing down this minute or you're grounded for a month!"

Sometimes Joanna sat on the floor of her bedroom with her ear pressed to the speaker, listening to the same song ten times in a row, a little louder each time. Once Esther caught her with her mouth pressed to the speaker. She was trying to swallow the sound or something, trying to feel Mick Jagger's full lips on her own. Esther hollered over the music, "Now what the hell are you doing? Have you lost your mind?" Joanna resisted the impulse to remind her mother about facing the music.

In university she listened solely to female vocalists: Carly Simon, Maria Muldaur, Joni Mitchell, Helen Reddy. They were strong independent women, unabashedly sexual, wise, intense, and loving. They loved men, yes, but they also loved themselves. When she grew up, she was going to be a strong serious self-respecting self-sufficient woman too.

When Joanna moved away from home she took her record collection with her, even the ones she seldom listened to any more. Esther went to Jerome's, the music store downtown, and bought herself albums by Janis Joplin, Helen Reddy, Carole King, and also Rod Stewart. She told Joanna this in a letter. She wrote: *I missed your music after you left. So now I put them on when I do the housework. They make me feel better.*

Joanna tried to imagine her mother boogying through the house with the vacuum cleaner, Janis Joplin wailing over its roar. Or her mother down on her knees cleaning the oven, scrubbing at the gunk in the back corners while Carole King crooned all around her. The oven, with Esther's head in it, was full of toxic fumes and Carole's mellifluous lament. In her return letter Joanna said she thought it was great that Esther liked good music after all (*ha ha!*). She did not ask her mother what it was that she needed to feel better about.

Now that Joanna had no one to fight with about it, music was not a determining factor in her life. Like everyone, she had favourite songs and artists. She bought albums, but not excessively, and she never went to rock concerts because she didn't like crowds.

Henry played bass guitar with a local band, the Blue Notes. They rehearsed together two nights a week and, in between, Henry practised alone at home. He stood with his guitar in front of the stereo and played along to learn new songs. For one week straight he practised the first four lines of "Crossroads" from the old Cream album. He played it incessantly, lifting the needle with one finger, putting it down carefully back at the beginning. Until finally Joanna cried, "If you play that song one more time, I'm going to scream!" And then she did.

With Lewis she listened to sad slow ballads about love and all other subdivisions of damage people inflict upon themselves and each other. Their favourite was Leonard Cohen. They listened to him before, during, and after making love. Lewis had a lovely voice and sometimes he sang along, softly, wetly, into Joanna's ear while lying in her bed, stroking her thighs, massaging her back. Joanna also listened to Leonard Cohen alone and often crying after Lewis had gone home to his wife. Eventually she could not listen to Leonard Cohen at all.

Gordon listens almost exclusively to classical music. At first Joanna is embarrassed to admit that she knows nothing about it. Gordon assures her that he came to this knowledge through no fault of his own. His parents were both avid listeners and their house while he was growing up was always filled with symphonies, concertos, and arias. No caterwauling there. This is neither the first nor the last time that Joanna keenly envies him his upbringing. She knows this is a betrayal.

By way of consolation, he reminds her that he was the only child of intensely educated older parents: his mother, Millicent, wrote high school French textbooks and his father, Eugene, was professor of Medieval Studies at the university. While all the other normal boys his age were listening to Tina Turner and jerking off, he was appreciating Beethoven's Symphony No. 8 in F, Opus 93, studying declensions and conjugating highly irregular verbs. Now his parents have retired and moved out of the country, not to a trailer park in Florida, but to a villa in France. Mostly they leave Gordon and Joanna alone.

Gordon loves classical music and is happy, he says, to teach Joanna what he knows. She cannot read music. He says this is not necessary to appreciate the music. She can barely distinguish the sounds of the various instruments. She can pick out the piano well enough but the woodwinds and the strings are never clear to her ear. Thanks to Henry she can also identify the bass guitar, which is of course not useful in this instance. Gordon says she'll learn. He says learning to appreciate classical music is like learning to read French. All it takes is time, practice, and patience. Joanna remembers Esther saying that French was just like English, only backwards.

Joanna listens carefully to the music and to Gordon's detailed explanations of it. But soon enough she finds herself longing to listen without having also to appreciate or understand. She points out to Gordon that it is not necessary to understand the operation of the gasoline engine in order to drive a car safely and well. He says this is an illogical argument. He rolls his eyes and spouts off about the composition of Moussorgsky's *Pictures at an Exhibition.*

Eventually she does come to enjoy classical music. She listens to it while she is working in her studio and also while she is doing the housework. She likes this picture of herself: woman baking chocolate chip cookies to the sounds of Schumann's Symphony No.1, "Spring"; a serene slender woman in a clean kitchen, a pretty woman, but not flashy or overtly sexy, a woman who is obviously a mother, a happy mother, a good mother. She remembers Esther's apron, the one with the musical notes embroidered around the band and the bottom. She herself has drawn the line at aprons but still it is comforting to imagine herself in one. She is not barefoot and pregnant either. She is wearing fluffy pink slippers and suspects that Samuel, like herself and Gordon, is destined to be an only child.

But sometimes she gets restless. Sometimes she plays loud rock-and-roll all afternoon instead. She plays the old albums that used to be her favourites, rock-and-roll anthems of the past. She is repeatedly amazed to discover that she can still sing word for word the lyrics of songs she hasn't heard in fifteen years.

In the living room with the curtains closed she dances and sings at the top of her lungs. She thinks of this as her secret habit. She is careful to put the albums away afterwards, to turn the volume back down to a reasonable level. She does not go so far as to wipe away her finger-prints, but still, it is as if she were committing shameful crimes against the sanctity of marriage and motherhood. She does not imagine that good mothers are supposed to do such things. She remembers reading a letter to Ann Landers once—someone complaining about a woman who had several small children and liked to go dancing in discos—and Ann stated unequivocally that a mother of small children had no right to be found in a disco.

As a baby, Samuel is particularly fond of the Rolling Stones. When Joanna says, "Why don't we listen to Uncle Mick?" he grips the sides of his playpen in his blue bunny sleepers, swaying to the music, grin-ning and crowing and clapping his hands. But when he gets older he does not like the loud music any more. He cries and covers his ears. He will not clap or dance. He knows already, Joanna thinks, that it is dangerous somehow, that this mother dancing and singing all afternoon is out of control and up to no good.

Now she only listens to the old albums when he is at day care. She also listens alone to Bonnie Raitt, Tracy Chapman, Joan Armatrading, Patti Smith, Michelle Shocked: a new crop of female vocalists, strong, serious, loving, and wise like the others from an earlier time. But also more seductive, more political, not afraid to be straightforward, un-happy, and angry. Joanna no longer dances. Now she sits on the floor beside the stereo and listens carefully. This is the music she can un-derstand and appreciate. She sings along softly and sometimes she cries. After a while she doesn't play these songs any more. Of course nobody knows that she has stopped because nobody knew she was listening to them in the first place. After a while she listens only to classical music. After a while she understands and appreciates it.

4. Sickness

JOANNA HAD ALL the important childhood illnesses when she was in kindergarten. Esther said this was because she picked up germs from all those other unhealthy kids whose parents did not care enough to keep them home when they were sick.

In the fall there was chicken pox which drove Joanna repeatedly to hysteria with itchiness and left three permanent scars on her stomach, like the marks she imagined a bullet would leave on you: puckered, bloodless, white.

Just before Christmas there was German measles, which she thought had something to do with the war. She had nightmares about being hauled away to a prison camp by the Nazis because she had ugly red spots all over her face.

In February there was mumps, both sides of her neck hideously swollen and sore. She was still in bed for Valentine's Day. Esther made her put on her red flannelette nightie, propped her up with extra pillows, arranged all her stuffed animals around her, and handed her a pink heart-shaped box of chocolates. Then she took her picture, bulging glands, messy hair, puffy face and all. For some reason Esther especially liked this unattractive embarrassing picture. She kept it for years in a little silver frame on top of the TV.

At Easter there was red measles which was much more serious and scary than the others. Joanna had to stay in bed for a whole week in the dark because, Esther said, the disease made your eyes sensitive to strong light. "You don't want to go blind, do you?" Esther warned when Joanna whined.

Joanna did not go blind but she did get delirious with a fever of 104°F. Esther was afraid she would go into convulsions. This was in the days when doctors still made house calls. When Dr. Graham arrived in the middle of a sunny afternoon, Joanna couldn't remember who he was. It was Easter. In her delirium she'd been dreaming about Jesus risen from the grave in a halo of light. She knew about this from Sunday School. When Dr. Graham appeared in the doorway of her darkened room with the sunlight glowing in the kitchen behind him, Joanna thought he was the Son of God. She screamed hysterically because, as Esther liked to put it when she told and retold this story, she thought she was sent for. When Dr. Graham tried to calm her by reminding her that he was the one who had brought her into this world in the first place, Joanna screamed even louder and tried to crawl under the bed. Because, as she tried to explain to Esther later, if he'd been the one to bring her into this world, maybe he had come now to take her back out of it.

Joanna recovered, but a year later Dr. Graham died and, although she was old enough then to know about the difference between doctors and God, still she was relieved, as if Dr. Graham's demise might somehow increase her chances of immortality.

Joanna remained basically healthy through the rest of public school and Esther often said it was a good thing they'd got it all over with in one year.

When Joanna was well (which was most of the time) but didn't want to go to school, she fantasized about being sick for a long time, like the boy Colin in *The Secret Garden* which she had read four times. She imagined that such a life would be romantic and glamorous, poignantly tragic, and very cosy. She too, like Colin, would pass the days in a large darkened room filled with richly coloured rugs and handsome furniture. She too would read lavishly illustrated books about foreign lands, exotic creatures, formal gardens, and snake-charmers, while wrapped in a velvet dressing gown and propped against a dozen large pillows in a carved four-poster bed draped with brocade. She would ring a little silver bell and a nurse would magically appear with lemonade, ice cream, doughnuts, or a fresh batch of chocolate chip cookies. Her blankets would always be smooth and warm around her thin, weak, possibly crippled legs. Her pillows would always be cool. In this fantasy she had no parents and no friends.

When she was sick (which was seldom), it was nothing at all like *The Secret Garden*. Esther saw sickness as a shameful sign of weakness, probably moral weakness at that. It was all a case of mind over matter. If you were sick, you were probably just too lazy to get up and get busy. She also seemed to think that the best way to cure a sick person was to ignore her. If you were too sick to go to school, you were also too sick to read, talk, draw, drink lemonade, and eat cookies.

When Joanna was sick she had to spend the whole day flat on her back doing nothing. She got bored. She got hot. Her pillows got sweaty and wrinkled. She threw off the blankets. She got cold. She pulled the blankets back up. They got tangled in her legs, bunched in a lump under her back. She got hungry. Esther brought her flat, warm ginger ale and a bowl of tomato soup. She felt sick again. Esther brought her a bucket to throw up in and went to have a bath. When Clarence got home from work, Joanna was still too sick to get up for supper. By the time the dishes were done, she thought she might be well enough to watch a little TV. Esther said if she was too sick to come into the kitchen for supper, she was also too sick to come into the living room for TV.

By the next morning Joanna was all better. Esther said, "See?"

Although Joanna had never been seriously ill in her life, as she got older she began to worry more and more about her own good health. How long, realistically, could it be expected to last? It seemed too good to be true, considering that she had never done anything much to maintain it. She knew she didn't eat right often enough. A nutritious vegetarian meal one night was likely to be followed by a double cheeseburger, fries and gravy, and a chocolate milk shake the next. She hated any form of organized exercise and wouldn't be caught dead in a spandex suit flopping around with a bunch of overweight and overzealous women to an instrumental version of Abba. She drank too much coffee and not enough fruit juice. The only time she drank the suggested eight glasses of water a day was when she was hung over from drinking too much wine the night before.

When she felt well (which was most of the time) but tired of trying, coping, doing, she sometimes fantasized about having a terminal illness. Nothing messy, painful, or malodorous. Certainly not anything that involved vomiting, diarrhea, disfigurement, or a skin disorder. Rather, she imagined being inflicted with a mysterious painless disease which forced her to spend the rest of her sadly numbered days in bed wasting prettily away, growing paler and weaker, daily more delicate and rarefied, until she was hardly more than a vapour. Finally she would just dissolve altogether and evaporate up to heaven. In this fantasy she was frequently visited by many quietly sorrowful friends who could not imagine how they were going to live without her, and so they sat for hours by her bedside weeping and holding her limp, dry, nearly transparent little hands.

When she felt sick (which was seldom) she always assumed the worst, letting her imagination run away with her symptoms. Esther had often told her she had an overactive imagination. This made her think of Jeremy Hines, a boy in her Grade Four class who was called by the teacher "hyperactive." She imagined her own imagination to be like Jeremy: rambunctious and unco-ordinated, like a large yellow dog just leaving puppyhood, racing through rooms, knocking things over with its wildly wagging tail, licking people and chewing shoes. Maybe her imagination had a mean streak too, like Jeremy Hines, whose anger and frustration erupted unpredictably in fits of yelling, crying, banging on desks and walls, tearing up books and papers, tormenting the smaller children, and threatening to jump out the window and run away. Jeremy Hines was gone the next year, to a special school, the other boys said, for retards and troublemakers. Which was what Joanna imagined would happen to her if she didn't smarten up and teach her imagination to behave.

Now her imagination cruelly tormented her with the idea that almost any minor ailment could actually be cancer sneaking up on her. A sore throat, an upset stomach, an aching back, swelling anywhere, a disconcerting numbness in the toes of her right foot, a clump of broken discoloured veins on her right calf, even an abscessed tooth was probably not a simple dental problem but a cancerous growth in her mouth.

A recurring pain in her right breast offered three terminal possibilities to obsess about: breast cancer, lung cancer, or an impending myocardial infarction. When she finally summoned up her courage and went to see Dr. Millan, fully expecting to receive her death sentence, he said it was a pulled muscle. She had not thought of her breasts as having muscles. Rather, she had thought of them only as passive fleshy objects to be admired and caressed by men, sucked on by babies, and examined periodically for lumps.

Lewis, like Joanna, was a basically healthy person. The only illnesses he ever had were, he liked to say, self-inflicted, by which he meant hangovers. Not that he was a heavy drinker, but rather he seemed to be overly sensitive to alcohol's unpleasant after-effects and so paid a high price for even minor indulgences.

Coming over one morning after he and Wanda had been out drinking and dancing late the night before (while Joanna sat home alone watching TV in her housecoat, eating filberts and feeling sorry for herself), he flung himself melodramatically down on Joanna's bed and moaned, "Aspirin, bring me aspirin, I'm sick as a dog! I think I might throw up."

Joanna was not feeling sympathetic. In fact she was mentally playing the Other-Woman version of What's Wrong with This Picture?: the childhood game in which you had to pick out the chicken with one foot, the car with three tires, or the woman with her nose on upside-down. In this case, was it not supposed to be the lover who enjoyed the glamour, the romance, the dancing, and, possibly, many expensive gifts purchased in guilt and paid for in cash so as to be untraceable? Was it not supposed to be the wife who provided the comfort, the aspirin, the clean clothes, the meals? Was it not supposed to be the wife who held his head while he puked up last night's dinner marinated with red wine?

She laughed at him. He was hurt. "Just feel my forehead," he begged pathetically. "I think I have a temperature."

Joanna laughed again and walked away.

"Oh, you can be so hard-hearted sometimes," Lewis whined.

Yes, Joanna thought as she rummaged in the medicine chest. Hard-hearted, yes, but never when it would do her any good.

Since Esther's death it seems that the people Clarence knows have been dropping like flies. He has become skilled at deciphering the code used in newspaper obituaries. *Suddenly* means a heart attack. *After a long illness* means cancer. He was stumped once by an obituary which said *Suddenly after a short illness*. For every bit of good news Joanna has to offer him in their weekly Sunday phone calls, Clarence counters with a story of disease and/or death.

All week long Joanna stores up cheerful things to tell him. She worries because he often sounds depressed. She wants to cheer him up. She wants to please him. She still wants to make him happy. She wants him to be as happy as she is so she doesn't have to feel guilty. Sometimes she even makes a list so she doesn't forget anything.

When there's no important news, she concentrates on telling him things she thinks he can relate to: I weeded and watered the garden. I did five loads of laundry. I waxed the living room floor. I'm just getting over a bad cold. Gordon mowed the lawn. We had a thunderstorm last night. Samuel had a nightmare.

Talking to Clarence can be like talking to a child, although it is much more charming in children. She cannot very well explain the principles of conversation to him the way she does to Samuel, telling him that generally a conversation means first one person talks, then the other person talks, then the first person talks some more, and usually both people are talking about the same thing.

Maybe her father makes a list beforehand too, a list of all the people he knows who are sick and dying this week. Mostly Joanna has never heard of these people before. Sometimes, though, they are his neighbours, people Joanna saw every single day when she was growing up, and now when he says their names she cannot remember their faces.

When Joanna says, "Samuel went to a birthday party," her father says, "Great, I'll bet he had fun. Mrs. Bodnarchuk from down the street died on Thursday. The ambulance came in the middle of the night and took her away. She hadn't been good for a long time. It was her heart. Or was it her lungs? I forget. I never did get back to sleep."

Sometimes the sick and dying are people she can't recall at all, much to Clarence's consternation. Joanna says, "Gordon got a raise."

Clarence says, "Remember the woman at the corner store who used to sell me Cherry Blossoms?"

Joanna says, "No, I don't."

"She was pretty," Clarence prods, "and always smiling."

Joanna says, "Sort of, maybe I sort of remember."

"Well, anyway," Clarence says huffily, "she was so pretty and she killed herself last week. They say she shot herself in the head. You'd wonder where she got the gun."

Sometimes Joanna thinks that if she said she'd won the Nobel Prize, her father would say, "Oh, that's nice. Mr. James from Simpson Street just had brain surgery." She knows she is being uncharitable. She knows he can't help it. She knows he is frightened. But she also knows there is nothing she can do. She would like to reassure him. Instead she keeps committing crimes against him: the crimes of being young, healthy, happy, and hopeful. Secretly, neither of them can deny the fact that he is old, lonely, bored, and he will not live forever.

Another Sunday morning phone call. Clarence speaks briefly to Gordon, who answered the phone, and then at some length to Samuel. When Joanna gets on, Gordon and Samuel go out to play in the backyard.

She says, although Samuel has already told him this, "We had a terrible thunderstorm last night. I was scared. I've always been afraid of storms and I still am."

Clarence says, "I don't remember that, you being scared of storms." Joanna can hear Gordon and Samuel hooting and hollering through the screens.

She says, "I planted the window boxes yesterday. With pale pink impatiens and Crystal Palace lobelia. They're a deep blue-purple, the lobelia. When the sun hits them, they almost seem to glow."

Clarence says, "Your mother had those, the lobelia." Gordon and

Samuel are tossing the soccer ball into the air, leaping and darting around the bushes like birds in their green and yellow T-shirts.

She says, "Oh, I don't remember." In five minutes she will be outside with Gordon and Samuel and she will try to bounce the soccer ball off her head the way they do on TV and Samuel will fall into the fragrant grass, clutching himself with laughter.

Clarence says, "Well, she did. She loved them. Remember the butcher at Safeway? You went to school with his son. He was killed in a car accident last Monday night."

In five more minutes she will be able to hang up gracefully and go back to her young, healthy, happy, hopeful family. In five more minutes she will hang up feeling guilty, depressed, and afraid. How is it that her father cannot remember her fear of thunderstorms, the way the first low rumble in the west put a bubble of anxiety in her throat and a knot of tension in her stomach? How is it that she cannot remember her mother's lobelia glowing in the gentle evening light? How is it that she and Clarence lived in the same house for twenty-two years and now they don't remember any of the same things? How is it that all their respective memories are things the other has forgotten?

It is as if she and her father are remembering altogether different lives. Which, of course, they are.

5. Man

man *n.* 1. a human being, specif., *a)* a primate (*Homo sapiens*) characterized by an erect stance, an opposable thumb, the ability to make and use specialized tools, articulate speech, and a well-developed brain capable of abstract thought, *b)* a member of any extinct species of this family [Neanderthal *man*]. 2. mankind; the human race. 3. an adult male person. 4. *a)* a male servant, subordinate, or employee, *b)* a member of the military, esp. a rank-and-file soldier or sailor. 5. *a)* a husband, *b)* a lover or suitor. 6. a person possessing qualities generally regarded as manly, such as strength, courage, etc. *See also* MAN ABOUT TOWN, MAN-AT-ARMS, MAN-EATER, MAN FRIDAY, MAN-

HANDLE, MANHOOD, MAN-HOUR, MANHUNT, MAN IN THE STREET, MAN-MADE, MAN OF GOD, MAN OF LETTERS, MAN OF STRAW, MAN OF THE WORLD, MAN-OF-WAR, MANPOWER.

6. Deep

"STILL WATERS RUN deep," Clarence often said, usually in Joanna's defence when Esther was chastising her for sulking again. Any prolonged period of silence on Joanna's part (except when she was sleeping) was interpreted by her mother as another episode of adolescent angst: unnecessary, unhealthy, and calculated largely to annoy her. It did not seem to occur to Esther that maybe Joanna was just thinking—and not about her. If, in her own defence, Joanna said, "I'm just thinking," Esther said, "Quit your mooning around. You think too much for your own good."

She also said, at various times, "You're too honest for your own good. You're too trusting for your own good. You're too smart for your own good." As if even the virtues must be measured out in titrated doses, for fear perhaps of using your goodness up too soon, as if it were a fixed quantity which must be meted out over the course of your lifetime. Esther believed in avoidance of excess in all things. She often warned Joanna (and Clarence too) about indulging in "too much of a good thing." Too much turkey would give you a stomachache, too much cheese would make you constipated, too much ice cream would rot your teeth, too much sunshine would give you heat stroke, too much trust would break your heart, and too much thinking would . . . would what? Rot your brain? Too much honesty and they (whoever *they* were) would get the better of you. Somehow you would be victimized by truth in the end. To find yourself a victim was, according to Esther, no less shameful than being a villain. Both fates were somehow connected to excess. Victims, villains, and excess. Be careful. Be quiet. Be good.

"You think too much," Esther said. Joanna was in the living room, in the middle of a long hot Sunday afternoon, weighed down by the heat, her family, this little house, the curtains closed against the sunlight all up and down the empty street. All of it kept pressing down upon her until she thought she would scream with the airtight seriousness of Sunday. "You think too much for your own good," Esther said, standing in the archway between the living room and the kitchen with a dishtowel in her hand. She could not bear to see anybody doing nothing. Thinking should not be considered an activity in its own right. Rather, it was something you should do while doing something else, something more practical, more reasonable, more important.

"Still waters run deep," Clarence said, coming in from the front yard where he'd been out moving the sprinkler around so it would hit the begonias ranged in clay pots up and down the steps.

"One of these days she'll drown herself," Esther said, as if Joanna had suddenly left the room or gone deaf.

On weekend nights Joanna and Henry went downtown to the Neapolitan Bar and Grill to party with their friends. The Neapolitan was the usual meeting place, filled every night with the same faces, regulars who seldom seriously considered going elsewhere. It was the kind of place where you could go any time and always find someone to sit with. The bartender, Jake, knew everyone and also what each person liked to drink and he would ask you what was the matter if you ordered something different.

The Neapolitan was not the kind of place strangers would often come into. Outside it was run-down, dingy, and somewhat lopsided, as the foundations settled unevenly year after year into the soft earth. Over those years the stucco had been every colour imaginable and was now a generic beige, shadowed in spots with the previous green, blue, and pumpkin colours beneath.

Inside it was also run-down and dingy, dark even in the daytime, smoky, crowded, and noisy with the music from the jukebox and the clatter of pool balls from the two tables at the back. The small round tables were set close together and covered with terry cloth to sop up the spilled drinks. The grill was a hole in the wall in the back corner where they slapped together hamburgers, french fries, and burritos. Jake stocked only standard liquors, nothing fancy, no liqueurs (except peppermint schnapps for hangovers), no imported beer, two cheap Canadian wines, a red and a white, and he didn't do cocktails.

The truth was Joanna would never have ventured into the Neapolitan either if it hadn't been for the music. The last weekend of every month there was a live band. She'd gone in originally to hear the Blue Notes, a local band everybody was raving about, which was how she'd met Henry in the first place. He played bass in the band. They were not an especially good band but they were energetic and enthusiastic.

She'd gone in with three women friends from work (she was a temporary secretary for a real estate company just then) and they'd been lucky enough to get a table near the front. She'd fallen in love with the way Henry held his guitar. Or the way his eyes shone in the half-darkened smoky room. Or the way he didn't seem to care that he couldn't sing very well. She had fallen in love with something about him, something specific that afterwards she could never put her finger on. But later, every time she saw him up on stage, the feeling came back and her heart jumped up.

At the end of that first night Henry had come and sat down with them, introduced himself, ordered a round, and sung (off-key, quietly) into Joanna's left ear that Kenny Rogers song, "Don't Fall in Love with a Dreamer." When he wasn't playing his guitar, he said, he was driving a dump truck for a local construction company. Two months later they were living together. It was all so easy, no wonder she couldn't remember later exactly how it had happened. Later, when people asked them how they'd met, Henry said, "She picked me up in a bar," and Joanna said, "I did." She remained surprised to find herself living with a dump-truck driver named Henry. Not that there was anything intrinsically wrong with either of these things, the trade or the name. It was just that she had never thought to picture herself in this position.

Now it was Friday night and another band was playing as fast and as loud as they could. Everyone was dancing and singing and drinking to excess. Around ten o'clock two strangers came in. The woman had big hair dyed brassy red, a black leather jacket, red lipstick, blue mascara, earrings that looked like knives. The man was short and slim with round shoulders, glasses, a moustache, average. They found a small table near where Joanna and Henry were sitting with their friends.

They were Henry's friends really, other men with long hair and shaggy beards like Henry, other musicians and dump-truck drivers, a carpenter, a roofer, a plumber. Often Joanna was the only woman in the group. Occasionally one of the other men had a date, but not often and never the same woman twice. They were divorced or they were confirmed bachelors. They referred to themselves as "the boys." Joanna knew they liked her well enough, for a woman. She was a good sport, for a woman. She never complained about the bad language, the interminable arguments about unions, the odour of diesel fuel which hung in the air all around them. Whenever Pete the roofer got really drunk and stood on the table to do his glass-eating trick, she laughed as loudly as the rest of them. Whenever Luke the carpenter did his straw trick (he could stick a small plastic drinking straw all the way up his left nostril and then make it come out his mouth), she applauded as wildly as the rest of them. She was hardly squeamish at all, for a woman. She did not tell them they were gruesome or gross.

But Joanna was feeling restless and bored with Henry and his friends. She had been hoping for two months now that Henry would change, because if he didn't, she thought she was going to have to break up with him. They had been together for nearly two years. She wanted him to be neater, cleaner, more creative, more ambitious. She wanted him to drink less and read more, sleep less and exercise more, party less and help out around the house more, watch less TV and eat more vegetables. Much of what she had found charming and refreshing about him at the outset of their relationship now bugged the hell out of her. She wanted him to grow up, settle down, and find another group of friends.

In fact Henry *had* changed. He had trimmed his beard, cleaned the oven, stopped putting four teaspoons of sugar in his coffee, started lifting weights and watching PBS. He had stopped dragging this annoying bunch of losers home with him at all hours of the day or night.

He was reading *Madame Bovary* because she had said it was a great book. He was trying to understand her art. At least once a day now he asked her how it was going, and last week he had even suggested they go to see the new show at the Gallery Nouvelle. But when the day came he had an abscessed tooth, which was hardly his fault, but Joanna was angry anyway and so she went alone. After the show she had gone down to the Neapolitan because she was mad and she wasn't there for ten minutes before Jake the bartender had called her to the phone. It was Henry, who said he felt so miserable, would she please come home and make him some chicken soup? She had told him there was a can of chicken noodle in the cupboard.

He had said at least twice recently that maybe he didn't want to be a truck driver all his life after all. So yes, he was trying to change. But what if he *did* change and she still wasn't happy with him?

He knew she was unhappy. She wasn't exactly hiding her feelings. But they hadn't yet seriously acknowledged the inevitability of breaking up. Henry, she thought, was still trying to jolly her out of it. Yesterday he had given her a funny card for no reason: *Don't worry! One of these days we'll see the light at the end of the tunnel . . . and with our luck it'll be an oncoming train!*

Now Henry was asking her to dance, but she said she was too hot, too thirsty, she thought she'd just sit and sip on her beer. Really she was eavesdropping on the strangers at the next table. Clearly, they were not getting along. The redhead was leaning across the table towards the man and her mouth was getting thinner and harder. He stared more deeply into his glass as she berated him. When the band paused between songs, Joanna heard the words "asshole," "fuck face," "bastard," "how could you?" And several times a name which the woman spat out with such vehemence that Joanna could not be sure if it was Lonny, Bonnie, or Connie. Then the man was mumbling into his moustache at some length. Neither of them noticed that Joanna was listening.

Suddenly the redhead cried, "Deep? You want deep? I'll show you deep!" In what seemed to be a single movement, she jumped to her feet, smashed the glass ashtray in half against the side of the table and dragged it down the full length of his face. Then she ran out the door as the man put his hands over his face and the blood flowed through his fingers.

As Joanna watched the man bleeding and half the bar running towards him and Jake behind the bar picking up the phone to call the police, she made the single sound "O," deflated, defeated, unfinished, her lips still wet from her last sip of beer staying that shape for a long time after the sound was out. Then she was pounding Henry on the arm and crying, "Do something! Do something!"

He said, quietly, "What?"

Joanna was having a show of her new collages at the Gallery Nouvelle. She was nervous and excited. About a variety of things. Mostly about the show, of course. But also about Lewis with whom she had been sleeping for seven months. He was coming tonight to the show with Wanda. Joanna had been torn up for two weeks about it, hating herself for having come to the point where being in the same room with Lewis and Wanda was better than not being with him at all.

"Tell her not to come," she had pleaded repeatedly.

"I can't."

"Why not?"

"You know."

"I know."

All their other artist friends would be there too, to be supportive and to avail themselves of the free wine and food. There would also be a number of prominent community professionals who might actually buy something. Certainly none of the other artists could afford to.

Just before eight o'clock the guests began to arrive in groups of two or three. Lewis and Wanda appeared at quarter after eight. Joanna, having endured several other similar situations during the past seven months, had perfected her technique of remaining in motion around the room, chatting with one cluster of guests, then moving graciously on to the next, hugging old friends, introducing herself politely to new faces, all of this without ever losing track of Lewis (and Wanda) but without yet having to speak to him (them) directly. That encounter was best postponed until she had screwed up her confidence, had a bit too much wine, and could enter fully into the spirit of the masquerade.

Sometimes she lurked beside the hors d'oeuvres table and helped herself to the free wine. Sometimes she stood quietly behind clumps of strangers as they examined her work. Most people were impressed and paid her compliments. But some people said, "I think it must be upside-down." "What is that green blob in the corner?" "What's her name again?" She knew she should not be listening to them. It was foolish, unprofessional, and faintly masochistic. It was like a scab you could not keep yourself from picking till it bled.

A fat pale man in a beige suit peered for a long time at a piece she had called *Time Zones*. The base of the collage was a large antique map of the world upon which Joanna had pasted photographs of various objects stereotypically indigenous to certain areas: tulips on the Netherlands, penguins on Antarctica, oil wells and camels on the Middle East, cars, dollar bills, stereos, and hand guns across most of North America. She had also pasted, on the oceans and seas, many pictures of clock and watch faces and parts of actual watch mechanisms: tiny gears and springs, small and large clock hands sprouting from the Atlantic, the Pacific, the Red Sea, the Dead Sea, the Suez Canal.

The woman with the fat pale man was also fat and pale, wearing a blue silk dress. They both looked a little glazed, having stared at *Time Zones* for so long. Finally the man grunted and said, "I don't get it." Joanna had thought *Time Zones* was obvious, maybe too obvious in its thematic implications.

The woman said, "Well, you know, it's this modern art. It's like this new math. Why do they keep changing everything? Why can't they just leave well enough alone? This modern art, it's not supposed to mean anything. It's not even supposed to *be* anything really. You're not supposed to know what you're looking at. It's deep. It's like this modern poetry. It doesn't rhyme. I've always liked rhymes. And I'd sooner have a nice landscape, trees and water, sun and some horses, maybe birds, over my new chesterfield."

Joanna saw in her head the picture which had hung over her parents' chesterfield when she was a child. White horses whipped into a frenzy

beneath a stormy overwrought deep blue sky behind, the lead stallion
about to rear up with his nostrils flared and his long mane flying in
the cruel blue wind.

"Yes," the man said, shaking his head. "Yes, you're right. It's too
deep for me."

Joanna looked down at their feet as they made their way to the door.
Instinctively she scanned the room for Lewis, looking for moral support.
Just as she spotted him near the Exit sign, he leaned down to whisper
in Wanda's ear. He put his large hand around her small shoulder. She
pressed her palm against his chest. They were smiling, nearly hugging.
Joanna's stomach clenched and sliced open, hard and hot, as if she'd
swallowed a chunk of her wineglass.

For the first time in years she remembered the redhead and the
ashtray in the Neapolitan. *Deep?* she thought. *You want deep? I'll show
you deep!* She wondered how it had felt to slash open that man's face,
that small average mumbling man, that fat pale stupid man, that tall
handsome man over there being so nice to his wife.

She wished she knew what jail that redheaded woman was in. Maybe
she wasn't in jail at all. Maybe she had gotten away with it. Maybe she
was just going on with her life like everyone else, eating cheese, drinking wine, going to art galleries (probably not), going to seedy bars
then, drinking draft beer and dancing, or maybe she had been completely changed by the ashtray incident. Maybe she was a social worker
now, or a probation officer, maybe she was a kindergarten teacher or
maybe she had married that small average mumbling man, his face far
more interesting now with the scar, maybe she was the mother of twins,
changing diapers, baking cookies, spending whole afternoons in the
park in the sun while the babies slept in their stroller in the shade
beside the swings. Maybe her hair wasn't even red any more, maybe
she had let it grow back to its original mousy brown.

The ashtray slashing that night was the most drastic and dramatic
thing Joanna had ever seen in her whole life and, like all the other true
deep dramas, it hadn't even made the newspaper. She remembered
searching for it the next day in the evening after supper, sitting on the
couch beside Henry, and even though she was rattling the pages all
around him, he didn't ask what she was looking for. Instead he asked

if she wanted to go down to the Neapolitan. She said no. They stayed home and watched TV instead, an old movie which she could not remember the name of now but it was one of those sinking-ship movies where they're launching the lifeboats and, try as they might, there is never enough room for everyone and so the captain (a distinguished rotund grey-haired man looking snappy, heroic, and efficient in his tidy white uniform) plants his feet firmly in the middle of the panic and yells, "Women and children first!" There was a good reason for this hierarchy of rescue but Joanna could never be sure what it was. They had watched the movie and gone to bed. She could not remember if they made love. Probably not, because she was busy thinking that yes, it was quite possible that even if someone did change in all the ways you thought you wanted him to, you still might not be happy with him. Yes, it was quite possible to love someone and then stop.

But now she loved Lewis and she could not stop.

At home alone later after the show she tried to cry but couldn't. She hated crying. It made her feel ridiculous, the tears and the snot got smeared all over her face, and she sounded, as Esther had once pointed out, like a sick moose. She could not cry the way they did in those old movies, gently, softly, sweetly, warm tears sliding down a pretty face, wounded eyes growing wider and wider . . . darker and darker . . . fade to black in the arms of a handsome, sympathetic, well-dressed or naked man. When she cried, she curled up in a ball on the bed and pounded her fists, her hair got all messed up, and she swore the whole time through her sobs. It was pathetic.

She ate the last piece of pizza left over from supper and then tidied up the kitchen. Washing her face, she thought about Lewis and Wanda getting ready for bed at their house, still chatting about the show or planning what they would do tomorrow. Brushing her teeth, she thought about the fat pale man and his wife having a last glass of sherry and a bit of ripe cheese while still trying to decode the mysteries of modern art and what should they hang over the new chesterfield (which was, no doubt, crushed velvet or plaid). Sitting on the toilet, she thought about her collages hanging in the empty gallery with the door locked now, the lights off and a few uneaten chunks of cheese curling up on the crystal platters.

She put on her flannelette nightgown and went to bed.

She awoke to the sound of the telephone ringing. It rang a dozen times into the dark kitchen. She knew it would be Lewis, calling from their downstairs phone now that Wanda was upstairs asleep.

Lewis calling from a dark room to apologize, his hand cupping the receiver like a flame in the wind.

Lewis calling to whisper, "I'm sorry, I'm sorry." He might be crying. He might say, "I'm sorry, I'm crying, I'm sorry." He often said on the phone that he was crying but she could never hear it in his voice. He said that was how he cried, without sound, without tears. She thought he knew nothing about crying and how it should be done, with anguish and snot, with heat and a headache afterwards.

It would be Lewis calling at three in the morning to say, "I'm sorry, I'm sorry, I never meant to hurt you." As if that made everything all right. As if not *meaning* to hurt someone must lessen the depth of the pain you had so unwittingly inflicted upon them. As if hurting someone when you hadn't meant to was not a criminal act after all. As if the aftermath of pain was merely an incidental by-product, like the unidentifiable remains they stuff wieners with.

7. Soft

"YOU'RE SOFT IN the head, woman," Henry said. "But hard, oh so hard in the heart." It was raining. They were getting ready for bed.

They had agreed to break up. Henry would move out, Joanna would keep the basement apartment, which had, after all, been hers in the first place. Henry was packed and ready to go, his clothes stuffed into three green garbage bags which sat now on top of his stereo on the front porch. He'd rented a room in a sleazy downtown hotel until he could find a place of his own.

They had been living together for nearly two years. They had been deciding to break up for the past two months. For the first month, the discussion had gone like this:

Joanna said, "I want to get married and have babies."

Henry said, "I'll never get married and I don't like kids."

Then they both said these things several more times, usually at two in the morning over a bottle of scotch or a case of cold beer. They repeated themselves until they were exhausted from anger or hysteria and then they went to bed.

For the second month, the discussion had gone like this:

Henry said, "Maybe we should get married and have babies."

Joanna said, "No, I don't think so."

Henry said, "But I thought that's what you wanted."

Joanna said, "I did."

Henry said, "I've changed."

Joanna said, "Yes."

Now the decision was made, Henry was leaving, and they were making love for the last time.

"Nobody will ever love you as much as I do," Henry said, not unkindly, as he slipped his hand between her wet thighs.

"You're probably right," Joanna said, spreading her legs and guiding his fingers inside.

"You're soft in the head, woman," Henry said. "But hard, oh so hard in the heart."

Joanna imagined she would have occasion in the future to recall these words. They had a nice prophetic ring to them. Joanna suspected that Henry imagined that she would never let herself be completely happy. He often told her that she expected too much of people, especially of the people she loved. Perhaps he was right. Perhaps she expected too much of life in general. She was unwilling to either admit or alter this possibly fatal flaw in her outlook. They both imagined they would be friends forever.

8. Eating

JOANNA ALWAYS WAS a picky eater. Raw tomatoes were all right, for instance, in sandwiches on white buttered toast with salt and pepper, but not on plain white bread because the juice made the bread go soggy and pink. Ketchup, which Esther called "catsup" and which Clarence slopped all over everything, was utterly revolting. Tomato juice and Campbell's tomato soup were also all right. She liked a little glass of tomato juice at breakfast, not to drink but to dip her buttered toast in, two slices cut precisely in half and then into eight equal fingers, dipping-size. She liked tomato soup for lunch, especially in the wintertime, with soda crackers, not mushed up in it but on a plate beside. When they had spaghetti for supper, Joanna had her noodles plain with butter and some salt.

Esther said, "How can you turn your nose up at something you've never even tasted?"

Joanna said, "I can tell by the smell that I don't like it."

"But it smells good," Esther insisted.

"Not to me."

She did not like pineapple, bananas, coconut, blueberries, grapes, broccoli, Brussels sprouts, spinach, mayonnaise, vinegar, mushrooms, egg salad sandwiches, fruitcake, peanuts, cabbage, mashed potatoes, vegetable soup, peaches, pork chops, peas, boiled eggs, beets, potato salad, dill pickles, liver, prunes, turnips, green beans, sweet-and-sour spareribs, porridge, maraschino cherries, marmalade, tapioca, sardines, horseradish, black licorice, creamed corn, or yams.

She liked grilled cheese sandwiches, chicken drumsticks, corn on the cob, barbecued steak, lemon meringue pie, hot dogs, pretzels, raw carrots, cream puffs, rice, pears, Delicious apples, pomegranates, turkey, red licorice, macaroni, bacon, potato puffs, peanut butter and Cheez Whiz on white toast, watermelon, butter tarts, grape jelly, mandarin oranges, rhubarb with sugar, waffles with butter and real maple syrup, chocolate milk shakes and hot fudge sundaes from the Dairy Queen. She also liked fish which they had every Friday although they were not Catholic.

She had never tasted asparagus, sour cream, sauerkraut, lamb chops, clams, zucchini, lobster, shrimp, blue cheese, buttermilk, oysters, black olives, pickled eggs, ravioli, tartar sauce, or snails. And she did not intend to.

She did not like strawberries because those little picky things on the outside stuck in her teeth. She did not like raspberries any more since she bit into one with a white worm curled up in the hole. She did not like orange juice with pulp. She did not like marshmallows unless they were roasted or floating in a mug of hot chocolate. She especially did not like those miniature marshmallows featured in the Kraft commercials during "The Ed Sullivan Show." They were shown in various bizarre dessert concoctions which Esther unfortunately occasionally felt compelled to try.

She also didn't like things that were all mixed up together. Lasagna, chili, beef stew, chicken pot pie, tuna casserole—simply the sight of these made her gag. She especially hated Esther's jellied salad which they had every Thursday: a mould of green Jell-O with shredded carrots, chopped celery, and sliced green olives suspended in it.

Esther tried to explain to her that all the food ends up mixed together in your stomach anyway. Joanna said she did not want to think about this. Esther got out her cookbook and read aloud the recipe for the Thursday night casserole they had with the hateful jellied salad. The casserole was called American Chop Suey. It contained hamburger, onion, white rice, elbow macaroni, and Campbell's tomato soup.

"See!" Esther said triumphantly. "There's not a thing in there that you don't like. Rice, you love rice! Macaroni, your favourite!"

"But not *together*. I don't like them *together*," Joanna moaned.

It was Wednesday. They would have the casserole and the jellied salad tomorrow night. There was always an argument before, during, and/or after the Thursday evening meal. It was starting already, it was starting early, it was only Wednesday. Sometimes there were tears on Thursday, hers, her mother's, or both.

The tension began like prickly heat, a vague burning, a little itch. Clarence slopped ketchup all over his plate. Esther informed them that she had put green pepper in the jellied salad just to be different. Joanna moved the pile of casserole from the left side of her plate to the right. Esther helped herself to more salad, declaring it delicious. Joanna moved the mound of lumpy green Jell-O from the right side of her plate to the left. Clarence's mouth got closer and closer to his plate as he shovelled in the food. By now they could not even look at each other. There seemed to be another presence in the kitchen, a mealtime miasma which was making them all mean and miserable.

Clarence and Esther were finished. Clarence stood up and burped enthusiastically. Esther put their plates in the sink and did not even offer to make tea. Joanna was left sitting alone at the table with her brown plaid plate still in front of her, still full of food, cold now and played with, so it was even more disgusting. She was usually sitting there for another two hours, promising herself that when she had children of her own she would never ever force them to eat.

Esther was hissing, "You will sit there until you eat it! You will sit there until bedtime for all I care!" Then she shut herself in the bedroom where, Joanna supposed with some grim satisfaction, she would lie facedown on the shiny orange bedspread, gritting her false teeth and weeping, dabbing her wet cheeks with the several Kleenexes she kept tucked in her bra because in those days women's slacks and blouses did not have pockets.

Clarence was in the living room, oblivious, immune, or exempt, lying on the chesterfield watching television and dozing and snoring, or having another whisky and Coke, working on the cryptogram, deciphering a ribbon of gibberish—QXKFXC ZMEKN OVTOCONEV NCOHXF WONKAYAHXKQ YOWABZ WXOBV—to reveal some obscure and useless sentence—TENDER YOUNG ASPARAGUS GRACED MAGNIFICENT FAMILY MEALS.

Sometimes Joanna managed to choke down most of her meal and then her mother was temporarily mollified. Other times, when the food and Joanna were still sitting there at nine o'clock, Esther would stomp out of the bedroom and noisily scrape the remains of Joanna's meal into the garbage can, muttering about starving children across the ocean. To which Joanna once cried, more in despair than anger, "Well then, mail it to them!"

In bed afterwards she was hungry. She supposed she had won something. But what? She did not feel victorious. She could hear her parents in the kitchen doing the dishes and then in the living room, watching TV, reading the newspaper, Clarence still working on the cryptogram or his paint-by-numbers, Esther sewing or working on her stamp collection, both of them going about the rest of their evening as if nothing had happened. Joanna did not feel triumphant. She felt hungry, lonely, and frightened.

One Friday, after another miserable Thursday evening, Clarence surprised them at breakfast by suggesting they go out for dinner that
night. Maybe he was not oblivious after all. He put his arm around
Esther and said, "Maybe you could use a break." Maybe they all could.
Esther in the curve of his embrace looked up at him with shiny grateful
eyes and kissed his cheek. Joanna looked away. She could not have said
what was more disturbing: when they got all sappy like this or when
they were arguing. Which in their case meant Esther giving Clarence
the silent treatment for a day or two, sometimes longer, once for a
whole week when Clarence went for drinks after work on a Friday with
the men from the mill and he didn't come home until after midnight,
drunk as a skunk, and threw up in the kitchen sink. Esther cleaned it
up and said nothing. Esther said nothing for a whole week. Until the
next Saturday when they all went grocery shopping as usual and everything slid back to normal again. Joanna had never heard them actually arguing out loud. The silent treatment made her so nervous that
she often wished they would just yell at each other and throw things
and get it over with.

When Clarence got home from work that Friday, they all got dressed
up and went to the Winston Hotel, which was only a few blocks away,
in the business district of the neighbourhood. They were seated at a
table for four in the dingy dining room. The waitress, her face like a
Hush Puppy shoe, whisked away the extra place setting without looking at them. Heavy plates and chunky silverware were set on paper
placemats with coloured pictures of fancy drinks on them, drinks with
names like Singapore Sling, Stinger, Sidecar, Bloody Mary, Tom Col-
lins, Harvey Wallbanger. These were called "cocktails," Joanna knew,
a smutty-sounding word with suggestions she did not dare examine for
fear of bursting into a fit of red-faced giggling right at the table and
falling off her chair. Esther and Clarence studied their menus which
were large pink plasticized cards with a typewritten list of today's spe-
cials paper-clipped inside. They ordered drinks. There was bland cheerful music seeping from somewhere near the kitchen into the half-full
room. They were happy. They were very hungry. Clarence wanted the
salmon steak. Esther wanted the roast pork. Joanna wanted a hot dog.

Esther whispered, "It's not that kind of place. Order something serious."

Joanna whined, "But I want a hot dog, with french fries and gravy."

Esther hissed, "Roast beef, roast beef, order the roast beef!"

Joanna moaned, "But I want—"

Esther snarled, "You will never be happy, will you? I can never please you, can I?" Which Joanna could not understand because it had been her father's idea to come here in the first place and what was or wasn't on the menu had nothing whatsoever to do with Esther anyway. She could not understand why her mother thought she was in charge of (or to blame for) absolutely everything.

When the roast beef arrived, it wasn't even as good as what Esther made at home on Sundays. Joanna thought about mentioning this but the mealtime silence which so often engulfed them at home had them in its grip here now too and so she said nothing. They could not speak. They could not look at each other. Clarence slopped ketchup all over his plate. Esther slopped sour cream all over her baked potato. Joanna moved the dry meat from the left side of her plate to the right. Clarence's mouth got closer and closer to his plate as he shovelled in the food. Joanna moved the stringy meat back again. Esther looked out the window. Joanna's throat was closing. She looked with furtive longing at the other families at the other tables. They were talking, they were even laughing, they were tasting tidbits of each other's entrées. When the little girl in the high chair two tables over spilled her milk, the mother just smiled and the father gaily waved for the waitress. Two tables over in the other direction, another family of three, the boy about ten, Joanna's age, was loudly and joyfully reliving the movie they'd seen the night before. These were happy families. These were families in love. Joanna wished she could die and be reborn into one of them.

Her parents ordered coffee. The waitress took their plates away, hers too, not seeming to notice or mind that her meal had been mostly rearranged rather than eaten. At least here, Joanna thought, her mother would not rush off to the bedroom crying and her father would not fall asleep and snore. At least here she would not have to sit at the table until bedtime, watching the world gently darken outside the window, watching the streetlights come on, watching her whole life, as yet unlived, pass before her bleary unloved eyes. At least here she could still have dessert before she had to go home and face the music.

Whenever Joanna and Lewis had the chance to spend the whole evening together, they ordered Chinese food from the Bamboo Gardens down-town, free delivery. The Chinese writing on the menu was like hiero-glyphics, mysterious and promising. Half an hour later, two big brown paper bags arrived, steaming and heavy with Styrofoam containers and plastic packets of plum and soya sauce.

They spread the food all over the coffee table and curled up on the couch to eat. They ate like two pigs, filling up their plates again before they were even half-empty, being greedy and messy, as if there weren't enough food arrayed around them for six people.

What Joanna really wanted was to get to the fortune cookies at the end, to those single sentences of reflective wisdom or prophetic guid-ance, Oriental oracles encapsulated in a bow of sugar, almonds, and flour. She observed the superstition that the fortune would be rendered invalid if you simply pulled it out, in the way that if you said your birthday cake wish out loud, it would never come true. You had to eat away the cookie to free the fortune inside.

They were like newspaper horoscopes. The positive relevant ones gave her a shiver of optimistic excitement: *There are big changes for you but you will be happy. This person loves you sincerely. Happy event will take place shortly in your home.* Of course there were no truly dire fortunes, the creators of these morsels either being chronically optimistic by nature or having been warned sternly at the outset that nobody wants a cookie that says: *Your lover will leave you next month. You will spend the rest of your life alone and miserable. You will die a tragic and painful death by the end of the week.* As with the newspaper horoscopes, Joanna could easily disregard the more irrelevant messages: *You will make a profitable in-vestment. You are next in line for promotion. Simplicity and clarity should be your theme in dress.*

Lewis too thought the fortunes were like newspaper horoscopes: just plain silly. He yanked his out unceremoniously and read them aloud, laughing and rolling his eyes. He crumpled them into little balls and dropped them into one of the empty Styrofoam containers. From which Joanna rescued them when she cleared the table, smoothed them out and saved them all, noting the date on the back. She kept them in an envelope behind the spices. She thought she would do something with them some day, although she could not have said what and in fact she never did.

Gordon takes great pleasure in food, both its preparation and its consumption. He is a good cook, his specialty being a sumptuous Spanish paella, rich with chicken, shrimp, clams, and artichoke hearts. He carves a mean turkey. He likes almost everything, anchovies, oysters, and oatmeal being the quite reasonable exceptions. He does not expect a hot meal waiting on the table every night when he gets home from work. If Joanna is still in her studio when he arrives, he either starts supper himself (without feeling compelled to point out what a hero he is for doing so) or orders a pizza. Joanna's friends envy her. Sometimes she thinks she even envies herself. In the early days of their marriage, when Joanna occasionally felt obligated to apologize for these lapses in domestic responsibility, Gordon would just roll his eyes and peel another potato.

He even professes to enjoy grocery shopping and doing the dishes, although sometimes Joanna suspects this is something he knows modern men are supposed to say. He is always humming when he rolls up his shirtsleeves and plunges into the dishwater up to the elbows. He even has his own favourite brand of dish soap, which is blue and costs twice as much as the generic yellow lemon-scented stuff which Joanna occasionally buys by mistake. His disappointment when this happens is palpable although he says nothing, afraid, Joanna supposes, of sounding like a demented housewife in a TV commercial, swooning over the new improved brand of laundry soap, denouncing the old inadequate kind and her own stupidity for having used it for fifteen years, her husband and six children having spent the best years of their lives trotting around in sweat-stained T-shirts and greying underwear.

Gordon is much better at grocery shopping than she is. Maybe he really does enjoy it. He strolls heartily down the aisles. He chats amiably with the little old ladies who invariably park their carts so no one else can get by while they squint through their trifocals at ingredient listings, preparation directions, and price-per-unit calculations. He fondles the fruit, paws through the loose mushrooms for the most perfect specimens, and taps a dozen melons before selecting the best one—the one, Joanna thinks nastily, that will be ripe in exactly forty-seven minutes, which is how long it will take to finish up here and get the damn thing home. He loves to try new products and conducts serious conversations about the economy, the government, and the weather with the woman installed at a table at the end of the frozen food aisle, who is offering free samples of low-cholesterol cocktail wieners, high-fibre cereal with oat bran and almonds, or tiny paper cuplets of hand-squeezed pulp-loaded orange juice. It is the best (and the most expensive) orange juice in the world and the cuplets are just like the hospital ones they bring your pills in. He calls the cashiers by name. They all wear little plastic tags. Their names are Doris, Daisy, Joanie, and Mo. They tell him about their varicose veins, their children's zany antics, their second cousin's baby shower, and the best way to prepare a leg of fresh New Zealand lamb.

Joanna, on the other hand, just wants to get it over with. Shopping alone, clutching her list and gritting her teeth, she bulls her way through the aisles, snatching off the shelves as fast as she can only the items she's written down, preferably without having to bring her cart to a full stop. She buys mushrooms in a blue plastic tub, six tomatoes in a cardboard carton, apples in a bag, and the melon on the top. She averts her eyes and shakes her head whenever she passes the free-sample lady. At the checkout she reads the magazine headlines and studies the sugarless-gum display with her wallet open.

In the early days of their marriage they went late at night to the twenty-four-hour A&P on Barrie Street. There were few shoppers then, most normal people being at home asleep in bed. At midnight the other shoppers were serious quiet childless couples like themselves. Or else they were university students, slightly drunk and silly, loading up on chips and Cheezies and enough mix to get them through the rest of the party. Sometimes in the winter there were one or two dirty homeless men who had come in to get out of the cold and so they were spending an hour buying a loaf of day-old bread.

Now they go on Friday night or Saturday afternoon, like everybody else. Like all the other children in the store, Samuel cries and fusses, dirties his diaper, throws his bottle, an apple, and a jar of mayonnaise on the floor. A bored young man with spiked hair comes to mop it up. Gordon enjoys himself while Joanna gets more and more depressed: by the ever-escalating prices, by the thought of having to unpack and put away all this expensive stuff when they get home, by the knowledge that she has become the kind of person who spends Friday night at the A&P. She feels boring, normal, and defeated.

As they drive home through the rain at dusk, a Bruce Cockburn song called "Trouble with Normal" comes on the radio. After the song has ended and the broadcast has moved on to exuberant commercials for life insurance, heating oil, and Pepto-Bismol, then to depressing international news about another civil war in the Third World, another American evangelist accused of sexual transgressions, and another child abducted in Toronto (that evil city), Cockburn's lyrics continue to play like a refrain or a rebuke inside her head. Samuel in the back seat is singing "Three Blind Mice": "They all ran after the farmer's wife/She cut off their tails with a carving knife."

At home she will put the groceries away, get Samuel bathed and into bed. Then she will have a bath herself while Gordon reads and dozes on the couch. In the bathtub she will mourn briefly for all she has lost and all that she has gained.

Samuel is a picky eater too. The transition from milk and apple juice to solid food is a rough one. Joanna has, like most modern mothers, high ideals about nutrition. Her child will never want for healthy homemade food. Her child will never be forced to eat that commercial crap in the little jars, mushy, weird-coloured slop laced with sugar, salt, and who knows what other poisons. She buys a hand grinder and a book about how to make your own baby food. She spends hours cooking and then pummelling carrots, apples, potatoes, garden-fresh peas, lima beans, turnips, and squash. She prepares gourmet infant meals which Samuel promptly spits all over her. He likes bananas. That's all. Bananas mushed up with milk. Everything else ends up in his or her hair.

On Samuel's first birthday, Joanna makes him a special supper. She puts the tomatoes in boiling water, then dips them in cold water and peels them, picks out every single seed, boils them down, purées them in the blender. She boils the spaghetti noodles till they are very soft and cuts them lovingly into tiny Samuel-size bites. She arranges it all in his special Beatrix Potter bowl and lets it cool. Gordon puts Samuel in the high chair and Joanna puts the bowl on the tray. Samuel waves his arms at his meal and gurgles happily. Joanna feels like a good mother, a very good mother, a damn-near perfect mother. Gordon hovers around the high chair with the camera ready. Samuel puts the full bowl upside-down on top of his head. The food slides down his face. He throws the bowl on the floor and waves his arms around some more. Gordon is roaring with laughter. Samuel is crowing and smearing the tomato sauce and noodles all over his face. Joanna is laughing too and pointing, saying, "Smile for Daddy now, smile! Say cheese!"

But down on her hands and knees, sponging the slop off the linoleum, she begins to cry softly, softly, so softly that nobody notices, and in the morning, first thing, she goes to the A&P and loads up the cart with two dozen little glass jars.

9. Mountain

LEWIS AND WANDA were going to the Rockies for a ski week in March. This was a trip they made every year. They loved skiing. They loved mountains.

Three days before their departure, Lewis asked Joanna if she would house-sit for them: they'd been broken into once before and they were worried. Joanna agreed.

An hour later Lewis called back and said, "No. Please forgive me. I wasn't thinking clearly. It would be too painful for you."

But Joanna said, "No, I want to do it, let me."

They left on Thursday afternoon. Lewis called from the airport to say goodbye one more time. He had, he said, told Wanda he was going to the washroom. Into the telephone he said, "You know I won't be able to write, probably not even a postcard. You understand," and Joanna said, "Yes, I understand." It was hard to believe that words could ever cross those mountains anyway and still make sense on the other side. Words would be snowbound, banging up against icebergs and rock faces, solid straight through. He might as well be going to another planet for all that she could reach him there. Inside the mountains, the silence, she supposed, would be as vast as the space. She thought about the Frank Slide eighty years ago when the side of Turtle Mountain came loose in the Crowsnest Pass and the rock covered railways, roads, houses, and farms, the whole sleeping town of Frank, Alberta, mothers, fathers, children, lovers, dogs, cats, cows, and goldfish. The new highway went over the spot now—she'd seen somebody's vacation snapshots of it once. There was nothing to see but a vast grey field of boulders and a historical plaque commemorating the disaster. Everything must be imagined, including the bodies, like words, still locked within the unreliable, unyielding earth.

Joanna had never been to the mountains herself. She didn't like travelling. She didn't know how to ski and had no desire to learn. If she and Lewis ever ended up together, she figured then maybe she would.

Into the telephone now he said, "I love you," and in the background Joanna could hear a tumult of travellers and then his flight being called.

"I love you, yes, I do love you," she said, encouraged by the sound of his voice. Maybe he really would leave Wanda someday. She had to keep hoping for that. She'd said to him once (in anger, but truthfully), "I want to be your lover, not your mistress." A lover, she figured, was always propelled by anticipation and passion, by a picture of a future very different from today. A mistress, on the other hand, was calm and self-contained, well-dressed and quite satisfied with two afternoons a week, having mastered her problematic expectations and gone on with her separate successful life. A lover would be wild-eyed and volatile, subject to hysteria, insomnia, substance abuse, perched always on the brink of weeping or wailing, of delivering an ultimatum or taking it back. A mistress would have her rendezvous pencilled into her leather-bound monogrammed appointment book.

On Friday Joanna was busy all day, had a meeting with a new gallery owner that ran late, drinks downtown afterwards, but she thought often of Lewis and Wanda's house sitting there empty, not bleak but still, the beams shifting imperceptibly in the cold weather, then settling again with something like a sigh. She was comforted by the image of each uninhabited room with every article in its place: every table, chair, and knick-knack fairly gleaming with harmony as in a painting, a still life with flowers and fruit in a hand-turned wooden bowl. She did not think much about skiing or gondolas or hot-rum toddies, woolly sweaters and rosy cheeks in front of a fieldstone fireplace. This trip had been planned last winter, long before she and Lewis became lovers. There was nothing she could do. It, like many things lately, was out of her control.

On Saturday she went to the library and borrowed books about mountains. Maybe this way she could reach him. Maybe this way she could find out what she needed to know. They were heavy hard-covered coffee-table books with large glossy pages of thrilling full-colour photographs briefly captioned with useful and intriguing snippets of information.

There were no people in these pictures, at least no live ones, only ghosts and the occasional daring mountain goat. There was certainly no sign of Lewis schussing down the slopes in his red balaclava, lime-green gaiters, and black-mirrored goggles, looking like an alien attempting to fly. There was certainly no sign of Wanda, either whisking and whispering down behind him or stuck whining at the top because she was afraid. Certainly, no matter how long Joanna looked at the pictures, none of her questions would be answered in them. They might as well be hieroglyphics.

On Sunday around suppertime she went over to the house. It had snowed during the night, two or three pristine inches everywhere, white city snow which would soon enough be muddied brown, not blue mountain snow which might remain unseen, unsullied, for years. She drove her car back and forth in the driveway several times. Lewis had asked her to do this to make the house look lived-in. Then she parked her car snug up behind theirs, a nondescript blue mid-size, plugged in, she noticed, with a perfectly coiled orange extension cord. She could imagine Lewis carefully plugging it in while he and Wanda waited for the taxi to the airport, could see him checking the connection once, twice, patting the hood as he walked away, and her throat swelled with a sudden excess of emotion.

She swept the snow off the front steps with the broom he'd left by the side of the house, took the accumulated mail out of the box, and felt the neighbours watching her.

She unlocked the front door the way he'd shown her. It was a sticky lock and she had to jiggle the key several times to release it. She took off her jacket and boots (her socks too, for no reason) and left them in the foyer.

In the living room she perched on the arm of the sofa beside the fig tree and the floor lamp with the stained-glass shade. She had been here many times before, to dinner, to parties. She had endured whole evenings in this room, long hours made bearable by meaningful glances over the edges of coffee cups and crystal liqueur glasses, long hours made keen by the threat or temptation of giving herself away.

Now the hardwood floor glowed warmly immaculate beneath her bare feet and she could see the streetlights coming on through the white sheers hung across the front bay window. She flipped automatically through the sheaf of envelopes in her hand: bills mostly, junk mail, something from the tax department for Lewis, a bulky letter in a mauve envelope for Wanda, a bank statement addressed to them both, a postcard with a picture of palm trees, green water, white sand. She read the card without conscience, for postcards, by their peculiarly public nature, seem to be fair enough game for curious eyes. It said, among other things, *Remember the time we were all down here together? Remember the mangoes? We miss you. Let's do it again soon! Love always, Don and Susie.* Joanna was obscurely hurt to think that Lewis had never mentioned these people, obviously longtime continuing friends with whom he had shared meals, parties probably, whole holidays, maybe even secrets.

She left the mail on the coffee table beside an aesthetically arranged seashell collection, a blue ceramic bowl full of walnuts, and the last three issues of *Ski Magazine*.

In the kitchen she found a note from Wanda stuck to the fridge with a ceramic magnet in the remarkably lifelike shape of a lobster. Beside it was a snapshot of Lewis and Wanda drinking out of Styrofoam cups at a picnic table in the pines. The note explained when to water the plants, when to put out the garbage, and how to unlock the liquor cabinet. It also contained the name and number of the ski chalet where they could be reached in case of an emergency. She did not read this part because she did not want to be tempted to get hysterical and call him.

Stuck up beside the note with another magnet, this one in the shape of a pineapple, was a full-colour brochure for the chalet. In the pictures, the mountains were alternately rosy and protective or black and white and dangerous. It occurred to Joanna that if Lewis really did want to get rid of Wanda, it would be easily enough accomplished in the mountains: just a little nudge and Wanda would go straight over the edge, surprised and still smiling, Lewis left perched on the summit alone with his skis braced and his eyes shut, to not see the look on her face when she started to tumble, head over heels and screaming, falling so far that when she hit the bottom, Lewis would hear nothing. If a tree falls in the forest and there's no one there to hear it, does it make a sound?

But Joanna wasn't sure that Lewis really did want to get rid of Wanda. At least he didn't want to *actively* get rid of Wanda. Once he said he wished that she too would fall in love with someone else and leave him and then nobody could ever construe the whole sad situation as being in any way his fault. Then he would not have to spend the rest of his life feeling guilty and, after a decent interval, six months at least, he and Joanna could get together publicly and nobody, least of all Wanda, would ever suspect that they'd been sleeping together all along. Once he said he wished Wanda would just disappear and be done with it.

Maybe an avalanche would be the answer, Wanda's removal taken clear out of Lewis's hands, Wanda's small body dragged off by tumbling tonnes of snow travelling at one hundred kilometres per hour, Wanda's small body scooped up and then deposited at the bottom of the slope to be dug up by search dogs in the summer, every bone in her body broken, her poles and goggles still attached.

Joanna opened the fridge and poked around: eggs, milk, plain yogurt, apples, tomatoes, an orange the size of a grapefruit, a chunk of white cheese with blue mould on one side. She was momentarily awash in a wave of nausea or fatigue.

"Tired," she said into the empty house. "I am bone tired."

She leaned against the stainless steel sink and looked out the window into the backyard where the bright moon on the white snow cast an eerie edge of light across the shrubbery, the blackened raspberry canes, the bird feeder hung from the poplar tree.

She poured herself a drink of brandy and went up the stairs with the snifter cupped in both hands. Her legs, she noticed as if from a great and precarious height, were trembling.

In Lewis's studio she browsed through the books on the shelf, leafed through a pile of receipts and scrap paper in a wire basket on top of the filing cabinet. She thought fleetingly that he might have left her a note somewhere, a message somehow, something to signal that he knew she was there. But no, that was foolish. How could he possibly have managed (or risked) such a thing?

She examined his brushes and paint tubes which were meticulously arranged on a small metal table to the right of the easel. The brushes were placed in precise descending order according to width. The paint tubes were laid out in an accurate spectrum from dark to light. She picked the tube of Chinese blue from its proper position and wedged it in between Verona brown and raw sienna. Then she moved it back.

Lewis's paintings were propped all around the room in various stages of completion. She had often expressed envy at his ability to work on several paintings simultaneously. Personally she felt compelled to finish one piece before beginning another. She was the same way about books, reading one at a time all the way to the end before picking up a new one. Lewis was the opposite, reading five or six different books at once, a novel by Milan Kundera, poetry by Leonard Cohen, a biography of Salvador Dali, a travelogue of the Greek Islands, *Man and His Symbols* by Carl Jung. Joanna thought they must get all mixed up in his mind, like poorly done watercolours bleeding into each other so everything ended up an ugly muddied brown. She said that if she tried reading that way, Carl Jung and Salvador Dali would end up drinking ouzo in a taverna on the island of Rhodes, reciting Cohen's poetry and debating Kundera's concept of eternal return.

Lewis just laughed and said his mind didn't work that way, he didn't let things get muddled up, he'd trained himself to keep things in separate compartments to hold disorder at bay. In light of their current situation, Joanna did not like to contemplate the contents of these compartments in too much detail. She knew there was one with her name on it.

Now she sat down on the floor beside the wicker wastebasket which was half-full of balls of crumpled yellow paper. She was a little disgusted with herself when she began opening each one as if it were a gift, but then she convinced herself that anyone in such a circumstance would have done exactly the same thing, whether they cared to admit it or not. She carefully smoothed out each page on the floor between her outstretched legs, smiling fondly at the sight of his precise handwriting. They were mostly notes to himself: *Don't forget to plug the car in. Get skis tuned up. Pick up dry cleaning. Pay phone bill. Cancel newspaper. Buy condoms.*

She carefully crumpled the pieces of paper up again and dropped them one by one back into the basket.

As she crossed the hall and entered the bedroom, the night-light, which was hooked to a timer, came on suddenly. She had never been in this room before.

Their wedding picture sat on top of the bureau in a silver frame. Wanda had white flowers in her hair and Lewis had his arm around her slim shoulders. In the background there were mountains, rosy and protective, the same mountains as in the ski chalet brochure. Joanna realized that she'd never asked Lewis where they got married. This was just one of many questions she'd never asked him, for fear of having to face up to the answers which would be stuck then forever inside her brain. Now it made sense, this ritual annual trip to the mountains. They probably rented the very same room, the one advertised in the brochure, the one with a Jacuzzi, a heart-shaped bed, mirrors on the ceiling, and matching velour bathrobes provided free of charge. They probably thought of it as a renewal, a rejuvenation of their vows. To her it was a return to the scene of the crime.

Beside the wedding picture was a leather-bound journal which she opened in the middle to find Wanda's handwriting covering page after page and so she did not read it. There was also an envelope of photographs marked CHRISTMAS which she did not look at.

In the top drawer of the bureau there was a tangle of socks, underwear, belts and scarves, an elegant lacy camisole. In the bottom drawer there were carefully folded shorts and T-shirts, a shiny red bathing suit smelling salty, waiting for summer which was bound to come upon them again just as it always did.

On the bedside table there was a box of pink Kleenex, a pair of gold earrings, a small digital clock with insistent red numbers, two empty water glasses, and a miscellaneous jumble of coins and paper clips, matchbooks, and sugarless gum.

The bed was small, a well-cared-for antique with carved head- and footboards. It was covered with a colourful quilt, obviously handmade, probably by somebody's grandmother. There were four fluffy pillows in pure white cotton cases. She could not imagine which side of the bed Lewis slept on.

She turned off the night-light and lay down exactly in the center of the bed. She pulled the quilt around herself and looked at the ceiling, resting the brandy snifter in both hands on her chest. In a while she set the glass on the bedside table and then she fell asleep in the perfectly peaceful house.

10. House

ESTHER AND CLARENCE lived in what was known as "a wartime house." Although Joanna knew this only meant it had been built during the war, sometimes it felt like a fortress, a haven of safety which occasionally appeared in her dreams, surrounded by barbed wire, mine-fields, and soldiers who could not see them, they were so well hidden, so cleverly barricaded behind its sturdy impenetrable walls.

The little house on Mary Street was the middle one in a row of seven identical little houses. It was square, covered in white asphalt shingles (later replaced with immaculate aluminum siding) with green wooden steps front and back (later replaced at the front with wrought-iron railings and hollow concrete steps) and green shingles on the roof (later replaced with black shingles which sparkled in the sun). Over the years, all of the houses changed eventually as the owners worked hard, made money, and added porches, patios, picture windows, and carports. Some families had more babies and built on bedrooms or they got dogs and built little houses for them out back. Some families moved away and then their houses were filled up with new people who changed things yet again just to suit themselves. But for a time the seven little houses on Mary Street were all exactly the same and Joanna just naturally assumed that everybody everywhere lived the way they did. Eventually she came to hate the little house at 126 Mary Street, but for a long time she loved it and all the six others exactly the same.

Originally the house consisted of five rooms: the living room, two small bedrooms, and the bathroom, all opening off the kitchen which was the biggest room in the house. There was an attic but no real basement, just a dugout which was intermittently inhabited by fertile families of grey mice so that Clarence had to go down and set traps with bits of bread and cheese. He always managed to dispose of the soft furry corpses when Joanna wasn't around.

After muttering about it for years, Clarence finally made Esther happy and took to renovating, knocking out a wall and doubling the size of the living room, putting in a picture window, and adding two rooms onto the back: a bigger bedroom for them and what they referred to as "the utility room," which housed the washer and dryer and several white metal cabinets of varying sizes for storing canned goods, pots and pans, sheets and towels, and the vacuum cleaner.

That summer Joanna got a dollhouse for her seventh birthday. It was the house she had been dreaming of: two storeys made of tin, four rooms on each floor, with all the necessary details printed right on: paintings, curtains, carpets, a red-brick fireplace with orange flames in the living room, books in floor-to-ceiling brown shelves in the den, blue towels in the bathroom, a blank TV screen in the family room, a clock in the kitchen set forever at 3:15. The outside of the house was done in Colonial style, with black shutters at every window and permanently pruned green bushes all around the bottom. There was a set of miniature plastic furniture for each of the eight rooms. Joanna spent hours rearranging, redecorating, moving the sleeping black cat from the bay window in the living room to the biggest bed upstairs, and wishing, always wishing, for a rocking chair, a new chesterfield, a real swinging cradle for the baby.

The trouble was there was no baby. No baby, no mommy, no daddy, no nothing. The only living thing in the whole perfect house was Blackie the cat and he was asleep. Joanna fairly soon tired of trying to imagine a family into those orderly well-furnished rooms. She could never quite decide what their names were from one day to the next. They would not sit still, always changing, surprising, disappointing, or scaring her. Sometimes the daddy was tall, dark, and handsome, a teacher, smart, kind, and generous. Sometimes he was bald and fat, a butcher whose white apron across his big belly was always splattered with blood so that even his own children were half-scared of him. Sometimes these children were clean and happy, safe and sound. Sometimes they got sick, had nightmares, hit each other, broke things and got sent to their rooms for the rest of the afternoon. Sometimes the baby was rosy and sweet, a little angel who sucked her thumb and gurgled. Sometimes she cried all day and all night. Sometimes the mommy was cheerful and pretty, with her hair done up in beautiful black curls and her lipstick on while she baked chocolate chip cookies and hummed in the sunlit fragrant kitchen. Sometimes the mommy had bags under her eyes, her hair left in curlers all day as she sat in the bay window in her housecoat and cried. Sometimes she told the whole bunch of them to go away and leave her alone.

Sometimes there were no children at all, just the mommy and the daddy alone in that big house with nothing to do.

Soon enough the perfect dollhouse went the way of all exhausted toys: first to the top shelf of Joanna's bedroom closet where it gathered dust and the odd spiderweb, reminding her of an abandoned house she'd seen once with empty black windows that had frightened her, the front door dangling open as if someone had just left in a hurry, a torn white curtain flapping through a broken upstairs window like a flag. She got all shivery trying to imagine a house with nobody living in it. It was like trying to imagine her own self dead.

Then the perfect dollhouse went up to the attic and she seldom thought of it again.

When Joanna got to Grade Eight, she had to take Home Ec once a week. She, like all the other thirteen-year-old girls she knew, was glad. Enough of all that other useless stuff. Now they were going to learn something important. Now they were going to learn how to cook, clean, sew, and clip coupons. Now they were going to learn how to keep house.

They began in September with cooking. The teacher, Miss Murchie, led them step-by-step through the mechanics of preparing a nutritious but inexpensive family meal. They spent one whole class going through recipes and planning the menu. Democratically they settled on salmon croquettes, peas and carrots, coleslaw, and Jubilee fruit salad for dessert. They spent the next class drawing up the grocery list with the aid of the local newspaper from which they determined which store had the best bargains on which items. Miss Murchie did not mention that this method of grocery shopping would involve driving all over town all afternoon just to save six cents on the cabbage, twelve cents on the grapes, and twenty-three whole cents on the salmon.

Because each Home Ec class was only fifty minutes, they actually made these dishes one at a time. They learned that each recipe must be followed to the letter in the right order and that there was a specific time limit allotted for each consecutive step, which Miss Murchie clocked with her stopwatch. They learned that dry ingredients must not be measured in the same cup as liquid ingredients. They learned that a carrot must not be chopped with the same knife as an apple. They learned how to peel grapes. They learned the all-important difference between a pinch and a dash. Last but not least, they learned how to set the table so that even a simple meal looked like a veritable banquet.

Four classes later they learned how to do the dishes. Joanna had been helping Esther with the dishes every night for years. Esther washed and Joanna dried and put away, the two of them gazing out the window, listening to the radio and humming along, or maybe Esther was talking about what happened on her soap opera that afternoon or wondering why the climbing roses on the trellis weren't blooming yet, or maybe Joanna was telling her that Susie Arneson didn't like Dennis Jackowski any more, now she liked Phillip Churchill instead, or hoping that tomorrow's History test would be multiple choice and not true or false. Meanwhile the dishes always got done and it never occurred to Joanna that there might be a trick to any of it.

Now she learned in Home Ec that they had been doing the dishes all wrong. What you were supposed to do was the cutlery first and then the cups and glasses because these were the items that went right into your mouth. Then you could do the plates, saucers, bowls, et cetera. Finally you finished up with the pots and pans, but not before you'd drained and then refilled the sink with fresh soapy water. Also, speaking of sinks, you were supposed to have two: one for washing and one for rinsing. You were supposed to wear rubber gloves to protect your skin and jewellery.

Upon hearing all this, Esther just snorted and said she'd been doing the dishes for forty years (in one sink with her bare hands, no less— she considered rubber gloves a pretentious affectation of those who fancied themselves upper class) and she had no intention of changing now. If the old way had been good enough for the last forty years, it would be good enough for the next forty. She'd said as much about the new math too.

Joanna had to admit her mother had a good point. She was suspicious too of the fact that, in total, it had taken a team of twenty girls six whole weeks to prepare one nutritious but inexpensive family meal. At this rate, Joanna suspected, the poor little family would have starved to death long before it was time to don the rubber gloves.

Next the class went on to a more promising project called "Planning Your Dream Home." First each girl selected a floor plan from a fat book, then enlarged and transcribed her plan onto a sheet of bristol board using the appropriate drafting symbols for windows, doors, electrical outlets, and plumbing fixtures. They were given little indication as to how these houses would actually be constructed. This work, it was assumed, would be done by men, men who knew, as if by magic, how to pour concrete, erect walls, run wires, lay pipes, and shingle roofs. The girls in Home Ec, who would become women and so did not need to concern themselves with such abstractions, were required to do the interior decorating. Much of this would also need to be realized by men, men who would apply paint and wallpaper, lay carpet and tile, and move the furniture around until they got it right. These men were not expected to have a say in choosing these items. Rather they had only to assemble and admire them as the women directed. The function of these men of the future, it seemed, was the execution of the women's dreams. They would also provide the necessary financing without complaint.

Miss Murchie gave the girls a dozen wallpaper books and a shoe box full of paint chips from which to select their colour schemes. They were to find the furnishings on their own.

For weeks Joanna spent hours each evening combing through old magazines and catalogues. With her mother's manicure scissors, she clipped beds, tables, cabinets, shelves, desks, couches, footstools, stoves, fridges, and chairs of all kinds. Then she arranged the pieces in the appropriate rooms. Of course the objects were not in proportion or perspective, so that in the living room the oak coffee table was three times the size of the flowered love seat, and in the kitchen the matching almond fridge and stove took up most of the floor space while the table and chairs were an inch square in the corner. In this way the dream home took on a seductive surreal quality, like a scene from *Alice in Wonderland*.

Joanna dreamed about the project the night before she handed it in. In the dream she found herself inside her own dream home come to three-dimensional life. Moving from room to room, she changed size accordingly as the perspective lines dissolved and reformed around her. There were vanishing points everywhere, askew and awry, disappearing, as was their habit, into thin air. In Art class she had been learning about vanishing points. In real life she knew about perspective and putting things in it.

perspective *n.* 1. the art of drawing objects or a scene on a flat surface so as to show them as they appear to the eye with reference to relative position, size, depth, or distance. 2. *a)* a mental point of view of the relative importance of things or events, *b)* the ability to see things in their true relationship. 3. a distant vista or view.

In real life she already knew that you cannot ever see things as they really are. The farther away an object is, the smaller it appears. She knew that a four-storey building six blocks away looks smaller than a matchbox in the palm of your hand. She knew that past the vanishing point all objects are equal: invisible. She did not know yet if these apparent paradoxes were caprices of reality or vision or both.

In the dream the floors of her house were spongy and her head brushed the ceiling as she grew to fit the furniture in the living room. She shrank to the size of a peanut as she stretched out on the four-poster bed in the master bedroom. She would not have been surprised to find the Cheshire cat asleep at her tiny cold feet. She got an A+ on this project without ever having mentioned the dream.

When Joanna first began sleeping with Henry, he was living in an unfinished house with two other men. It was a prefab house, what the men called "a package." It had arrived originally on a huge flatbed truck, all the pieces precut and numbered like a giant wooden puzzle. It came with a thick manual of diagrams and directions on how to assemble the pieces in the correct order so they would turn themselves into a finished house.

Luke, who owned the house (and the as-yet-unassembled pieces still stacked in the backyard), had begun building two years earlier when he was still married and planning to live happily ever after. But then his wife ran off with another man. After that Luke was laid off from his job at a local construction company and went on unemployment. He rented out the bedrooms to his friends to help pay the mortgage. He was a quiet man, filled now with love and pain in equally debilitating quantities. He was still building in fits and starts, when he felt like it, when he could afford it.

When the men got motivated, they put more parts of the house together: another wall, a door, a few sheets of drywall, tile on the bathroom walls, baseboards in the kitchen, a railing on the basement stairs. When Joanna went over, she might find the living room enclosed where there had only been open beams before. Or there was a full-fledged door on the bathroom where there had been only a curtain hung from nails, and she knew the men could hear her peeing and putting in her diaphragm before bed. Once she went over late at night and found Henry sleeping in a different room altogether because they were working on his. Waking in the middle of the night, she couldn't find the bathroom.

She never knew what to expect when she went there. The house was like a person whose mood you could never count on. One day this person would hug you and laugh, the next day she would cut you in the street. It wore her down. Henry began by mutual agreement to sleep at her place instead, although she had only a single bed. Joanna said she felt better there, with the walls and floors complete and unchanging around her. Somehow she imagined that in a solid finished house their relationship would be solid too. During the next month most of Henry's stuff ended up in her apartment, and it soon seemed silly to be paying rent on a room he didn't live in so he gave Luke notice and then they were officially living together. They said they'd buy a bigger bed soon but they never did.

Lewis had fantasies about the house he and Joanna would live in some day. It was modelled on a restored stone house on Pembroke Street near the waterfront. Their dream house too would have real red shutters, window boxes overflowing with purple lobelia and pale pink impatiens, dense vines growing up the sunny southern wall. They dreamed aloud about this house until it was perfect in every detail and they were living happily ever after in each beautifully appointed heritage room.

They did not allow their fantasy to be tainted by the troublesome realities of finance or circumstance. Lewis never asked Joanna, "How will we afford it, both of us artists with no visible means of support?" Joanna never asked Lewis, "Aren't you forgetting something? What about your wife?" In this fantasy, Joanna dealt with Wanda the way Esther dealt with photographs of herself that she didn't like: she cut herself out with the manicure scissors and often sent the rest on to Joanna who had grown accustomed to receiving these odd-sized remnants of her parents' lives.

One day when Joanna happened to pass the old stone house on Pembroke Street, there was a For Sale sign out front. She nearly wrecked the car. She drove around the block four times to be sure.

At home she could not call Lewis because Wanda was home from work that day, sick with the flu. (He had called first thing in the morning to tell her this, to say he would not be able to come over that afternoon as planned. He called from the drugstore where he had gone to buy Milk of Magnesia.) Instead Joanna called the real estate agent whose name was on the sign. She told the agent that she and her husband were interested in viewing the stone house on Pembroke Street. The agent said the asking price was $329,000. Joanna said that was no problem. They made an appointment for the afternoon after next (surely Wanda would be better by then).

Lewis called again around suppertime. He was at the corner store this time, buying a newspaper and some ginger ale. Wanda was on the mend. Joanna told him about the house, the price, the appointment. He was silent. He was horrified. He was angry. He said, "Are you out of your mind?" He refused to go and look at the house.

Joanna said, "Fuck you then. I'll go and see it by myself."

When she arrived at the appointed time, the agent was waiting on the front steps. The real red shutters were open, the window boxes were overflowing, and the vine on the south wall was lush in the sunlight. Joanna waved at the woman and then drove away.

After Joanna and Gordon have bought their big house on Laverty Street, they quickly discover that they are not especially good at household management. They have never been home owners before, and much as they are theoretically thrilled with their new elevated status they are terribly daunted by the realities of maintenance, upkeep, and repair. Joanna is surprised to discover that Gordon doesn't know any more about these things than she does. She realizes that she has been nursing her own sexist stereotypes, assuming that all men are mechanically inclined, born with a basic knowledge of plumbing, electricity, and home heating.

Much as they love their house, they are a little afraid of it too. Joanna is seized with a paralysing panic when things break down or might. She dreams of the furnace and/or the hot-water tank exploding, the wiring sizzling inside the walls, the chimney catching fire, the sewer backing up all over the basement. She never worried about such things when she was renting, as if her transient status effectively exonerated her from responsibility for the workings of the place and also, by extrapolation, from the threat of personal injury or possible death due to the malfunction of said workings. Now there is no landlord to call.

Often she overhears other people (older, wiser people who have been home owners for years, women in camel hair coats in the grocery store lineup, red-faced matter-of-fact men in hunting caps at the bank) discussing such household catastrophes. Their voices thrill with the details of disaster. She speeds home afterwards, running yellow lights, with a knot in her stomach. She is convinced that when she rounds the corner of their street (tires squealing), it will be to find several large firetrucks in the driveway, a dozen firemen in yellow hats scaling the walls, hacking the roof open with their silver axes to release mushroom clouds of hot black smoke. Each time this does not happen, each time she returns to find the house as she left it (patient, empty, and cool), her knees go weak with relief and she whispers small prayers of thanksgiving.

She remembers five years ago when Henry's friend Doug's house blew up. A work crew had been digging up the street in front of Doug's house when they hit a gas line. He said later that he had been lying on the couch watching TV when he felt the house grow suddenly cold and unnaturally still. He jumped through the window of the back door just as it blew sky-high. When Joanna and Henry walked over to have a look, they saw the side walls blown out, the roof collapsed, and the front wall lying flat in the front yard with the curtains still on the rods above the broken windows. Insulation lay in puffy pink bats all over the yard. There were also plants blown out of their pots, records whole but with no labels tossed onto the grass like Frisbees, a broken aquarium with no fish in sight, a Canadian flag tacked to what had been the ceiling, a stereo turntable with its guts hanging out, and a wooden door, closed, still in its frame in the wall which lay flat on the grass.

Joanna quickly discovers that a large part of home ownership involves calling repairmen (usually three or four times before she can reach them) and then waiting for them. She spends whole days stuck in the house when she might have been out. The truth is she probably wouldn't have gone out anyway, she would have been working all day in her studio, but at least she wouldn't have felt so trapped and impatient. She hates waiting. She gets angrier by the hour, but when the guy finally shows up at quarter after five, she wants to sink to her knees and hug his smelly overalled legs. She wants to say, "Marry me! Marry me!" But she is already married. To a man who knows nothing about home maintenance. She wants to say, "Adopt me! Adopt me!" With a man like this around the house, she imagines she would never be worried again.

Lewis and Wanda's house is not far. Joanna drives by it fairly often, almost without thinking, almost, the car, it seems, sliding into cruise control and automatically following that route, which is the fastest, least congested way to get to or from downtown. Considering that they are nearly neighbours, it is surprising how seldom she and Lewis run into each other.

Lewis and Wanda's house always looks abandoned. No signs of life. Dark brown brick, empty black windows, garage doors closed, the lawn in the summer brown and shaggy, a few untrimmed shrubs, no flowers, the driveway in the winter seldom shovelled, dirty car tracks, no footprints. The only evidence of habitation is the mail occasionally poking out of the box and the garbage in bags at the curb if she happens to pass by early on a Wednesday. Otherwise, the house looks deserted, expressionless, hermetically sealed with secrets, vacant or evacuated.

Some days this makes her feel sad as she sails by with Samuel safely buckled up in the back, the radio blaring, the two of them humming along, or Samuel singing solo, off-key but enthusiastic. Some days, less charitable days, this makes her feel victorious, as if in the struggle to survive their calamitous romance, she has emerged the winner.

Her house fairly bursts with exuberance. She thinks this as she drives by it, something she does fairly often, shamefaced, feeling foolish to be driving slowly by her own house to admire it from the outside, the way she imagines passing strangers do. "Gee," Samuel teases as they pass, "I wonder who lives in that nice cosy house?"

There are riding toys in the driveway, the shovel in winter stuck in a snowbank, the green hose in summer unravelled across the front yard, a sawhorse and some lumber from Gordon's latest do-it-yourself project, bedding plants in flats ready to go into the ground, also the lawn mower plugged in, ready, clothes flapping on the line out back, the wheelbarrow filled with black dirt. All the windows are open like smiling mouths, emitting soft music and laughter. It is as if, Joanna thinks, the front door might be flung open at any moment and the lady of the house (her!) will be standing there waving and inviting you to come on in, have some coffee, fresh muffins, a cool glass of wine, strawberries from the garden, take off your shoes, lay down your burdens, have some more coffee, another glass of wine, bring the baby, the dog, your boyfriend, your mother, your husband, there's always enough, more than enough, there's always enough for everyone. In fact, she and Gordon live quite solitary lives but they do it because they want to, not because they have to.

11. Black

THE COLOUR OF the room you would like to lie down in for a few days, maybe a week, a small perfectly black room, the black you fall into when you turn out the light and your eyes have not yet adjusted to the darkness, that pitch-dark blind-black just before the objects begin to assume their shadowy shapes again, the dresser, the bed posts, the window, the doorknob, the ceiling, reforming piecemeal until you are surrounded again. A small room, perfectly black, also perfectly silent, so that you do not have to hear traffic or voices out in the street, the furnace, the fridge, the phone, footsteps, sirens, music, another person breathing and believing in you. A small black silent room with nothing in it but a bed, where you could lie suspended, not sleeping exactly but floating in and out of consciousness, your own or someone else's, for a string of unmarked hours during which you do not have to talk, eat, cook, clean, cry, dream, roll over, or go to the bathroom. A small black silent room where you never need anything, not forever, just for a few days, maybe a week, just long enough to find . . . long enough to find what? You're not sure but you know you've lost or are missing something, perhaps you never had it in the first place, or perhaps you left it somewhere, or maybe it is just hiding, under the couch, behind the TV, out back in the long grass, or down in the bushes at the limits of the city, but all they ever find in the wilderness these days are the dismembered body parts of murdered women and the moss-covered skulls of missing children, so of course you're afraid to look there for fear you might find a part of yourself you don't recognize. It must be like love, this mysterious missing link, the way you've always been told: "Don't worry about love. You'll know it when you find it." A small black silent room. You'll know it when you find yourself in it.

12. Mutton

RHYMES WITH *BUTTON*. Button, button, who's got the button?

Esther saved buttons in an old biscuit tin. Although she never talked about having lived through the Great Depression, this button-saving habit was part of that legacy. Whenever an item of clothing wore out or no longer fit, she carefully snipped off the buttons and put them in the tin. She also saved zippers, picking out the stitches one by one with her silver seam ripper, then putting the zipper in a bag already filled with others of all sizes and colours, curled around each other like benign snakes. The pieces of fabric were cut into squares and used as rags until they fell apart.

Occasionally Esther found a use for the old buttons, replacing those which had fallen off and been lost. But most often it was Joanna who dipped her hands deep into the button tin, pulling up whole handfuls and then letting them drop through her fingers like jewels. She could spend all afternoon playing with the buttons, counting and sorting, arranging and rearranging them by colour or size all over the kitchen floor. Sometimes she pretended they were money and played store.

Her favourites were the tiny pearl buttons, of which there were many, and one flat metal button, gold-coloured but hollow. On it was the raised figure of an ancient soldier, Greek or Roman, down on one knee in a tunic and a winged helmet. His left arm was outstretched, holding a small round shield. Hung from his right shoulder was a long stick or sword. Esther could not remember what garment this button might have come from.

Esther's habit of economy extended to many areas. She saved used paper bags, tinfoil, waxed paper, cardboard boxes of all sizes, wrapping paper, TV dinner trays, egg cartons, and string. She practised the three R's, Reduce, Reuse, Recycle, long before they became politically correct. She abhorred all manner of waste and extravagance. Later Joanna will appreciate this but at the time she found Esther's habits annoying (as if she were just being stingy) or embarrassing (as if they were so poor they couldn't afford to throw anything away).

Esther was only extravagant when it came to winter coats. If she must live in this God-forsaken frozen climate for six months of the year, then at least she would do it with style. She owned a magnificent fur coat which she kept in cold storage over the summer and, when the temperatures began to drop in the fall, retrieved and wore proudly all winter long. It was a mouton coat, so heavy that Joanna could barely lift it. One night when there was a power failure for eight hours three days after Christmas, Esther covered Joanna, asleep, with her mouton coat. When Joanna woke up in the morning she was sweaty and, with the weight of the coat upon her, she could hardly get out of bed.

It was a long time before Joanna understood that mouton was a fancy French word for mutton, which meant in fact sheep. She had imagined that a mouton must be a very rare and precious animal from which such elegant garments were made. Perhaps it lived in Antarctica, perhaps it was ten feet tall, perhaps it was like a unicorn with fur. Eventually she came to understand that the coat had been made from sheep, those fat dirty slow-moving animals she saw from the car when they drove in the country. She felt she had been tricked.

By this time Esther had a new winter coat, Persian lamb, with deep rolled cuffs and a stylish flare at the hem. Joanna was shocked. It was bad enough to have learned the truth about those diagrams of lambs she had coloured in the old cookbook. Now she had also to consider the fact that lambs were skinned and made into coats. She could not imagine how many little lambs had been killed before she knew what was going on. She could not imagine the extent of the brutality that went on in the world behind her back.

13. Comfort

JOANNA WAS FEELING a lot better. The sound of Lewis's name or the sight of a stranger on the street who remotely resembled him no longer caused her heart to dip alarmingly or her stomach to go hard as if she'd swallowed an apple whole. She thought she was almost over him now. It had been six months. She was feeling a lot better. She thought she might live after all.

After six months of celibacy, sex had been reduced in her memory to a remote and unlikely configuration of body parts. She went to bed alone each night in her flannelette nightie and her socks, with a book and sometimes a snack, a plate of cheese and crackers, a piece of cold pizza, a bowl of pretzels or chips. Trying in vain to imagine a hard hairy body onto the unrumpled expanse of mattress beside her, she was left feeling wooden but renascently pure.

For a time, she'd been convinced that she would never have sex again. She had imagined herself alone forever, dedicated to loving Lewis even though they could never be together. She would remain constant, chaste and faithful to him, to the memory of his love. She would be forever untouched by other human (probably sweaty and clumsy) hands. She would be like the woman in black at the end of the pier in *The French Lieutenant's Woman*, the motionless mythical Sarah Woodruff staring out to sea. However, her sense of humour often interfered with the perfection of this fantasy, frequently reminding her of an old cartoon she'd seen once which said that a tragic life was only romantic when it happened to somebody else.

Now Joanna supposed that her life would eventually settle back onto her, resuming much the same shape and form it had taken before she'd fallen in love with Lewis. Now she supposed that there would be whole days some day when she wouldn't even think of him, whole days when she might look back and think that nothing had happened, nothing had changed, and no, her life had not been ruined after all. Now she supposed that eventually she would have sex again but she could not quite yet imagine how all those squirming curves and bony hollows fit together in the first place. She worried that, if and when the time came, she wouldn't remember how it was done. She'd heard that making love was like riding a bicycle: once you'd learned, you never forgot. Joanna never had been much good at bicycle riding, especially those ones with multiple gears and hand brakes.

She worried that, if and when the time came, she would burst into laughter and ruin everything.

She thought she wouldn't take Lewis back now, not even if he came crawling and crying on his hands and knees. She played this whole scene out in her mind frequently, in exquisite and gratifying detail.

Lewis would come to her door in the early morning or just at dusk, either one of those times when the light has gone tentative and watery. It might have been raining, so that the streets were slick and that hole in the eavestroughing over her back door would be dripping cold water right down his neck. He would be frantic, penitent, his hair rumpled with distress, his hands held palms up before him, trembling. He would say, "I've left her. I love you. I cannot live without you for one more minute. Please be mine forever," and she would say, "No, thank you. You had your chance and you missed it," and then she would quietly but firmly shut the door in his crumpled face.

In the more vengeful version of this black fantasy, it was Wanda who had left him and, when Joanna politely refused to take him back, he was left alone to spend the rest of his meaningless life regretful and depressed in a rented room above a greasy spoon on the bad side of town.

Now it was Saturday afternoon and she thought she'd walk downtown. This was a longtime habit but one she'd given up after losing Lewis. For the last six months she'd been spending Saturdays at home, doing laundry all morning in her ugly grey track suit (the kind she'd always said she wouldn't be caught dead in), watching car racing, kickboxing, and golf all afternoon in the living room with the curtains closed, afraid to leave the house because she might run into *them* or because the phone might ring, it might be Lewis, he might be missing her and changing his mind. When the phone did ring, she was afraid to answer it because it might be Lewis or it might not be, and sometimes she just let it ring and then wondered all the rest of the day who it could have been.

Today was a breezy end-of-summer afternoon. The sun was bright but not hot, beginning already to assume its autumn clarity and crispness. She thought she'd go to the art store and stock up on supplies. She'd had a new collage in her head for a week: this was a sure sign of her return to health. For six whole months, all during the wet fragrant spring and on through the humid green summer, it seemed she hadn't had a thought in her head, creative or otherwise, only pain and anger and loneliness, all those unmanageable emotions which expand to fill the space available and then some.

Tomorrow she would start. It had to do with maps, road maps like those she'd collected as a child, sending away for them with coupons clipped from Esther's magazines: maps of the Yukon, Switzerland, Alberta and British Columbia, the Amazon River System, South Africa, Venezuela, all of them equally exotic and unlikely. Some of the maps came to her with courteous letters attached: *Have a wonderful trip, ma'am. Enjoy yourself with our very best wishes. Keep our country beautiful. We're happy to be at your service.* As if they thought she would really go, as if they thought she was a real person with real plans, a grown-up.

When each new map arrived, she would spread it out on her bed, memorizing mileage counts and place-names, peering at red highways, black railroads, twisty blue rivers both skinny and fat. She was always careful to remember how she'd unfolded each map so she could refold it properly when she was done.

The maps ended up in a box in her closet eventually, but still she kept sending for more, asking at gas stations and the Tourist Information Bureau until Esther said she was driving her crazy. Joanna became an expert at folding maps, if nothing else.

Clarence gave her a world atlas for her twelfth birthday and she studied it for hours, especially the pretty coloured maps shaded to show Vegetation, Topography, Agriculture, Industry and Resources, Average Temperature and Rainfall. There were lists too, which she copied into a special spiral notebook: Area, Population, Capital City, Highest Point, Monetary Unit, Major Languages, Major Religions. She knew off by heart the largest islands, the highest mountains, and the longest rivers of the world. But nobody ever asked her about these things and gradually she forgot them. When she grew up, she discovered that she had absolutely no desire to travel, an aversion she had probably inherited from Esther and Clarence, along with her dislike of cabbage, blue cheese, and Brussels sprouts, along with her mistrust of rich people, big cities, and horses.

This collage would begin with the old atlas. She was going to cut out bits and pieces of all her favourite countries and make a new one. She was going to call it *Journey to the Center of the Earth*, or maybe *Transport*. Either way, there was going to be a circle in the center, a black circle with fleshy pink edges, the way mouths had looked to her these past six months, men's mouths especially: opening, closing, talk-

ing, laughing, promising, eating like pigs, gurgling back beer: damp
black holes in the yellow sunshine. A black circle in the center, yes,
with fleshy pink edges like a mouth or the way she pictured her own
vagina now that Lewis had left her.

transport *vt.* 1. to carry or move from one place to another. 2. to carry
away with strong emotion; to cause ecstasy or exaltation; enrapture;
entrance. 3. to convey to a penal colony; banish; deport.

After the art store, she'd go down to the market for a basket of peaches,
a dozen farm-fresh eggs, some zucchini, green onions, and mushrooms.
She'd try that new Hearty Frittata recipe for supper. She'd buy herself
a bouquet of flowers. She would admire the food, the blossoms, and her
own independence while indulging in a glass of white wine with classical music on the stereo and maybe even a candle or two.

The market, as always, was crowded. There were clusters of people
at every stall, bouncing apples and tomatoes from hand to hand to
judge their weighty ripeness, pulling back hairy green corn husks to
peek at the sweet plump kernels inside. Farther over at the handicrafts
stalls, women were pressing handmade cotton pants and vests against
themselves and pirouetting. Babies in strollers were gooing and reaching chubby hands out to fluffy stuffed sheep and hand-painted wooden
trains. Men were smelling loaves of fresh bread while munching on
oatmeal cookies the size of plates. The canvas tarps of the stalls flapped
in the wind and somebody somewhere was playing a fiddle and singing.
Everybody was smiling and talking to total strangers about the gorgeous weather, the superior produce, and the stupid government.

Joanna concentrated on her purchases, determined not to let the rest
of the world's flamboyant coupled happiness make her depressed.

At a stall in the middle row she was contemplating buying a pair
of silver earrings in the shape of paintbrushes. She didn't really need
them but she thought she deserved a present.

She spotted Lewis and Wanda at the end of the row, bending over
a display of hand-turned wooden salad bowls. They were holding hands

and also a pink balloon. They were looking happy: they hadn't seen her yet. Her heart buckled. Afterwards she would think that one of the main things she'd learned from having an affair with a married man was how to spot *them* before they spotted her.

As she put the earrings down and started to walk away, Lewis turned and saw her. He grinned and automatically began to raise his hand but then Wanda turned too and he stopped himself and brushed away an invisible wasp instead. He shrugged as if to say, *What can I do?* and Joanna hated him for having once loved her.

Back on the street, she passed a construction site where many muscular dirty men in yellow hard hats stood around eating doughnuts and drinking coffee from Styrofoam cups. She had to walk around a brand-new shiny red dump truck which straddled the sidewalk, engine running. She patted its black bumper, thought of Henry and his smell of diesel fuel, his big dirty gentle hands. She laid her head for one moment on the hot red hood and then she walked away. One of the workers nodded and waved.

She passed a young woman, with long curly hair and gold granny glasses, perched on the stone fence of St. Paul's Cathedral, playing her guitar and singing in her bare feet. Before her in a wheelchair sat a bearded young man with tattoos and no legs. He was dropping dollar bills into the open guitar case and asking for another song.

Joanna went to Woolworth's, to the toy department in the basement. She bought a set of paint-by-number oil paintings: Artist Touch, Series Four, New England Coast. Two 12" x 16" paintings, 21 colours, artist's brush and complete instructions for $9.99. The instructions read: *Apply paint to all numbered areas until you have completed your picture. Allow about ten days for your painting to dry before framing. Your friends won't believe you painted it yourself!*

The pictures were just like the ones Clarence had done twenty years ago. In one, there was a tiny man fishing from a seawall in front of a tall red wooden building with a sea gull and sailboats in the background. In the other, three red rowboats were moored on the rocky shore of a blue-and-green lake, more sea gulls, some fir trees, and fog on the horizon.

At home, Joanna put on her nightgown at five o'clock. When she was young, home after school, sometimes she asked Esther if she could put on her slippers and her flannelette pyjamas, curl up in the big swivel chair and watch TV till supper. Mostly Esther wouldn't let her. Mostly Esther would say, "What if somebody comes over? What will they think?" This was around the time Esther made skinny long-legged Joanna wear two crinolines to school so the teacher wouldn't think her mother didn't feed her.

Now Joanna could do whatever she wanted. Now she could sit at the kitchen table in her nightgown and do paint-by-numbers till midnight if she wanted to. Though the oil paints were in plastic flip-top containers now instead of those tiny glass jars with gold screw-on lids, they still smelled exactly the same.

14. Hand

IT IS THE way men hold their hands, Joanna figures, that gives them away. It is the way they hold their hands in unguarded moments that exposes their tenderness, their vulnerability, and gives you a glimpse of all the fragility they've been trying so hard to hide.

The last year of high school there was a rumour going around that you could tell the size of a guy's *thing* by the size of his fingers. There was, so the theory went, a direct correlation between these appendages: short stubby fingers meant a short stubby *thing*, long skinny fingers meant a long skinny *thing*, and so on. You just had to decide what you liked the most: length or width. But how could you decide, Joanna wondered, when you'd never even touched one, let alone tried it on for size?

This theory, handy though it might have been, was soon (and then repeatedly) disproved. The first penis Joanna ever touched belonged to a boy named Thomas Hunt. Thomas was a short thin boy with short thin fingers. But when he unzipped his fly and his hard penis sprang out at her, it was long *and* wide. She didn't like to stare so she closed her hand around it, her fingers, it seemed, barely able to encircle it.

They were with another couple at the cottage of the other boy's parents. They were supposed to be at a basketball game, but this other boy, Stanley Evans, was wild and bossy in a charming way. He had his mother's car, a bottle of his father's whisky, and the keys to their cottage slipped secretly into his jacket pocket. Stanley was the kind of boy who could convince you to do things you wouldn't normally do, and so off they went.

At the cottage on Buck Lake, they drank all the rye and then Stanley led the other girl, Louisa, into the bedroom. Joanna didn't know Louisa very well but she did know (everybody knew) that Louisa and Stanley had been *doing it* for at least two months.

Joanna and Thomas necked on the couch and she let him put his hands up her blouse and down her shorts. Then she put her hand around his penis and held it carefully. She didn't know what would happen next: would it get even harder, even bigger, would it explode? Slowly, slowly, like a flower folding up for the night, it went soft and Thomas sighed. "Your hands are very cold," he said, but she knew he wasn't blaming her.

He tucked his penis, little and shy-looking now, back into his jeans. He was grinning and shrugging as if it didn't matter, but his hands held palms up before him, those short thin fingers spread, looked frightened and embarrassed.

They turned on the lights and played cribbage, scrupulously ignoring the sounds from the bedroom, till Stanley and Louisa were done and came back into the main room, rumpled and red-faced, holding hands proudly.

Joanna and Thomas went out several more times after that, to basketball games and movies, walking downtown sometimes on Friday night for chips and gravy, milk shakes or sundaes. They held hands, but that was all. High school ended, Stanley and Louisa got married, Thomas went away to university, and they were all relieved to be changing their lives, finding their way to the future.

Joanna, as Thomas had so politely pointed out, always had cold hands.

"Cold hands, warm heart," Clarence used to tease her, Joanna having just come inside for supper after building a snow fort in the front yard with Penny and Pamela, rosy-cheeked but disappointed because what she really wanted was a snow fort big enough to crawl right inside of, but the roof and the walls were always collapsing around her. Clarence would kneel before her on the braided porch rug and help her take off her snow boots and mittens. Then he would rub her tingling hands, one by one, between his two big dry palms, blowing on them too. His hands smelled like paper, his warm breath like whisky, and he said, "Cold hands, warm heart."

Joanna would flex her warming fingers and stare at them, looking for clues to the condition of her own heart. She knew that if you crossed your fingers behind your back when you were telling a little white lie, then somehow the lie didn't count. She also knew that if you kept your fingers crossed when you were hoping and praying for something, you were bound to have good luck. Esther said an itchy palm meant money was coming your way. Clearly there was magic in the hands.

An itchy nose was also significant. Esther at the stove making supper would scratch her nose and say, "Oh oh, I'm going to kiss a fool," and sometimes Clarence would sneak up behind her, put a hand on each shoulder, whirl her around, and kiss her right on the mouth. Sometimes Esther laughed and kissed him back. Sometimes she shrugged him off and pushed him away and then Clarence would make a face at Joanna, rolling his eyes and holding his hands out and open, helpless.

It is the way men hold their hands, Joanna figures, that gives their secrets away.

Henry putting his fist through the drywall in the bedroom when Joanna said she didn't want to live with him any more. Then he spread both hands on the wall above the ragged hole and rested his forehead on them. By bedtime his right hand was swollen and purple across the knuckles. Joanna put peroxide on the scrapes and wrapped it for him in a tensor bandage.

Lewis not washing his hands when he left Joanna's bed to go home to Wanda because he said he liked the smell of her on his fingers. Lewis at the market with Wanda reaching his hand up to wave and then brushing at the air instead.

It is the way men hold their hands, Joanna figures, that can leave you stricken with love.

Gordon holding Samuel after his bath, the moist naked baby curled into his bare shoulder like a kitten. Gordon's big brown hand spread across Samuel's neck and shoulders, holding up his wobbly head. Gordon nuzzling Samuel's neck, pressing his ear to Samuel's, which looks like a seashell, Gordon hoping perhaps to hear the ocean inside. Samuel tucking his feet up and falling asleep in his father's hands.

With children, it is not in the hands, Joanna has discovered, but the feet: those chubby feet so small she wonders how Samuel will ever learn to walk, those baby toes so pink and round like flower buds she is afraid for months to trim his nails for fear of cutting a toe right off.

Even now, the mere sight of Samuel's white-and-yellow plastic thongs abandoned in the doorway of her studio at five o'clock on an early September afternoon can bring her heart to her throat, can rip it right out nearly. It is Labour Day, the end of another summer, and Samuel will start school in the morning.

Joanna leaves the thongs where they are and goes back to the kitchen where Gordon and Samuel are playing Old Maid. Suddenly there is the roar of jet engines overhead, louder and louder, coming lower and lower as if they will crash right into the house. For a moment Joanna thinks, *This is it, this is the end, we are all going to die.* But Gordon says, happily, "It's the Snowbirds." From the kitchen window they can see front doors opening all up and down the street, their neighbours on their front steps craning their necks, the women in their aprons holding wooden spoons, a bunch of broccoli, a half-peeled potato, or a big silver pot lid like a shield, the men bare-chested with newspapers or beer in their hands, pointing.

Gordon, Joanna, and Samuel go out and stand at the end of their driveway, waiting for the planes to come round again. The lady next door waves and calls, "Thank God they're friendly!" The elderly couple at the end of the block are rolling their adult son out in his wheelchair, down the wooden ramp, pointing his droopy head in the right direction and holding it there.

They can hear the planes coming up behind the houses and the elm trees, but the sound seems to be coming from all directions at once and Samuel spins around on his bare feet, not knowing which way to look.

They come from behind, right over their house, nine silver planes in perfect formation, swooping with red-and-white smoke dissolving behind them. Samuel puts his hands over his ears and leaps up and down on the spot, crowing.

Joanna watched the Snowbirds with Clarence and Esther from their front yard thirty years ago. She was Samuel's age then and just as excited. Had she too run outside in her bare feet? Had she too clapped her hands and hollered and spun? Had she too thought the noise and the danger and the fear were half the fun? Did she really remember that day so clearly or was she making it up as she went along?

Gordon hoists Samuel onto his shoulders and they are both waving. Joanna has an unmanageable lump in her throat and wonders why it's always the happy memories that make her cry. Gordon notices her wet shiny eyes and pats her back gently, grinning.

She gets like this at parades too, especially at the Christmas parade. She can't help herself. The floats, the marching bands, the high-stepping horses, the clowns tossing candy at the children, the Shriners in their funny tasselled hats in their miniature tooting cars, the local car salesmen and the mayor waving from white convertibles, their breath white too in the November morning air.

Last year, by the time Santa Claus came round the corner, Joanna was ready to burst into tears. Santa was laughing and grinning and ho-ho-ho-ing while green elves and brown reindeer danced and tinkled all around his big red chair. It was the way he waved, she tried to explain to Gordon later, back home over hot chocolate and marshmallows. The way he waved, so innocent and yet imaginary, as if he really believed in himself and in the children too, none of them the least bit troubled by the fact that there was a Santa on every corner, in every shopping mall, in every old-time movie. Santa could do anything. Santa could be everywhere at once and all those reindeer too.

It was the way Samuel stood there waving back, stamping his cold little feet in his big blue snow boots on the sidewalk, insisting they stay till Santa was well out of sight. Joanna cried and Samuel said, "Don't cry, Mommy. Everything will be all right. Santa will bring you a nice present too," and Joanna cried even more with Gordon's arm around her, his left hand tucked into her parka pocket because he'd forgotten his gloves and Samuel, age four, was so sure of everything that it broke her fearful motherly heart.

With men it is the hands; with children, the feet. What then, she wonders as they troop back inside, the Snowbirds safely landed, the sky gone silent again, what then is it with women that gives their secrets away? It is not in their hands or their feet. Women, it seems, are more likely to be aware of these extremities, self-consciously waving and pointing them, fondly pampering and painting them.

Except for Joanna who has bitten her fingernails since she was five, bitten them incorrigibly right down, as they say, to the quick. For a time the state of Joanna's fingernails was the bane of her mother's existence. Esther shaking her head and saying, "You'd bite your toenails if you could get them up to your mouth!" Joanna not mentioning that she had tried it once but couldn't manage it. Esther painting Joanna's nails every morning with a foul-tasting brown liquid which made her fingers look as if they were stained with nicotine. Joanna not mentioning that after the first couple of bites you got used to the taste. Esther making Joanna wear a pair of white cotton gloves to bed every night. Joanna not mentioning that the only time she *didn't* bite her nails was when she was asleep.

She still bites them and once in a while, when Samuel catches her with her fingers in her mouth, he clucks his tongue like Esther used to and says, "Oh, Mommy, don't be such a baby!" But other than that, her nails are no longer an issue.

It is not in the way women hold their hands or their feet. It is not even in the way they hold their mouths when they're angry or their shoulders when they're frightened. It is, Joanna thinks, in the way they are always holding their breath.

15. Short

"LIFE IS TOO short," Clarence often warned Joanna when she was sulking through the long boring hours of another Sunday, wishing she could hurry and grow up because she was still labouring under the mistaken impression that adults could do whatever they liked. "Stop wishing your life away," her father said, not unkindly. "Make the most of what you've got." "There's no time like the present." "Life is too short." Et cetera, et cetera, and many other platitudes which Joanna found impossible to believe.

When she got older and moved away from home, she had to admit that her father had a point. Also her mother, who had often warned her that once she got past twenty-one, the years would just get shorter and shorter until the day she died.

Sometimes now Joanna feels that her life is passing before her very eyes even as she is engaged in the time-consuming process of living it. Now that she is a bona fide adult, an artist, a wife, and a mother, not only does it strike Joanna that yes, life is too short, but, after a difficult day and a few glasses of wine, it also often seems that life is elsewhere.

Life meaning: 1. an elegant late dinner in a posh restaurant where the chefs are French, the food is superb, the wine is overpriced and sublime, and nobody needs to have their food cut up or go to the bathroom the minute the meal arrives and nobody has to leave early because the babysitter has to be home by eleven.

Life meaning: 2. a Mediterranean cruise on a ship the size of an apartment building where immaculately groomed waiters deliver drinks and meals all day long and no children under twelve are allowed on board (also, it would appear from the brochure, no uninteresting or unattractive people of any age, nor anybody with an unsightly wardrobe and no suntan).

Life meaning: 3. a temperate summer afternoon spent at the new

patio table under the blue-and-white umbrella which has an unmistak-
ably festive French air about it and four matching chairs, a whole afternoon spent reading, drawing, and dozing without feeling obliged to
weed the garden, mow the lawn, hang out the clothes, untangle the
badminton net, find the red croquet mallet, or clean the cat poop out
of the sandbox.

Life not meaning: 1. a long hot simultaneously boring and terrifying
afternoon spent at the park while your child and forty-seven others
fight, pee their pants, slop their ice-cream cones all over their shirts,
and flirt with broken bones, concussions, sudden death, and/or permanent disability on swings, slides, teeter-totters, monkey bars, and an
assortment of other diabolical playground equipment from which one
of them is bound to plunge headfirst the minute you open the book
you have optimistically brought along in your bag, which also contains
toys, Band-Aids, apple juice, Kleenex, a Batman hat, rocks, feathers,
and an acorn, thus handily disproving the notion you once held that
after your son was toilet-trained, you wouldn't have to lug that stupid
bag all over the place, the only difference now being that it doesn't
have diapers in it any more.

Life not meaning: 2. the furnace, the fridge, the washer, and the car
all breaking down in the same week, thus cleaning out most of your
savings in repair bills, and when your son spends all day Saturday
begging for a remote-control aircraft carrier for seventy-five dollars
which he saw advertised between cartoons, you tell him he can't have
it because you're broke, and when you ask him, "Do you know what
broke means?" he replies readily, "Sure, like glass, broken glass. Like
when I knock my drink off the table with my elbow and then there's
broken glass and sticky apple juice all over your nice clean floor and
you are so mad your face gets all red."

Life not meaning: 3. yet another weekend spent doing the laundry,
mowing the lawn, washing the dishes, cleaning the toilet, dusting the
bookshelves, cleaning out the fridge and disinfecting all those plastic
containers that have been sitting in the back for a month, and so on
and so on and so on and so, on and on and on, until you fall asleep in
front of the TV in the middle of the news and then you go to bed

where you make love or not and then dream about a small gold locket your mother gave you when you started school, engraved with your initials, and you put a picture of yourself inside but the locket was lost twenty years ago, in a sandbox, the school yard, the garden, or gone down the drain, and in the dream you find yourself naked with a fine gold chain hanging empty around your slender neck.

Life not meaning: 4. washing the kitchen floor at ten o'clock on Friday night.

Joanna is down on her hands and knees, up to her elbows in the hateful soapy water, muttering, "I hate this, I hate this, I hate this God-damn floor." Which is not true. She loves this God-damn floor, chose the tiles and laid them herself, with Gordon's help, slowly, lovingly, the pattern emerging square by square beneath their hands. She loves this God-damn floor every single time she looks at it.

Gordon says, "Why wash it now then?"

She says nothing. What does he know? Men don't see the dirt like women do. Men can't even see what needs to be done unless you point it out to them. He probably wants to go to bed and make love or something.

He persists. "You don't have to do it now, do you?"

"Yes," she says. "Yes, I do, I have to do it right now." Which is also not true. But she keeps scrubbing and muttering with her head down. Her hands in the bucket are wrinkled, the cleanser gives her a rash, she couldn't find the rubber gloves, her hair is hanging over her eyes, her knees on the hard floor hurt, her shoulders are shaking as if she is crying but she's not. She knows that if she tries to explain herself she will only sound ridiculous and then Gordon will sweet-talk her out of being miserable. She knows that she is being difficult but she does not want to stop. She knows she is having what Esther called "a snit" and she intends to make it last.

She knows damn well there are many people whose lives must be even more trifling and meaningless than hers.

There are the people, for instance, who write to Ann Landers in a rage because they were invited to a wedding and asked to bring money instead of a gift. Plus they were told to leave their loathsome children at home. Or they are insulted because the salesclerk at the dress shop said they were too fat, too old, and too ugly to wear a miniskirt. Their six-year-old grandson never thanked them for last year's Christmas present. Their fiancée forgot to mention that she was married before, has three children living with their father in Alaska, and was in jail twice in Vermont for shoplifting.

Well yes, Joanna reads Ann Landers too but she would never dream of writing to her and she often disagrees with her sensible syndicated advice.

There are the people, for instance, who regularly call the radio phone-in garden show to ask the horticultural expert why their forsythia only bloomed on one branch this year, how to keep the squirrels from eating their lily bulbs, how to transplant a fifteen-foot-high apple tree without killing it, how to prune a cedar bush into the shape of a poodle. Their voices on the airwaves are urgent. They have been trying all week to get through to the gardening guru who remains calm and pronounces the Latin names like reverent incantations.

Well yes, Joanna listens to the garden show too but only because it comes on right after lunch while she's stuck at the sink doing dishes.

There are the people, for instance, who read the tabloids every week and believe them. They even do the quizzes which proclaim to reveal your personality through your driving habits or how you eat hot dogs. They learn that their shoe size predicts their longevity, the longest lives going to size 7 women and size 11 men. Pregnant readers are pleased to discover that they can determine the sex of the baby by regulating the food they eat. Those wanting a boy should eat mostly fruits and vegetables, especially carrots and bananas. Those wanting a girl should limit their consumption of fruits and vegetables and concentrate instead on milk, cheese, and yogurt.

Well yes, Joanna reads the tabloids too but she doesn't believe a word of it. She buys them when she's bored in the supermarket check-out line. She clips the best headlines and sticks them on the fridge: MELTING WOMAN TO WED! ADAM & EVE'S SKELETONS FOUND—IN COLORADO! SATAN ESCAPES FROM HELL—VIA ALASKA OIL RIG!

This last article features a full-page photograph of a huge cloud of black smoke billowing from a flaming rig. Satan's face is clearly visible in the cloud formations: open growling mouth, jagged dripping fangs. Thirteen oil workers dead. Seeing is believing. Didn't she believe once that the cows, camels, bears, and lambs she saw in the clouds above the backyard on Mary Street were as likely to be real as anything else? Didn't she often see the man in the moon and wonder how he got there, what his name was, where his arms and legs were? Isn't she still as eager for answers as any of these people composing letters to Ann over breakfast, finishing their lunch in time to catch the garden show, settling in after supper with their socks rolled down around their swollen ankles to read the *Weekly World News*? Doesn't she too still believe that somewhere out there, somewhere elsewhere, there are experts who know everything and people who are perfectly happy with their lives?

The kitchen floor is finished now. Gordon has given up and gone to bed. Her snit has lifted, along with the ground-in dirt, cracker crumbs, and sticky spots with fluff stuck to them. Perhaps her snit has escaped like Satan and is hovering even now in a crabby-faced cloud over the house, causing all the neighbours to quiver and gasp, running to their telephones to dial 9-1-1 or the *Weekly World News.*

Life may or may not be elsewhere. But certainly she must admit that yes, it is too short, just as Clarence said. This wisdom however is hard to hang on to when you've thrown yourself headfirst into a snit, a bucket of hot soapy water, or life, daily life, in your size 7 shoes.

16. Fruit

WHEN JOANNA FIRST heard the word "melancholy," she thought it must be a fruit. She first heard the word from Esther: Esther saying to Clarence, "Some people *like* melancholy. They love it, they thrive on it. Me, I prefer peace." Joanna thought she said "peas." She figured *melancholy* must be a cross between *melon* and *cauliflower.*

She was at an age where she was just beginning to realize that words don't always mean what they seem to. Take *cauliflower,* for instance.

She'd only recently discovered that cauliflower was neither a flower nor a dog. Esther had explained to her that Lassie on TV was a collie dog. Cauliflower, she figured, must have something to do with Lassie.

They never had cauliflower at their house because Clarence only liked it with cheese sauce and Esther said cheese sauce took too long and was always lumpy anyway. Joanna finally ate cauliflower one night at Penny and Pamela's (with cheese sauce, yes) and she was surprised to discover that it was a vegetable, white and blossom-shaped, a little on the mushy side. Melancholy, Joanna imagined, would be juicy and sweet like honeydew melons but not green, orange like cantaloupe. Once she suggested they have melancholy for dessert. Esther just laughed and they had peaches instead. Perhaps melancholy was similar: furry and fragile, easily bruised. The feel of the peach fuzz made her shiver, like fingernails on a chalkboard.

Later on, of course, she learned what melancholy really meant.

melancholy *n.* 1. [*Obs.*] orig., black bile: in medieval times considered to be one of the four humours of the body, said to come from the kidneys or spleen, and to cause irritability, sullenness, sadness, and depression. 2. a tendency to be sad, dejected, or depressed. 3. sad, meditative musing; pensiveness.

When Joanna hit puberty just as Esther hit menopause, Esther said, many times, accusing and angry, "Why are you always so melancholy? You're just like your father."

Finally Joanna said, "Well, he can't be that bad. You married him, didn't you?"

Clarence went around the house for days after that singing "My Melancholy Baby." Even Esther had to laugh.

One afternoon after sex Lewis was still depressed. They were sitting at her kitchen table in their housecoats, hers pink chenille and his plush white terry cloth, a Christmas gift from Joanna which she kept in her own closet because of course he could hardly take it home to Wanda.

When Joanna suggested he simply tell Wanda he'd bought it for himself, he said no, he didn't like to lie to her. When Joanna laughed unkindly and said it was a little late for scruples, he said he didn't like to lie to her about little things when the big lies he was telling her were so dangerous.

Now they were sitting at Joanna's kitchen table in their housecoats at three in the August afternoon with the blinds closed, the doors locked, and the answering machine on. They were drinking scotch and water. Was this, Joanna wondered, what their great love had reduced them to?

She did not like to wonder this out loud for fear she was right and maybe Lewis had just never seen it that way before, and once she'd stupidly pointed it out to him, maybe he would suddenly see the light and go back to Wanda with his tail between his legs because it was The Right Thing To Do. That was how it most often happened in those romantic movies she watched compulsively on the VCR now and hated: those morality movies in which the illicit lovers (illicit, of course, because he was married or she was married or they were both married, to perfectly nice people who did not deserve this betrayal) loved and suffered and then loved some more, until finally one of them, the heroic one, ended the affair and walked nobly but sadly away (usually through a train station, an airport, or a rainstorm) because it was The Right Thing To Do. Joanna lived in terror that Lewis too might some day be overcome by this particular strain of nobility and leave her.

Indeed, Lewis was more depressed than usual today, swirling his dwindling drink around in his glass and brooding extensively about love and life. How many kinds of love were there? If he still loved Wanda (and he *did*, he had never once said he didn't love her), but he loved Joanna too, how was that possible? How could he love two women at one time? There was not enough of him to go around. How could he live without Joanna? How could he live without Wanda? Assuming that love was real, then what was it for?

Sometimes Joanna thought they were so busy inspecting their lives that they scarcely had time left to live, let alone enjoy, them.

Inevitably, all of this self-examination would lead to a deeper and broader depression, some tears, another drink, and either more sex or more questions. What is the purpose of passion? What is the power of guilt? And finally, what is the meaning of life?

This afternoon Lewis looked deep into his scotch and said, "It's as if Wanda and I were living in the Garden of Eden until you came along and changed everything."

What, Joanna wondered, did this make her? The serpent, that well-known, well-hated slimy insidious reptile? Or the apple? That delicious and dangerous, forbidden and perishable fruit? The Bible never said it was an apple anyway, it was just a fruit, it could have been anything, it could have been an orange, an apricot, a grapefruit. It could have been a kumquat.

"The Garden of Eden, my ass!" she said. "You were more like *Babes in Toyland*, the two of you like children playing house, Wanda in her apron, cooking up your supper, you the good husband in your slippers, reading the paper. You the great artist and she was always there stroking your ego and telling you how wonderful you are."

She didn't know what she was talking about but she couldn't stop. She was making it all up out of pieces of her anger, her envy, and her loneliness. Lewis never said much about his daily other life, having learned early on that the thought of him and Wanda having a quiet supper together (fresh pasta, green salad, warm buns, and white wine) could throw Joanna into just as much of a jealous frenzied resentful rage as the thought of them making love while she went to bed once again with a book. The details of their domestic habits were as dangerous and damaging to her as the spectre of their sex life.

"You don't know what you're talking about," Lewis said now. "You don't know anything. You've never been married."

"I wasn't stupid enough to fall for that crap."

"If you're so smart, then why aren't you happy?"

"You're not happy either, asshole!"

Was this what their great love had reduced them to: a level of such mutual misery that the worst thing they could accuse each other of was unhappiness?

Joanna cried and Lewis got dressed.

"Do you mean to tell me," she sobbed, "that now you're just going to walk away and leave me here like this, you rotten bastard?"

"Yes," he said. "I have to go home. Wanda will be wondering where I am."

"So now you're going to go home and play good husband?"

"Yes," he said, "I am."

"What a farce!"

"Yes," he said, "it is."

Joanna grabbed a grapefruit from the wicker basket in the center of the kitchen table and heaved it at him. But he was already out the door and the grapefruit split wide open when it hit the solid wood, spurting pink pulp and sticky juice everywhere. She wished it were his head.

When Joanna calls home to tell Clarence that she and Gordon are getting married, Clarence says, "That's good. He's a good man. A little melancholy maybe, but I like him anyway. He seems to be very level-headed."

Clarence comes for the wedding, which is a simple civil ceremony at the courthouse downtown. If this is a disappointment to Clarence, he does not say so. He also does not say anything about melancholy. He says, "I'm proud of you, dear," although he does not say exactly for what. After the ceremony, the wedding party goes to the Long Street Diner for a fancy dinner and then back to Joanna and Gordon's apartment for champagne and cake, a chocolate cake because Joanna does not like fruitcake. On top of the cake, there are two white plastic doves with ribbons of all colours cascading from their beaks. Joanna and Gordon have been living together in Joanna's apartment for six months. If this arrangement bothered Clarence, he did not say so. In a few more months, they will buy the big house on Laverty Street.

When Joanna is pregnant with Samuel, a woman in prenatal class says, "Giving birth is like trying to shit out a grapefruit." Joanna wonders why this woman is taking the class when she already has three kids.

After Samuel is born, after twenty-four hours in labour and eleven of those on the delivery table, Joanna thinks: *Watermelon. More like trying to shit out a watermelon.*

For months afterwards whenever she lays the baby down to sleep in his bassinet, she cradles his head in her hands and it is heavy but wobbly, like a piece of fruit, round and sweet-smelling, rolling and perishable. She cannot touch or look too closely at the soft spot which pulses in the middle of his head like a heart. She cannot bear to think of his brain inside, intricate and convoluted, so unprotected. Soon his skull closes over and he learns to hold his head up. Sometimes Joanna considers the size of his growing head with surprise at the thought of it ever having come out from between her own two legs.

Samuel, age four, is deeply involved in the process of naming things. Always he is asking, "What's this?" Always Joanna is telling him nouns: cantaloupe, caterpillar, hippopotamus, onion, elevator, earring, pantyhose, diamond, pomegranate.

Joanna feels either inspired by the newness of everything as seen through his eyes or exhausted by the thought of how much he has to learn, of how many words she knows that are cluttering up her brain. Is the brain infinitely expandable, always enlarging to accommodate the information available? Or will it get full some day and shut down?

Often now Samuel wants more information than she is able to give.

"What's this?"

"A tree."

"I *know* that. What kind of tree?"

"I don't know."

"Why not?"

Sometimes he asks the names of things he already knows, as if seeking reassurance that things do stay the same, that what he does know is still correct from one day to the next.

"What's this?"

Garbage can, kitten, crayon, helicopter, apple, freight train, pear.

"What's this?"

"Truck."

"I *know* that. Why is it a truck?"

They are in the kitchen making supper. Joanna is at the counter slicing strawberries. Samuel is beside her on his plastic Sesame Street stepstool so he can see and reach.

"What are these again?"

"Strawberries."

"What does that mean?"

"What do you mean, 'What does that mean'?"

"I mean, What does a strawberry *mean*?" He is impatient and then offended when Joanna laughs. She is going to say that a strawberry doesn't mean anything, but of course that's not strictly true.

strawberry *n.* 1. the small, juicy, red, fleshy accessory fruit of a stolon-bearing plant (genus Fragaria) of the rose family.

"A strawberry just *is*," she tries lamely to explain, doubting that Samuel will be satisfied with this.

But he is. "Oh I get it," he says. "Strawberries aren't *supposed* to mean anything. All they have to do is be red and taste good. A strawberry means a strawberry."

Again Joanna laughs and he is proud of himself. It occurs to her that this is what she should have told Lewis seven years ago when he was fussing around about the meaning of love, the meaning of life. She should have said, "We don't go around asking, 'What is the meaning of a strawberry?' so why do we all keep asking, 'What is the meaning of life?' The answer is the same. So why don't we just shut up and live it? Why don't you just shut up and let me love you?"

17. Butterfly

THE SUMMER SAMUEL is one year old, he is afraid of trees. This fear comes over him after an ugly incident with the large potted fig tree in the living room. He is not walking alone yet, is still pulling himself up to stand. When he tries to pull himself up at the fig tree, it tips, he loses his balance and goes face-first into the dirt and the leaves. For several months after this he carefully skirts all trees everywhere, as if they too are likely to fall on him. Joanna is amazed by the fact that he knows that the huge evergreen out front, the vast and rustling weeping willow at the corner, and the potted fig in the living room are, despite their different shapes and sizes, all still trees. How does he know this? How does he know that the German shepherd down the street, the tiny Chihuahua in a magazine ad, and Pluto in the Mickey Mouse cartoon are all still dogs? How does he know about dogness, treeness, essence? His fear of trees passes of its own accord.

The next summer, when he is two, he is afraid of long grass. The feel of it tickling his calves makes him scream. "Bugs!" he cries. He thinks there are bugs crawling up his legs. This motivates Gordon to keep the lawn more neatly mown. But still all summer long Samuel plays in the driveway, on the steps or the sidewalk. He likes to sit on the warm concrete with his toys spread all around him. Joanna says, "I guess he'll never be a country boy. He'll probably end up living in downtown Toronto, not a blade of grass or a tree in sight!" But this fear too passes of its own accord.

When he is three, he becomes (and remains) afraid of all flying insects, especially bumblebees and butterflies. Joanna can sympathize about the bumblebees. She is afraid of them too, their fat bodies buzzing past her head when she works in the garden. She ducks and flails her arms. Samuel does the same thing, shrieking. It is part of his inheritance.

But butterflies are beautiful. She cannot understand the problem. He is especially afraid of the large orange monarchs. She tells him they don't bite, they just flutter by. But as always, when he is afraid, he will not let himself be reassured by her mere words. She fusses over how he will not take her word for anything. This will no doubt serve him well in later life but right now it is annoying. She buys him books about insects, storybooks in which all manner of insects don hats, coats, trousers, spectacles, and are brought to anthropomorphic life, speaking simple English, having adventures, families, and little ladybug friends. He says bugs can't talk. He says ladybugs are okay. She buys him

informative nonfiction books filled with lavish photographs. He says
the close-ups of butterfly heads look like monsters.

Finally she gives him a monarch butterfly she has kept in a jar for
five years. She found it once on the side of the road, dead and perfect,
just lying there as if asleep. For several days the jar sits on his dresser
where he eyes it cautiously. Finally he asks her if she will open it and
let him touch the butterfly. When he touches the orange-and-black
wings, they crumble and turn to butterfly dust in his fingers. He laughs
and takes to playing butterfly all over the house, swooping from room
to room, flapping his arms in much the same way as when he plays sea
gull but without the sound effects. He wants to know what sound does
a butterfly make. She says she'll have to look it up. He says that when
he has butterflies in his stomach, he thinks they are real, trapped inside
him like bugs in a jar. He wants to know how they get in there, how
they get out, how can they breathe, and are they eating the inside of
his stomach? Could she look all this up too?

Reading up on butterflies, she discovers that they have long been
believed to be the souls of the dead. According to superstition, if you
see a butterfly at night, it is an omen of death. Also, butterflies are
cannibals.

By the time she has gathered this dismaying information, Samuel
has lost both his interest and his fear. He says it is moths now that
worry him. What is that white stuff on their wings, is it magic dust,
is it poison? Will a moth die if he touches it, will he die if a moth
touches him? He says they fly at him just like they do at a light bulb.
He says they are trying to fly into his mouth. Joanna says why would
they want to do that? He says maybe there's a light in his stomach.
Maybe it comes on when he opens his mouth, the way the fridge light
comes on when you open the door. Joanna says she's never heard of
such a thing. He says maybe the moths know something she doesn't.

18. Smooth

ESTHER WAS PROUD of her smooth skin. She nursed a legitimate pride
in her face which did not seem to venture into vanity. It was true. She

always looked ten years younger than her real age. She liked to tell people how old she was and then watch their eyes widen with disbelief. Even Joanna eventually had to admit that her mother looked better than all the other mothers she knew. Her face was clear and creamy, wrinkle-free. No crow's-feet, no frown lines, no laugh or smile lines either. Which was not to say she didn't do these things. Of course she did and, in fact, her face was usually mobilized with emotions, often conflicting. It was just that somehow they didn't sink in, at least not into her skin.

She was always creaming and oiling her face, replenishing her moisturizer five or six times a day, applying a special heavier cream at night, trying all the latest lotions on the market but then returning to her old favourites in the end. Once a month she smeared a foul-smelling concoction on her upper lip to remove her moustache. Sitting at the kitchen table waiting for the depilatory to burn off the tiny black hairs, she invariably retold the story of a woman she'd seen once on the bus who had not only a full-fledged moustache, but sideburns too, curly black sideburns on both cheeks.

Joanna, like most teenagers, had pimples, mostly on her chin and her forehead. Occasionally a big juicy white one would sprout in the middle of the blackheads which covered her nose. She could spend an hour in front of the bathroom mirror, moaning and sighing over the advanced state of her ugliness, dabbing hopelessly at the bumps with the latest acne cream which Esther had picked up at the drugstore along with another jar of moisturizer for herself.

"I had pimples too, you know, when I was your age," Esther offered from the other side of the bathroom door. "Maybe you'll be lucky when you're older, maybe you will inherit my skin." She was only trying to help, Joanna knew that, but she was too smug and too smooth to be of much consolation.

Joanna did not inherit her mother's skin. Her skin was just like her father's: rather red, rather rough if looked at from a certain sunlit angle, marked by patches of tiny red broken veins on each cheek. But what looked rugged on her father, Joanna hated on herself.

"But you look so healthy," Henry said.

Joanna said, "But I would give anything, absolutely anything, to have skin like Mary Louise." Mary Louise Dupont was a friend of theirs whose skin was pale and smooth and perfect, with just a faint blush of pink at the cheeks, no freckles, no pimples, no broken veins, never a blackhead in sight. "Just look at her," Joanna said. "Isn't she beautiful?"

"Yes," Henry said. "But so are you."

"No, I'm not."

"Yes, you are."

"No, I'm not."

"Yes, you are."

"But wouldn't you love me more if I had skin like hers?"

"No, I wouldn't."

"Yes, you would."

"No, I wouldn't."

"Yes, you would."

"But you know what they say, Joanna—beauty is only skin-deep."

"Yes, stupid. And it's my skin that's the problem."

"Shit."

"You," Lewis said after the first time they made love, "you have the smoothest skin in the world." Joanna was lying on her stomach beside him and he was trailing one hand up and down the whole length of her back. She wondered briefly what other women's skin was like but decided not to ask for fear of bringing Wanda to mind. She was fairly purring. Maybe it was true. Maybe she had inherited her mother's skin after all, although she was sure this was not quite what Esther had had in mind.

Thinking about skin again later—not, of course, at this particular moment when she was surrounded by so much of it, smooth, yes, hers and Lewis's too, also rosy, damp, tingling (hers) and tight, tanned, delicious (his)—Joanna realized she had no idea how Esther felt about the skin on the other parts of her body. There had been some mention of stretch marks and a certain preoccupation Esther had with the brown

spots on the backs of her hands which she said were not age spots but
something she had acquired while pregnant, sitting on the back step
in the sunshine waiting for Joanna to be born. Sometimes she said this
fondly, other times meanly, as if the spots were some kind of stigmata.
Joanna herself had never thought much about the skin on the other
parts of her mother's body. In fact she had never thought much about
her mother having other parts, or having a body at all for that matter.
Mothers, in those days and still, were generally considered to be sexless,
shapeless, and celibate. It was as if all pregnancies had been generated
by immaculate conception and, the eventual birth having been accomplished, all carnality and lasciviousness had been permanently expelled
along with the placenta. Passing a pregnant woman on the street, you
did not imagine her formerly svelte body wrapped around that of some
hairy eager man, engorged and engrossed in the throes of passion. Passing a mother with her newborn cradled in her arms, you did not imagine her spread out on the delivery table, sweating and squealing or
screaming. Especially you could never imagine your own mother with
your own head coming out between her legs. Especially you could never
imagine that your own parents would ever need to have sex again now
that they had you.

After another afternoon session of voluptuous love-making, Lewis
and Joanna were both in the bathroom, Lewis just getting out of the
shower before he headed home to Wanda, Joanna peering into the
mirror, trying to fix up her face and her hair before she headed downtown to do some errands. She was dabbing makeup on the patch of
broken veins on her left cheek. Lewis shrieked, "What are you doing?"

Joanna said, "Well, I'm covering up these veins on my cheek."

"My God," Lewis said, "I just can't believe you would do such a
thing," as if she were guilty of some heinous crime or at least of some
serious transgression, even worse than adultery.

Joanna was embarrassed and indignant and she stopped covering up
her veins.

After they stopped sleeping together, she started again. But every
time she did it, she thought of Lewis and felt foolish. Every time she
admired her own smooth skin (while lolling about in the bathtub or
sliding in between the smooth sheets, occasionally convinced that she

would die if she did not soon find someone to touch and admire her),
she thought of Lewis and was briefly but utterly disabled with despair.
These memories were unfortunate but unavoidable. It was annoying,
she thought, the way you could not pick and choose among your memories, selecting the ones you wished to savour and treasure (and perhaps
embroider gracefully) while simultaneously discarding the sad sloppy
detritus. It should, she figured, be merely a matter of mind over matter,
mind over mind.

She should not have to think of Lewis every time she forgot to empty
the kitchen garbage can and there he was in her mind, curling up his
aquiline nose at the odour, crying out, "My God, Joanna, this is disgusting!" She should not have to think of him every time she pulled
out the sink stopper after doing the dishes and all the soggy bits of
supper went down the drain and Lewis said, "You're supposed to leave
the stopper in to catch all that, you know." She should not have to
think of him every time she thought of her own smooth skin.

These memories were like genetic inheritances, half of them from
people you had never even met: your father's eyes, your mother's forehead, your grandfather's double-jointed elbows, your great-grandmother's
trick knee, or your second cousin's allergy to lima beans. These memories, like these inheritances, would never go away. You would never
be rid of them, you just had to make your way around them, incorporate
them, or try to eradicate them with weekly visits to your therapist.
Joanna had resigned herself to being stuck with her father's eyes, her
mother's forehead, and her memories of Lewis forever.

Gordon has that kind of smooth tight skin with which, it seems, only
men are blessed. Always he looks scrubbed and shiny, as if he has just
stepped out of the shower, the sunshine, or a month's vacation in the
mountains. He has no blemishes, no freckles, no blackheads. His face
is so smooth you might even think he had no pores.

Joanna admires his skin and he admires hers. "You," he says after
they've been making love for months, "you have the smoothest skin in
the world."

"What does other women's skin feel like?" she asks.

"Rough, dry, scaly, flaky. Sometimes they have little bumps on their bums."

"Oh yuck!" She believes him unconditionally. She is a superior being. She stretches and rubs her smooth long legs all over him until he gets hard again. Of course she has the smoothest skin in the world—she inherited it from her mother.

She does not think about Lewis until later in the evening, while she and Gordon are finishing the supper dishes and she pulls out the stopper and lets all that soggy gunk go down the drain. There is a piece of pasta that won't go so she pushes it down with her fingers. Gordon doesn't notice. She thinks about Lewis as she wipes the counters and the stove. She thinks about how she didn't even think of him when Gordon stroked and marvelled at her smooth skin and then put his penis back in. She thinks with surprise about how memories are maybe not permanent after all. If time does not have the power to heal all wounds, perhaps it can change all memories to make them more manageable. Perhaps it does have the power to obliterate whole moments altogether. Of course it does. Of course it is true, as William James said, that forgetting is as important as remembering.

19. Command

"YOUR WISH," SAID Lewis, "is my command." He was giving her a massage with fragrant frangipani oil. She'd complained of sore shoulders and a kink in the small of her back. She'd been working since morning for six hours straight on a collage called Parts of Speech. Hunched over her art table, she had cut and pasted dozens of pictures of mouths: mouths open, laughing, screaming, eating; mouths closed, pursed, hissing, frowning, waiting. Some of these mouths were in agony. Some of them were in ecstasy. Sometimes you couldn't tell which was which. From these mouths came words at all angles, words of all kinds: nouns, pronouns, adjectives, adverbs, and verbs.

Simple words like: house, bread, salt, spider, red, cheese, green, window, white, table, black, chair.

Complex words like: trouble, dream, wish, I, me, you, he, she, it, they, them, the.

Gentle words like: comfort, sweet, summer, woman, child, sleep, pray, play, peace, truly, surely, purely.

Fierce words like: pain, power, passion.

"Your wish," said Lewis, "is my command," and then he rubbed her back, neck, shoulders, and bum with slippery sweet oil until she slid into a gentle stupor.

She thought about wishes and commands and how he was just being funny, how he was also lying, because of course her wish was not for a massage. Her wish was that he would leave Wanda, arrive on her doorstep with all his worldly belongings, move right in, and then they could proceed to live happily ever after. This possibility was beginning to look more and more unlikely, and in her more realistic (that is, completely depressed) moments Joanna had to consider her growing suspicion that if he ever did leave Wanda, he would then be so guilt-ridden and morally tormented that he would never allow himself to be happy again.

Joanna thought about the commands she'd really like to give him. Commands, orders, ultimatums: *Tell her. Leave her. Be mine.*

In elementary school she'd learned all about commands in English class: Make the bed. Do the dishes. Eat your spinach. Walk the dog. Do your homework. Brush your teeth. Be a good girl.

She'd learned how, although such sentences might at first glance appear to be grammatically incorrect, incomplete fragments, because they seem to have no subject, in truth the subject is there, implied, unspoken. Remember that the subject of all commands is *you,* the invisible but omnipresent second person.

In high school, everything, including English Grammar, became more complicated: connecting words became conjunctions, questions became interrogative sentences, wishes ("if only . . . ") became conditional phrases, and commands became imperatives. In her French Grammar textbook it said: *"L'IMPERATIF: Entrez!* Come in! *Buvons!* Let's drink! *Sortez!* Get out! The imperative is not a tense. It is a mood."

THE IMPERATIVE: Love me. Leave her. Marry me. Make me happy. Do the right thing.

She'd also learned how, in certain cases of the imperative, a single verb could stand alone and function as a complete English sentence. According to Mrs. Crocker, her teacher, this provided ample proof for the suggestion that verbs are the most vital words in the English language. "A thorough understanding of verbs," Mrs. Crocker said, "will serve you well in any situation."

For instance: Help!

In this case, both the subject (you) and the object (me) are implied. It is the verb that is urgent, active, and full of both danger and promise.

Later she will learn that in the language of love there are no nouns, only verbs and pronouns: to love, to have loved, to be loved, to have been loved, I love, you love, she loves, he loves, they love, we love, we did love, we had love, we will love, we would love, if only.

There are also, occasionally, adverbs: truly, madly, deeply, eternally, endlessly, desperately, sweetly, softly, sadly, stupidly.

Later still she will learn that of course this is not true. Later she will learn that in the language of love all words are equal.

20. Chair

EVER SINCE SHE'D moved away from home and got a place of her own, Joanna had wanted a wicker chair. When she finally went out and bought one four years later, bearing it home like a trophy in her little car with the hatchback up and tied with a bungee cord to the bumper, she wondered why she'd waited so long.

Her basement apartment had come partially furnished: bed, dresser, couch and chair, scarred coffee table, and an unsteady metal TV stand. Whatever else she needed, she had picked up cheap at garage sales and flea markets or scrounged from friends who were replacing their old stuff. There was something daunting about home furnishings, a fear not of the objects themselves but of their purchase. She could not imagine herself walking into a major department store and then walking out again with something so cumbersome and intimidating, something so *final,* as a love seat, a dining-room table, or a self-defrosting refrigerator. Such purchases, such *commitments,* were more properly made, it seemed, by people who were really grown up, who were settled, self-satisfied, and married to some other practical, patient adult who would quite happily debate the pros and cons of Scotchgarding, cubic footage, energy-saving devices, six chairs or four, should the fridge door open right or left—all of these details discussed lovingly while holding hands in front of an aggressive well-dressed salesman on commission. Joanna, who still did not know what she wanted out of life, could not imagine acquiring by herself these accoutrements of adulthood, attractive though they might be, and then having to drag them around with her for the rest of her life, the way travellers drag those gigantic suitcases on wheels behind them through airports and train stations.

Alternately, Joanna took her inability to commit to furniture and major appliances as an indication of her free-spirited independence and thriftiness or as a sign of arrested development. She'd read a magazine article once which revealed that many single women have similar problems: buying a couch or a fridge of your own when you are single seems to be an admission that you will never have a husband and a permanent home that requires real furniture.

She set up the white wicker chair in the corner of her studio space. Because her apartment was small, her working area was half of the long narrow living room. When she finished working for the evening, she would curl up in the wicker chair below the west window. She read or wrote letters, sipped a cup of hot chocolate or a glass of white wine, all the while admiring the chair and the picture of herself sitting in it. She hated to admit how much pure pleasure she took in a mere material possession. Loving that chair was undoubtedly shallow and conspicuously consumeristic. She would have been hardly surprised to find herself dreaming about it.

When she did in fact see a chair in her dreams, it was not the white wicker chair. It was an electric chair which she'd seen on TV once when she was little and her parents had accidentally let her watch "Naked City," the city under scrutiny being New York or Chicago or some other of those evil American metropolises. In the dream she couldn't see who was in the electric chair, but there were sizzling sparks, much jerking and twitching and screaming while the audience applauded and cheered. At the end of the dream, as at the end of the program, a coda in white block letters appeared on the screen: THE INCIDENTS POR-TRAYED IN THE PRECEDING PROGRAM ARE TRUE. ONLY THE NAMES HAVE BEEN CHANGED TO PROTECT THE INNOCENT.

By the time she and Gordon have moved into their house on Laverty Street, the wicker chair is warped and worn and Joanna is finally able to admit that much as she once loved the chair, it has never been very comfortable.

For the first year in the new house the chair sits in the basement, gathering dust and spiderwebs, a little mildew on the burgundy cor-duroy cushion. They pile things on it: a box of scratched LPs, a bag of newborn baby sleepers which Samuel seems to grow out of every two weeks, a torn lampshade, a pair of Clarence's plaid felt slippers left behind at Christmas.

The next summer they bring the chair up, clean it off, buy a new flowered cushion, and put it outside on the front porch. For a week Joanna sits in it every evening after supper, reading the newspaper and once again admiring the chair and the picture of herself sitting in it. Gordon plays with Samuel underneath the evergreens. She admires them too and also the smell of the mock orange bushes all around the porch. But after a week she has to admit that the chair is no more comfortable now than it ever was. They leave it on the porch, though, because it looks nice there, homey and faithful.

Two weeks later, pulling into the driveway after a trip downtown for groceries, Joanna suddenly realizes that the chair is gone. For half an hour, she searches the yard foolishly, thinking that somebody is playing a practical joke on her, having hidden the chair in the shed, behind the forsythia, under the front porch. For five whole minutes she stares at the empty backyard as if the missing chair will materialize at any moment. She examines the place where it sat, looking for clues, footprints, fingerprints, a note. Finally she has to admit that it is not a joke, she is not a detective, and the chair has been stolen.

For weeks afterwards she is nervous to think that somebody walked onto the front porch and stole that chair right out from under their sleeping little noses. For weeks afterwards, pushing Samuel in his stroller around the quiet neighbourhood, she is peering into backyards and open garages, watching for her chair.

Then she forgets about it altogether. Until some people in a house on Duncan Street two blocks over put a whole set of white wicker furniture out on their front porch, a love seat, two chairs, and a matching round table. She thinks about warning them. They're all sitting out there, playing Monopoly, drinking pink lemonade, and laughing. She keeps walking. Every time she passes the house, she thinks she really should go in and warn them. But she never does and their wicker furniture stays put, untouched and intact. She envies them, not so much for their furniture as for their luck and their charmed lives which, she imagines, will be played out smoothly and happily, immune as they seem to be to theft, danger, and random despair.

21. Sweet

JOANNA WAS NEVER FOND of sweet things. As a child, given the choice of a treat, she would always rather have a bag of chips than a chocolate bar. Except for the Cherry Blossoms which Clarence sometimes bought her on his way home from working overtime. She also liked chocolate milk shakes and hot-fudge sundaes from the Dairy Queen. These too were most often brought home by her father and so she ate them happily. But afterwards she felt sick to her stomach.

When she was an adolescent, it seemed to be an advantage because, unlike Penny and Pamela, she was not having to constantly fight off chocolate cravings for fear of getting pimples. Their theory was that chocolate raised the temperature of your blood to the boiling point and then your skin erupted under the pressure. In the end Joanna got pimples anyway. Sometimes the three of them got together and squeezed each other's pimples even though Esther said squeezing them would leave you scarred for life.

Esther said maybe Joanna didn't like sweet things because she was sweet enough already. At first Joanna thought this was a compliment but eventually she realized it was not. It was just like the way Esther always said, whenever Joanna had a new outfit, "Anything looks good on a model." There was that time in university when Joanna was waiting at the corner for the bus on a winter afternoon all bundled up in her new blue parka with white rabbit fur around the hood. In the wind her dark curly hair was tangled in the white fur and her cheeks were rosy red. Her mother's friend Agnes passed by but Joanna did not notice her. When Agnes called Esther that evening she told her she'd seen such a pretty girl at the bus stop, such a very pretty girl, that she had stopped to take a second look. Lo and behold it was Joanna. Esther thought this was hilarious. "Imagine that," she said several times. "Imagine that! You should be flattered." As if Joanna had somehow tricked Agnes, had fooled her into thinking that she was somebody else, somebody pretty.

After Joanna moved away from home, she met a lot of women who bragged about their obsession with chocolate. They liked to call themselves "chocoholics." They said there should be a self-help group. They sat together in various kitchens and restaurants, giggling and confiding the extent of their addictions. They traded recipes and waxed nostalgic, drooling slightly, over a piece of Black Forest cake they'd had six years before. These women were well past the age of pimples so they worried about their weight instead. They said they gained ten pounds just thinking about it. They said every bite of chocolate went straight to their hips.

Chocolate, in spite of its perils, was something you were *supposed to* like. Joanna discovered it increasingly difficult to admit, even to close friends, that she didn't. Upon hearing such a shameful confession, these women's usually friendly faces would contort into grimaces of distrust, disbelief, and sympathy. You would think their lips were double-jointed. You would think they'd just heard her confess that she didn't like babies, flowers, or sex.

They said, "But wouldn't you just die for a piece of double chocolate cheesecake?"

She said, "No."

They flinched. They faltered. They looked her over long and hard as if she'd suddenly sprouted an extra head or a beehive hairdo. They struggled to make sense of her. They felt betrayed. They tried to convert her.

They said, "But wouldn't you just love to sink your teeth into something dark and sweet and sinful?"

She said, "No. I don't like sweet things. Three bites of chocolate and I feel like throwing up." They clucked their tongues in disbelief.

Revenge is sweet, so they say. After Lewis dumped her she thought about revenge. Maybe the chocolate-licking women thought about it too, while digging in with guilty gusto, sucking up every last shred of sugary evidence. Revenge must be sweet because Joanna found that whenever she tried to plot her revenge against Lewis and Wanda or both, she felt nauseous and feverish afterwards. Maybe indulging in revenge, like indulging in chocolate, brought your blood to the boiling point. Maybe indulging in revenge would cause your whole face to break out into juicy pustules, the kind that squirt all over the mirror when you squeeze them. Or maybe your hips would blow up like balloons. Maybe indulging in revenge would leave you scarred for life.

22. Whistle

ON THE WAY home from school, Joanna was whistled at by a dirty half-dressed man in a yellow hard hat. He was leaning against a blue dump truck with three other men, also half-dressed, dirty, in yellow hard hats. It was nearly the end of June and Joanna would be starting high school in September. These four men were working on the street a block away from her house. They had been there all week. Usually when she passed them, they were down inside a large hole with just the tops of their hard hats showing, bobbing like yellow bubbles just below street level. She would have liked to look down the hole but she was shy and didn't want to draw attention to herself. Plus she figured she was too old to be impressed by such things. Often there were three or four children jiggling around the hole, inching as close to the edge as they dared, peering down, oohing and aahing. Adults, on the other hand, walked past without looking at either the men or the hole. Forced to manoeuvre their cars around the hole or idle in the heat till the flagman waved them through, these adults looked merely irritated, hot, and bored.

Today the workmen were leaning against the blue dump truck, drinking coffee out of long silver thermoses like giant bullets. One man was drinking orange juice out of a jug. The juice dribbled down his chin and onto his bare hairy chest. They had all taken off their shirts in the heat. The man who whistled at Joanna was wiping the sweat off his face with his balled-up T-shirt.

Joanna looked reflexively in his direction and saw that he was young, handsome, and very brown. When she looked away in confusion and tripped over an uneven sidewalk crack, he hooted and the four men began laughing and talking in a foreign language.

She walked the last block home as fast as she could. In the kitchen she slammed her schoolbooks down on the table. When Esther asked her what was wrong, she told her what had happened. "It was disgusting," Joanna cried, "just disgusting!"

Her mother chuckled knowingly. "Oh, you'll change your mind about that when you're a little older."

"I will not," Joanna said.

"Yes, you will," Esther said. "They think you're pretty cute."

"I don't care what they think."

"You will."

"I won't."

The next night after supper Joanna took a walk down the street and had a good look in that hole. It was deserted, unguarded except by yellow wooden barricades and an orange-and-black striped metal sign with a flashing light on top. The workmen were long gone, home to their suppers, their children, their girlfriends, their wives. The blue dump truck was gone too. Draped over one of the yellow barricades was a dirty sweat-stained T-shirt, flapping like a flag in the breeze.

Down inside the hole were pipes of varying sizes and colours, a mysterious network of appendages to which every house on the street was connected. Joanna thought of a doctor show she'd seen on TV where the dying man in the neat white bed had tubes coming out of his nose, mouth, and arms.

She took the T-shirt off the barricade and carried it home where she hid it under the back step. The next morning when Esther had gone out shopping, Joanna fished out the shirt and smelled it. She put it on and admired herself, naked beneath, in the mirror on the back of the bathroom door.

Two days later, the same men, one of them anyway, maybe the same one, whistled at Esther on her way home from the bus stop. She'd been downtown all afternoon shopping again. She burst into the kitchen flushed and flirtatious, laden with packages. "Well, they whistled at me too," she announced. "I guess I've still got it after all." Joanna rolled her eyes scornfully.

Esther was cheerful and coy all evening long. Clarence teased her mercilessly, whistling at her every time she walked across the room. Esther loved it and wiggled her hips in response. Joanna was embarrassed by their pathetic foolishness. She was also angry. If those men would whistle at her mother, they would whistle at anyone. She had never thought of her mother as pretty and she did not want to. If anyone had asked her to describe her mother (why would they?), she would have said short with dark curly hair and glasses. This described most of the mothers she knew. She could not have said whether they were pretty or ugly or what.

She took a detour to and from school until the work was done, the hole filled in and paved over, nothing left to look at but a large square of smooth black asphalt in the middle of the street.

23. Woman

woman *n.* 1. a female adult human being, as opposed to MAN. 2. women collectively. 3. a female servant. 4. *a)* a wife, *b)* a sweetheart or mistress; a female lover or sexual partner. **5.** a man with qualities traditionally regarded as feminine, such as timidity, weakness, tendency to gossip, etc. **6.** womanly qualities or characteristics; femininity. *See also* WOMANHOOD, WOMANISH, WOMANIZE, WOMAN-KIND, WOMANLIKE, WOMAN OF THE WORLD, WOMAN SUFFRAGE.

24. Cold

HOT. HOT. OF course it was hot when Joanna and Lewis began their romance. Joanna never thought of it as an *affair*. An affair seemed to her a tawdry thing, sleazy, hard-hearted, and contemptible.

affair *n.* 1. a thing to be done; business; a concern, a matter. 2. [*pl.*] matters of business or commerce; public matters. 3. any incident or occurrence, esp. a scandal. 4. a social gathering or function.

An affair was an enterprise embarked upon by fools and then abandoned abruptly without undue expenditure of emotion or anguish. An affair, it seemed to Joanna, had little to do with love.

affair *n.* 5. a sexual, usually temporary, relationship between two people not married to each other; an amour.

Always she thought of her relationship with Lewis as a *romance*, the long tender story of two fairly young lovers in which every little thing was significant, bittersweet, and heart-rending.

romance *n.* 1. orig., a long narrative in verse, or later prose, relating the adventures of chivalric heroes. 2. an imaginative, fictitious tale of exciting and extraordinary adventures, esp. one set in a remote time or place.

She liked to think that between them there would always be passion, kindness, and hope. They were hot. They would always be hot. They had not meant to hurt Wanda but they had been swept away by the heat. Sometimes Joanna liked to think it was nobody's fault. It was fate.

romance *n.* **3.** a sense of mystery and wonder surrounding the mutual attraction of love. **4.** *Music,* a short lyrical piece of an informal or sentimental nature. **5.** a wild exaggeration; an inventive falsehood or fabrication with no real substance.

It was August. Everyone said it was the hottest summer ever but the truth was it was the hottest summer in three years. (The collective memory for weather is uniformly short: a hot summer is always the hottest, a cold winter is always the coldest, a wet fall is always the wettest, and a late spring is always the latest ever.) The last hottest summer had been in 1979 when Joanna was living with Henry, and after three straight weeks of both heat and humidity in excess of the one-hundred mark, Henry said, "It's so hot it feels like the whole world is going to implode."

Indeed it was the following spring when the Mount St. Helens volcano erupted. Was this a case of synchronicity or coincidence? Coincidence is usually perceived as flim-flam, a fluke, a device used in bad novels to manipulate the plot. Synchronicity, on the other hand, is regarded as evidence of the mystical union of metaphysical forces, a glimpse of the grand purposeful plan of the universe. Synchronicity carries in it a sense that all things happen for a reason, whereas coincidence produces a sneaking suspicion that they don't, that everything is merely a matter of chance. What then about weather, volcanoes, love?

This year all of July and August was drenched with sweat. Everyone felt battered by the remorseless sunshine. Joanna did not like the hot weather any better now than she ever had: it still made her listless and crabby, gave her heat rash and pimples, made her sticky, childish, and mean. The only saving grace now was that since overexposure to the sun had been determined as the leading cause of skin cancer, she was blamelessly released from the obligation to get a good tan.

This year was like those forest fire summers twenty years ago when the oppressive heat became ominous and the unrelenting sunshine was clouded in the west by a layer of smoke. The heat hung on, the rain never came. Millions of acres were burning out of control. Small towns were evacuated. The smell of smoke was everywhere, in everybody's clothes and hair. Sheets dried on the clothesline were smoke-scented and spotted with soot. When the wind changed for the worse, innocent travellers were stopped on the highway and, as if in a war zone, all able-bodied men were conscripted into the fire-fighting service.

This year, once again, the heat became the enemy, insidious and omnipotent, building daily to some ultimate catastrophe. There was always the tension of a thunderstorm in the air, brooding and building but never breaking. Joanna couldn't remember what it was like to be cold.

In the middle of August she went to an opening at the Gallery Nouvelle downtown. Lewis and Wanda were there too. They had all known each other for two years.

For two years the sexual attraction between Joanna and Lewis had sputtered and sparkled. It was an exhilarating tension which did not seem to require that either of them act upon it, an electrical attraction which, it seemed, could build and build and never break. Because they were both artists (Lewis did oil paintings which were intricate abstracts in unusual unsettling colour combinations with weighty intelligent titles like *Plato's Theory of Desire* or *Language and Reality*), there were many opportunities for innocent-enough phone calls about grant applications, galleries, supplies, and the larger aesthetic questions. Sometimes they talked for an hour or more.

Whenever possible, Joanna manoeuvred situations so she could see Lewis for a few hours, with or without Wanda, at openings, parties, lectures. She could no longer convince herself that she did not have ulterior motives. Once they went out dancing with a group of other friends. Wanda was not fond of dancing and did not seem to notice that Lewis danced with Joanna almost every song. Two or three times

Joanna purposely went to a restaurant where Lewis had mentioned they would be dining with weekend visitors from out of town. No one seemed to find her sudden appearances unusual or suspicious.

After such an encounter with Lewis, Joanna invariably felt enlivened and inspired. She felt she could cope with anything: malfunctioning household appliances, disagreeable store clerks, negative reviews of her work, poverty, persistent phone calls from the credit card company. Nothing fazed her. She could smile her way through anything and then forget all about it. Water off a duck's back. She pictured perfectly round globules sliding gently down her iridescent feathers, shots of sunlight sparking off into the opaque emotional atmosphere. A fat blue duck in a rainstorm, quacking and smiling as the water drops rolled around it like precious gemstones in the grass.

After an encounter with Lewis, Joanna was likely to have erotic dreams about him all night long so that in the morning she awoke wet between the legs, light-hearted and hopeful for hours on end.

At the August opening, they all knew (although not especially well) the man whose work was being shown. His name was Walter Hicks and his paintings were large softly coloured nudes in magnified close-up, so that breasts, hips, and thighs were like sand dunes or clouds, pubic hair like tangled vines, and navels like shadowy magical caverns leading most likely to the eighth wonder of the world.

As at all such events, everyone was kind to the artist, generous with their enthusiasm for the new work as the gallery owner brought him free drinks and steered him gently from group to admiring group. There had been a recent rumour that Walter Hicks was ill, terminally ill some said, but as everyone congratulated him, patted his arm, and gazed into his face for signs of disintegration, Walter Hicks looked merely tired and shy with black smudges under his eyes and a slight tremor in his hands, both of which could just as likely have been symptoms of the occasion as of disease or impending death.

As the evening wound down, someone suggested they adjourn to a nearby jazz club, Baby Fat's. Joanna said she'd love to. Lewis said he'd love to. Wanda said she was too tired and would just go on home, not to worry.

Eight or ten people went across to Baby Fat's and the others went their separate ways. Walking to the bar, Joanna was fussing silently about the seating arrangements: how to discreetly manage things so that she and Lewis could sit side by side. But when they arrived, it was easy. Everyone seemed to assume that the two of them should sit together. Joanna took this as a positive sign.

They had several cool drinks and discussed the show, the heat, the rumours about Walter Hicks's health, the heat, the music, the heat. The bar was not air-conditioned and all the doors and windows stood open, admitting the sounds and smells of the downtown streets: exhaust fumes, sirens, footsteps, laughter, and the murky humidity so thick it had a smell of its own. They were all laughing and sweating, their tall drinks sweating too as they held them against their flushed cheeks.

As they grew more animated, Joanna's and Lewis's hands kept falling to each other with apparently casual touches on forearm, shoulder, knee-cap, thigh. They were sitting on an ever-increasing slant, all of her body leaning in towards Lewis and his towards her. The triangle of negotiable space between them grew smaller and smaller, a mere slit finally of smoky air. A latecomer joined them uninvited around mid-night. He pulled over a chair from an empty table and thrust it right between them. Lewis glared at him so hard that he went and sat some-where else.

Joanna went down the basement to the bathroom and splashed cold water on her face and neck, even into her hair and underneath her cotton dress. When she came out, Lewis was standing in the alcove at the end of the dimly lit hallway. They kissed for a long time with Joanna's back, bare in her sundress, pressed against the cinder-block wall and the cool jazz trumpet playing just over their heads.

Upstairs the party was ending. People were paying up and wandering away in groups of two or three. Joanna said she had a bottle of good scotch at home, would anybody like to come over? Lewis said he'd love to. The others said no thanks.

In the living room they shared a drink. Lewis lifted the skirt of her sundress and gently buried his face in her thighs. They made love on the couch half-dressed. Then they took off all their clothes and Joanna spilled the drink. Lewis licked it off and they made love again in the bedroom. Lewis got up at four o'clock and had a shower. They made love in the bathroom. Lewis had another shower, got dressed, and went home.

The next day there was no contact between them. Joanna spent the morning in bed, trying and failing to sleep. She spent the afternoon walking around downtown in a morass of guilt, regret, and arousal. She spent the evening in her studio, trying and failing to work. She could not imagine what Lewis was doing.

The next day she called him when she knew Wanda was at work. She said she wished it had never happened. He said he wished she didn't feel that way. She said they were treacherous sinners, whether or not they believed in God. He said she was probably right. She said she couldn't go on with him, it would be too hard seeing him with Wanda, watching them always walking away. He said he wished she'd reconsider. She said no. He said he'd like to come over and talk about it. She said no. He said all right then.

She called him back. He came right over. They made love in the bedroom three times in a row. She cried and said she loved him. He said yes, he loved her too.

"What are we going to do?" she asked.

"What else *can* we do?" he asked. For a long time she thought he was right.

The heat continued without pause. It really was the hottest summer ever. Day after day all-time high temperatures were recorded, marvelled at, and barely endured. Day after day Joanna and Lewis made love all afternoon, sweating and sliding all over each other until Joanna, happily, could no longer imagine what it was like to be cold, lonely, or calm. She'd read a theory somewhere that people can never remember what sex is really like and so they have to keep doing it over and over again. It might have been Henry Miller who said this. Perhaps it was true. Perhaps people's memories for sex were no better than for weather.

It was a summer strafed with accidental, random, and meaningless deaths. Each week there seemed to be yet another victim, all of them young, unprepared and completely surprised in the act of dying. There were teenagers killed instantly in head-on collisions with transport trucks at three in the morning on winding empty country roads north of the city. There were young fathers in power boats and hip-waders drowned while fishing on the long weekend in small hitherto harmless lakes to the west. There was a mother of two hit by a bus, a baby suffocated on a water-bed, an innocent bystander shot to death during a drug deal, a ten-year-old girl killed when her mother's car was hit by mistake in a high-speed police chase. Through no apparent fault of its own, the whole city that summer seemed to be in mortal danger.

Each week in the newspaper there were detailed articles about these people who had died, sad stories in which these poor victims were invariably described as *very outgoing and personable . . . a dear friend to everyone . . . a model student loved by all . . . always kind to animals . . . always giving . . . always loving . . . always happy . . . always hopeful.*

Only the good die young. Or was it that only the young in death might become good so that everything which had gone before was transformed and perfected by the phoenix of their own mortality?

Joanna and Lewis read these newspaper articles together, hidden away in her quiet apartment where they could feel horrified, frightened, and sorry, but still safe. Joanna supposed that Lewis must read them again at home with Wanda too, perhaps over supper, perhaps later over coffee and sweet liqueur, perhaps later still in bed when it was too hot to sleep. He probably comforted Wanda just as he comforted her. Joanna supposed all this but tried not to dwell on it as she reread the stories alone after Lewis had left, studying them carefully for signs, premonitions, portents, warnings, reason. Such randomness was beyond contemplation, filled her with a malignant lump of fear. If only she could figure out why these things had happened, what these poor people had done wrong, what they should have done instead to better their chances of attaining long, if not eternal, life. If only she could convince herself that such tragedies could have been prevented, she might not have to come to the conclusion to which all this evidence was pointing: she might not have to realize that life itself was beyond our control, beyond all of our cleverly erected and carefully tended scaffoldings of power and safety. She was not ready to abandon the illusion that if only you did the right thing at the right time in the right way, that if only you could figure out what the rules were and then obey them word for word, your life would go the way you wanted it to and you would be exempt from tragedy, catastrophe, and random death. Then you would also be exempt from fear.

Forever after, her love for Lewis would be mixed up in her memory with these meaningless deaths, with all loss and leaving and fear, with the unbearable ominous heat.

Walter Hicks died that summer too. He was thirty-four years old and he died of pancreatic cancer. The day of the funeral Wanda was away. Lewis said that he and Joanna could sit together at the service but they could not go there together. Joanna often did not follow these fine calibrations of acceptable behaviour.

There were things Lewis would do and things he would not. He would meet Joanna, as if by accident, for a drink downtown but he would not arrive at the bar with her. He would meet her for a drink but never for lunch. He would kiss her in parking lots but never on the street. He would not ever hold her hand in public. He would lie to Wanda about where he'd been all afternoon but he would not lie to her in the evening.

There were lines he would cross and lines he would not. He would tell Joanna when Wanda was going out of town but only after she was gone, so as not to seem too happy about it. He would tell her what he and Wanda had done on the weekend but never beforehand, so as not to hurt her too much. He would tell her when they had an argument, but not what it was about, who started it, who cried, or who won.

There was a great deal of fancy footwork involved which Joanna was forced to follow. It was like learning ballroom dancing from an intricate pattern of footprints and arrows drawn in chalk on the floor. Although she did not always understand how these lines were drawn, she did understand that they were the measures by which Lewis convinced himself he was not a complete bastard.

So she agreed: they would sit together at the funeral but they would not arrive together. Lewis would come to her apartment an hour early and they would have a drink. Then they would leave her place separately and meet downtown at the church. Joanna wondered what difference it could possibly make. She assumed that everybody knew they were lovers anyway. Lewis said it made all the difference in the world. He was sure nobody knew. He seemed equally sure nobody would ever know unless he told them.

When Lewis arrived at three o'clock, Joanna was ironing. She had been ironing for an hour in the heat. She was sweaty and miserable. She had ironed six different outfits because she could not decide what to wear. It was still hot, very hot, too damn hot for black. Besides, she hadn't really known Walter Hicks that well. It might be presumptuous of her to don full-scale mourning. Lewis said, "What does it matter?"

She could see he thought she was being trivial. She could see that he had always thought she was above such petty concerns. She remembered the afternoon he had arrived unexpectedly to find her vacuuming. He had watched her with wonder and said, "I could never have pictured *you* vacuuming."

She laughed at his incredulity and said, "Well, who did you think did it? I do dishes and toilets too."

"Well, yes," he'd said stupidly, "I suppose you do."

Joanna had to admit she was flattered by this image he had of her as some hothouse flower or an exotic bird whose hands were never contaminated by evil chemical cleansers, whose thoughts never sank to the menial drudgery of groceries, housekeeping, and the endless eradication of dirt, and whose whole brilliant mind must never be sullied by the ineffable tedium of daily life.

Now she said, not unkindly, "It matters to me." She poured drinks and ironed some more. She finally settled on a very conservative pale grey shirtdress left over from her bank teller days.

"It's fine," Lewis said. "It's beautiful, you are always beautiful." He held her beside the ironing board, burying his face in her damp curly hair. He said, "I can smell you in the heat." They made love on the cool kitchen floor, not taking off their clothes, just rearranging them so they could get at each other.

Lewis left first. They met at the church and sat together in a pew near the back. Joanna wondered if they smelled of sex. All around them people were weeping softly and Joanna cried too. She hadn't known Walter Hicks very well but she liked to think he would have understood, perhaps even applauded, their need to make love, loud animal inelegant love, in the face of death and losing everything. Love, it seemed, was the only defence they could muster. Love, it seemed, was the only defiance left to any of them.

Joanna could not imagine being with Lewis in the winter. She worried that it was somehow the heat that held them together. Maybe when the winter came, they would turn back into themselves, into the simple admirable selves they'd been before they fell in love. The months of their romance might become nothing more than an unlikely hallucination, a steamy half-remembered dream. But the summer ended, the autumn passed, Christmas, then New Year's, and still they remained lovers, true lovers, bound.

In the winter, Lewis loved to skate. Joanna loved it too, but only at night, only alone. Once or twice a week around ten o'clock she would gather up her skates and walk the few blocks to Patterson Park where there were two regulation hockey rinks encircled by a general skating area. In the late afternoon and early evening all available ice surfaces were noisy and jumping with children of all sizes and levels of ability, skimming past or flopping down at unpredictable moments in their colourful well-padded snowsuits. There were picturesque rosy-cheeked couples in hand-knit his-and-hers skating sweaters, holding mittened hands and gliding gracefully round and round, grinning at each other. On the hockey rinks, there were aggressive athletic young men (of which Lewis was often one) on pick-up teams body-checking each other with gusto and slapping the puck against the boards so hard that the wood rang like crystal in the frozen air.

Late one February afternoon Joanna walked over to the rink. Lewis had said he was going to play hockey for an hour before supper. Joanna didn't bring her skates. She didn't want to skate, she only wanted to see him, and she wanted it to look like a coincidence, her arriving there just as he was stealing the puck in his nice tight sweatpants, racing head-down towards the net in his woolly fisherman-knit sweater, scoring a goal in all his lean splendour.

She stood back from the boards and watched him play for five minutes before he spotted her. He skated over, flushed and sweaty, clutching his black-taped stick like an oar or a weapon. He said, "I knew you'd come." Was she that predictable? Was he that sure of her? Was he that sure of himself?

He said, "I mean, I hoped you would come," but the other players were hollering for him so he just shrugged and skated away. Joanna regretted having stepped out of their secret romance and into the rest of his world. She hated him briefly for knowing her so well, for knowing that she couldn't stay away. She hated him for supposing that now she would hang around to watch him play, stamping her feet in the cold, cheering him on, admiring him and aching inside. She turned away and went home. How long, she wondered, would it take him to even notice she was gone?

The next day he told her that Wanda had shown up at the rink not five minutes after she'd left. "You must never come there again," he said. "It's too risky." Another line drawn.

And so she never did. But she kept on with her solitary night skating. The ice was empty then, and as she laced up her skates on a snowbank, the ice and the stars sparkled simultaneously into the silence and her breath was white upon the darkness. She skated round and round, aimlessly, endlessly round and round, like the plastic ballerina which had twirled on top of a tiny mirror in her first jewellery box, spinning frantically at first to the accelerated strains of *Swan Lake*, then slowly, more slowly, until dancer and music together ran down and stopped.

As a child she'd always skated in the dark. After supper, after homework, she had walked across the railroad tracks to Montgomery Park with her white figure skates slung over her shoulder, the blades tucked into their red plastic guards. She put them on in the shack. She tucked her snow boots with the skate guards stuck inside them underneath the green wooden bench and hit the ice. Sometimes Penny and Pamela came too. If not, she skated alone, forwards, backwards, practising her figure-eights until they were perfect. Back in the shack to warm up, the girls compared skates, whose teeth were sharper, what were they for anyway, why didn't the boys' skates have teeth, why were the boys' skates black?

Around nine o'clock or so, Clarence would walk over and watch them skate, he smoking with his hands in his pockets, Joanna embarrassed because none of the other fathers were there, but happy too, showing off for him, letting him unlace her skates back in the shack, letting him rub her half-frozen feet, letting him carry the skates over his shoulder as they walked in silence down the dark railroad tracks home.

Joanna and Samuel have just driven Clarence to the airport. They are driving home down dark icy streets clogged with creeping cars spewing clouds of exhaust and occasionally spinning their wheels furiously, in- effectually, like dogs losing traction on a stretch of shiny linoleum. It is the coldest night of the winter so far. The Christmas visit is over again and Joanna is more than ready to resume her real life. She feels guilty for feeling relieved to have put her father on that plane and sent him home to his empty little house.

It has been seven years since Esther died. It has been seven years since her romance with Lewis ended. Joanna always thinks of these two losses together. She is always mixing up her mother and her lover in her head, although they never met, never would or could have, never will now. Lewis had been away for the weekend with Wanda when Joanna got the call from Clarence. Clarence not crying but choking as he told her her mother was dead. Joanna crying alone, then calling Clarence's neighbour to go over and comfort him. She went downtown to the travel agent to book her flight home the next day. When the agent asked, "Business or pleasure?" Joanna said, "Neither. My mother died." The agent was embarrassed and could not look at her when the ticket and the cheque changed hands.

Samuel in the back seat now is a little sniffly and teary-eyed. Clarence was too when he shuffled through Security and set off the metal detector because he'd forgotten to take his keys out of his pocket. Samuel is consoled when Joanna says, "Don't worry, he'll be back again next

Christmas, maybe we'll see him in the summer, he'll call tonight for sure, don't worry."

But as the years go by, Joanna wonders if each Christmas will be the last. She thinks of how Clarence shuffles now, of how each time she sees him, he has aged in the interim, losing ground when she's not looking. She is swamped by mixed emotions. Are there any other kind?

As they draw closer to the house (where Gordon will be home from work by now, waiting to warm them with laughter, hugs, hot chocolate, spaghetti sauce bubbling on the back burner), they pass a lone figure trudging down the sidewalk where the snow has frozen into treacherous ruts and furrows. It is a woman in a long padded parka, a white scarf wrapped round and round her head and her face so that only her eyes are showing. She holds one red mitten over her mouth. It is Wanda.

What on earth is she doing walking in the dark on the coldest night of the year? Where is she going? What is she running from? No, she's not running, she's just picking her way through the ice, she's just walking slowly away. How could Lewis let her out on a night like this? Joanna has always thought of Wanda as delicate, fragile and frail, looking pale and thin like a plant. Now, after seven years, she sees that Wanda is tougher than anyone would ever guess, than anyone, including Lewis, would ever give her credit for.

Now she is swamped with guilt, more guilt, and tenderness. But if she rolls down the window and opens her mouth to offer Wanda a ride, she thinks she will spit out blood, her own blood, or poison, her own poisoned blood, or semen, gallons of the semen she swallowed seven years ago.

25. Slow

WHEN JOANNA FIRST starts seeing Gordon, she wants to proceed with caution. Fools rush in, haste makes waste, the tortoise and the hare, slow and steady wins the race, all of that. "I want to go slow," she says to him often. The fact that they have already slept together, are in fact in bed together when she first says this, does not strike her as contradictory.

"Slowly," Gordon says.

"Yes, I want to go slow," Joanna repeats.

"*Slowly*," Gordon says again and Joanna realizes that he is correcting her grammar rather than agreeing with her.

She wants to stay in control this time. It has been a full year since her romance with Lewis ended. Her feelings for Gordon are not at all like those she had for Lewis. Although it seems unfair and unfaithful, she cannot help comparing the two, not the men themselves so much as her own feelings for them. Then, with Lewis, she felt consumed, engulfed, enveloped. Ablaze, awash, aflame. Overwhelmed, overpowered, overcome. Now, with Gordon, she feels calm, quiet, satisfied, secure, confident, content, tender, and damn near serene. She does not want her love this time to have anything to do with fire, water, or power. She does not want to be railroaded, steamrolled, or swept away—by tidal wave, hurricane, tornado, volcano, cyclone, monsoon, typhoon, or any other unmanageable force of nature. Now she is hoping against hope that she can be in love and not insane.

With Lewis she had either been higher than high or lower than low. There had been scarcely any middle ground, that bland flat territory she had in fact scorned as the habitual uninspired residence of lesser mortals. She was fond of saying then that contentment was for cows. Now she craves that legendary middle ground.

She has, she supposes, grown up. But occasionally, on sleepless nights or fretful mornings with the prospect of another calm and orderly day unrolling before her, she wonders if she has *given* up. What is the difference between acceptance and resignation? If Lewis was the grand passion of her life (and she is pretty sure he was, cannot imagine love getting grander or more passionate than that), then where does that leave Gordon?

She has told Gordon about her affair with Lewis in some (though not graphic) detail. Gordon appears to accept the possibility that she may still have some residual feelings for Lewis. He says they are not feelings so much as memories of feelings, which is a whole different thing. If he is jealous, he keeps it to himself. He says we all have our baggage. He says her feelings for Lewis do not necessarily take away from her feelings for him. She is impressed by his maturity and only occasionally wants to shake him.

She is afraid, not of being hurt, but of being overwhelmed. She thinks that saying they should go slowly will actually make it true. As if, contrary to popular proverbial wisdom, her words will speak louder than her actions and she will be protected from her own obsessive romantic urgency.

Gordon agrees with her, affably. "Yes, you're right. We should go slowly. We've both made mistakes before. This time we can get it right if we're careful." This decided, they make love again and fall asleep.

They are at Gordon's apartment, a small one-bedroom suite on the fourth floor of an unremarkable eight-storey building. All the apartments have balconies surrounded with black cast-iron railings and cluttered with lawn chairs, bicycles, and barbecues. Some people have put up window boxes filled with red geraniums. Other people hang their laundry on the railing instead. Inside all the apartments are identical, one- and two-bedroom models, the basic floor plan flipped right or left.

In Gordon's apartment all the walls are white and all the furniture is brown. The couch is brown plaid which, unfortunately, reminds Joanna of her mother's dinner plates. It is a large manly couch, a bulky brown plaid atoll in the middle of the nearly empty living room. She has seen this couch in the apartments of many other single men. Although Gordon has lived here for several years, the apartment still looks unfinished. He has not yet gotten around to decorating. There are framed prints and paintings leaning against the walls, still waiting to be hung. There are many cardboard boxes stacked in the storage closet, still waiting to be unpacked. There are books in precarious piles, still waiting to be shelved. For that matter, there is a bookcase in a large flat box, still waiting to be assembled.

In Gordon's bedroom there is a king-size bed and an eight-drawer double dresser. On the floor there is a jumble of clothes, books, magazines, and unopened junk mail. Under the bed among the hairy dustballs there are three pairs of underwear, two dirty plates, one dirty sock, many dirty Kleenexes, and one used condom which has been there so long it's gone hard like a curious fossil. It reminds her of the dead baby birds she used to see on the sidewalk on the way to school, their tiny opalescent bodies curled up and crispy. Joanna knows what is under Gordon's bed because sometimes when she has spent the night and Gordon has gone off to work early in the morning, she stays and sleeps a little longer, warmly cocooned in the middle of the vast bed, the blankets which smell like him pressed to her nose. She sleeps a little longer and then she snoops.

She snoops with a lump of guilt in her throat and an exhilarating knot of suspense in her stomach. She sips a mug of coffee and looks under the bed. She munches on a piece of brown toast and goes through all eight of his dresser drawers. She is looking for secrets: love letters, photographs, diaries, clues to Gordon's other life. What makes her think Gordon has another life? What does she expect to find? A wedding picture perhaps, him arm in arm with a wife he forgot to mention? Cancelled support payment cheques for six children in Alaska? A box of syringes and a Baggie full of heroin? A series of full-colour photographs of him engaged in sexual intercourse with a dog, a horse, a leopard, or eight-year-old Siamese twins? A warrant for his arrest for an unspecified but major international crime? A gun and a box of silver bullets, half-empty? A skeleton in the closet, so to speak? Well, perhaps not a whole skeleton, not in a dresser drawer. Perhaps a set of finger bones strung on a twenty-four-carat gold chain.

In seven of the drawers, she finds clothes, many clothes, all clean and ironed and neatly folded, arranged according to season. In the top left drawer she finds balls of socks and underwear, a badly tarnished peace sign medallion, a bundle of paid utility bills, a catalogue of hand-tied fishing flies, and a box of wooden matches.

Is it possible that Gordon has already told her everything she needs to know? Is it possible that Gordon has nothing to hide? That she has nothing to fear? That he will be boring and she will like it?

For the first month Joanna keeps snooping and warning him that she wants to go slowly. Then she begins to lose her fear. They spend more time at her place because it is cosier and better equipped. It begins to look like they are going to live together. It begins to look like they are going to live together happily ever after. They are not exactly planning this out loud but after two months it has begun to look like the next logical step.

In retrospect, Joanna will have to admit that, despite her warnings, the only thing slow about it was the way Gordon liked to put his penis into her, slowly, drawing it out again slowly, back inside slowly, slowly, until she thought she would scream and sometimes did as she came four, five, six, seven times.

26. Wish

AT VARIOUS TIMES in her life Joanna has wished for various things, invoking various traditional methods to make her dreams come true.

She has blown out many candles on many birthday cakes and then wished like crazy for a piano, a set of encyclopedias, a pure white Persian kitten, a pink satin blouse like Penny's.

She has snapped many wishbones from many turkeys and then wished like mad for a date, a thousand dollars, new parents, peace on earth, good will towards men.

She has spotted many twinkling stars and chanted many times: *Starlight, star bright,/First star I see tonight,/I wish I may, I wish I might,/Have the wish I wish tonight.*

She has tossed many shiny pennies into many allegedly magical fountains and wishing wells, then wished fervently for a car, a husband, new hair, a good night's sleep.

On certain occasions, Joanna has wished she was somebody else.

In the dream Joanna has just been given the one thing in the world she has always wanted the most. In the dream she knows exactly what it is, but when she wakes up she can't remember, left only with a sense of serene pleasure, an image of whiteness which suffuses her whole morning with gentle satisfaction and thanksgiving.

Sometimes now Joanna thinks she has everything she has ever wished for in her entire life.

27. River

JOANNA REMEMBERS SITTING on the banks of a river with a man. At the secluded spot where they sat on a wide flat rock with their knees drawn up to their chins, the water spread out before them in a deep still pool. Farther down there was a waterfall, its headlong turbulence hidden around a corner but filling their heads with a rushing sound which was either comforting or frightening.

Joanna was not an outdoor person then and she is still not. She thinks of herself as an indoor person. She feels more comfortable in buildings, with four walls, a floor, and a ceiling around her. Outdoors she feels exposed and self-conscious, as if she were being watched and found foolish. Outdoors she feels clumsy, unsteady, and light-headed, as if she might fall over any minute for no reason. She knows that being outdoors, communing with nature, is supposed to be relaxing, replenishing, generally good for the soul, but she always ends up feeling sulky and sometimes even tearful with wanting to go home. This young man with his pale skin and soft white hands was probably not an outdoor person either and yet, unaccountably, there they were.

She remembers that she was wearing tight white shorts and a skimpy green halter top with a yellow apple embroidered on the front. The man too was wearing shorts and no shirt, so that when he stood to skip rocks across the quiet pool his shoulders were shiny in the heat. He was tall beside her in the sun, casting a cool shadow across her. She remembers wishing that he would sit back down and put his arm around her. He did.

She remembers thinking that maybe wishing *could* make your dreams come true. Then they talked about the notion that you can never step into the same river twice. He was a serious young man, brooding and intense, a deep-thinking young man who was often preoccupied with the contents of his own excellent mind and frequently depressed in a philosophical manner, flinging his long-fingered delicate hands about in paroxysms of existential despair. They were in university, had met in a second-year philosophy course.

She remembers nodding and smiling wisely while he talked, but inside her a voice was chanting, *I love you, I love you, I love you.* Also she was hoping he didn't get into the question, if a tree falls in the forest and there's no one there to hear it, does it make a sound? He was inordinately fond of this discussion. There were trees all around them, not falling, not making a sound save that of the wind in their leaves.

Today he did not question the trees or what they might or might not do when there was no one around. Instead he told her about his high school friend who had drowned in this same river, perhaps in this very spot. There was no way of knowing because the boy was alone when it happened, gone for a swim in the middle of a hot August night. He said he was still haunted by the image of his friend's body going over the falls. He said he could not free his mind from the idea that river equals death.

Joanna remembers nodding and making sympathetic mewing sounds but her crotch was getting tender and wet and she was wishing that he would reach over and undo the ribbon of her halter top and lick her smooth small breasts. She was wishing that he would press her back into that flat wide rock and ravish her. But she knew that wishing this time wouldn't work. This was not the kind of thing this young man would ever do. She also knew that this sad story was bound to lead him to a discussion of either the River Styx, that river which circles Hades nine times and across which the dead must be ferried, or the River Lethe, that river of forgetfulness, that river of oblivion which leaves travellers unable to remember who they are or where they've come from once they've reached the other side.

She suspects now that she never did have sex with this young man. At least she hopes not, because much as she can remember the river, the heat, and the dead boy, she cannot remember his name.

28. White

THE COLOUR OF the snow in which you make angels all afternoon three days before Christmas. Your snowsuit is red, your hat and mittens are blue, your mother is inside ironing, you can see her through the picture window and from the outside she looks beautiful and friendly, maybe even happy, maybe she is humming. You are lonely but peaceful. You make angels all over the front yard and then go through the white picket gate and make them again all over the back until there are dozens and dozens, some of their wing-tips touching, so that when your father comes home from work just at dark, he claps his hands and says to your mother, "Aren't we lucky? There are angels all over the yard. Does this mean we are saved?" You are too young yet to know much about the need for salvation, but as the darkness fills in the angels you imagine them rising, fine feathery shadows floating up to the roof of your house where they will perch all night long with their wings wrapped around their knees (do angels have knees?) and also around dozens of perfect Christmas presents especially for you.

The colour of the snow in which you make angels with your lover. Your jacket is purple, his mittens are black, and as you step carefully into his angel, he kisses you full on the mouth in broad daylight in your own backyard which, after all the secrecy, lies, and afternoon ren-dezvous, is such a flagrant disregard of the danger, such a dramatic declaration of desire, that you might as well be making love in the driveway for all the world to see. You take this kiss as a sign, a sign from God that yes, he really will leave his wife and the two of you will live happily ever after together. But he does not leave her, not today. Today he goes home to her once again, sad, he says, depressed, devas-tated even, guilty and ashamed of his own cowardice, he says, with white snow in his black hair, and you are left alone with six angels prostrate in your own backyard.

The colour of the snow in which you make angels with your son. His snowsuit is blue, his hat and mittens have penguins on them, and he is giggling and rolling around with snow in his mouth and his eyes and you do not have the heart to tell him that his angel looks more like an elephant. You tell him it is perfect, he is perfect, a perfect angel. He says, "That's not what you called me this morning when I knocked over the milk." He, like you, is too smart for his own good.

The colour of the snow in which you have made angels all your life. No matter what else, the snow is always white. No matter where you go, what you do, who you love, how well or poorly you love them, the snow in which you make angels will always be white.

29. Beautiful

"YOU'VE GOT BEAUTIFUL eyes, little girl," Clarence often said. "Just like your mother."

Esther said, "Don't you roll those big brown eyes at me."

"You have beautiful eyes," Thomas Hunt told Joanna while his penis softened in her hand.

"You have beautiful eyes," Henry told her across the breakfast table when she knew damn well they were puffy and red from having been up late drinking and arguing the night before.

"You have beautiful eyes," Lewis said, at least a thousand times, every time he looked at her, it seemed, every time they made love. "You should get contacts," he often suggested.

But Joanna would just roll those eyes and laugh, saying, "No thanks, I've got enough trouble. At least this way I've got my glasses to hide behind when I need to."

Sometimes after Lewis left her (if you could call it that: after all, he'd never really been *with* her, he'd always been with Wanda, just sleeping with Joanna on the side, if you could call it that; usually they did it from the top or the bottom or the back, occasionally standing up, very seldom on the side), Joanna would stand in the bathroom and peer at her own eyes in the mirror. Yes, they were big (big enough) and brown (brown enough) but they looked ordinary to her. She could not see in them what other people (mostly men) proclaimed to see. This was akin to trying to tickle yourself. It just never worked.

"Please don't tell me I have beautiful eyes," Joanna says.

"All right, I won't," Gordon says. They have just met, they are drinking margaritas at a party, flirting and flitting around each other like butterflies. As far as looks go, Gordon is not Joanna's type but she likes him anyway. He is a graphic designer, currently working for a local book publisher. She has seen him around but this is the first time they've actually met.

"Tell me something I haven't already heard," Joanna says.

"You have a beautiful nose," Gordon says.

"Thank you," Joanna says. "I'm sick to death of hearing about my eyes."

"Ah yes," Gordon says, "the eyes, the windows of the soul."

"I hope not," Joanna says. Her soul is her business. She does not want people peering into it whenever they feel like it.

Sometimes there are eyes in her dreams. Her own eyes, brown. Other people's eyes, other colours. Crying eyes, smiling, laughing, staring, accusing eyes. Closed eyes, somebody sleeping or dead. Eyes with no face. A face with no eyes. Once she dreams of her eyes being poked out with a hot stick but she can't tell who is holding the stick. Once she dreams of having her eyes scooped out with a spoon and then thrown against the wall where they bounce and blink but she can't tell who is holding the spoon. Often she dreams that she has gone blind.

Clarence, cradling Samuel, six weeks old, says, "Yes, he's definitely got your eyes."

Joanna says, "Oh no."

30. Window

JOANNA'S BEDROOM WINDOW faced directly into the kitchen window of the house next door. This house in those days was owned by a young couple named Sandra and Larry Irving. They had a new baby girl with the unlikely name of Cassandra. Esther said it was a shame to saddle a sweet little baby with a weird name like that. Clarence said the baby would grow into it. Joanna thought it was glamorous. A girl with a name like that was bound to grow up and be somebody. Herself, she'd been trying lately to convince people to call her by her middle name, Isabelle, which she thought had more promise, more flair than her first. Esther said she was being silly. Clarence called her Izzie just to make her mad.

From her bedroom window, Joanna could peek right into Sandra and Larry's kitchen. She knelt on her bed to spy on Sandra at her kitchen sink doing the supper dishes while Larry bounced the baby on his knee behind her. Sandra and Larry's kitchen was exactly the same as theirs. They even had the same sheer white frilly curtains with a venetian blind underneath. If Joanna squinted, she could see the flowers on their wallpaper and the mountains in the picture hung over their kitchen table. At night in the summer through the screens, she could hear Sandra and Larry laughing, singing to Cassandra, arguing half-heartedly once about buying a new car when the old one was still good.

Joanna, falling asleep every night with her bedroom door propped open a few inches to let in the light of the kitchen because she was afraid of the dark, found it comforting to imagine the seven houses on their side of the block squatting in a row, theirs in the middle, flanked on each side by three other families doing (or so she imagined) all the same things in the evening in all the same rooms with all their windows lit-up yellow squares against the accumulating darkness. She imagined other mothers doing the dishes or ironing in their bright kitchens, other fathers doing paint-by-numbers or crossword puzzles in their cosy living rooms, other children curled up in their bedrooms listening to cars passing in the street, the occasional snatch of music or voices raised in laughter, sometimes the sound of a bicycle or footsteps hurrying home.

She imagined that after all the children were fast asleep, all the parents watched the same TV show and then went to bed all at the same time, all the lights winking out in all the houses as the whole block settled simultaneously into sleep.

Sometimes on a stormy night, when she could hear the wind driving the rain against her window, Joanna lay stiff and breathless in her bed, sweating with the knowledge that nothing but a flimsy, infinitely fragile pane of glass stood between her and the fury outside. She kept both her fists and her eyes clenched against the lightning, and when the thunder rattled the windowpane, she thought she would faint with fear.

Living in the basement apartment, Joanna quickly learned to recognize her visitors by their shoes and the look of their legs from the knee down. The apartment was in an ordinary suburban three-bedroom red-brick house with a two-car garage. One of Joanna's living-room windows looked into the garage where she could see hoses, rakes, shovels, and two black tires on her landlady's small yellow car. Occasionally neighbourhood cats got accidentally shut in the garage. They looked in the window at her, meowing. Her landlady was a retired schoolteacher, widowed many years before. She lived quietly and expected Joanna to do the same.

In the winter, bright but not warm sunshine came through the bare branches of the lilac bushes in front, casting a tangled pattern upon the far wall of Joanna's living room, lobes of light changed into discs or gold coins on the dark wood panelling. Some winters the snowbanks got so high she couldn't see over them. Inside there was an inch and a half of ice on the bottom of the windowpane.

In the spring, the lilacs came into bud and sprouted small tender leaves which infused the whole room first with a soft green light and then, as the bushes blossomed, a dreamy mauve fragrance. By midsummer, the bushes were covered with dark green shiny leaves, the room was always in shadow, and again Joanna could hardly see the street. But with the forced intimacy of hot summer nights, screen doors and windows flung wide open hoping for a breeze, she could smell the bushes and the damp black earth, she could hear the noises of the neighbourhood at night. She could hear footsteps, laughter, a boy bouncing a basketball as he walked past. Sometimes she heard a mysterious tidbit of conversation which might recur that night in her dreams:

"I wouldn't if I were you."

"I don't blame you."

"He's been like that for years."

"Are you crazy?"

Mostly she could hear the couple in the house across the street fighting, always fighting, usually outside in their driveway. It was impossible to keep secrets in the summertime. For months she didn't even know their names, but she knew all about their money problems, the man's ex-wife, the woman's crazy mother, the time the man got picked up for impaired driving, the good job he used to have until he got himself fired and it was all his own damn fault. She even knew about their sex life and how the woman had been trying to get pregnant for a year but couldn't, and that was probably his fault too.

By the end of August, they were at it every night. They would yell and yell at each other in the driveway until finally one of them, sometimes him, sometimes her, cried, "I'm going to leave you! Just you see if I don't!" and then the other one yelled, "Go ahead! Leave me! See if I care!" Then there was the sound of one car door slamming, the engine gunned hard, the tires spitting up gravel as one of them, sometimes him, sometimes her, made their getaway. The one left behind, deserted in the driveway, would call out after the speeding car. The woman would call, "David, don't!" Or the man would say, "Sherry," with no exclamation at all in his voice. This was how Joanna finally came to know their names.

Early the next morning, six or seven o'clock, when Joanna was still in bed or just getting up, shuffling around the kitchen in her underwear because it was already hot, too hot to drink coffee really but she would have it anyway, then the car would come back quietly. It was a big old two-toned Chevrolet, the kind of car that used to be known as a boat, now usually referred to as a gas-guzzler. The car would pull slowly into the driveway, and one of them, sometimes him, sometimes her, would get out and go up the steps to the front door and knock and wait until it was opened, then step inside, pull the door softly shut, and stay there all day with the curtains closed.

When Joanna flew home for Esther's funeral, she discovered that the Irvings' house next door was owned now by a real estate agency that rented it out. Clarence said he had told her about this but she had forgotten. "They rent it out," Clarence said, shaking his head, "to anybody who comes along. Riff-raff."

The house was run-down now, shingles lifting, paint peeling, windows cracked and clouded with dirt. Bricks were falling out of the chimney and the front steps were rotting away. The grass was seldom mowed—the tenants, it seemed, expected the real estate people to do it, and the real estate people expected the tenants to do it, and so it almost never got done.

Clarence said, "It always made your mother mad to see that mess next door. And now she's dead."

The night after the funeral, there was a commotion next door. Joanna, sleeping uneasily in her old bedroom, dreaming of coffins and doves, was awakened at three in the morning by a woman yelling, a door slamming, then fists pounding and a man crying out, "I love you, damn it! Please let me in! I promise I'll never hurt you again." His voice echoed in the small space between the houses.

Then came car brakes in the street, two doors opening, then slamming shut. Red lights flashed around her bedroom.

Joanna got up on her knees and peeked through the curtains. Two policemen had the man up against the wall below the kitchen window. His arms and legs were spread and they were feeling him up and down. They were all silent. The woman watched from the window above.

Clarence came up behind Joanna. He knelt on the bed beside her and together they watched as the policemen turned the man around. He stumbled, nearly falling into their arms, so they propped him against the wall and put the handcuffs on.

"Drunk," Clarence whispered. "He always comes around when he's drunk. His name is Frank. I've heard her call him Frank."

The policemen led Frank up the sidewalk between the houses. Joanna and Clarence sneaked into the front room and peeked through the curtains there. They could hear the police radio crackling as the cops pushed Frank into the back seat. They got in the front and the interior light flicked on. One cop spoke into the radio while the other made notes. Frank in the back seat held his head in his handcuffed hands. His shoulders were heaving as if he were crying or trying to throw up. Red lights still flashing, the cruiser drove away.

"See?" Clarence said, and they went back to their beds.

After she stopped seeing Lewis, Joanna took to driving past his house at odd hours of the day and night, sometimes very early in the morning when she supposed they were still in bed. She never knew what she was hoping to see but she cruised past slowly and studied the front of their house, looking for clues.

Perhaps she thought the position of the curtains in the windows would tell her what was really happening inside. Sometimes the curtains of what she knew to be the spare bedroom were closed and she hoped this meant they were sleeping in separate rooms.

One night, returning very late from an evening out with friends, she saw that all of Lewis and Wanda's lights were still on, upstairs and down, the whole house blazing. She hoped this meant they were finally having it out, weeping and wailing from room to room, Wanda trailing Lewis upstairs and down, shouting accusations and throwing things.

What she really hoped to see was the window of Lewis's studio standing wide open, the curtains billowing out like sails, and his easel, his canvases, his brushes, and paints all in a heap on the front lawn with his shirts, socks, and underwear scattered everywhere.

What she really did see was a pair of dirty white runners curled up slightly at the toes on the front step, a Persian carpet draped over the railing to air, three bags of garbage waiting to be walked to the curb, their blue recycling box filled with bottles, cans, and newspapers. Once there were at least a dozen cases of empty beer bottles neatly stacked, a brand she'd never known Lewis liked.

The last time she drove past on purpose, it was four months since Lewis had told Wanda the truth, and there they were, large as life, on a sunny Saturday morning out on the front step drinking coffee. Wanda was sitting on the top step in a pretty blue blouse reading the morning paper aloud to Lewis who was stretched on his back beside her on the warm concrete in the green shirt which was Joanna's favourite. Behind them Joanna could see clean pink sheets and all their underwear flapping on the clothesline in the backyard. She could also see that she was the furthest thing from either of their minds.

One of the things Joanna and Gordon like best about their house on Laverty Street is its big kitchen with the windows facing the street. So many of the houses they looked at had tiny dark kitchens stashed to the back or the side, utilitarian little rooms with space only for the requisite appliances and a stingy bit of countertop. These kitchens usually had just one window, most often over the sink looking out at the brick wall of the house next door. These kitchens were like bathrooms, necessary but shameful somehow, best kept hidden from the public eye.

It is an older suburban neighbourhood with many large trees and mostly two-storey red-brick houses set close together. To the north the neighbourhood deteriorates quickly. To the south it escalates slowly, edging by increments all the way to the very upper-class area on the waterfront. They are in the middle where the houses are well-tended with flowers in the front yards, clean relatively new cars in the driveways, wooden decks and fences in the back. Many of their neighbours are retired people.

After they have bought the house, while they are still waiting for the previous owners to move out, Joanna and Gordon drive by it often, usually late in the evening, and through the kitchen windows they can see these people gathered around the table eating or just talking, their faces warmed by the yellow light of a wicker lamp hung from the ceiling above them. One night the house is in darkness, they think there's nobody home, and then, moving mysteriously across the room as if self-propelled, there comes a birthday cake lit up with dozens of flickering candles and they can hear these strangers singing right out on the street.

Their kitchen is large and bright with plenty of room for cooking and eating. It is a room to spend time in. People, Joanna has discovered, generally fall into two distinct categories as far as rooms go: there are kitchen people and there are living-room people. This distinction is most pronounced at parties where the guests unconsciously gravitate to one room or the other, so that by the middle of the evening there would seem to be two separate parties in progress. There are always more people in the kitchen.

At their housewarming party, for instance, three weeks after they've moved in, the kitchen is quickly clogged up with guests hovering around the table where the hors d'oeuvres are laid out, lounging against the counters, the stove, and every empty inch of wall space, somebody always in front of the refrigerator, somebody perched on the edge of the sink, all of them with drinks and crackers in hand, laughing and smoking and munching and admiring the big windows, the smoky blue blinds, Joanna's collages all over the walls.

The more they talk, the more boisterous they become, each with a funny story about houses they've lived in or escaped from, renovations they've done or dreamed of, real estate agents they've hated or loved, everything needing to be told at least twice at top volume to be sure nobody misses it. Joanna in the midst of it thinks this is the best party she's ever had, maybe the best party she's ever been to. Several of the kitchen people say as much as they help themselves to another beer, another cracker, another carrot stick.

The living-room people are sitting around politely nursing their drinks and conversing knowledgeably about mortgages, interest rates, and the very best plumber in town. They keep opening the windows to clear out the cigarette smoke which is drifting in from the rowdy kitchen. They keep turning down the music so they can hear themselves think. Until finally one of the kitchen people goes into the living room, rolls up the rug, puts some rock-and-roll music on the stereo and starts dancing. Joanna and Gordon join in energetically but Joanna feels a little self-conscious to find herself all dressed up and dancing in her bare feet in her own living room, which so far has been used mostly for quiet evenings watching TV or her and Gordon curled up on the couch reading after Samuel has been put to bed.

The truth is she seldom ventures into the living room during the day, except first thing in the morning to open the curtains so the plants won't die in the dark, and sometimes in the afternoon, especially when it rains and then she closes the curtains and snuggles under a woolly afghan on the couch, daydreaming or napping cosily for an hour (which, she has often thought, is one of the biggest advantages to working at home). But usually she works all day in her studio upstairs at the back of the house. Sometimes, though, when she's thinking about a new project or when she feels lonely, too isolated working at home alone while the rest of the world goes on (or goes wild or goes crazy or, for all she knows, goes away) without her, she sits at the kitchen table and looks out the window instead.

Laverty Street is very quiet during the day, a pocket of middle-class life which is not a shortcut to anywhere and so there's not much traffic. Sometimes the retired couple across the street is out working on their already immaculate yard or coming home from the shopping center with bags of stuff, once a new barbecue, a lawn mower, a pink toilet.

Sometimes there are people walking by, talking with their heads down, sometimes pointing and looking up. Then Joanna gets close to the window and peers up too, with a feeling of excitement and wondering what she is expecting to see: a flying saucer? an enemy fighter plane? a jet coming down in hideous flames?

Most often what she does see is a migrating V of Canada geese or a glossy fat crow with something four-legged and furry dangling from its beak, or once just at suppertime a gracefully arching jet trail being spun in slow motion out of a minuscule metallic speck like the silken strand of a spiderweb and Samuel, pointing, cries, "Look, he's making a white rainbow!" Sometimes it really is a rainbow. Everybody loves rainbows. Once she sees the Goodyear blimp.

She thinks she might do a collage called *Kitchen Window*. In it she will include trees, birds, squirrels, a rainbow, real blades of grass, real maple leaves going orange in the autumn. There will also be bicycles, cars, garbage cans, a lawn mower, a pink toilet, a pot of gold, a man crying, and yes, of course, the Goodyear blimp. It will contain windows too, many windows with faces looking out, and she will cover the whole thing with fine white cheesecloth like a screen. In one corner, there will be real shards of broken glass.

Many times when Joanna looks up, there is nothing at all, just a bowl of blue sky, and she feels acutely disappointed, also a little embarrassed as if she has been tricked.

31. Rough

DAISY THE CAT was born in a barn and she never quite got used to living in a house. No matter how hard Joanna loved her, no matter how completely Clarence ignored her, and no matter how often Esther hollered at her or smacked her with the fly-swatter, Daisy remained wild at heart for all of her short life. She ran up and down the living-room drapes as if they were trees. She would eat anything that had been left momentarily unattended. She ate a whole package of frozen calves' liver left out to thaw. She ate half a chocolate cake left out to cool before icing. She ate straight through the rind of a cantaloupe to get at the juicy fruit inside. At night she slept with Joanna, stretched flat out sucking on the ribbons at the neck of her nightie, kneading her chest with both paws, licking her cheeks with her rough pink tongue. Esther said she did this because she'd been weaned too soon. Joanna loved her with all her heart, which sometimes she thought of as wild.

They got Daisy from a man Clarence worked with at the paper mill. His name was Ed Hartley and he lived with his crippled wife on a farm west of town. The Hartleys had no children but they had cows, horses, chickens, geese, a Shetland pony named Pete, four dogs named Mutt, Jeff, Big, and Little, and many nameless cats.

Clarence, Esther, and Joanna drove out one Sunday afternoon to choose a kitten. The kittens were too young really to be given away but their mother had been accidentally stepped on by a horse.

The Hartleys lived in a small square building covered with tar paper. This building was originally meant to be the garage for their big new house which, at this stage, was a concrete foundation sticking four feet out of the ground with the window holes boarded over. Clarence said the big house had been at this stage for ten years. Meanwhile the Hartleys had set up housekeeping in the garage. There was a sagging plywood ramp up to the door. Inside, it was all one room, with the sleeping area curtained off in a corner. The floor was covered with odd-shaped pieces of linoleum in different patterns, held together with black electrical tape. The room was not very clean. There did not appear to be a bathroom, so Joanna was glad they weren't staying long.

While Clarence and Mr. Hartley took Joanna out to the barn to pick her kitten, Esther stayed behind to have tea with Mrs. Hartley who was a small, rumpled, cheerful woman in a large wheelchair. Her legs hung from the chair seat like the legs of a monkey doll Joanna had had as a baby, a doll made of men's grey work socks, stuffed with old nylons, its long legs spongy and floppy with soft large lumps. As they walked out to the barn, Joanna could not imagine what her mother might find to say to such a woman in such a house.

Near the barn there was a barbed-wire fence Mr. Hartley said was electrified. It kept the cows and horses in, he said, and the wild critters out. It would not shock them bad enough to kill them, just enough to teach them a lesson. Joanna had received a small electric shock once when plugging in the iron for Esther and she remembered how the current had felt running up her skinny arm and how all the little hairs stood on end.

In the barn, Joanna patted and cuddled each of the four kittens in turn. She chose the white one because right away it purred and licked her chin with its rough pink tongue.

On the way home, Joanna in the back seat was busy with her kitten, rubbing her chin, deciding on a name, pressing her face against the soft white fur. Up front Esther said, "That poor woman. What a rough life she's had." She said this in a voice Joanna had seldom heard her use before: a soft sad voice, trembling almost with genuine sympathy and admiration perhaps for all that Mrs. Hartley had been through and survived.

A few months later Joanna came home from school to find Daisy sleepy and wobbling around the kitchen with a red cut on her belly. Esther said Daisy had hurt herself on a wire fence. Joanna thought of the Hartleys' electrified fence. Later still, she realized that, in fact, Daisy had been taken to the vet and spayed while she was at school.

When Daisy was a year old, she was hit by a car right in front of their house one sunny Saturday afternoon. Joanna saw it happen from the picture window. She ran into the street and held Daisy's bloodied body in her arms as the death car sped away.

Daisy, she knew, was the only living creature on the face of the earth who had ever loved and understood her. Now she was gone. That night Joanna began writing a kind of diary, a series of letters to Daisy, on the gold-embossed parchment writing paper she had received that year for her twelfth birthday. She kept these letters hidden in a box behind the books on her middle shelf so Esther wouldn't find them.

Esther said there would be no more pets after Daisy because it hurt too much when they died. Later Joanna will understand that this was not a good enough reason. She will learn about falling in love while knowing full well your heart may be broken. She will learn about fighting for your life every day while knowing full well we are all going to die.

For years afterwards, whenever she hears someone say, "Boy, that's rough!" upon hearing bad news, or "He's had a rough life," upon hearing of someone else's repeated tragedies, Joanna will think of Mrs. Hartley and Daisy and her rough pink tongue.

She will think of Daisy's death and her father saying, "Honey, I know it's rough," while she leaned against him, sobbing into his brown sweater which was also rough and smelled of autumn leaves and earth.

She will think of the mysterious scar on Daisy's white belly, of Mr. Hartley's electrified fence, and Mrs. Hartley's legs dangling like a monkey doll's from her shiny wheelchair.

32. Citizen

"It is very important," Esther often said, "to be a good citizen." She was not an especially civic-minded person in the usual sense of the word. She often didn't even bother to vote because, as she said, she and Clarence had been voting for opposing candidates for twenty-five years so their votes cancelled each other out. She thought the mayor was an asshole but this did not strike her as a misfortune she could do anything about. She was, it seemed, comfortably resigned to a state of political impotence. Let somebody else worry about such issues, somebody, the implication was, who had nothing better to do with their time. Nothing ever changed much anyway no matter who got in. And really, what did it all have to do with her in the end?

Politics aside, however, there was, according to Esther, an extensive list of requirements for good citizenship. To be a good citizen you must keep your lawn mowed, your shrubs pruned, your hedges trimmed, and your garden weeded. You must eliminate every single dandelion from your property by dragging around a solid weed-killer bar once a week.

You must keep the outside of your house clean. This involved hosing down the dust and vacuuming up the spiderwebs around the doors and windows. You must get your storm windows up in October and down again at the end of April. You must have the trim, if not the whole thing, freshly painted, preferably in a new colour, every other year. You must keep your eavestroughing clear and your fall leaves raked, even though it was your stupid neighbours' stupid tree that dropped its leaves all over your yard. (It was a well-kept secret that Esther had finally succeeded in killing the Irvings' messy maple tree by watering its roots with turpentine and Javex in the middle of the night.)

You must keep the snow shovelled all winter long, including the public sidewalk out front. You must put salt on the steps so the mailman didn't slip on the ice and break his neck and sue you. If you had a dog, you must keep it tied up and perfectly quiet at all times. You must pay all your bills on time, including the paperboy when he came to collect.

You must obey all laws about everything, especially traffic laws about which Esther, although she'd never learned to drive herself, was very conscientious. The only laws which could be safely circumvented with a clear conscience were those involving customs declarations at the border crossing from the United States. Once a year they went down to Duluth to buy sheets and towels and shoes at J. C. Penney's and it was okay to hide these items on the way back so they didn't have to pay the duty. This contraband was justified, it seemed, by the unfortunate fact that, through no fault of their own, they lived in a country where the prices were higher, the exchange rate never worked in their favour, and the textile selection was miserably inadequate.

The qualities of a good citizen had a tendency to expand and accumulate until they bled into a correlative list of qualities necessary to be a good person. The borderlines between these two ideals were blurry and Joanna had trouble keeping track of the difference. Was a good citizen necessarily a good person and vice versa? Could a good person be a bad citizen? Could a good citizen be a bad person?

A great many of the requisites for good personhood hinged upon cleanliness. Your house must be kept spotless at all times. This required daily, if not hourly, maintenance. Esther swept the kitchen and all other uncarpeted floors twice a day. She dusted and vacuumed every afternoon. She laundered her rags as carefully as if they were handembroidered linen heirlooms. She was quite visibly proud of her comprehensive collection of household cleansers, disinfectants, and detergents, which she kept in a locked cupboard under the sink as if they were priceless antiques.

Joanna was often conscripted into the ever-escalating campaign against dirt. She was sent onto the back step to shake the bedroom rugs and all the grit from them flew back into her face. She was sent into the bathroom armed with a rag and a bottle of Windex and she'd better not leave any streaks. She was sat down at the kitchen table with a sharp knife to pick out all the crumbs and sticky stuff jammed in between the tabletop and the rim. Her bedroom was a favourite target for Esther's outrage. "This room," Esther would say, standing in the doorway with her arms crossed, one foot tapping, mouth grim, "this room looks like a dog's breakfast." Or she said, "This room looks like a cyclone hit it." Which left Joanna grinning at the image of cans of Dr. Ballard's and a dozen Milk-Bone biscuits being swept away in a windstorm. "Stop smiling and start cleaning," Esther said. Joanna set grimly to it, reminded once again that cleanliness, like most important things, was not supposed to be funny.

Every Monday Esther did the laundry. This involved a complicated process of sorting by colour, fabric, and several other mysterious characteristics of clothing which Joanna never quite figured out. Once satisfactorily sorted, the dirty clothes lay in limp expectant piles all over the floor. The washing process itself involved adding a variety of fragrant powders and liquids to the churning water in accurate measures at precise and somehow precarious moments.

Esther would already be hard at it Monday morning when Joanna left for school, usually still at it when she came home again for lunch. Esther would wave her into the kitchen to fix herself a sandwich, while reminding her that wringer washers were still the best but they were dangerous too, requiring her undivided attention, and she was living proof, having had her left arm accidentally put through the wringer right up to the elbow when she was young. Luckily there was no permanent damage. But there could have been. She could have been crippled for life. As it was, the only lingering effect was the way her arm ached in the cold or the damp.

This was before they had a dryer, and when Joanna came home from school at four o'clock, Esther would be out on the back step hanging up the last of it, humming with clothespins in her mouth. The whole backyard on a bright windy day was filled with a fragrant flapping chaos of colours like a flock of giant exotic birds.

When the wringer washer finally gave out, Esther allowed herself to be convinced (by Clarence and an eager appliance salesman on commission at Simpsons-Sears) that an automatic washing machine would save her a great deal of precious time and energy, leaving her more freedom to pursue her other interests. They might as well get the matching dryer too, which would eliminate the aggravation of all that hanging up and taking in, all that worrying about the weather, roving sea gulls and thieving crows, that nasty grit which floated over from the smelly paper mill. Best of all, the salesman said, a dryer would eliminate forever that unsightly low-class look of clothes on the line, your underwear and the stains on your sheets displayed to the entire nosy neighbourhood. Although Esther informed him that *her* sheets were *never* stained and *she* washed *her* underwear by hand, they bought the dryer too.

After that, when Joanna came home from school on Mondays, it was to find Esther in the living room ironing and watching "Another World." Ironing used to be a Tuesday job but the new washer and dryer saved her so much time that now she could do it on Monday. Although it obviously pleased Esther to be getting a jump on things, even Joanna could see that with the new labour-saving appliances some-how the challenge had gone out of the job, and with it the joy her mother had taken in her weekly victory over dirt.

Now on Tuesday she cleaned the bathroom instead, vigorously scrub-bing the tub and the sink, confidently ignoring the TV commercials which warned that abrasive cleansers would damage the porcelain. They got rid of the dirt, that was the main thing. She spent a lot of time working on the toilet, muttering about men and why couldn't they aim straight, never mind remember to put the seat down. Once a month she replaced the little container in the tank which made the water blue, a bright pretty blue which turned a murky green when Joanna peed into it.

Although she was ambivalent about God, Esther had utterly and exultantly embraced the notion that cleanliness was next to godliness. The imperatives of household maintenance were not unlike command-ments. Failure to obey them indicated sheer and shameful laziness and anyone who allowed her home to fall into filth was bound to suffer the consequences: guilt, shame, and divine punishment. These command-ments were primarily binding upon women because they took care of such things. It was the women who had the instinct and the talent, men having so patently and repeatedly proven themselves to be sloppy, unreliable, and virtually useless in the sanitary struggles of daily life. Men didn't even *see* the dirt, so how on earth could they be expected to know what to do about it?

It was a small step from household cleanliness to personal hygiene. There were many rules in this area too. Esther was always nagging Joanna to brush her teeth, comb her hair, wash her hands and face, clean the sleep out of her eyes. She said the same things to Clarence sometimes too. She supervised Joanna's baths for more years than she needed to, long after Joanna was out of danger of slipping beneath the surface and drowning herself. Years later she was still standing on the other side of the closed bathroom door, reminding Joanna to wash between her toes, behind her ears, to scrub her neck and her elbows, especially her elbows which always looked dirty and rough, provoking Esther to go at them periodically with a lotion called Pretty Feet which was supposed to repair such unsightly areas by chafing off the dead skin. It left Joanna's elbows red and raw as if they'd been burned.

"And don't forget," Esther always whispered, "to wash *possible*," which was what she called her crotch.

Joanna wore a clean outfit to school every day, which Esther chose and laid out on her bed while Joanna was eating her breakfast. Esther liked to think of Joanna as the best-dressed girl in her school, but the truth was the other girls teased her about her wardrobe and she longed to wear the same grubby dress three days in a row like everybody else. Of course there was the thing about clean underwear every day in case you got in an accident and you wouldn't want all those doctors and nurses to see your dirty panties, would you? A sight, Joanna couldn't help but think, which would be unlikely to faze them anyway if the rest of you was covered with blood, your bones were sticking out, and your guts or your brains were slopping all over the place.

It was hard to keep track of all these things, hard to remember what was important. By the time she reached adolescence, Joanna had decided, like most teenagers, that her mother was nuts.

Joanna sometimes surprises herself now by still obeying (or at least trying to, or at least feeling guilty for not) some of Esther's rules and regulations. It is disconcerting enough to hear her mother's voice coming occasionally out of her own mouth. *Wash your face brush your teeth*

change your shirt you look like an orphan clean up your room pick up these
stupid toys before somebody trips and breaks their neck this room looks like a
cyclone hit it if you don't pick up these stupid toys right this minute they're
going in the garbage were you born in a barn or what? It is even more
astonishing to find herself hollering wholeheartedly at Gordon for not
having mowed the lawn for two weeks: "Just look at those dandelions
and there's a thistle back there the size of a rosebush! We've become
the disgrace of the neighbourhood!" Then refusing to speak to him all
evening after he says calmly, "Why, dear, if it's that important to you,
why don't you do it yourself?"

It's not *supposed* to be important. It's supposed to be one of those
trivialities which only shallow bourgeois people fuss over because
they've got nothing more meaningful to occupy their minds. It's not
supposed to matter but it does, and sometimes she dreams about dandelions, thistles, dirty dishes in the sink, piles of laundry mildewing
all over the basement, centipedes breeding under the bed, windows so
dirty she can't see out, snow in the driveway so deep she can't get out,
dirt so thick she can't breathe and she dies. Once she dreams there are
nine loaves of mouldy bread in the cupboard.

She still finds it hard to remember what is important. Certainly the
importance of any number of big things is quite clear: famine relief,
nuclear disarmament, gun control, child abuse, family violence, world
peace, love, truth, freedom, and the environment. She has a list clipped
from the newspaper, ONE HUNDRED WAYS TO SAVE OUR EN-
VIRONMENT, taped to the inside of one kitchen cupboard door. The
list begins with *Reduce consumption whenever possible*, moves on through
Keep the lint screen in the dryer clean, Diligently repair all leaks and drips as
soon as they occur, and *Eat lower on the food chain*. It ends with *Reduce stress*
in your life and *Have fun and be joyful*. She really tries, she really does,
but sometimes the pressure of trying to be environmentally correct gets
to her. Sometimes she has relapses and throws away a perfectly good
glass jar, eats a greasy double cheeseburger out of a Styrofoam box, goes
berserk in the grocery store and buys individually wrapped processed
cheese sticks for Samuel, a T-bone steak for Gordon, and a jumbo roll
of pink paper towels for herself. Sometimes she falls headfirst into a

bucket of stress like quicksand and forgets all about having fun and being joyful, while also being good to the planet.

Then there is the shifting middle ground of those things which may or may not be important in the long run, which are crucial to one person and inconsequential to the next, which seem essential and life-sustaining one day and downright stupid the next. This category includes money, a new car, sex, laughter, friendship, save the whales (the elephants, the whooping cranes, the ostriches), gardening, music, ballet, art, literature, and all other forms of happiness.

Finally there are all those things which are no doubt meaningless but also no doubt important whether you think they should be or not. How is it, Joanna often wonders, that so many meaningless moments can also be so important?

How is it, for instance, that purchasing, carrying home, and then putting up in the kitchen three wicker plant baskets (multicoloured, mostly purple, pink, and turquoise, in graduated sizes with hoop handles, flat on one side, to hang on the wall) can fill her with such pride of ownership, such joy of home decorating, that she calls Gordon at work to tell him what she got? For weeks afterwards every time she sees the baskets she smiles, and she likes them so much she goes back to the store and buys another set for the bathroom and this time they're on sale, twenty per cent off, and this makes her even happier. How is it that the herbs she snips from the plants she has put in these baskets taste so much better than they did when they were just sitting on the windowsill in square green plastic pots? How is it that when the basil dies she feels like a failure?

How is it that when she's finished five loads of laundry, all of it dried and folded and piled on the bed, she is filled with such an ardent sense of accomplishment, filled with such immense satisfaction, that she presses Samuel's soft sweatshirts to her nose and inhales the fresh clean scent just like some dumb housewife in a TV commercial who is convinced she's discovered the meaning of life?

How is it that when she comes home from the market on Saturday afternoon with bags of fresh fruit, she immediately spends twenty minutes washing and polishing the Empire apples and the Bartlett pears, humming and smiling and admiring their plump round bodies, their tight fragrant skins, arranging them carefully in the big wicker basket like a bouquet of flowers? How is it that this makes her feel like such a good, happy, and generous person? How is it that when Samuel sees them, hugs her and says, "Oh, Mommy, I love you, you're such a good Mommy," for once she actually believes him? As they sit at the table crunching, Samuel eating an apple out of one hand and a pear out of the other, how is it that she feels so confident, so clear, in such complete quiet benevolent control of her own small (but significant) corner of the world?

How is it, let's face it, that the black clingy cotton shirt she picked up half-price at Benetton's can make her feel so sexy, so attractive, surely the most desirable woman in the world? She strides along the downtown streets in this new shirt and her flowered stretchies, her hair is swinging, her crotch is tender and damp, she is smiling at strange men, certain that behind her back they are sighing and swooning with aggravated unrequited lust, will probably have erotic dreams about her for weeks, and their poor droopy wives will wonder what's gone wrong.

Isn't she an artist, a mother, a modern woman? Isn't she supposed to be above such things?

Yes, how hard it is to remember what is important. Is something important necessarily meaningful as well? Can something that is meaningless be important anyway? What is the connection between meaning and importance? What if there isn't one? What is the meaning of meaning? What if there isn't one? What if everything is meaningful and we just don't know it yet? What if not everything is a moral issue after all? What if it is? What if her mother was wrong and not all of a person's actions come complete with a moral quotient? What if her mother was right? What if there is no point in trying to remember what is important? What if it doesn't matter? What if everything is important?

If everything is important, how can we ever hold it all clear in our minds? What if it turns out that all the things in life that she thought were important aren't? Or what if all the things in her life that she was good at, all the things she took pride and pleasure in, all the things she practised and practised and finally perfected, turn out to be meaningless and unimportant? What if it turns out that all the times she said, "It doesn't matter," she was wrong? What if it turns out that all the times she said, "It doesn't matter," she was right?

The questions keep multiplying and reproducing themselves, as if by fission, like monstrous amoebas run amok. This is like Samuel always coming to her with questions to which he already knows the answers. Strings of questions: Is it raining? Is it windy? Are you drinking coffee? Are you getting dressed? What's your first name? What's my last name? Are you my real mother? Do you love me? Will you always be my mother? Will you always love me?

Sometimes she tries to explain that this is not how questions work, how you're supposed to ask questions about things you don't know yet, not things you can see very well with your own two eyes, how there are many important questions worth asking but these are not some of them. Instead of answering, she asks him, "What do you think?" and he says, "I don't know, I can't remember, sometimes I just don't know what I know."

One morning after another barrage of questions about the perfectly obvious, Joanna says, "Oh, honey, no more, this just makes me tired," and he says, "Me too, Mommy, sometimes I just get so tired of the inside of my head." Which Joanna and Gordon think is charming and precocious, but when she tells it to Clarence on the phone he is alarmed and says, "I hope this doesn't mean he's going to be mentally disturbed."

Sometimes Joanna gets so impatient with Samuel's questions that she snaps at him in sheer frustration: "I don't know, I don't care, it doesn't matter, stop it!" Sometimes she tries to tease him by giving the wrong answers but he gets so impatient he cries. Then she tries to explain that there are many things in life worth crying about but this isn't one of them. Then he wants to know what is.

33. Foot

HENRY HAD, WITHOUT a doubt, the smelliest feet in the world. He liked to say so himself. He was proud of them. He figured he would have made it into *The Guinness Book of World Records* if only they'd had the good sense to add the category. A brand-new pair of cowboy boots on Henry's feet for a day and a half smelled like a pair of runners that had been worn twenty-four hours a day without socks for the last ten years. Henry's shoes had to be removed before entering the apartment and left outside the door.

Depending on the brand, his socks either rotted away in great ragged spreading holes or went stiff like little woollen corpses. Joanna was in charge of hauling all their dirty clothes down to the laundromat once a week which was a chore she didn't mind but she absolutely adamantly unconditionally refused to wash Henry's socks. Henry solved this problem by throwing his socks away at the end of the week, buying new ones in big bags by the dozen for only ten dollars.

The first time he stayed over, he left his shoes outside the door with the socks tucked inside them, went immediately to the bathroom and washed his feet for ten minutes while Joanna put on some romantic music, poured two glasses of wine, and dabbed perfume on her pulse points. When he came barefoot into the living room smelling of strawberry soap and took her in his arms to waltz slowly to the bedroom, she thought this foot-washing routine was a charming exotic (or eccentric) ritual which he might have learned in some foreign country, Japan or Finland or some equally peregrine land.

Some months later, they were downtown partying with some friends at the Neapolitan and Henry (in his favourite T-shirt, black with white block lettering which said INSTANT ASSHOLE: JUST ADD AL-COHOL) said he wanted to dance. He stood up, took off his work boots, and tucked them neatly under the table which then cleared instantly, everyone up and scattering, holding their noses and waving their hands. This was a story Henry loved to tell later, whenever anybody asked him why he didn't dance much any more. Every time he told it, the story got better and better until finally it wasn't just their table that had emptied, but the whole damn bar, in a virtual stampede (it was a wonder nobody got trampled to death!) to the door and then everybody ran outside, dozens of them, turning green and gasping for air, huddling together in the pouring rain. Joanna, who thought she would die of embarrassment every time he told this story, said only, "It wasn't raining."

Henry had a way with stories. He could turn the most trivial incident into a hilarious anecdote which he improved and embroidered with each retelling. He was fond of funny sayings which he managed to work into every story. "She was two axe-handles and a plug of tobacco wide," he would say of an overweight woman. "Strong like bull, smart like suitcase," he said of those he considered less than brilliant. A person who had died was either "done like dinner" or "tits up in the rhubarb." Of those who found themselves embroiled in self-inflicted trouble, he said, "If the shit fits, wear it." Whenever he and Joanna were off to the Neapolitan for the evening, he would say, at least twice, "Let's get drunk and get a personality on!" At first Joanna found this habit charming but after a while it became almost as irritating as the smell of his feet.

Years later, whenever Joanna caught a whiff of someone else's foul foot odour (in the summer in the park, in the shoe store at the mall, at a party, people dancing through the kitchen in their socks), she would think of Henry and cringe.

Years later still. Joanna has just come in from digging the garden with Samuel and he is proudly showing her the seedlings they started in the house, his own garden in flats, sunflowers and sweet peas already three inches tall and his carrots sprouting in clumps like green hair. She is just resting at the kitchen table for a minute, reading the paper, sipping some pink lemonade, and she catches a whiff of her own bare feet, sweaty and sticking to the cool linoleum. She thinks about Henry. She hasn't talked to him for years. He lives in Toronto now, has a wife, a job, a baby and everything—all the things he swore he never wanted, all the things she could not imagine him having. She thinks about Henry, his smelly feet, his stupid T-shirt, and for a minute she misses him. For a minute she wonders what her life would have been like if she'd married him. She has no regrets. She's just curious, mostly about all the people she might have been and will never be now.

34. Spider

"KILL IT, KILL IT!" Esther shrieked. There was a daddy longlegs in the bathtub. Spiders, as far as Joanna could figure, were the only things in the world that her mother was afraid of.

"But if I kill it," Clarence teased, holding a Kleenex ready six inches above the spider, "it will rain."

"I don't care if it rains," Esther hissed through clenched teeth. "Just kill the damn thing!"

"It's just a little spider," Henry said. "It won't hurt you."

"Kill it, kill it!" Joanna cried.

"I don't want to kill it," Lewis said. "Live and let live." He guided the fat hairy spider onto a piece of paper and carefully carried it outside and released it into the long grass. "What do you do when I'm not here?" he asked Joanna.

"I kill them with my shoe," she said grimly.

"I hate spiders with all my heart," Samuel says.

"Why?" Joanna asks.

"Because they're ugly," he says.

She was just tucking him into bed when he spotted a small spider nestled in the farthest corner of the ceiling. "Kill it, kill it!" he cried.

Joanna is perched precariously on a stool with a Kleenex in her hand. She could have called Gordon to come and do it but she doesn't want to pass her fear of spiders on to her son. It may, however, already be too late.

The spider is pale grey, almost white, almost transparent. She shudders when she squeezes it into the Kleenex. It crunches a bit.

"Let's see! Let's see the guts!" Samuel cries.

She sits down on the side of his bed and unfolds the Kleenex to reveal a grey smear, two or three legs still intact. Samuel is disappointed. "There's no blood," he says and curls back into his blankets with his snuggly bear.

At 3:00 A.M. he wakes up crying, having dreams, naturally enough, about spiders, all kinds of them he says, dangling from the ceiling, crawling up his legs, banging on the window with their little spider fists. They were coming out of his ears, chewing on his eyebrows, spinning webs out of his hair. There was one, he says, as big as a cat, a big grey cat, wearing a hat and carrying a pencil that turned into a gun. She lies down beside him in his skinny bed. By way of consolation she would like to say she was dreaming about spiders too. But in fact she was not. In fact she was dreaming that she had moved back to her old basement apartment. In the dream she had Samuel with her but Gordon was no longer around. In the dream this did not seem to present a problem.

She tells Samuel that spiders won't hurt him, spiders are nothing to be scared of. She tells him to think about nice things instead: sailboats, sunshine, cookies, flowers, popcorn, puppies, cheese. She falls asleep beside him and for the remaining hours of the night neither one of them dreams about spiders. Waking in the morning snuggled warm against her back, Samuel says he dreamed that she was sleeping beside him all night long and, sure enough, here she is. He says, "You make all my dreams come true," and Joanna would like to believe, even briefly, that he is right.

35. Needle

ESTHER SAID HER mother had died from blood poisoning contracted when she stuck her hand into a mending basket full of her father's socks. A dirty darning needle went right into the palm of her hand. In those days there were no antibiotics and the infection was fatal. Although Esther did not talk much about her childhood, Joanna knew that she had loved her mother and hated her father. This anecdote was offered as proof of what a bastard he had been—for certainly, if it had not been for his holey socks, her mother would have lived. Perhaps forever.

Her father had died a year later of cirrhosis of the liver. Esther, the youngest child, was thus orphaned at the age of fourteen. But she had three older sisters who finished raising her. Most of this task had fallen to Frances, the oldest, who was twenty-four at the time. Frances now lived in Vancouver and she and Esther kept in touch by letters and phone calls, although they did not visit owing to the distance and the expense involved to bridge it.

The two other sisters, Florence and Joan, lived in other cities too, Florence in Toronto (that evil city) and Joan with her American husband in Phoenix, Arizona. Florence and Joan were just Christmas cards now, theirs the first to arrive each year early in December, often without even a note inside, just their names signed at the bottom, along with the names of their husbands and children, cousins Joanna had never met. One of the aunts (Joanna cannot remember now which one) favoured Christmas cards illustrated by people who had no arms and so they painted with their mouths or their feet. Every year Esther made veiled comments about these cards, implying that although they were admirable they were also odd and somehow inappropriate.

There were other veiled comments about Florence and Joan. Florence was always referred to as "Poor Florence" for reasons which remained unspecified. Perhaps she was to be pitied because she lived in Toronto. Joan was always called "snooty" because her American husband owned a large hotel in Phoenix and they were quite wealthy.

This lack of familial connection was not caused by an actual feud or rift or anything like that. It seemed due merely to lack of interest and effort on everyone's part. "We've never been a close family," Esther often said proudly, the way another person would say just the opposite.

Clarence's family was not close either. His father had died of stomach cancer before Joanna was born and his mother had been hit by a car and killed when Joanna was eighteen months old. She had been waiting for a bus in the winter when a car coming round the corner had spun out of control on the icy road and crushed her against a metal hydro pole.

Clarence had one brother, Evan, who was two years older and who lived with his wife and three children in Halifax. Clarence had fond memories of Evan from when they were growing up and from when they were both soldiers in the Second World War. But there was nothing, it seemed, between childhood and the war, and little after that. They too were not good at keeping in touch much beyond Christmas cards and the occasional long-distance phone call which made Clarence nervous so that he hunched over the phone and yelled into the receiver to be sure of making himself heard across all those miles. Evan died when Joanna was seven. He had suffered a heart attack while shovelling his driveway. Clarence flew alone to Halifax for the funeral. It was the first time he had been on an airplane since flying back to Canada with Evan at the end of the war. Evan's wife, Angela, remarried a few years later, and after this Clarence completely lost touch with her and the children—more relatives Joanna did not know.

As an only child, she was often lonely, especially at Christmas, when she longed for a large noisy energetic family gathered round the table, passing turkey and mashed potatoes, laughing, arguing about who was the best carver, who made the best pies, whose turn it was to say grace. She imagined a dozen people at least, of all shapes and sizes, something like the Waltons on TV. She fantasized that she would some day be reunited with all her long-lost relatives whom she would recognize instantly from her parents' old photographs. The fantasy did not extend much beyond this meal because Joanna could not imagine what else that many people would do all together in a house at once.

Growing up, Joanna always had a sense of herself as a solitary child, a potential orphan. She worried about what would happen to her if her parents died. Much as she liked to fantasize about these unknown relatives, they were total strangers and she did not really want to live with them. She imagined all kinds of fatal calamities which might befall either Esther or Clarence or both of them. She especially worried whenever Clarence went out to shovel snow for fear of finding him facedown in a snowbank an hour later, stone-cold dead with the shovel frozen to his hands. She was immediately alarmed every time Esther hauled out the mending basket and stationed herself in front of the TV with a darning needle three inches long and a burned-out light bulb which she inserted into the foot of Clarence's work socks so she could mend the holes neatly with thick grey wool. Sometimes Joanna secretly checked the contents of the mending basket just to be sure there were no dirty needles imbedded in her father's socks.

Eventually Esther abandoned mending socks altogether because, for all the time it took and the price of socks these days, it was not worth it. Later when Joanna was working part-time at Simpsons-Sears, Clarence bought a snowblower. In fact Joanna bought it in her name so she could get her staff discount. By this time, however, she knew there were more dangerous things to worry about than needles and snow.

36. Red

THE COLOUR OF THE BLOOD which fills your mouth when you get your tongue stuck to the car door handle in the winter and your father yanks you off, then rushes you inside the house to your mother who laughs and makes you drink warm milk which does nothing but turn your blood pink and this is the first you have known of a wound which a kiss or a Band-Aid cannot fix.

The colour behind your eyelids when you close them in a well-lit room, a small sunny kitchen perhaps, where you are listening to your lover tell you that his wife will die if he leaves her, you understanding for once and for all that there will be no easy way out, and the red behind your eyelids is a colour only you will ever see.

The colour of your son's cheeks after a long walk in the winter, you pulling him gently over snowbanks on the wooden sled behind you, the sled which was yours when you were little and now your father has fixed it up, repainted all the red parts, for this new child who doesn't care of course where the sled came from, cares only that it slides silently and sometimes throws snow up into his face and by the time you get home he is all rosy and laughing, and when you see your own face in the mirror you are surprised to discover that you too are all rosy and laughing, every bit as happy and handsome as he is, and maybe this is what you have been hoping for all along.

37. Sleep

WHENEVER JOANNA HAS insomnia, she can just picture a mouth in her brain. Not a whole mouth exactly, more like a full set of false teeth: pearly whites set into perfectly pink gums, disembodied but very energetic, clacking and chattering away with a miserable tormenting mind of their own. They are like the plastic toy she saw once in a novelty shop: a set of teeth atop a pair of tiny yellow sneakers with black laces like sutures, and when you wound the key at the back the sneakers tapped blindly across the tabletop while the teeth clacked cheerfully. Obviously this contraption was meant to be amusing but it gave Joanna the creeps, reminding her of a black-and-white horror movie she'd seen years ago called *The Brain That Wouldn't Die*.

Two or three nights a week usually, and Sunday night always, these intrepid teeth start up their chattering inside her brain. In addition to the clacking teeth, there is also sometimes, but not always, a buzzing as of flies, the big ones, bluebottles. The teeth and/or the flies usually begin somewhere between 3:00 and 4:00 A.M. They persist until half an hour before it is time to get up at which point Joanna finally falls into a deep sleep and then the alarm clock rings, just when she is sure she could have slept forever.

Having long ago discovered that there is a helpful book for every conceivable occasion, Joanna has taken to reading up on the subject, borrowing library books with promising titles like *The Five Types of Sleeplessness and How to Overcome Them* and *Natural Sleep (How to Get Your Share)*. She has become casually conversant with all the scientific research on alpha waves, delta waves, and REM sleep. She knows the specific names of the five forms insomnia may take. She has had all of them, sometimes all in the same night. She is interested to learn that Sunday night insomnia is a common syndrome among people who like to sleep late Sunday mornings and then, presumably, spend the day lolling around on the couch watching Sunday afternoon football or pay TV, pigging out on pretzels and guzzling beer. This must mean that religious people who get up early Sunday, trundle off to the morning service, and then spend the rest of the day vigorously atoning for their sins will be spared not only eternal damnation but also the devilish torment of sleeplessness.

Long ago she gave up on the time-honoured solutions of drinking warm milk and counting sheep. Warm milk only makes her tongue feel furry. And sheep—well, who cares about sheep anyway? Who bestowed those magical sleep-inducing powers upon them in the first place? Some dumb shepherd, no doubt, who was bored and kept falling asleep on the job and had to blame it on someone.

For a while she put aside her skepticism and tried some of the remedies and suggestions outlined in the books. They recommended mental alphabetical games as an instrument for focusing your thoughts and so inducing sleep.

Make an alphabetical list of fruit. A: Apple. B: Banana. C: Cantaloupe. D: Dates. E: Eggplant. Is the eggplant a fruit or a vegetable? What was the name of that Greek restaurant where they had the great moussaka? And what was that wonderful dessert called? Baklava, that's it. Should eggplant more properly be referred to by its French name, aubergine? In which case, it should have come under A. *Buzz. Clack.* Her mind is wandering again.

Instead she ends up making an unalphabetized list of all the things she thinks, worries, and fusses about when she should be sleeping.

If it gets too hot, will the propane tank for the new gas barbecue explode . . . the kitchen floor hasn't been washed for two months . . . Samuel still cannot recognize the letter W . . . the furnace sounds funny . . . the roof needs patching . . . she doesn't write to Clarence often enough . . . her new collage is probably a meaningless waste of time and glue . . . the fuel bill is past due, also the phone bill and the property taxes . . . she was impatient and crabby with Samuel all day

. . . she still hasn't made a will . . . what will she do with all of Clarence's stuff when he dies . . . a year ago she started stripping the back door for repainting and it's still not done . . . she wants to paint it green . . . what if Samuel can't find a job when he grows up . . . she hasn't filed her income tax yet . . . Gordon is breathing funny . . . what if Samuel becomes a drug addict and ends up in a crack house in Toronto (that evil city) . . . the car needs a new muffler, has in fact needed a new muffler for nearly six months . . . what is Lewis's middle name . . . the windows are filthy . . . the driveway needs resurfacing . . . there's no milk for breakfast . . . that mole on her left thigh looks bigger and darker . . . trying to remember Lewis's middle name, she has forgotten the colour of Henry's eyes . . . Samuel watches too much TV . . . some day every single person who is alive at this very moment will be dead . . . she drinks too much coffee, must switch to herbal tea instead . . . trying to remember the colour of Henry's eyes, she has forgotten the name of that man she dated later who refused to eat in restaurants for fear his notoriously noisy stomach would gurgle and embarrass him to death . . . she has a pain in her right kidney . . . Samuel wants to know where they will go when they die . . . Clarence is alone alone all alone . . . Samuel wants to know where he was before he was born . . . she forgot to clean the toilet . . . so many questions lately to which she must answer "I don't know" or else fall back on that ever-useful parental "Because" . . . she hasn't sold a collage in six months . . . something to fall back on, she should have learned short-hand . . . what's that sound, a squirrel, the wind, a marauding psy-chokiller . . . do secretaries still take shorthand or is it all done magically now with machines like a trick done with mirrors . . . why is Samuel afraid of swings . . . the man with the gurgling stomach was named Kevin . . . another four-year-old has disappeared in Toronto (that evil city) and what if it happens here . . . Samuel eats too much candy . . . did she ever tell Gordon about Kevin or had she kept it a secret . . . what did it matter anyway . . . secrets are like lies . . . you have to remember who you told what . . . you have to keep your stories straight . . . would Gordon mind about her sleeping with Kevin ten years ago . . . or would he mind more that she'd never mentioned it

. . . did the fact that she might never have mentioned it mean that sleeping with Kevin had been too important or too irrelevant or just too embarrassing . . . she's always believed that honesty is the best policy . . . what if it isn't . . . why is she such a lousy liar . . . what will she say when Samuel discovers the truth about Santa Claus and the Easter Bunny . . . what will she do when Samuel realizes she doesn't know everything . . . what are his chances of living to be old, let alone happily ever after . . . what's that smell, smoke, is it smoke? . . . if it gets too hot, will the propane tank for the new gas barbecue explode and kill us all or will it explode in the other direction and kill the new baby of the couple across the back lane?

The books recommended getting out of bed and doing something boring if you have been awake for more than thirty minutes. Joanna sits at the kitchen table, flipping through the newspaper, gets started on the crossword puzzle, and is wide awake again. She goes into the living room and clicks through all the channels. There is the perky blonde woman on the weather channel who is fairly hysterical with enthusiastic promises of sunshine in Miami for the rest of the week. There are black-and-white reruns of "Hazel" and "Leave It to Beaver." There are frenetic smoky rock videos which she watches with the sound turned off because the music is bound to stir her up too much and set her to wondering when was the last time she went to a party . . . a *real* party with loud music, flagrant substance abuse, and dancing so wild the floorboards were jumping . . . not the kind of party people have nowadays with elaborate hors d'oeuvres, a choice of mineral waters, and *The Phantom of the Opera* or the soothing sounds of whales on the CD player . . . when was the last time she even went to one of those so-called parties . . . how come nobody has parties any more . . . when did she stop wanting to go to parties . . . when was the last time she had a party herself . . . what was the name of that guy who came to her and Henry's Christmas party, and when the police came to the door because the neighbours had called about the music again, this guy invited them in for a beer and then threw up in the dieffenbachia?

Now she does nothing but suffer through the sleepless hours, wondering why they are referred to as "the wee small hours" when clearly they are the largest hours in the world.

Gordon sleeps well but tries to be sympathetic. He asks, "What are you worrying about?"

She says, "Everything."

He asks, "What can I do?"

She says, "Nothing."

He asks, "What are you afraid of?"

This is the real question. Joanna knows the answer will come to her eventually. This is akin to those annoying questions that come up in casual conversation: who wrote that book about the dancing bear, who sang that song about onions, who starred in that movie about Vietnam? Then everybody racks their brains but no one can come up with the answer though it's on the tips of all their tongues. Joanna thinks of this as "The Rita Coolidge Syndrome" because of the time she and Henry tried for three weeks to remember the name of the woman who'd made that album with Kris Kristofferson in 1973, the one called *Full Moon*. Sure enough, the answer came to her at three in the morning and she sat bolt upright in bed, crowing, "Rita Coolidge! Rita Coolidge!"

Now the question is, what are you afraid of? She knows it will come to her some day and she knows it won't be Rita Coolidge.

Much as she longs to be one of them, Joanna holds an abiding mistrust of all people who sleep soundly. With all the reasons in the world to worry, how could they? They must be kidding themselves, missing the point, or just plain shallow. Henry, despite his many other charming attributes, was one of them, a sound sleeper who said with irritating self-righteousness every morning at breakfast, "Wow, I slept like a log!" Until Joanna, flopping and fussing around beside him night after night, came to picture him that way: a solid immovable object flat on his back in the bed, his legs stretched straight out, arms folded corpse-like across his chest, his long hair spread all over the pillow (*both* pillows) like branches, his eyes and nostrils like knot-holes, his wide-open snoring mouth like one of those tree cavities in which woodpeckers nest and small children hide things.

On calmer, less resentful nights when she wasn't actively hating him for his peaceful slumber, she was reminded of the Sleeping Giant, a rocky peninsula in Lake Superior at the mouth of Thunder Bay. Viewed from the shore or the air, the rock formation takes on the shape of a giant sleeping on his back, arms folded across his chest. According to Ojibwa legend, this is the warrior Nanna Bijou at rest, turned to stone by the wrath of Gitche Manitou, the great spirit who created the world. As a child she had treasured a postcard picture of the cape with the sleeping body of an Ojibwa warrior superimposed upon the rock in headdress, moccasins, war paint and all.

Samuel, naturally enough, in the first year of his life, sleeps like a baby: that is to say, lightly, unreliably, and never long enough. Sometimes the three of them are up half the night. This is generally infuriating but occasionally it takes on a festive atmosphere, the three of them puttering around in the bright kitchen in the middle of the dark night, Gordon making popcorn and hot chocolate, Joanna singing into Samuel's sleepy ears. One night when Samuel has gas, they all go out to the car and drive around the block a dozen times in their pyjamas singing "Rockabye Baby."

Before long Samuel is sleeping through the night. Gordon is too. But Joanna is often still stuck in the quagmire of sleeplessness.

Samuel at four wants to know where he goes when he's asleep. Joanna remembers asking Esther the same question and Esther replied by reciting the traditional children's bedtime prayer: *Now I lay me down to sleep/I pray the Lord my soul to keep./If I should die before I wake/I pray the Lord my soul to take.* Joanna had never considered the possibility of dying in her sleep. The prospect terrified her every night for weeks afterwards. Perhaps this had been the start of her insomnia in the first place.

Now, in answer to Samuel's question, she says, "I don't know."

He says, "But where do my eyes go? Where does my voice go? They have to go somewhere, don't they?" She does not tell him about the children's prayer.

She too has come to see sleep as a place, a pure and simple place, probably white, which she will get to some day. She is still optimistic that such a place can be found. She does not know if she must go forward or backward to reach it.

Must she go back to those nights when she lay tucked up safe in her little bed, the kitchen light coming in a crack softly, Esther and Clarence in the front room talking quietly, the open window admitting the comforting sound of Mr. Nystrom mowing his lawn, and June bugs bounced off the screen? She had a ritual in those days which, like all rituals, made her feel safe enough to sleep. Check under the bed, close the closet door tight, then jump into bed and pull the tightly tucked-in sheets out at the bottom so they wrapped all around her feet. This was necessary ever since Penny and Pamela had told her the story of a little boy in Toronto (that evil city) who slept with his feet hanging out and a rat chewed his toes off. Unfortunately Joanna is less able now to believe in the magic of rituals, although she does still shut the closet door tight just in case.

Must she go even further back to that night she doesn't remember, but there it is in the photo album: herself a toddler, sprawled sound asleep in her crib with her Davy Crockett coonskin cap on her head resting on the big panda bear Clarence won at the Ex, her arms around her yellow stuffed dog Wyatt Earp, and the bunny rabbit decal is smiling on the wooden headboard?

Or does she have to go forward to some future time when everything will be clear, all memories will be meaningful, and yes, she will be living a long and happy life?

38. Anger

EVERY MORNING JOANNA awakens to the seven o'clock news on the radio. Although this daily deluge of international information is often a depressing way to start the day, still she prefers it to the rock-and-roll station where the music is frenetic and the deejays are all pumped up with perkiness. Just the sound of their relentlessly jovial voices makes her want to stay in bed.

This morning she awakens just in time to catch the tail end of the lead story: another uprising in another country which is of course distressing to hear about but distant enough to be an intellectual exercise in political empathy—how terrible, how horrible, those poor people, it couldn't happen here. Joanna cannot always hold on to this reassuring delusion of immunity. She hears these days (every day, it seems) about murder, rape, torture, child abduction and molestation in this, her very own country. Sometimes these atrocities occur in this, her very own city which she has always wanted to think of as safe, sane, solid, and good.

Even here a five-year-old child has been abducted from his very own neighbourhood. They cannot find him, they are still looking, afraid of what they may discover in the forest, in the river, in the basement of his apartment building, in the dumpster behind Mac's Milk. Even here a woman has been raped and then bludgeoned to death with a hammer in her very own home at three in the afternoon. Even here women and children have been advised to take extra safety measures for their own protection. Even here they have all been infected with fear.

Joanna hears people still trying desperately to convince themselves that they are safe. She overhears them in the bank, in the grocery store, in the underground parking lot while looking over their shoulders. They say, "It was a bad neighbourhood . . . I heard she was a drug addict . . . I heard the child was unsupervised." For although they must now admit that yes, it *can* happen here, still they cling furiously to the belief that it cannot happen to *them*. Still they erect their totems of safety. Still they will not admit that they are afraid.

This morning the carefully modulated noncommittal voice of the news announcer says, "Police are now patrolling city streets to prevent outbursts of anger."

Still half-asleep, Joanna thinks, *Yes, this is how it should be.* She imagines policemen in pairs walking the streets on the keen lookout for anger. They are on special assignment to stop the slaughter. They have dogs specially trained to sniff out and track down the smell of anger, a smell, she imagines, like hot metal or burning rubber.

All over the city there are pockets of anger like boils about to burst.

There are anxious frustrated motorists stuck in traffic, leaning on their horns and giving each other the finger. There is a man beating his dog, his daughter, his wife. There is a man beating his head against the wall, a perfectly perpendicular suburban wall covered with aluminum siding, red brick, white stucco. All over the city there are furious mothers slapping down the dinner plates, slapping their children's chubby hands for picking their noses or playing with themselves, for grabbing a chocolate bar in the grocery store, for swearing, spitting, or hitting. Slapping them for crying, saying, "I'll give you something to cry about!"

There is a heartbroken wife who has just discovered her husband's infidelity. She has lost her head and is standing even now over his sated sleeping body, ready to plunge a knife straight into his unfaithful handsome heart. At this moment the policemen fling open the door with their guns drawn. But they are smiling, they say politely, "Excuse me, ma'am, but you're under arrest. You're under arrest for anger."

The wife gives herself over gratefully into their sensible qualified hands. The husband sleeps on. The wife is weeping. The policemen are patting her shoulders, her hair. The tracking dog is licking her trembling hands. She says, "I was just so angry, I was just so afraid." The policemen say, "Don't worry, it will be all right, pull yourself together, we're here to help you, no one would blame you, we're here, we're here, we're here in the nick of time."

Joanna gets up and puts the coffee on. Gordon is already in the shower. She can hear him singing. Samuel is awake and talking to his teddy bear. For the moment not one of them is angry or afraid.

Given the choice Joanna knows she would rather be angry than afraid. She also knows that she has never been one without the other. Like most women, she is afraid of being angry and she is angry at having to be afraid. More and more often now, she finds herself furious with fear. Now she understands why no one ever asked Esther what she was so mad about.

39. Carpet

JOANNA BOUGHT A fake Persian carpet for the living room of her basement apartment. When she and Gordon move into their house on Laverty Street eight years later there is no real place for the carpet which is worn now and badly stained, so they put it in the basement which is unfinished yet but they hope to build a rec room some day and the carpet will come in handy then.

It is six months or more before Joanna goes into that part of the basement again. The necessities (laundry, storage, furnace, hot-water tank) are all at the other end. The carpet, by this time, is covered with mildew, black and grey in some places, yellow, like pollen, in others. Luckily it is time for the twice-a-year city-wide pick-up of junk so they roll up the rotten carpet, tie it with twine, and place it at the end of the driveway with their other junk: two rusted toasters, two broken vacuum cleaners, and a twisted iron bed-frame which they found in the basement when they moved in.

The next morning at breakfast they see that the carpet is gone. The rest of the junk is still there. The city truck won't be around till later in the day, maybe not until the next day or the next. Lots of people are cruising the streets in pick-up trucks and vans, scavenging other people's junk, shaking their heads, no doubt, and clucking their practical tongues at the perfectly good stuff some dissipated people throw away. Whoever carted off their carpet is in for a big surprise.

The next morning they look out the window at breakfast and there is their carpet, carefully tied and leaning up against the junk (stove with no door and no elements, TV set with no glass and no guts) of the house across the street.

Joanna sits at the kitchen table all morning planning a new collage and just before lunch she sees the city workers in overalls and black gloves heaving the carpet and everything else into the back of an overflowing truck.

40. Girl

girl *n.* 1. a female child. 2. a young, or relatively young, unmarried woman. 3. a female servant or employee. 4. a woman of any age, married or single. 5. a sweetheart; also, one's wife. *See also* GIRL FRIDAY,

GIRLFRIEND, GIRL GUIDE, GIRLHOOD, GIRLIE, GIRLISH, GIRL SCOUT.

41. High

SCHOOL. WOODBINE HIGH SCHOOL. Also known as Woodbine Collegiate and Vocational Institute, WCVI.

Although she did not think she had minded it that much at the time, Joanna still has dreams about high school twenty years later. They are nightmares really, personal, athletic, and academic in nature, nerve-racking dreams of disgrace and forgetting. She dreams at various times that she has arrived for classes at WCVI only to discover that she has forgotten her homework, her room number, her blue gym suit with her name embroidered on the back, her shoes, her bra, her panties, her teacher's name, her own name. Or parts of her body have gone missing: her right hand, her eyebrows, her nose, her breasts, her left leg from the knee down. Occasionally she arrives stark naked and nobody notices. Or she arrives stark naked and everybody laughs so she rips all the pages out of her math notebook and tries to stick them to her body.

Sometimes the school itself has gone missing and she arrives to find an empty lot, a lake, or a shopping mall in its place. Or else the school is there but all the doors have been locked, moved, or covered over with red bricks. Sometimes she gets inside the building all right but then her classroom is gone or the stairs are missing or moving like a down escalator gone berserk, so that no matter how long she climbs them she can never reach the top. Then she gets sent to the principal's office and is suspended for a week for being late.

Gordon assures Joanna that such dreams are very common. "Everybody has high school dreams," he says. "We were all traumatized by high school whether we knew it or not. People who don't dream about high school missed the point." By way of consolation, Gordon says he has high school dreams too, same dreams, different school. Sometimes he too dreams that the school building has disappeared and in its place there is a used-car lot. Sometimes he dreams that he is undressing in the locker room after a basketball game with all the other exuberant sweaty boys, and when he removes his gym shorts he finds that his penis has fallen off. Or else his penis is still there but the other boys start snapping at him with their wet towels and then it falls off and somebody steps on it or throws it down the toilet.

Joanna does not find it particularly consoling to think that her nightmares are run of the mill. That night she has an even worse nightmare in which she is trapped inside someone else's high school dream.

In the beginning of this dream, she is flying effortlessly above the rooftops of an unidentified city. It is night and the windows of the houses are warm yellow squares singing into the unquiet dark, into the unbridled night where anything might happen. But she is not afraid. She is flying, she is above all danger. She is airborne and immune. Then she is inside the bedroom of one house and in the bed is a boy named Robert Malone with whom she went to high school. He was the boy that every girl dreamed of. He was not very smart but he was a skier. Every day in the winter he came to school in a different ski sweater with matching turtleneck. He was always tanned. He looked like Jean-Claude Killy. His parents were well-off and every year Robert got a whole new set of ski equipment, always the best make, top of the line. He dated cheerleaders and volleyball players.

In the dream Joanna slips into Robert Malone's bed. He is, she sees, not a boy any more. He is a slightly balding middle-aged man in cotton striped pyjamas. He had a nice wife and three kids but she divorced him and he only sees the kids on weekends. He is an insurance salesman. His ex-wife Barbie was a cheerleader but now she is a cashier at the A&P on the corner of Brock and Niagara. They are, Joanna realizes in the dream, the kind of people whose lives peaked in high school and it's been downhill ever since.

Robert Malone is dreaming too. He is dreaming about high school. He is dreaming that he is skiing down the front staircase of WCVI which is covered in three feet of fresh powder snow. He is having a wonderful time and there are girls everywhere, girls who at first appear to be angels with red-and-white wings but who, on second thought, are cheerleaders with red-and-white pompoms. Joanna is somehow

WORKING   167

trapped inside Robert Malone's body and she is terrified. She does not
know how to ski. The snow is flying everywhere and her mouth is full
of it. She knows this is not even her own dream but still she cannot
wake up. As you might expect, Robert Malone suddenly takes off and
then they are flying so high they cannot see the ground. They are flying
to the moon. Robert Malone has turned back into a handsome teenager
and Joanna is aging rapidly.

42. Working

IN THE LAST year of high school Joanna worked in Ladies Wear at
Simpsons-Sears, two nights a week and all day Saturday. She also
worked there during the summer. She had been wanting to work for
three years, pestering Esther to let her apply for a job at the old folks'
home where Penny and Pamela worked part-time serving supper and
doing dishes. Esther said she was too young to work. "What's your
rush?" Esther said. "You'll be working for the rest of your life."

working *adj.* 1. that works. 2. used in or taken up by work. 3. on
which further work may be based. 4. of an animal used for work, not
kept as a pet. 5. twitching or jerking convulsively with emotion: said
of the face.

Once Joanna had the job in Ladies Wear, Esther thought it was wonderful. She bragged about it to her friends. Not only did Joanna get a
staff discount on everything in the store now, but she was doing so
well that she was probably going to be promoted to head of the department by the end of the summer. This of course was not true. Joanna
was not a particularly good salesperson. She could not bring herself to
tell overweight middle-aged women trying on dresses ten years too
young and three sizes too small that they looked marvellous. Instead
she smiled sweetly, nodded gently, and thought about other things
while these women bought whatever they wanted anyway. She could
take neither credit nor blame for their sartorial decisions. She occasion-

ally worried that she would lose control and tell one of these women that she was fat, ugly, and stupid. She did not enjoy working at Simpsons-Sears but her mother enjoyed it immensely. Because, Joanna suspected, this job was the most hopeful indication yet that she was going to turn out normal.

What she often thought about while watching her customers try on clothes was a childhood fantasy she'd had about this store. Unlike many children she had never seriously considered running away from home. In retrospect she wondered at her own lack of initiative. Perhaps even then she had felt ashamed of herself for being unhappy. Even then she knew she had much to be grateful for. And if ever she was in danger of forgetting this when she was younger, Esther was quick to remind her. There were many many children worse off than she was. Of course there were those starving children she saw in TV commercials, their naked brown bellies distended, flies crawling into their noses and eyes, hungry dehydrated children too weak to cry. There were also, Joanna had observed, unfortunate children much closer to home, children she knew who came to school unfed, unwashed, possibly unloved. These children got in trouble. These children got blamed for everything. These children got lice. These were children on welfare, Esther said, whose fathers drank and beat them and ran around with bad women, children whose mothers never cooked or cleaned but lay around all day in their underwear watching soap operas and eating chocolates till their teeth fell out. "You're lucky and don't you forget it!" Esther warned. Joanna alternated between feeling guilty for being lucky and feeling guilty for being ungrateful for being lucky.

When she did fantasize about running away from home as a child, it was always to the Simpsons-Sears store that she imagined she would go. She figured she could live there undetected for years as long as she was tidy and quiet. During the day she would just roam around and blend in with the regular shoppers. On Sundays and at night she would have the run of the place. She would wear pretty dresses off the racks, with an endless supply of pink leotards and black patent leather shoes. She would take food from the cafeteria upstairs—she didn't eat much anyway, they'd never miss a cheese sandwich here, a hamburger there. She would watch ten or twelve televisions at once, all on different channels. She would sleep in one of the display beds with matching frilly spread and sham. Of course there were bathrooms and once a week she would bathe in one of the tubs in the plumbing department, probably the pink one. And the toys—of course, there were the toys.

In the Simpsons-Sears store, she was sure, she could quite easily live happily ever after.

Working there, she quickly discovered, was another matter altogether. Now she knew they had a night watchman who patrolled the premises and the bathtubs weren't hooked up anyway. The job itself was dull. Every day she worried that working at a dull, trivial, ordinary job would turn her into a dull, trivial, ordinary person.

working *n.* 1. the action of work. 2. twitching or agitated movement, as of the face. 3. slow or gradual progress involving great effort. 4. the functioning processes of the mind. 5. [*pl.*] the part of a mine or quarry where work is done.

When she occasionally complained after work that she was bored and her feet hurt, Esther again reminded her that she was lucky. "You're lucky to have a job," she said, "and a clean easy job at that. You could be in a factory. Or a coal mine. Then you'd know what work is! Don't be so lazy! Working isn't supposed to be fun." Since neither Esther nor Joanna had ever set foot in a factory or a coal mine, this argument struck Joanna as more relevant to the sixteenth century than to 1972. "Look at your father," Esther lectured on. "He's worked at the paper mill for twenty-two years. Soon he'll be getting his gold watch. He's a smart man, he could have been anything. He could have been an accountant! But no. He has worked hard all his life and look where it's got him."

Yes, indeed. Look. Where?

43. Sour

JOANNA HATED SOUR cream, the thought of it, the name of it, the look of it. She hated the whole concept of sour cream. She had to turn her

head when her parents smeared it all over their baked potatoes at supper. She had accidentally drunk sour milk once. And she had seen
Esther emptying a carton of milk left out too long in the summer, the
foul-smelling stuff neither solid nor liquid slopping down the drain.
She did not see why sour cream should be much different. She could
not imagine why anyone in their right mind would eat such a thing
on purpose. At least it didn't smell.

"Don't be such a sourpuss," Esther often said, so often in fact that
Joanna began to imagine her whole face gone white and curdled, neither
liquid nor quite solid, but like a pussycat too, like a fat blob of sour
cream with whiskers and a small pink nose.

Once in the bakery department of the grocery store she had seen a
loaf of bread called sourdough which she supposed must be a nasty
surprise for unsuspecting buyers. Imagine taking a big bite of fresh
bread only to find a huge clot of sour cream hidden in the middle, the
way they hide red jelly inside of doughnuts and when you bite into
them the jelly gushes out the sides like thick sweet blood. Esther said
sourdough bread had nothing to do with sour cream but Joanna was
not convinced. Fortunately Esther never bought the stuff anyway.

Joanna also hated the sweet-and-sour spareribs which Esther made
by pouring a whole bottle of sweet-and-sour sauce over a pile of spareribs and then baking them in the oven for an hour. In this case it was
not just the sourness she hated. It was also the sweetness, the chunks
in the sauce, and the ribs themselves which, by the time Esther was
finished with them, were just bones with a few mouthfuls of stringy
meat stuck on them.

After both Esther and Clarence got false teeth, they did not have the
spareribs very often any more. By this time Joanna had discovered Chinese restaurants and realized that it was only her mother's version of
sweet-and-sour that she disliked.

Much later she will also acquire a taste for sour cream, just as Esther
predicted. This eventuality, like most of the future, is not something
she could ever have imagined beforehand.

44. Earth

LEWIS SAID, "I would go to the ends of the earth for you." They were in Joanna's bed in the middle of a hot August afternoon. They had just made love and were lying naked side by side flat on their backs, feeling sweaty and weak. Joanna was reflecting that, because of the illicit nature of their relationship, they seemed to be always doing one of three things: getting ready to make love, making love, or resting up after having made love.

She smiled and sighed when he said this about the ends of the earth. Although she loved him truly (there was no longer any doubt about that—they had often examined themselves in exact detail to be sure they were not just driven by lust, loneliness, or the excitement of living dangerously), she was occasionally taken aback by the romantic clichés which had taken to falling from his heretofore witty and original lips. Although Joanna was charmed by these sentiments, she was still sane enough to be skeptical too. Saying he would go to the ends of the earth was all well and good. Be that as it may, he would still nevertheless not go downtown with her for dinner. He had to go home and cook dinner for Wanda who would be home from work in fourteen minutes.

Joanna went downtown for Mexican food. Over her enchiladas and refried beans, she thought about the ends of the earth, which of course did not exist. She imagined the earth like a ball of taffy pulled out between two enormous celestial hands until the ends were nearly transparent, sticky and stringy, that familiar reliable orb pulled to the outer limits, too thin to support life or love as we know it. She imagined these sticky insubstantial strands crowded with intrepid true lovers determined to prove themselves, having actually gone to the ends of the earth just like they always said they would. Only to find there nothing to hang on to. Only to find themselves suspended above the abyss, clinging by their toenails to translucent gummy threads from which they were plummeting one by one like dead birds dropping out of a nuclear sky.

45. Trouble

JOANNA DOES NOT believe in secrets, which is probably why she can never keep them. Even Esther used to tell her that she was too honest for her own good, that she'd better learn how to lie (but not to her, of course) if she wanted to survive, let alone get anywhere, in this crazy world. Even then, Joanna knew that Esther was wrong. It was not the truth, but secrets, that would get you in trouble.

trouble *n.* 1. a state of mental distress; worry; perplexity; difficulty; bother. 2. *a)* a misfortune; mishap; calamity, *b)* a distressing, vexatious, or embarrassing experience or circumstance, *c)* a condition of being out of order, needing repair [tire *trouble*].

Certainly a secret, any secret, was exciting. The exquisite tension of keeping it, of walking around for days bearing the secret inside you like a treasure or a pearl. Then the mouth-watering pleasure of telling it, of watching the eyes of the person you'd told bug out and shine with shock.

But Joanna knew that every time she'd kept a secret she'd been promptly punished. This cause-and-effect relationship, she assumed, was one of those immutable laws of the universe which would continue to be true forever. (She was too young yet to know that truth, like all other natural and mental phenomena, was subject to change, interpretation, revision, and error.)

There was the time she cheated on her Geography test and copied the name Lake Nipissing from the boy at the next desk and a week later somebody drowned in that very lake.

The time she slept over at Penny and Pamela's and she never told her mother how they spent the whole night with a flashlight reading *True Story, True Romance, True Confessions,* and one week later Daisy the cat got run over by a car right in front of their house.

Not long after that, Joanna's art teacher, Miss March, gathered the whole class together with paper, sharp pencils, and masonite boards and they all dribbled over to Branding Park where they each chose a spot and sat down cross-legged on the grass. Joanna drew the biggest climbing tree. She remembered to draw with her whole arm, not just her wrist, the way Miss March had said, and there were pencil smudges on her elbow and the palms of both hands. It was the best drawing she'd ever done and Miss March pinned it up in the art room where it stayed all year long.

That very weekend the climbing tree was split in two by lightning in the middle of the night. It fell across the road, its insides the colour of peaches or banana skins. In the morning city workers swarmed all over it like termites. A truck hauled the pieces away and by lunchtime it was all gone and they'd painted the big stump green.

In Joanna's mind, this was akin to the consequences of secrets. The tense excitement she'd felt while drawing the perfect tree was not unlike the feeling she had while reading those dirty magazines. The only difference was that with the magazines that feeling was mostly between her legs and with the drawing it was somewhere else, higher up, and bigger, just below her ribs and some in her chest too. Both of these incidents had something to do with power and punishment, she knew that, but she couldn't yet figure out the connection.

The worst time was when she stole a pair of black silk panties from Woolworth's (not doll clothes, a puzzle, or a pack of gum, but *panties;* not pink or white or lacy, but *black,* big and brazen enough to fit a full-grown fancy woman, not a skinny twelve-year-old girl with no bum). Nobody ever found out. But two weeks later Esther had to go into the hospital for something called a hysterectomy. She had a disease; she was going to have an operation and they were going to take the diseased part out. "Woman's trouble," Clarence called it, shyly but with a hint of dismissal in his voice too, as if it were nothing really, as if it were all in Esther's head.

Esther afterwards was supposed to spend six weeks getting her strength back. Joanna had never seen her mother sleeping in the daytime before and it was frightening, the sight of Esther bundled on the chesterfield all day long, with her hair uncombed, no makeup on, dozing with her mouth half-open and wet. This experience of illness was a terrible blow to Esther's self-image and she did not suffer such hu-

miliation gladly. Although she had been told to lie around and recu-
perate for six full weeks, she was up and back to normal again in less
than one. Joanna would have liked to see the scar but she knew better
than to ask.

She'd given up early pumping her mother for information. Trying
to get the truth out of Esther was more like pulling taffy than teeth.
She'd give a little and then she'd pull back so Joanna was left with
these long thin loops of knowledge, sweet because so tantalizing, sticky
because she could not let go of them. Joanna never had been fond of
sweets.

She knew, for instance, that her mother had had other boyfriends
before Clarence came along, but she didn't know their names, what
they looked like, what had happened to them in the end. She knew
that Esther had worked as a waitress once, but she didn't know where,
when, or what it was like. She knew that Esther had had a baby before
her, a long time ago, a blue baby born dead, but she didn't know if it
was a boy or a girl and she couldn't figure out how you could be born
and dead at the same time. She knew that Esther had been thirty-five
when she was born, an age at which, as Esther often said, having a
baby was dangerous and/or downright embarrassing. But she never said
why. When Shirley Hutchinson down the street got pregnant at nearly
fifty years of age, Esther was appalled and discreetly averted her eyes
whenever Shirley and her belly lumbered proudly past. When she did
talk to Shirley, Esther stared straight over her shoulder and scrupulously
avoided noticing that her stomach was sticking out a foot in front
of her.

When it came to sex, Esther gave Joanna a book to read, a book
she'd ordered from a women's magazine. Esther handed Joanna the book
out of the blue and told her to read and remember it. "I don't want
you getting in trouble," she said angrily. It was clear that she would
not entertain questions or confusion.

Put out by the company that made Kotex or Tampax (why did all
these things end with *x,* just like sex?), it was a thin pink-covered
volume filled with drawings of happy hugging families and dimpled
big-eyed babies. There was also a diagram of a woman's insides which

seemed to be filled up at the bottom with something shaped like a set of bagpipes. Joanna knew this was the part her mother had had taken out. There were arrows with words pointing to the various parts. One arrow said *Fallopian tube* but what it pointed to looked more like a flower than a tube, a fernlike blossom on a curvy stem, something you'd expect to find growing underwater, its pale green fronds waving and nodding at the fish.

Although the book talked a lot about penises, there was no corresponding diagram of the man and so Joanna figured the look of a penis must be a secret or something too ugly to be closely examined. She knew that the penis was on the outside of the man's body while all the woman's organs were neatly tucked up inside, out of sight, out of mind. She thought women were lucky this way, to have everything so cleanly contained. Just think, Esther was now missing whole parts of her insides and nobody could tell by looking at her that there was just a space where those bagpipes had been.

trouble *n.* 3. a person, event, or thing that causes affliction, annoyance, distress, etc. 4. public disturbance; civil disorder or unrest; agitation. 5. effort or exertion. 6. an illness; ailment; disease.

Joanna grew up to become the kind of person other people will tell absolutely anything to. She often wonders what it is about her that causes people to confide in her. Why can't they see that she is just a blabbermouth?

There was the time at a party with Henry and his friend Derek's girlfriend Wendy told Joanna that she'd had a baby, a girl, when she was sixteen. She'd given the baby up for adoption but not before she'd had a look at her, even though you weren't supposed to do that. Now every year in the spring at the time of her daughter's birthday, she walked around peering into the faces of small children, not wanting her back really, but just wondering what she looked like, what her name was.

There was the time Joanna and Lewis were at the secret bar they went to where nobody knew he was married and the waitress sat down to have a beer with them after her shift and she told Joanna how she'd had an abortion last summer and never told her husband. He thought she'd gone in to have an ovarian cyst removed, or something like that, you know—one of those *woman* things.

There was the time Phoebe Patterson, a woman Joanna had worked with briefly, was committed to the psychiatric hospital. She'd had a nervous breakdown. She was suffering from psychotic delusions of grandeur: she thought she was Mother Theresa, Madame Curie, or Marilyn Monroe. Joanna wondered for a long time about nervous breakdowns: what were the symptoms, how did it feel? How would she know if she was having one? Sometimes she wished she *would* have one, just to get it over with, to be able to fall apart and be put away where she could rest for a while and be waited on, pampered, where a nice nurse would do her hair, cut her toenails, and maybe even feed her. But how could she ever have one if nobody would tell her what it was really like?

It is, Joanna figures, the things nobody told you that you will most want or need to know in the end. It is the secrets you've hung on to that will keep you awake at night eventually.

secret *n.* 1. something unknown or known only to a certain person or persons and purposely kept from others. 2. something not revealed or explained; a mystery. 3. the true cause or explanation for something which is not obvious [the *secret* of one's success].

"You," Henry said after the first time they made love, "you, Joanna, are an exquisite fuck."

"Thank you," Joanna said quietly, as if Henry had said, "My, what a lovely dress!"

"Thank you," Joanna said simply, having learned that when someone gives you a compliment it is no longer considered charming to say, "What, this old thing?" Now, whenever someone gave her a sartorial compliment, she countered by saying, "Thank you, I got it at Second Fiddle for five ninety-nine."

In this case, she said, "Thank you," and left it at that.

Much as it was gratifying to think of herself as an exquisite fuck, she couldn't help but wonder if this was really something she could take credit for. After all, when it came right down to it, she really had nothing to compare herself to. It was not as if she and her female friends, close though they might be, sat around saying, Well . . . how do *you* do it? How do *you* move *your* hips? Do you whisper dirty words in his ear? Which words? When? Do you like it from behind?

"You," Henry went on to say, "are the best kisser I have ever kissed."

Joanna said, "How do other women kiss?"

Henry said, "Differently."

This told Joanna nothing.

The women she knew, she realized, also told each other nothing. They did not say, How do you kiss? Where do you put your arms, your legs? How far do you take his cock into your mouth? Even if they did ask this last question, they would not say "cock." They would say "penis" because they were polite well-brought-up women who prided themselves on being anatomically, if not sartorially, correct and they would not say the c-word even if they had one in their mouths.

Joanna and her friends were only joking when they asked each other, "Do you spit or swallow?" It was a rhetorical question. They did not really want to know. They did not want to picture their dear gentle friends clutching some man's bare back, moaning, maybe drooling, eyes glazed over with unbridled passion. They could not picture their dear gentle friends' faces contorted with ecstasy.

When they talked about sex, they compared results. They did not compare technique.

Results meant: Did he pay your cab fare home? Did he call you the next day? Did he fall forever in love with you? Did he ask you to the dance next Saturday night?

Technique would have meant: Did he groan when he first put it in? Did he call your name (or God's or somebody else's) when he came? Did he come? Did you? How long did it take? How many times? Who was counting?

Joanna never did get up the nerve to tell anyone that Henry said she was an exquisite fuck. What if he was wrong? What if he was right? How could she ever know?

secret *adj.* 1. *a)* kept from general knowledge, *b)* abstruse; concerning occult or mystical matters. 2. remote; secluded; private. 3. keeping one's affairs to oneself. 4. mysterious or esoteric. 5. in a clandestine manner; concealed from notice; hidden.

A Saturday morning, 8:45. Lewis was rubbing his penis between Joanna's legs and her back was arched. Wanda was away for the weekend. Joanna was moaning and looking straight into his eyes when the phone rang.

It was Esther. "Finally," she said triumphantly, "finally I got the truth out of Agnes."

Who the hell was Agnes, Joanna thought, naked, aching. Oh yes, Agnes, her mother's friend, Agnes from the bridge club.

"Finally," Esther gloated. "She's kept it a secret all these years. But now I've got it."

What she had was Agnes's secret special family recipe for a dessert called Yum Yum Good. Agnes brought this concoction to everything: to bridge club, to funerals, bake sales, and afternoon teas. Everybody loved it but Agnes just smiled like a magician who will not reveal the tricks of the trade to anyone under any circumstances. Finally, Esther had wormed it out of her. She insisted now on reading the recipe into the telephone. She insisted now that Joanna immediately copy it down. For the sake of keeping peace in the family, Joanna, still naked, found pencil and paper and listened.

YUM YUM GOOD

Crust:

24 graham wafers crushed (or 1 3/4 cups crumbs)

1/2 cup melted butter

1/3 cup white sugar

Dissolve sugar and butter by creaming. Add to crumbs and pat into 8- or 9-inch pan, saving enough for topping.

Filling:

16 marshmallows

1 1/2 4-oz. Cadbury Dairy Milk chocolate bars

1/2 cup milk

1 cup whipping cream

Melt marshmallows, chocolate, and milk together in double boiler. Cool. Whip whipping cream very stiff. Combine with chocolate mixture. Spoon over crust and sprinkle on topping. Refrigerate overnight.

Afterwards Joanna wondered what had possessed her to answer the phone in the first place. Who was she expecting anyway? A stranger giving away a million dollars if only she could correctly answer the skill-testing question: 467 + 289 - 14 x 999 = ? The Nobel Prize nominating committee telling her she was in the running? Wanda accusing and crying and cursing so that finally the truth would out, the secret would explode into all of their startled ghastly faces, and they could at long last get on with their lives, whatever they were going to be? Who was she expecting anyway? Who on earth could she have thought would have something more important to say than Lewis at that moment looking straight into her eyes and telling her that he loved her to death?

Afterwards Joanna bought an answering machine, and whenever Lewis came over she turned it on the minute she saw him coming up her driveway. They would lie there in her bed listening to the voices speaking into the machine in the kitchen, listening to the unsuspecting voices of business associates, bill collectors, or friends. Joanna and Lewis would lie there in her big bed in her blue bedroom like spies, listening and giggling and safe, so they thought, from the unsuspecting rest of the world.

One such snuggly afternoon, Lewis told Joanna a secret about Wanda. He told her that Wanda still sucked her thumb when she went to bed.

"No wonder we never make love any more," Lewis said mournfully. "Can you imagine having sex with somebody sucking their thumb?"

Joanna did not laugh nearly as hard as she wanted to. She also did not tell Lewis that she too still sucked her thumb, her left thumb, had sucked it so long, in fact, that it was now smaller than her right.

It was an innocent-enough secret, Wanda's thumb-sucking, and yet Joanna managed to throw this knowledge back at Lewis later, turning it on him in an argument just the way she swore she never would. They were naked in Joanna's bed. They were arguing because Lewis had told Joanna he'd already made love to Wanda, not once but twice, that morning, so maybe now he couldn't or maybe now they shouldn't because it just didn't seem right.

Joanna said, "What happened? Did she stop sucking her thumb?"

When Lewis said, "I never should have told you that. I feel like I've betrayed her," Joanna laughed in his face and then cried on his naked chest.

Then Lewis went home for supper with Wanda. Joanna went downtown for groceries. Waiting in the checkout line at the A&P, she overheard the woman in front of her hissing at her husband, "Of course she's got trouble, she's always got trouble. But don't you go feeling sorry for her! It's no secret. She brought it all on herself." Joanna wondered if it might not be the people who bring their trouble on themselves who need and deserve the most sympathy in the end.

After the affair was over, Joanna never did get up the nerve to tell anyone how the loss of Lewis had ruined her whole world. How she could not even masturbate any more without crying. Who would she tell?

After the affair was over, Joanna thought about how time is supposed to heal all wounds. How time, like some antibiotic ointment faithfully and regularly applied to the affected area four times a day, is supposed to be the magic anodyne which will eventually render one's scar tissue down to innocuous layers thin as rice paper. But what if it doesn't? What if it only makes it worse? Ah yes, the exquisite torment of time and the truth.

exquisite *adj.* 1. carefully done or elaborately made [an *exquisite* design]. 2. of great beauty and delicacy [*exquisite* lace]. 3. consummate;

extreme; of highest quality [*exquisite* technique]. 4. keenly sensitive; fastidious; discriminating [an *exquisite* ear for music]. 5. acutely suscep- tible to; sharply intense; keenly felt [*exquisite* pain].

On the delivery table for eleven hours trying to give birth to Samuel with Gordon there as her coach, Joanna says all the things she was told in prenatal class that she would say and that she swore she never would.

She says, "I hate you! This is all your fault! I'll never sleep with you again! I hate you! Why did you do this to me? I hate you! Why can't you help me? I hate you! Go away! Please don't leave me! I love you!"

When Samuel is barely one month old, Joanna realizes there were a lot of things they didn't tell her in prenatal class. They didn't tell her how some days it would be too much trouble to even comb her hair, let alone change her smelly milk-stained blouse, let alone even consider making love to a man, any man. They didn't tell her how some nights, awake with him again at 4:00 A.M., she would think of how easy it would be to accidentally put the pillow over his face and hold it there, and no one would ever know what had really happened. They didn't tell her how after she'd imagined suffocating him, then she would sit the rest of the night beside his bassinet watching him breathe, weeping with guilt. They didn't tell her how a little tiny baby would change every single detail (past, present, and future) of her entire life.

46. Soldier

DESPITE ALL PHOTOGRAPHIC evidence to the contrary, Joanna can never quite believe that her father fought in the war. There are dozens of war pictures which were never pasted into the album with the rest. In fact, the album does not begin until 1954, the year Joanna was born. All the earlier prints and negatives were stored in a shoe box in the original developers' envelopes in no apparent order. Because Esther kept threat- ening to throw the box away (she was tired of moving it around, she never looked at those old pictures any more anyway, who would want to?), Joanna took them with her when she left home.

Being an artist, now she has ulterior motives beyond her instinctive needs for archival order and memory. She still believes that if these needs are eventually satisfied, from them will issue clarity, meaning, and a coherent sense of reality. She might use the war pictures in a series of collages.

They are in an orange envelope with Esther's name on the top. Joanna sorts through them, selects the best ones, and then arranges them page by page in a new photo album, sticking them down with those black paper corners so she can still lift them out to read Clarence's handwritten notes on the back.

PAGE ONE:

A shadowy man riding in a wagon drawn by a white horse down a wet cobblestone street. An old car disappearing in the opposite direction. Tall vine-covered buildings on either side, sunlight on stone, the shadow of a tree. The village is not named. Perhaps this is where Clarence and his soldier buddies were so hungry they ate olives right off the tree and made themselves sick.

An empty city street, modern, with large brick buildings and part of a viaduct on the right. In the center beneath a leafless tree, a round metal structure sits on the sidewalk, open on one side, with lattice work and iron leaves ringing its domed top. No matter how many times Joanna looks at this picture she thinks of it as an elaborate European phone booth, despite the fact that Clarence has written *Italian Urinal* on the back. She cannot imagine her shy father peeing in this place, let alone taking a snapshot of it to send back to Esther in Canada waiting at home.

Harbour in Naples: Smooth grey water, placid but crowded with intricately rigged ships puffing black smoke. On the left a freighter, docks, and large piles of something that looks like salt. A fluffy white cloud coasting in the center of the sky.

PAGE TWO:

A statue of two naked people kissing on a marble pedestal. The woman is draped from the waist down. She has her arms around the man's waist. He has one hand up to her face as if he were kissing her and putting his fingers in her mouth at the same time. His blurry genitals look like grapes.

Another statue of a naked woman also on a pedestal looking to the right, her left hand spread across her crotch, her right hand hovering protectively below her full breasts.

A third statue, a fountain. A cherubic little boy with dimpled arms and legs peeing proudly in a steady stream. On the back it says: *The Little Boy of Brussels.*

The interior of an enormous unidentified basilica with soaring vaulted carved and painted ceilings, Corinthian columns, shining stone floor. Two diminutive priests strolling in black, two soldiers in uniform, another man in the middle in a white hat. Joanna can make out letters carved into the stone near the dome: *NI CAELORVM TV ES PETRVS.* She does not read Latin but she likes the sound of it.

When did Clarence do all this sightseeing and picture taking, all this art appreciation between battles? It is as difficult to picture her father in this church as it is to imagine him in his tank, in the trenches, in mud or smoking rubble up to his knees. It is as difficult to picture him down on his knees praying as it is to imagine him killing Germans.

PAGE THREE:

The Colosseum in Rome, the wide boulevard in front nearly empty of vehicular traffic save two army jeeps on the right. There are several bicycles, one motor scooter, and many pedestrians: six men in white uniforms, a soldier in shorts, a woman with long dark hair and a newspaper, another woman balancing a large package on her head. The ruined ancient structure looms over the street as if it too had been damaged in this long war.

A bombed-out building, rubble piled all around it, timbers, rocks, and wires heaped upon its collapsed roof. Joanna recalls (and cannot completely cast off) her childhood confusion, her sense that everything must have happened at once, as if it were all the same war.

Clarence and another soldier both in uniform leaning against an undamaged building. Between them is a small scruffy dog and a short plump woman in a striped belted dress. Her breasts are very round and large, the left one hanging lower than the right so she looks lopsided. They are all smiling. Clarence has his arm around the woman, who has neat dark hair and an open peasant face. The back of this picture is blank. It gets mixed up in Joanna's mind with the one of the bombed-out building. Bombs. Shells. Bombshells. Is this woman a bombshell? War, women, sex, death, and other surprises. She never does ask Clarence about the woman in this photograph.

PAGE FOUR:

A picturesque shot of a rolling valley, misty mountains fading into an overexposed sky. Joanna can make out sun-struck buildings, undulating fields, roads like ribbons or veins. On the back it says: *Bertchesgaden, Germany, 1945, taken from Hitler's balcony.*

Another soldier, not Clarence, posed in front of a bombed-out building. Beside him a sign: GOERING'S HOME. This time it is the ground which has been overexposed, faded to white, so the soldier seems to be standing on air.

Esther posing on the front step of their white house in a white suit, padded shoulders, black blouse, big shiny earrings, legs crossed at the knee, arms crossed at the wrist, waiting, while Clarence takes pictures from Hitler's balcony and gives his heart over maybe to unknown bombshells.

PAGE FIVE:

Holland, 1945: Clarence's head sticking out of a Sherman tank, its top open like the lid of a tin can, a cigarette dangling from his mouth, radio headphones like earmuffs.

Our crew, October 6, 1945: Clarence and four other out-of-focus young men kneeling, squatting, standing in front of the tank.

My tank, Cecil III: the enormous muddy machine lined up with four identical others in a field of dirt. The gun of her father's tank sticking straight up. Now it looks like an erect penis but when she was younger, it only looked like a big scary gun.

PAGE SIX:

Two vertical shots of the same brick building, undamaged, many windows, white curtains, striped awnings. Apartments, a hospital, an orphanage, what? In the first picture, three buxom serious women on the sidewalk in front with a baby in a white bonnet in a black carriage and a little boy on a tricycle. In the second picture, seven little boys out front, all in shorts and argyle knee-socks. On the back of both of these it is written: *In remembrance of the ending of the war on the 5th of May 1945.*

Inexplicably (or naturally) enough, Gordon has been reading a book called *Decisive Battles of World War II*. There are many maps and pictures, chapters on the Blitzkrieg, the Battles of Britain, Midway, El Alamein, Stalingrad, Monte Cassino. Joanna knows for sure that Clarence was in this last one. She studies the photographs looking for her father's face. Could that be him inside a rolling Sherman tank? Could that be him running through the ruins of Cassino Town? She is overwhelmed by the growing knowledge of what he went through, what he never talks about, what he must have done to survive.

It is Sunday morning. Samuel is looking at the book with her, full of questions. "Is that Grandpa's war? Why isn't Grandpa in the pictures? We don't like guns, do we, Mommy?"

Currently there is a war documentary series running on TV on Saturday afternoons. Joanna will not let Samuel watch it, its horrific impact on the mind of a five-year-old outweighing, she figures, its educational value. Samuel says, "We don't like war, do we, Mommy? We just hate that show." Either it gives him nightmares or he thinks it's just another program like "Superman," "Batman," or "G.I. Joe."

When the phone rings, it is Clarence making his weekly call. He says, "I went to Kmart yesterday and got Samuel some school clothes." He says, "The tomatoes are great this year, just great." He says, "I cooked pork chops for supper last night and were they ever good! I'm really getting the hang of this cooking thing. Your mother sure would be surprised."

Her father is not the man at Monte Cassino, the man smoking calmly in the tin-can tank, the man peeing cavalierly in an Italian urinal. Her father is the man who buys school clothes for his only grandson, the man who grows tomatoes in the garden, cooks pork chops and is proud of them.

No. Her father is the man at Monte Cassino, the man who put his arms around unknown bombshells, the man who took pictures of churches and statuary in the middle of a war, the man who appreciated the panoramic view from Adolf Hitler's balcony. Her father *is not* the man who cooks pork chops to surprise a woman who has been dead for eight years.

The questions she asks him are: Did you get my last letter? Did

Mrs. Nystrom have her operation yet? Are you going to watch the baseball game this afternoon? Why don't you get those bunions looked at? Do you want to talk to Samuel?

The questions she does not ask are: Who was that woman you were hugging in Italy? What happened to the other men in your tank? What were you doing on Hitler's balcony? What was the name of that church?

And why, when he finally hangs up after discussing the weather, the rising price of gasoline and a murder/suicide in Toronto (that evil city), does she feel so stupid, so frightened, so angry?

She hangs up wishing he would remarry. If nothing else, it would give him someone else to worry about. It would also give her someone else to worry about *him* with. But this notion seems never to have occurred to Clarence. It is as if Esther's death were the end of possibility. As if he were now suspended in time, unable to go back, unwilling to go forward, afraid to take a step, afraid to make a change, afraid of remembering, afraid of forgetting. Afraid. Joanna realizes that she has no idea of what it is like to be old.

47. Cabbage

ESTHER WAS ALWAYS a snob about cabbage. She said it was something that poor people ate. She said the smell of boiling cabbage would stink up the house for days.

About cabbage (as well as cucumbers, green peppers, and peanut butter), Esther also said, "I can't eat it. It repeats on me." In another context, she often said of her friend Agnes from the bridge club, "One of the things I just can't stand about Agnes is the way she always repeats herself." Joanna felt the giggles bubbling up inside her as she pictured Agnes opening her mouth to bid at the bridge game and, instead of words, out came a cabbage, and another, and another, till the whole room was filled with them.

Grocery shopping one Saturday afternoon, Esther told Joanna to make herself useful and go pick out a good head of lettuce. In the produce aisle, the cabbage was right beside the lettuce. While Joanna tried to figure out what exactly constituted a *good* head of lettuce, a woman, in a worn cloth coat, beat-up shoes, and stockings sagged down around her ankles, was picking through the precarious pyramid of cabbages. Finally she pulled one from the middle and the whole thing gave way. There were cabbages everywhere, rolling around Joanna's feet, down the produce aisle, under people's shopping carts, and the woman just walked away. Esther glared at Joanna as if it had been her fault and then she said, inexplicably, "See?"

Twenty years later Joanna dreams about those rolling cabbages. In the dream the cabbages turn into heads when they hit the floor: real heads, perfect pale green heads, with eyes, noses, and horror-struck mouths. It is a full-fledged cabbage nightmare.

Gordon just laughs. He, like most people, has no strong feelings about cabbage one way or the other. He can take it or leave it, although he did say once that he thought purple cabbage was rather pretty. Sliced through the middle and looked at in cross-section, it is, he said, not unlike the cross-section of an upside-down volcano, the purple parts being like veins of lava running through rock, ready to erupt at any given moment. Or perhaps it's more like a fingerprint magnified a thousand times. Either way he is sure that cabbages are like snowflakes and human beings: no two of them exactly alike, each one of them precisely individual, and that in itself could be considered remarkable.

Joanna is working on a series of collages about fruits and vegetables, so it's no wonder she's dreaming about cabbages. She finds herself paying an abnormal amount of attention to the aesthetic, in addition to the nutritional, value of produce. Picking a peach, a tomato, an apple, or yes, a purple cabbage, takes a lot longer when you have to contemplate its beauty and symbolic significance as well as its ripeness and price per kilo. It is a matter of the way you look at things determining what you see. It is a botanic extrapolation of the power of mind over matter. Cabbages as human heads, geological formations, or fingerprints: anything is possible.

She brings her cabbages home from the grocery store and sets them up around her studio. After she has contemplated them, she will take them to the kitchen and turn them back into food: cabbage rolls, cabbage soup, cabbage strudel, coleslaw. After a week Gordon will suggest it's time to move on to cauliflower, broccoli, perhaps some sweet peppers which are available in all colours just now.

48. Hard

"YOU'RE SOFT IN the head, woman," Henry said. "But hard, oh so hard, in the heart." It was midnight. They were getting ready for bed.

They had agreed to break up. Henry was packed and ready to go. Because everything in the apartment belonged to Joanna anyway, it didn't look much different. He'd rented a room in a sleazy downtown hotel until he could find a place of his own.

"You're soft in the head, woman," Henry said. "But hard, oh so hard, in the heart."

"Yes," Joanna whispered, although she could not have said what she was agreeing to: his words or the way he was licking her stomach. She could picture her head like a soft-boiled egg and her heart like a fist.

"I'll never love anyone as much as I love you," Henry said as he slipped his hand between her wet thighs.

"Yes you will, sure you will," Joanna said, spreading her legs and guiding his fingers inside.

"No, never," he said, "not in my heart of hearts." She pictured him holding a giant hand of cards from that porno deck he'd bought in Las Vegas, all he had to show for his trip. Jack of Hearts, Queen of Hearts, King of Hearts, Heart of Hearts.

They imagined they would be friends forever. They could not imagine that Henry would live in that sleazy hotel room for nearly a year, at which point he would meet and suddenly marry a woman named Linda from Toronto and move there. They could not imagine how hard it would be to stay friends after having been lovers and, later, how hard it would be to keep in touch once Henry and his new wife had moved away.

49. Eagle

IN AESOP'S FABLES there was the story of the eagle and the crow. A young crow perched on a rock near a flock of sheep sees an eagle swoop down, pick up a lamb, and then fly back to its nest. The crow tries to do the same thing but chooses as his prey a huge ram which he cannot budge. Realizing his mistake, the crow tries to fly away but his claws are tangled in the ram's wool. A shepherd sees his predicament, pulls him off, clips his wings, and gives him to the children for a pet. The moral of this story was: *Know yourself! Do not undertake more than you are able.*

This advice seemed to contradict much of the other advice Joanna was given, those pithy maxims of encouragement: *Where there's a will, there's a way* and *If at first you don't succeed, try, try again!* From this perspective the crow would have been considered a quitter. The paradoxical nature of these various words of wisdom was confusing but it was the exclamatory injunction, *Know yourself!* that really worried her.

How was she supposed to know herself when every day she felt different? During the course of any given week, she thought of herself as pretty, ugly, stupid, smart, quiet, noisy, kind, nasty, generous, stingy, cheerful, crabby, lazy, hard-working, hateful, lovable, weak, strong, serious, and silly. She did not see how she could be all of these things. She imagined that nobody else could be as changeable and uncertain as she was. Perhaps when she grew up, she would be the same person every day. But for now the only things about herself that she knew for sure from day to day were the facts that she had dark brown curly hair and big brown eyes. But then again her eyes were blue when she was born and her mother dyed her hair.

The command *Know yourself!* was like Mrs. Crocker in English class always assigning the weekly composition on Friday afternoon with the cheerful admonition, "Write about what you know!" Then she would have them turn to a list of topic sentences in the textbook, a list from which they must choose one from sentences like:

1. I have found from experience that the world can be seen and appreciated from my own doorstep.
2. "Where there's a will, there's a way" is illustrated by the lives of many poor boys who have become famous.
3. We find the most colourful jewels in Woolworth's.
4. There are many disturbers of the peace.
5. There are mind poisons, just as there are body poisons.
6. The endeavour of education to keep pace with the rapidly growing ignorance appears to be quite hopeless, since there are year by year so many new things of which to be ignorant.

Joanna knew nothing about jewels, poison, or disturbing the peace. She did not know any poor boys who had become famous. From her own doorstep, all she could see was the neatly mown grass, her mother's carefully tended flower garden, and, occasionally, the neighbours' orange tomcat eyeing innocent sparrows or washing himself in the sun. She felt ignorant about everything important, including her own true self. She thought she was more like the crow, an ordinary pitiful nuisance, hardly at all like the regal self-satisfied eagle.

She thought of the eagle as an indigenously and exclusively American bird. Because they lived close to the U.S. border, most of the TV channels they received were beamed up from the south. She knew more about Minnesota than she did about Manitoba, more about Paul Bunyan and his blue ox Babe than about Louis Riel and his Red River Rebellion. In her mind the eagle was always perched atop a giant silver flagpole from which the self-confident Stars and Stripes waved strenuously.

Here they had the beaver instead, a pudgy awkward rodent with webbed feet, orange teeth, and a tendency to excrete intestinal parasites into the drinking water. Here they'd had until recently the Union Jack which she had drawn every year in elementary school, measured and outlined carefully with a ruler and then coloured in with red, white, and blue pencil crayons while the teacher explained once again what it stood for. But it was the flag of England really, not Canada. There was another flag called the Red Ensign, but nobody flew it. Then the government decided it was time for a new flag, so now they had the red maple leaf on a white background which nobody liked.

Joanna was fifteen the summer of 1969 when the Americans first walked on the moon and the whole world watched it on TV. Neil Armstrong stepped from the lunar module Eagle onto the surface of the moon at Tranquility Base and the whole world heard him say, "That's one small step for a man, one giant leap for mankind." Joanna was sleeping over that night at Penny and Pamela's. Their parents and their little brother Billy had gone away for the weekend. The three girls were having a slumber party, eating chips and stealing sips of whisky from the Texas Mickey Mr. Nystrom had won at a fishing derby. They were dancing in their baby dolls around the TV set when Neil Armstrong took his giant leap. They thought they were drunk and took turns swooning into each other's arms, crying, "The Eagle has landed! My God, thank God, the Eagle has landed!" while the astronauts tramped around on the moon far above them in their spacesuits, setting up their experiments, unveiling a plaque, and planting the American flag in lunar soil.

Two days before the moon landing, Senator Edward M. Kennedy had driven his car off a bridge on Chappaquiddick Island in the middle of the night. The young woman with him, a twenty-eight-year-old Washington secretary named Mary Jo Kopechne, had died. Senator Kennedy had not reported the accident to the police until the next morning. The whole world was shocked. The Kennedys, the perfect precious doomed Kennedys, were in the news again. "Their poor mother," Esther said.

Four days after the Eagle had landed, the astronauts were back on earth, safe and sound. That night Clarence drove Joanna, Penny, and Pamela downtown to see the new movie *Easy Rider*. Joanna fell immediately in love with the handsome renegade biker Peter Fonda, and when he and Dennis Hopper were shot to pieces at the end, she was so stunned that afterwards she could not remember leaving the theatre, getting back into Clarence's car, and riding home again. The next day Senator Kennedy pleaded guilty to the charge of leaving the scene of an accident. He received a two-month suspended sentence and a year's probation. The whole world was relieved. Esther said if he'd been an ordinary man, he would have gone to jail.

Two weeks later actress Sharon Tate and four other people were found murdered in her Hollywood Hills mansion. Sharon Tate was pregnant at the time which made the brutal crime even more horrific.

A week after that it was Woodstock, half a million hippies gathered on Max Yasgur's farm to listen to rock music, dance naked, do drugs, and make love, not war. Once again the whole world watched history being made on television. Joanna watched it too, sulking in front of the TV set, feeling too young, too boring, too ordinary, too Canadian, to be part of the excitement. Everything important and interesting, it seemed, happened south of the border. No wonder she knew nothing.

That night she dreamed of the American flag up there waving, stuck in the moon, omnipotent and arrogant with giant eagles swooping all around it. The lunar surface was crowded with long-haired men, bare-breasted women in brightly coloured skirts, and naked babies eating dirt. In the background there was loud music, Janis Joplin wailing in her whisky voice, Country Joe and the Fish singing bad words out loud, Jimi Hendrix cranking out his psychedelic guitar version of "The Star-Spangled Banner." There was also Senator Kennedy swimming with his mother and Sharon Tate searching under a bush for a crying baby. Joanna herself rode through this dream on the back of Peter Fonda's Harley which had a gold eagle painted on the gas tank. They passed her own parents weeping, a pale beaver gnawing a tree, and a crowd of people singing "O Canada" and saluting the red-and-white flag.

The following year four students were killed and nine others injured at Kent State University, Ohio, gunned down by the National Guard while protesting the entry of American troops into Cambodia. As it turned out, the dead students had not been participating in the demonstration. Jimi Hendrix and Janis Joplin died of drug overdoses in the fall.

The day after Janis Joplin's death in Los Angeles, James Cross, British trade commissioner in Montreal, was kidnapped by the FLQ. Five days later Pierre Laporte, Quebec Minister of Labour, was also kidnapped. On October 16, the federal government implemented the War Measures Act. Over 450 people were detained in Quebec. The following day the body of Pierre Laporte was found in the trunk of a car near St. Hubert airport.

Although Joanna had never been to Ohio, Los Angeles, or Montreal, she knew that she too was under siege. Even safe boring Canada had been invaded by anger. Peter Fonda was nowhere in sight.

50. Stomach

OFTEN ON A sultry summer afternoon there were half a dozen prepubescent girls lying facedown in the street in front of Joanna's house. Often Joanna was one of them. They had just come from the Branding Park swimming pool. Their bathing suits were still wet on their slender bodies. The more developed (and so more daring) girls wore bikinis with breast cups. Their hair was dry but flattened by the rubber bathing caps they were forced to wear according to pool regulations. Joanna's cap was festooned with floppy rubber flowers in all colours. The girls' eyes were bloodshot and stinging from the chlorinated pool water. Some of their ears were still plugged as if they had just stepped off an airplane. They spread their beach towels in the street and then lay down upon them, pressing their damp stomachs against the hot asphalt where they slowly steamed dry.

Soon after came the young boys who had watched their exodus from the pool and then followed a few minutes later. They strolled down the sidewalk ogling and whistling, the bolder ones flitting through the prostrate girls, flicking their wet towels at the air above their giggling shoulder blades. Once an older boy, a high school boy, rode through them on his bicycle, weaving around their naked outstretched arms and legs as if they were a slalom course.

At the sound of an approaching car, the girls would leap up and scatter like birds, startled pigeons or doves let loose from a magician's black hat. They clutched their towels and caps against their stomachs as if suddenly discovering themselves stark naked in the street. If the car was driven by a man, usually he would toot and wave as he passed. If it was a woman driver, she would just ignore them and grimly proceed.

Meanwhile the boys ran on to their homes, making rude noises and snapping their towels at each other now, harder, connecting, leaving red welts across bony shoulders, long straight thighs, flat brown stomachs. All of their bodies were hairless, boys and girls both, still straddling the spiky fence between innocence and hirsute hormonal knowledge.

Later, sometimes, in the middle of the night, older teenagers would climb the chain-link fence around the pool and swim unsupervised in the dark. They were yelling, screaming, singing, waking up the whole neighbourhood. If Joanna got up on her knees on her bed and peeked through her curtains at just the right angle, she could see them leaping and diving, their apparently naked bodies twisting and glinting like fish in the moonlight, the water exploding up around them like fireworks or a fountain of displaced diamonds. They played until the disgruntled neighbours called the police and the cruiser came sliding towards them, circling, silent, with its red lights flashing.

All of Henry's friends had beer bellies of which they were inordinately fond. Friday nights at the Neapolitan, Pete the roofer would take hold of his gut in both hands and shake it at Joanna. "This," he said, "this here belly is the only thing I own that's really paid for." Luke the carpenter would lean back in his chair to better display his stomach which strained vaingloriously against his red plaid flannel shirt. Sometimes there were buttons missing and his hairy navel showed. He often unconsciously caressed his belly, stroking it, patting, adjusting it like very pregnant women do. "Bought and paid for by UIC," he said.

Henry himself was in pretty good shape. He credited this to the fact that, up until five years or so ago, he had religiously lifted weights and worked out on the bench press. But then he'd had to sell the weights and the press because he was broke. Now he'd given up exercise altogether because it cut too much into his drinking time. Now, he said, he was committed to leading a thoroughly dissipated life. He knew it would catch up with him some day. He warned Joanna that one morning she would wake up beside a three-hundred-and-fifty-pound pool of fat with his heart, his liver, and the remains of his stomach in a bucket beside the bed.

They had these big-bellied men over for Christmas dinner. Originally Joanna was not keen on this idea but Henry reminded her persistently that they had nowhere else to go. Finally she relented and took pity on them. They ate heartily for what seemed like hours. Afterwards they lay around on the living-room floor moaning and burping and unbuttoning their pants. While Henry and Joanna did the dishes, they dozed off. Then Henry tiptoed around them with the Polaroid camera Joanna had given him for Christmas and took pictures of their bellies flopping over their belts. He insisted that these photographs remain stuck up on the fridge. He wanted, he said, to be reminded of where he was headed. He never did get around to taking pictures of the Christmas tree, the decorations, or any of the other festive paraphernalia.

Lewis was proud of his flat hard stomach. Also of his long muscular legs, his tight trim buttocks, and his well-formed biceps which he did not, fortunately, go so far as to flex in front of her. He worked out twice a week and jogged the other days, two miles from his house to the congested polluted streets of downtown and back. Joanna often wondered why he didn't run through the park, by the waterfront, or even just through the quiet neighbourhood. Wouldn't that be safer, wouldn't that be healthier? Eventually he admitted that he rather liked the look of himself in his black tank top and thigh-length spandex shorts. No baggy grey sweats for him. He preferred to run where he could be seen and see himself too, reflected in the storefront windows as he cantered by. He confessed that a woman had once said he ran like a fine young stallion.

"What woman?" Joanna said. They were making love on a Wednesday afternoon. Why did he always make such incendiary remarks when they were right in the middle of it?

"Oh, just some woman."

"Not Wanda."

"No, not Wanda. Just some woman I used to know."

"How well did you know her?"

"Not in the biblical sense. I never slept with her, if that's what you mean."

"Why not?"

"She was married."

"Was she in love with you?"

"I don't know. I don't think so. Forget I ever mentioned her. She just liked to look at my muscles."

"I'll show you muscles," Joanna said and clutched his softening penis as hard as she could with the muscles of her vagina. He was astounded and aroused.

"How on earth do you do that? I didn't know you could do that."

"There are lots of things you don't know about me. I practise."

"When?"

"Walking around downtown, waiting in line at the bank, when I'm bored and buying lettuce at the A&P."

Lewis is laughing and coming at the same time. Afterwards they curl up together in Joanna's big bed and she rests her head on his stomach. She cannot begrudge him his vanity for long. It *is* flat. It *is* hard. She does not have the heart to tell him that sometimes she wishes it were softer, flabby even, more like a pillow instead of a table upon which to lay her head. She does not have the heart to tell him that sometimes when she sees a fat man on the street, she has to fight off the urge to run and bury her head in his bulk, which she imagines would be plush and furry, docile, yeastily fragrant and unassailably safe.

The way to a man's heart is through his stomach.

It is Christmas Eve. Clarence has been here for three days. Samuel is fairly crazed with anticipation. He thinks his grandpa and Santa Claus are pals because whenever Grandpa comes to visit, Santa isn't far behind. He knows he will be allowed to open one present after supper.

The rest must wait until morning. After supper they will also bake cookies for Santa and they will leave eight equal pieces of carrot in the driveway for the reindeer. Samuel is in the living room headfirst under the Christmas tree, shaking and pinching and sniffing his gifts. His little behind is stuck up in the air, wiggling. Gordon says he looks like a puppy. Samuel barks and shakes a present in his teeth.

Joanna is in the kitchen making chili and corn bread. She is making the chili very mild so that Samuel will be able to eat it and also because Clarence has mentioned that he's had some trouble with his stomach lately. Also his bowels. Joanna doesn't like to ask for details. Inquiring after the state of her father's digestive system would seem to be an irrevocable unconscionable invasion of privacy. She goes easy on the chili powder. She asks him if he's hungry. He says yes. Very.

She is still at the point in the visit where she is trying to impress him with her culinary skills. She is still at the point in her life where she is trying to please him. She's read the self-help books, she knows that this need adult children have to win parental approval can be destructive. It is yet another form of unrequited love. She knows she should just be getting on with letting go. She knows that her family was not nearly as dysfunctional as some. Certainly she was never physically or sexually abused. Sometimes she feels guilty for feeling so damaged. What right does she have to complain? What right does she have to be scarred for life?

She does not always trust her own memory but then again it is all she has. What if she did have a happy childhood and just can't remember it? Sometimes she thinks, with no offence to those who have actually suffered through one, that unhappy childhoods are in style now. Perhaps she just wants to be like everybody else. But the truth is that her parents did not get divorced, her father did not beat her or her mother, he was never unemployed or (as far as she knows) unfaithful, she seldom ever even heard them arguing out loud. They were probably just an ordinary family. They had probably done the best they could. So why does she feel so bad?

Perhaps in those days parents were blissfully ignorant of the indelible damage they were doing, the scars to the bone they were leaving, the lifelong havoc they were creating. Now the word *parent* has been elevated to verb status. In Joanna's twenty-year-old dictionary it is credited only with being a noun. There is a passing reference to its adjectival use in reference to corporations and their subsidiaries.

Now that they must parent positively, mothers and fathers everywhere (but especially mothers) have become diabolically self-conscious, forever calculating the irremediable ramifications of their every move, every mood, every admonition. They read books, they watch videos, they take courses on how to parent. In none of these avenues of instruction are they ever told to trust their own instincts. It would appear that instincts, maternal or otherwise, may well be fraudulent, misguided, or downright dangerous. Doing what comes naturally will no doubt turn out to be wrong. They are told they must develop complex psychologically correct strategies for dealing with their children. They are supposed to give them messages (not rules), reminders (not orders), frozen yogurt (not ice cream). They must always reward good behaviour. They must never react to bad. There is no such thing as *bad*. They must not criticize. They must scrupulously avoid the use of such negative, authoritarian, ego-eroding, self-esteem-destroying epithets as: "Don't!" "Stop it!" and "No!" They must explain every little thing. They must negotiate. They must not expect too much. They must not expect too little. Nobody knows how much is too much or how little is too little.

The children are powerful. The parents are paralysed, held hostage by a heightened awareness of their children's fragility, by the spectre of their own childhood unhappiness, and by the certainty that if they do the wrong thing, their children will become drug addicts, car thieves, or psychokillers.

And here is Joanna, thirty-five years old and still desperate for her father's acknowledgement, encouragement, respect. Still she just wants to hear him say, "Good for you, honey. Good for you." She wants to hear him say it over and over and mean it. She wants him to make up for all the other times he never said it. He did say once, at her wedding, that he was proud of her. She is still waiting for him to say it again.

He says, "I just can't eat this johnny-cake. You call it corn bread. I

call it johnny-cake and I had too much of it in the war." He puts a
piece with one bite out of it back on the serving plate. He goes on to
tell (once again) the story of how his stomach shrank in the war. Joanna
has noticed that the older he gets, the more he talks about the war. As
if it were the most important thing that ever happened to him. Maybe
it was. He tells how when he finally landed back on Canadian soil, all
he could think of was a big juicy steak with baked potato and all the
trimmings, but when he had the plate in front of him, all he could eat
was three or four bites and then he felt sick. Joanna thinks of how it
is his life now that is shrinking, dwindling down year after year to a
matter of maintenance and passing the time, with intermittent obsessive respect paid to the weather and the unreliability of aging internal
organs (both of which are natural phenomena, inevitable, irrevocable,
and out of his control).

Samuel, having bolted his chili and two pieces of corn bread, leaps
up from the table and sticks out his tummy as far as he can. "Mommy,
Mommy, I'm full, feel how full I am."

Joanna, Gordon, and Clarence take turns patting his stomach. Clarence says, "You look like Santa Claus, with a big fat belly like a bowl
full of jelly."

Samuel says, "I'm not Santa Claus. I'm having a baby." He runs off
to the stash of presents under the tree.

Clarence is visibly shocked. Joanna knows that in his day, a five-
year-old child had no business knowing where babies come from.

She says, "Times have changed, Dad."

He says, "That's the problem."

She assures him that although Samuel knows babies grow inside their
mothers' stomachs, he has as yet expressed no curiosity as to how they
get in there in the first place. Thanks to a variety of prime-time TV
programs about wolves, whales, and a woman giving birth in the back
of a taxi, he does know how they get out and how much it hurts.

He is in fact fascinated by the whole idea. He loves to haul out the
photo album and pore over the pictures of Joanna when she was pregnant. His favourite is one taken at a summer barbecue, two weeks before
he was born, and there is Joanna sitting on a tree stump with her shirt

pulled up to show herself off to the camera. A little boy about two years old whose name she cannot now remember has one eye pressed to her belly button, trying to get a look at the baby inside. Behind them are tall dark fir trees, a glint of water, the lake, and a smoking barbecue.

Samuel would like to know what she had to eat that day. Hamburgers, hot dogs, corn on the cob, or what? Joanna can hardly remember the occasion, the location, let alone the menu. She was, is still, mesmerized by the sight of her own blooming belly in the center of the frame. The skin is so tight it shines. Samuel supposes that with that big baby (him!) in there, there was no room for food anyway. As if pregnant women probably don't need to eat, are nourished instead by some kind of osmosis, feeding intravenously off the fledgling child within.

Samuel would like to know if there are pictures of *her* before she was born, pictures of his grandma with his mommy still growing in her tummy. Now that would be something to see. No, there are not. Esther hated having her picture taken (she said she was not photogenic) and would certainly not have allowed it when she was pregnant.

Now Samuel runs back into the kitchen ripping open the present he has chosen. It turns out to be a beautiful blue hand-knit sweater from the neighbours across the street. Samuel's eyes well up with disappointment. It is not a toy. He is whining to open another one, a *better* one. Joanna is annoyed and chides him for being greedy and ungrateful. Gordon and Clarence, in true manly fashion, look silently down at their empty chili bowls. Joanna is tired of having to be the big bad mommy. She relents. Samuel goes again to the Christmas tree and this time opens a gift from Clarence which turns out to be a Batman figure he has been hoping for. This is much better. He roars around the house happily flapping his arms, rescuing the innocents, killing off the bad guys, and revving up the Batmobile while the adults have coffee and dessert.

Clarence tells a Christmas story. One year when Joanna was little (he does not remember how old exactly) she set her alarm clock on Christmas Eve so she wouldn't sleep too late in the morning. After he and Esther got into bed that night, Esther said she had changed Joanna's clock so they wouldn't have to get up at such an ungodly hour. Clarence said, "How mean can you be? It's only one morning out of the whole year. What difference does it make?" To his surprise, Esther got up and changed the alarm clock back again.

Joanna has never heard this story before. She is touched and grateful. Clarence says, "You were lucky you had me to protect you."

After the dishes are cleared away, Joanna begins making cookies, her own favourite, Thimble Cookies, one of her mother's favourites too. She mixes the dough and shapes it into one-inch balls as the recipe, in Esther's handwriting, directs. Her father, her husband, and her son are in the living room watching TV. This does not strike her as a suitable Christmas Eve activity. She calls them into the kitchen to help. She is determined that this year she will not make Christmas happen all by herself. Gordon and Samuel are happy to help. Clarence is reluctant. She tells him he has to help because she wants to take pictures. She sets them all up around the table where the cookies are laid out on sheets. She has Gordon dip the balls in egg whites and then chopped walnuts. Clarence wields the thimble, pressing it into the center of each ball to make a hole which Samuel then fills up with strawberry jam. She takes pictures.

After the cookies have gone into the oven, Clarence says, "I hope your mother wasn't looking down on that."

Joanna laughs. "Why not?"

"Because," Clarence says, "I would never help *her* with the cookies." Joanna has always assumed that the reason he never helped was because Esther wouldn't let him. Now she sees that she knows nothing about them at all. For all these years she has blamed her mother for everything. Now she sees that this cannot possibly be true.

After the cookies are done, everyone has a sample. Samuel has three. Clarence declares them delicious. But they are not. They are crumbly and burnt on the bottom. They are not nearly as good as the ones Esther used to make.

After the pictures have been developed, Clarence goes through them slowly. When he comes to the ones of the cookie-making, he says, pointing to himself, "Who's that?"

"It's you!" Joanna exclaims.

"Oh, oh, yes, I see," Clarence says, embarrassed. "I just didn't recognize myself for a minute there."

After Christmas, after New Year's, after Clarence has gone back home, Joanna will realize that she has once again asked him all the wrong questions.

She has asked him: Are you hungry? Are you full? Will you help me with the cookies?

She has not asked him: Why was she always so mean? When did you stop protecting me? Why wouldn't you help her with the cookies?

51. Stem

ESTHER GREW BEGONIAS in pots on the front porch, one at each end of the four steps. They were new pots, white plastic to replace the old brown clay ones. They were also new steps, concrete to replace the old green wooden ones. The concrete steps were hollow and they rang when Joanna jumped up and down them, holding on to the black cast-iron railing on either side. The begonias were yellow, pink, white, and red. Their leaves were dark green and waxy, run through with big red veins. Their stems were hairy and nearly transparent. Sometimes in her exuberance, Joanna knocked one off, flower, leaves, stem and all. Sometimes Esther had a fit. Other times she just sighed, picked up the broken stem, and put it in a glass of water on the kitchen windowsill. The stem where it had been severed leaked a clear thin liquid which Joanna figured must be plant blood. Left in water long enough, the stem would sprout roots like little white hairs. Esther said if you planted the broken stem, it would grow into a whole new plant. But she never did this. When the water got smelly, she threw them away.

In the book about sex which Esther gave Joanna when she was twelve, there was a drawing of a woman's Fallopian tubes which reminded her of the broken begonia stems. The diagram was printed in black and white, but if it had been coloured she imagined the tubes

would be pale green, the eggs iridescent mother-of-pearl, and the waiting uterus a voluptuous resplendent red.

In Miss Berglund's Health class the following year she saw the female
reproductive system in full colour, life-size, on a poster. Of course the
Fallopian tubes were not green and the eggs were too small to be visible
to the naked eye. But yes, the uterus and its contents, regularly emptied
and flushed away, were red, dark red, viscous, mutinous, imminent red.

When she was eighteen and Thomas Hunt's penis (which had been
long and wide, intimidating, if not downright majestic, at first) went
soft in her cold tentative hand, she found herself thinking again about
begonias, broken stems, the way they would reroot if you left them
alone on the windowsill. They were both embarrassed. Thomas tucked
himself back into his pants and Joanna babbled on foolishly about
plants, gardens, her mother's green thumb, all the while imagining his
little penis nestled there in the humid darkness of his underwear, more
like a mushroom than the adroit sturdy stem they had both been
anticipating.

Lewis's penis, when she finally got her hands on it, did not go soft.
Instead it unfurled and grew slowly but steadily hard, filling up with
blood and desire and other fragrant fluids, like a flower blossoming in
one of those TV nature programs where the transformation from bud
to full bloom is telescoped by the camera into a two-minute action
sequence so that what appears to the viewer to be slow motion is in
fact fast motion, a result of the clever convenient manipulation of time
in the pursuit of clarity, knowledge, and power. What if, Joanna wondered, we each possessed individual power over the passage of time?
What if we could slow down those moments that slip by too quickly,
those moments like this one, Lewis putting his penis inside her, slowly,
sighing, wet? What if we could speed up those hours that seem to drag
on forever, hours like the ones to come, all those hours after they had
made love and Lewis had gone back home to his wife and Joanna would
be alone again, sore between the legs, perhaps still sighing, perhaps
still wet?

52. Lamp

THE ONLY ANTIQUE Esther owned was a lamp which had sat in her parents' parlour when she was a little girl. Both the globe and the base were made of frosted pink glass with a pattern of white wild roses. It was actually a coal-oil lamp, now just an ornament which Esther dusted grudgingly. The oil, the wick, the smoke, the smell—it was all too much trouble, Esther said. As for antiques in general, she couldn't see what all the fuss was about. A bunch of old junk, she said, which stupid people paid exorbitant prices for. If ever she'd had any other antiques, they were long gone by the time Joanna was old enough to appreciate furniture. They had all gone to the dump, replaced by modern fifties stuff.

Esther was not the least bit sentimental about the pink lamp, and when Joanna asked if she could have it when she grew up and got her own place, Esther said, "What would you want with that old thing?" But she agreed. Joanna loved the pink lamp because it made her think of elegant ladies in long dresses with bustles and muffs, dashing men in top hats and waistcoats, sleek high-stepping horses pulling fringed carriages. She thought of the pink lamp as a leftover from a gentler, simpler, more classical time. She sometimes thought she had been born in the wrong century. Esther felt compelled to remind her that in those days they did not have televisions, vacuum cleaners, stereos, or cars. They had outhouses. In those days children did not have Barbies, dollhouses, or any other fancy toys. She herself had had nothing to play with but a stick and a ball. And yes, she had walked four miles to school even in the coldest weather. At various times during her brief scholastic career (she had quit school after Grade Ten because in those days girls were not expected to pursue higher education—they were expected to pursue their homemaking skills in the hopes of eventually procuring themselves a good husband), she had frozen her ears, her fingers, and all of her toes. Other than that, she did not often tell stories of her own previous life.

Esther said there was no sense hanging on to the past. Those people who longed for the good old days had poor memories. Esther believed wholeheartedly in progress. She said she liked to stay abreast of things. She did not believe in nostalgia.

Like most children, Joanna seldom thought of her mother as having once been a child herself. She could not imagine it. When she was older and would have liked to know more, it was Esther, it seemed, who could not or would not remember or imagine any of it. Joanna did not know if this was a deliberate abdication of her own past or if it was merely a negligent lack of interest. People of Esther's generation did not look to their past lives as the cesspool of all their problems the way people Joanna's age did. They did not go to expensive therapists who encouraged them to plumb their own pasts in order to garner insight into their unsatisfying present lives. People of Esther's generation did not seem to realize that making peace with your past would allow you to enjoy your present and proceed fearlessly (more or less) into your own fulfilling future.

When Joanna moved away from home she took the pink lamp with her. Also the box of old photographs Esther had been threatening for years to throw away. Joanna rescued it and packed it in with her other belongings. But not before she sat down and went through the photographs. She tried to get her mother to look at them with her but Esther was not interested. She said, "What's done is done. Why not just leave well enough alone? Let sleeping dogs lie," and went on with her ironing.

Joanna went through the photographs one by one. To her they were not so much a homage to the past, a futile attempt to stop time dead in its tracks, but rather a demonstration of faith in the future. All families take such photographs, take them in the middle of daily life while looking towards that day (five, ten, fifteen, twenty years from now) when they will be able to sit down and look back at what is now the present and hopefully remember and make some sense of where they have come from, where they have been and never will be again. Such family photos presume a certain optimistic belief that yes, the future will eventually arrive and the present (good, bad, or indifferent) will have meanwhile spontaneously become the past and they will be immersed in a new present, even while gazing down with wonder at the inevitable alchemy of time.

The prints and negatives in the box were all jumbled together. There were notations on the backs of some: names, dates, places, by which to anchor and acclimate them, but most were blank. A photo of Esther posing in the middle of a stand of birch trees wearing an elegant black dress, black pumps, little white gloves, and carrying a box-shaped polka-dotted purse was followed by one of her older sister, Frances, twenty years earlier in a clown suit in a dark doorway with a small black dog at her feet. Of course all the photographs were black and white so the actual colours of their garments, their accessories, and the dog could only be imagined. The dress might have been blue, the purse might have been red, and the dog might well have been brown.

There was a shot of an unidentified babe-in-arms, its face out of focus, crying or smiling. A small boy in a cowboy hat in a field. The same boy in a Davy Crockett hat in the same field. A flock of children watching a miniature train. The small boy with the hats might be one of them. Clarence in the war, young and handsome in his uniform. A sharp-faced man in a white suit, black shirt, posing stylishly with a silver-tipped cane. A white dog on a heavy black chain with its tongue hanging out. A series of Christmas trees which all looked the same, only the rooms around them having changed. The pink lamp appeared in several shots, in different rooms, on different doily-covered tables, flanked by different people, or by the same people who were growing, aging, changing, while the lamp remained the same.

When Joanna asked what had become of the pretty handmade doilies upon which the lamp had sat, Esther said she didn't know. Esther said she didn't know who half these people were either. Joanna asked her why did she have a box full of photos of strangers then? Esther said they weren't strangers at the time. She was, it seemed, no better at hanging on to people than objects.

Later Joanna will discover that she is the same. When people move out of her immediate orbit, whether to another city, another neigh-bourhood, or a new stage of their lives, she doesn't know how to keep track of them. Perhaps she has inherited this or perhaps it is because she was an only child, always acutely aware of her solitary state. Perhaps instead of trying to counteract that state, as you might expect, by holding people close and fast forever, she tends rather to perpetuate it. It begins to dawn on her that she is lackadaisical about other people. They are tremendously important to her for a time and then they are not. She begins to see her life in sections, as separate pockets of time and affiliation. She comes to each stage anew, having burned her bridges behind her, not consciously but somehow it happens, so that none of the characters from one stage leak forward into the next. Except for her parents, of course. They are omnipresent. Although she can always recognize herself, going forward, looking back, she is not sure that other people could. *You wouldn't know me if you knew me now.* The various stages of her life are like marbles set side by side, just touching, and it is only at the end, after the last marble has been put in place, that she will be able to see the pattern they have created. At any given moment it is hard for her to remember how she got *here* from *there.* At any given moment it is hard for her to imagine how she has and hasn't changed.

When she looks again at Esther's old photographs (five, ten, fifteen, twenty years from now) she will see that they themselves are like lamps, shedding their stories effortlessly like light upon a table. But the stories they tell are always aging too so that five, ten, fifteen, twenty years from now what she will see in them will not remain the same. All memory is revisionist, all stories are apocryphal, all photographs hang suspended in the present tense. As if in aging, a photograph changes meaning according to how the viewer has aged and changed and yet remained the same. As if in aging, a photograph acquires rings like a tree, rings of light upon a small table the way the pink lamp once illuminated tables, corners, shadows, whole quiet rooms.

53. Dream

OFTEN JOANNA IS blessed or cursed with the ability to remember her dreams in vivid full-colour detail. Sometimes she tells them to Gordon and Samuel at breakfast. Sometimes their eyes glaze over. But still she persists, trying to track down the tangents which shoot off from her dream images like sparklers, like synapses firing in all directions at once.

Sometimes the more she tries to make sense of a dream, the more details she remembers, details which may or may not be important—how can she know? She has read the dream interpretation books trying to find out. She has spent time contemplating the vocabulary of dreams, a language of pictures, looking for clues. She has wondered about the dreams of blind people. Do they too see pictures in their sleeping heads? And what about the dreams of deaf people? Are they silent like old movies? Could it be that in dreams the deaf may hear and the blind may finally see? She has deconstructed her dreams, both degenerate and divine. She has puzzled over dreams in which she herself does not appear, dreams in which she knows she is dreaming but cannot wake up, dreams in which she is someone she does not recognize, dreams in which she cannot see, hear, move, or speak. She has investigated the symbolism of dream bananas, dream lions, dream oceans, dream houses, dream mothers, dream lovers, dream death.

Sometimes the harder she tries to remember a dream, the faster it dissolves before her very eyes. As if dreams were like snowflakes, perfect, pointed, each one unique, but you must get very close to see them, and the closer you get, the more they are melting away under the hot onslaught of your own eager breath. By the time she gets to the break-fast table, all she has left is a tidbit or two: a set of railroad tracks, a plate of spaghetti, a brown dog tied to a tree, sunlight on a young woman's neck, the smell of apples, a tall man saying, "Stop it." By the time she gets to the breakfast table, she has forgotten how to speak the language of dreams.

What if all language was like this? The way sometimes you can look at a word you've seen a thousand times and suddenly it doesn't make sense, is just a scramble of letters flung across the page. This enormous gaping moment of meaninglessness, this black hole of language, lasts only a second and then the letters obligingly re-form themselves, the word reappears, and you can go on with your reading, your learning, your life. But what if it doesn't? What if you read a whole book and the words do not go into the folds of your brain the way they're sup-

posed to, but just dissolve one by one like dreams, amounting to nothing but a blank space, an empty cavity, an open wound? What if when
you close the book, you can't remember a single word? And when you
open it again later, what if all the pages have gone blank? What if the
next time you are searching for a word, you never find it?

No matter how she tries to tell her dreams, she has only language
to work with, that inadequate, inexact, iridescent vehicle upon which
we must hang all of our lives, past, present, and future, sleeping, waking, and otherwise.

54. Yellow

THE COLOUR OF your mother's apron from the time when all mothers
wear aprons all day in the kitchen and she wipes her wet hands on
them before holding out her arms to you when you get home from
school at four o'clock.

No.

Your mother's apron is always white with embroidery around the
band and the bottom, purple grapes, blue teapots, red apples, or giant
black musical notes, and although she wears it all day in the kitchen,
she does not wipe her wet hands on it before embracing you. Instead
she wipes them on a dishtowel because she does not want to muck up
her pretty apron and sometimes she does not even say hello.

The colour of a coward's belly, the belly of your lover who will never
leave his wife no matter what happens or doesn't. No matter what
happens next.

No.

Your lover's belly is a rich creamy brown, like coffee with lots of
milk. Or it is golden, glistening, burnt sienna or umber, and hard.
Even in the wintertime his belly looks suntanned and oiled. When you
kiss it, your lover's belly is always warm. When you lick it, it always
tastes salty, as if he is so potent there is sperm oozing out of all his

pores. He may be potent but you are not and you know now that, no matter what you do, he will never leave his wife because he is convinced that if he does, she will die. You know now that when his wife licks his belly, it is also salty and warm and perhaps this is what he thinks keeps her alive.

The colour of the sun, a round yellow ball in the upper right-hand corner of all children's paintings. The trees are green, the sky is blue, the house is white, and the cat in the window is black.

No.

In your son's paintings, the sun is just as likely to be purple, pink, or an empty circle. The sky is blue, yes, but the trees are orange, red, and yellow because it is fall, he says, the house is brown because your house is brown, and the cat in the window is white. When you casually mention about the sun usually being yellow, he says, "No, it's not. Look." And of course he is right. The sun is not yellow. Most of the time the sun is no colour at all. The sun is a hole in the sky. You should not look directly at the sun. You have told him this many times. You have also told him that he can paint things however he sees them, however he likes. He says, "I can do it however I want."

Yellow. The colour of memory.

No.

The colour of everything you have forgotten. By accident or on purpose.

55. Bread

ESTHER THOUGHT BAKING bread was a waste of time. "Baking your own bread," she often said, "is backward. I just don't understand it in this day and age." This attitude also applied to making your own pie crust, squeezing your own oranges for juice, and when she saw on TV the inspirational little story of a woman who made her own soap, she fairly hooted with derision. "The next thing you know," she said, "that woman will be washing her clothes on a rock in the river and riding a horse to the grocery store." As if all such retro-domesticity were the province of primitive fools who preferred to do things the hard way. Who in their right mind would suffer through these trials of their own free will? Who in their right mind would go to all that trouble of kneading and rising and kneading the bread dough again and again, all day long, when they could have the bread already made, tasty, sliced, white, fresh enough, and delivered to the door three times a week before breakfast no less?

"I," Esther often proclaimed proudly, "have never baked bread in my life and do not intend to start." Joanna suspected that her mother must have baked bread when she was younger, living on the farm. But Esther never talked about those times. It was as if she had had two lives, this life and that life. The dividing line was never clear but certainly, in *this* life, she had never baked bread. She believed in the breadman who, along with the milkman and the mailman, formed the triumvirate of home-delivery demigods which kept modern life in motion.

As predictable as the appearance of these men at the door on their appointed rounds was Esther's appearance at Joanna's bedroom door whenever she had gone in there to read, to think, to work on her art, or just to have some modicum of privacy. Esther eyed the need to be alone with great suspicion and could always find an excuse to barge in. Then she would stand in the doorway and survey the room, searching for signs of aberrant behaviour. Then she would lean towards the desk where Joanna was usually seated, now curling her arm protectively around the page in front of her.

One of the first collages Joanna ever made at this desk began with a drawing in oil pastels of the kitchen table set for supper: pork chops and peas on three brown plaid plates on the yellow plastic placemats on the blue tabletop. Poised on either side of the middle plate was a pair of hands clutching the cutlery like spears. These hands, male hands, were not attached to arms. They ended at the wrists. On this plate beside the pork chops and peas was a small photograph of a naked woman which Joanna had secretly cut from one of Clarence's dirty magazines. The woman's body was twisted to the point of contortion so that both her breasts and her bum faced the camera. Perhaps she was double-jointed at the waist, like a department store mannequin who could be manipulated into all manner of acrobatic erotic postures. Below the drawing, in letters cut from newspapers and magazines, were the words: *Man cannot live by bread alone.*

Even then Joanna knew that she could never explain the picture or the message or any other important part of herself to her mother.

Living on her own, Joanna learned by trial and error (as most edifying things must be learned) how to bake her own bread. The cookbook she worked from explained every step in detail with diagrams and also informed her that the etymology of the word *lady* can be traced back to the Old English meaning *loaf-kneader.* All that kneading and rising and kneading the bread dough again really could take all day and she loved it. With the fragrant dough warm and malleable, alive in her hands, she felt comforted and connected to an unbroken stream of women throughout history. She thought about bread while she baked it. She thought about breaking bread, casting bread upon the waters. She thought about Communion bread and wine, the Body and Blood of Jesus served up to stalwart Sunday morning believers. She thought about the miracle of the loaves and fishes. She thought about the staff of life. She thought about Murphy's Law and how the bread never falls but on the buttered side.

By the time the bread was ready to come out of the oven, she felt cleansed and creative. She also thought smugly of Esther, as if her bread-baking were yet another form of adolescent rebellion. The apartment around her smelled wholesome, yeasty, and safe. She took a warm loaf to the landlady upstairs.

Even after Esther has died (or especially after Esther has died), Joanna thinks about her while she bakes bread. She imagines her looking down from heaven (if indeed there is such a place, if indeed her mother has gone there), shaking her head and clucking her tongue. Sometimes she has long silent conversations with her dead mother, in which she explains why she likes to bake bread, how it makes her feel. She also tells her about preservatives, whole wheat, fibre, as if she cannot help feeling that still she must justify herself to her mother. She always suspected that Esther, in life, would have liked to be omniscient. She assumes that now, in death, she probably is.

When Clarence comes to visit, she bakes him half a dozen loaves of whole-wheat bread one snowy December afternoon. He devours a whole warm loaf with lots of butter. "Remember," he asks, "when they used to deliver bread, milk too, in the morning to our house? Remember? Now that was good bread."

56. Justice

"IT'S JUST NOT fair," Joanna said.

"No, it's not," Lewis said. "There's no excuse for the way life is."

"But justice," Joanna said. "What about justice?"

"What about it?" Lewis did not say, but held her instead. They were in her bed and there was the sound of a soft rain on the window. It was midnight, one of the few times they were able to be together after dark, Wanda having gone out for the evening with friends. Lewis did not say which friends, where, and Joanna did not ask. But now he had to go home soon, now he couldn't stay much longer, now he held Joanna in his arms until she fell asleep and then he got up and fished around on the floor for his clothes.

But Joanna was only pretending to be asleep. She listened to him padding to the bathroom, turning on the shower for a quick rinse, brushing his teeth, then putting on his jacket and boots in the back porch, patting his pockets till his keys jingled, sighing and shutting the door softly behind him. Wanda would be none the wiser. And neither, thought Joanna, would he. When he called the next morning she would tell him that yes, she'd been sound asleep, no, she hadn't heard a thing. He'd told her once that he couldn't bear to think of her lying there awake, alone, while he went home and climbed into bed with his wife. He said he couldn't bear it. He said it wasn't fair. He also said there was no such thing as justice, poetic or otherwise.

All's fair in love and war. That's what Esther had told her often enough. Which was, Joanna realized now, a good enough excuse when you were the one in the wrong. It provided a handy general justification for your own bad behaviour and any subsequent pangs of guilt which might crop up. She suspected it was of little consolation when you were the one who'd been wronged. Certainly, when Wanda finally discovered the truth about Lewis's infidelity, she was unlikely to sit back and say, "Oh well, you know what they say: All's fair in love and war!"

Joanna did not know nearly as much about war as she did about love. But she did know there was a lot more to it than what she'd seen in her father's photographs of statues, churches, and children. She knew there were also battlefields. She knew that by participating in either of these past-times, being in love or at war, you were placing yourself in mortal danger. No matter what happened, you had to take sides.

57. Boy

boy *n.* 1. a male child to the age of physical maturity; youth; lad. 2. a man regarded as common, lowly, immature, or callow. 3. a young man; fellow; a familiar form of address. 4. a male servant; an underling; a patronizing term used esp. by Caucasians to non-whites. 5. a messenger; a helper. 6. a son. *See also* BOYFRIEND, BOYHOOD, BOYISH, BOY SCOUT, OH BOY.

58. Light

ON SEPTEMBER 21, 1986, at exactly 12:36 P.M., Samuel says his first word. (His first word, that is, after "Mama" and "Dada" which he has been saying since he was seven months old. His first *real* word you might say, as if "Mama" and "Dada" didn't really count for much.) On September 21, 1986, at exactly 12:36 P.M., Samuel says, "Light."

light *n.* 1. the form of electromagnetic radiation having a wavelength between about 400 and 750 nanometers which acts upon the eye, making sight possible: this energy is transmitted at a velocity of about 300,000 km per second.

Joanna has just changed his diaper. Having outgrown the change table, he is lying on her bed with a plastic change pad under him. Above the bed is a hanging lamp with a white wicker shade. It is a cloudy day and the lamp is on, slightly swinging. He points to it and says, "Light."

light *n.* 2. the rate of flow of light radiation with respect to the sense of sight: it is measured in *lumens.* 3. a source of illumination. 4. the natural agent which emanates from the sun; daylight.

He says it again. By way of encouragement, Joanna repeats it too. Out of sheer delight, she claps her hands. Samuel claps his hands too and says it again. Clapping their hands and laughing, they bat the word back and forth between them as if it were an illuminated ball.

Let other children, Joanna thinks, take the linguistic plunge with simple primary words: duck milk dog juice bunny baby kitty hat fish foot. Of course there is nothing intrinsically wrong with these words or the charming average children who say them. She does not mean to be judgemental. It's just that she has always known Samuel was special. She realizes that all new parents think their children are special. But this is different. She is right. He *is* special. Now she has the proof.

And God said, "Let there be light"; and there was light. And God saw that the light was good.

Samuel is no doubt destined for greatness.

light *n.* 5. mental illumination; knowledge; elucidation; enlightenment. 6. religious or spiritual illumination. 7. one whose brilliant record makes him a shining example for others. *See also* LIGHT-FOOTED, LIGHT-HEARTED, LIGHTSOME, LIGHT-YEAR.

What if, she wonders briefly, your child's first word was: shit fuck asshole hate damn die? She doesn't know what her own first word was. Is it that she asked her mother and Esther couldn't remember? Or is it (more likely) that she never thought to ask until now? Now that she is a mother herself, now that it is too late.

She gets the camera and takes several shots of Samuel flat on his back on the change pad. He is not saying "light" any more but it is as if the word were still hanging in the air above him, a cartoon word floating in a bubble near his head.

This photograph will go into the album along with all the other firsts she has faithfully recorded in the past fourteen months. Five, ten, fifteen, twenty years from now when she hauls out the album, people will assume that this is just another cute picture of Samuel smiling and waving his arms around. She will have to explain. How can you photograph language anyway? Perhaps the word *will* appear after all: a slight blur above his left ear, like a fingerprint on the negative or a revealing smudge on an X-ray which only she, like a trained doctor, will be able to interpret.

She has forgotten for now the warning another mother once gave her: "Don't be in a hurry for him to do things. Once he starts talking, he'll never shut up. Once he starts walking, you'll never catch him."

They are a long way yet from the day when Samuel has talked nonstop about nothing for an hour and Joanna says, "Boy, you talk a lot sometimes. You're just saying the same things over and over again. I think you're in love with the sound of your own voice."

Samuel thinks about this for a minute. Then he says, "Yes, I am."

They are a long way yet from the day when Samuel (frustrated with Clarence whose hearing is failing so he cannot catch half of what Samuel is saying but he will not admit he needs a hearing aid) says, "What's the matter with you, Grandpa? Are you death?" Joanna tries to explain the difference between *death* and *deaf*. Unconvinced, Samuel says, "It sounds the same to me."

For now Joanna does not have to contemplate the fact that this first word is just the beginning. Just the beginning of all the history ahead of him as he grows up and away from her, forward, ever forward, flowing or hurtling past her and beyond, out of reach and still running, still shining bright.

light-year *n. Astronomy,* the distance that light travels in a vacuum in one year, approximately 9,460,500,000,000 km.

59. Health

IN THOSE DAYS, at the end of elementary school, *Health* was a euphemism for Sex Education. They had this class once a week, on Friday afternoons. They gathered in a small classroom in the basement, boys and girls together but ignoring each other. Often they watched films with the floor-to-ceiling drapes drawn like blackout curtains. They sat in the dark giggling and jiggling with the sense of momentous secrets about to be revealed. The boys in the back made kissing and slurping sounds until the teacher came in.

She was a young woman named Miss Berglund who wore suede miniskirts, knee-high leather boots, and gauzy embroidered cotton blouses. She also taught Art to the younger children. She was a hippie and the frequent subject of school-yard gossip. She was said to be living in sin. She was said to be braless under those blouses. Or she was said to be a drug addict, which was the real reason why she always wore long sleeves—so the needle marks wouldn't show. She was several times said to be pregnant. When she once missed a full week of school she was said to be having a nervous breakdown, an overdose, an abortion. (A girl with a wild older sister contributed this last suggestion, and although most of the other girls had little idea what an abortion might actually be, they readily spread the rumour around.)

Some of the things they knew about Miss Berglund were actually true. Her first name was Deborah, hardly an unusual or incriminating name save for the fact that teachers were not really supposed to have first names like other people. She smoked cigarettes in the staff room during lunch and recess. They could smell it in her long brown hair, the smoke mixed with the smell of shampoo, as she brushed close to their desks on the way to the front of the room.

Almost everything they learned in Health class had to do with the respective reproductive systems. As if there were no other parts of the human body that were likely to go wrong or give you trouble. The posters which Miss Berglund frequently tapped with her pointer were life-size drawings of the male and female body. Only the genitalia and the internal reproductive organs were shown in full-colour detail inside these silhouettes. On the female the breasts were also filled in, the mammary glands behind the nipples like small pieces of broccoli. All other parts of these bodies were blank, including the heads. Miss Berglund carefully pointed out the various sexual organs which she called "genitals." This word made Joanna nervous, mixing up in her mind with other similar words: "genial," "gentle," "gentile." Miss Berglund said the names aloud, simply, quietly, as if they were just ordinary commonplace words. As if "penis," "scrotum," and "testicle," "vulva," "vagina," and "uterus" were household names, like "refrigerator," "elbow," or "spatula."

Despite her unconventional appearance and possibly immoral lifestyle, Miss Berglund taught Health very much in the conventional manner. To explain how a woman became pregnant, she said, "The man's sperm is introduced into the woman's vagina." What kind of an introduction was this? Hello. Hello. Pleased to meet you. Likewise, I'm sure.

Miss Berglund did not explain how this feat was specifically accomplished. She did not say, "The man sticks his penis inside the woman and wiggles it around until it explodes." What little information they were given was spotty and euphemistic, as if they were supposed to guess the rest. Which, of course, some of them did: the girls who got pregnant and left school, the boys who got crabs or worse and bragged about it. She did say that you should only have sex with a person you truly loved. She implied that there would only be one such person in a lifetime, one of a kind, one in a million. She did not say how you could tell if it was really love or what would happen if, whether by accident or on purpose, you had sex with a person you did not love. Perhaps you would be punished. Perhaps you would get pregnant or crabs or worse. *Worse* meant a venereal disease.

venereal *adj.* 1. having to do with sexual desire or intercourse. 2. of a disease transmitted by sexual intercourse [syphilis and gonorrhea are *venereal* diseases]. 3. *Astrology,* born under or influenced by the planet Venus.

Joanna remembered Reverend Doak at church trying to explain the difference between venial and mortal sins.

venial *adj.* 1. that may be forgiven or pardoned. 2. that may be overlooked; excusable. 3. *Theology,* a sin committed without full consent or knowledge of its seriousness and hence not totally depriving the soul of sanctifying grace; distinguished from MORTAL.

Although the tone of Miss Berglund's voice would imply that contracting a venereal disease was a shameful fate worse than death, perhaps she was mistaken. Perhaps it was nobody's fault, perhaps it was excusable, merely a venial sin.

"Finally," Miss Berglund said, with satisfaction in her voice, "after its long journey, the sperm is united with the egg." This reminded Joanna of those front-page newspaper stories where long-lost siblings, who had been separated by unfortunate circumstances at birth or in early childhood and had then lived the next sixty years entirely oblivious to each other on separate continents, were reunited now after an arduous transoceanic flight. In the newspaper photographs they were wizened and stooped, weeping into each other's arms at the airport, or they were seated side by side sipping tea in one or the other's living room, having just discovered that they had given their respective children the same names and they both enjoyed gardening. Sometimes the reunited pair was not long-lost siblings but childhood sweethearts who had lost track of each other after high school. Although they never stopped loving each other in the backs of their minds, they had both been happily married to other people for the past forty years. Now both their partners had died and they were back together, about to live happily ever after what little time they had left.

After elementary school, Joanna never saw Miss Berglund again. It was said that she had left the city. The likely reasons for this defection ran rampant for a while. It was said that she had been fired and was now a prostitute in Toronto (that evil city). Or she had run away with a rock-and-roll band. Or she was in jail, a home for unwed mothers, or a hippie commune run by an evil charismatic psychokiller. By the time the truth filtered through (Miss Berglund had not left town at all but had quit teaching to marry a dentist and they now lived in suburbia where they were putting up a picket fence, planting a garden, and expecting their first child who would be born a respectable time after the wedding, which had taken place not in a field of daisies but in a regular church with a white gown, four bridesmaids, and a flower girl), Joanna and the other girls had lost interest. Not in sex, but in Miss Berglund anyway.

Over the years, Joanna had an average number of ailments involving the reproductive system. Most of them were minor. Her periods were painful. She had a prolapsed ovary. One year she suffered from a spate of yeast infections. She treated her condition with a variety of prescription medications in both tablet and suppository form. She douched with plain yogurt. Finally she replaced all her nylon underwear with cotton and was cured. Once she had a terrifying lump in her left breast which turned out to be a false alarm. Most of her health worries had to do with birth control. The pill was unhealthy and dangerous. The IUD hurt. Men did not like condoms. Foam was too messy. She settled on a diaphragm which she practised placing properly. She had a well-thumbed copy of *Our Bodies, Ourselves*. As the book suggested, she looked at her own genitalia with a hand mirror. She reached up her vagina and located her cervix which did indeed feel like the end of somebody's nose.

Sometimes she enjoyed the mystery of the female reproductive system, a labyrinth of ligaments, tubes, and pouches, pockets of power tucked up inside her. They were private, invisible, self-contained, and could not betray or embarrass a woman the way the male organ could. Even the word *organ* struck her as peculiarly male: a flamboyant instrument for public performance, large, loud, and unpredictable.

Other times, when she had a vague pain in her abdomen or a mysterious discharge, she resented this arrangement. Men, she thought then, had it easy, with their parts all hanging out in front. They could always see if something was wrong. For a woman, there could be something festering away inside for years and she would never even know until it began to leak. Like her mother who had not suspected she had cancer until she went to the doctor and he said she needed a hysterectomy.

Joanna genuinely enjoys being pregnant with Samuel. She can honestly say that she has never felt healthier in her life. She does not suffer from morning sickness, heartburn, hemorrhoids, or backache. Although she gains nearly forty pounds, she does not feel encumbered. Although two months before her due date she already looks like she is about to give birth any minute and strangers on the street ask if she's having twins, she does not feel grotesque.

Occasionally she thinks about Health class. She feels just like that poster of the female body Miss Berglund used to point to: as if only her breasts and the marvellous contents of her abdomen are filled in in full-colour detail while all other parts of her anatomy are blank white space, smooth and shiny, including her head. Now she knows all the pieces of the puzzle Miss Berglund neglected to mention.

In prenatal class too they seem to be doling out bits of information and she must guess the rest. They say that labour pain is not like other pain. They say that afterwards she will forget all about it. She thinks this is highly unlikely. They concentrate on the actual event of giving birth. They do not say much about being a mother. This reminds Joanna of hopeful eager young brides who focus all their attention on the wedding day itself and never seem to spare much thought for all that may come after.

Two months before Samuel is born, Joanna has a dream about Miss Berglund, in which her former teacher is now a gynecologist. Her office is set up outdoors in a large field of daisies. She performs examinations beneath a large blue tarpaulin. Joanna, the pregnant patient, is lying on the metal table with her feet in the stirrups. The mound of her belly is so big she can barely see around it. Miss Berglund is wearing yellow rubber gloves. She says she has twelve children of her own now. Joanna says, "Wow! You must be very fertile!"

"Yes," Miss Berglund says proudly. "Yes, I am. Look." She lifts up her white doctor coat. Underneath she is naked and there is grass growing out of her thighs.

60. Bible

WHEN JOANNA WAS nine years old, she received a Bible for perfect attendance at the Moseby United Church Sunday School. It was black of course, the tissue-thin paper edged with red, and the words HOLY BIBLE WITH HELPS: REVISED STANDARD VERSION embossed on the spine in gold. Inside there were a dozen or more full-colour pictures of significant religious figures and events: *Jesus and the Children, Lot's Choice, Ecce Homo (Behold the Man)*. At the back were thirty pages of Bible Study Helps, including maps such as *Israel and Judah in the Time of Ahab and Jehoshaphat, The Missionary Journeys of Paul,* and *Egypt, Sinai, Canaan: The Exodus from Egypt*. On this last map the suggested route of the Hebrews was drawn in a red line with little arrows all along it. Inside the front cover there was a gold bookplate with Joanna's name on it, signed *Reverend Charles Doak, Minister*. Esther had carefully written in the date below: *September 1963*.

Joanna was very proud of this Bible. It was, she figured, her just reward for all those months (winter, summer, dry, wet) of walking the six blocks alone to Moseby United Church while her parents stayed in bed. All those months of walking back home again chewing on the church program which always caused Esther to worry that she was missing some essential vitamin or mineral from her diet and it was this nutritional lack which gave her the urge to eat paper. The truth was she liked the taste of it.

Joanna kept her Bible beside her bed. Often she patted it or kissed it before she went to sleep. What she liked best about it was the smell and the black ribbon bookmark glued right into the binding which she thought was very sophisticated and elegant.

Two months after Joanna got her Bible, President Kennedy was shot to death in Dallas. Much later she will remember that she first heard the news of the assassination in Woolworth's downtown. Esther was buying Christmas gifts and Joanna was trailing her up and down the aisles, bored and overheated in her winter clothes. She will remember pretending to look through the costume jewellery, the pastel nylon panties, the packages of stamps for collectors. She knew she wouldn't be able to convince Esther to buy her anything so she didn't even try. She will remember standing for a long time in front of the fish tanks at the back where there was a goldfish that had grown to the size of a trout. She thought it must be a hundred years old. She will remember that as the news came over the store's loudspeaker she was whining and wanting to sit down at the lunch counter for a double Coke float. She will remember that everyone and everything stopped. Then started up again a few minutes later. She will remember staring at the horrible look on her mother's face and then they did go to the lunch counter where everyone was talking at once and one woman was crying out loud while eating a piece of cherry pie. She will remember thinking as she stepped back into the street afterwards that everything looked the same but was not.

Much later she will question this memory. Everybody of her generation has a memory of this day, November 22, 1963. It is a question they still ask each other twenty or more years later, by which time President Kennedy has become familiarly known by his initials. "Where were you when JFK was shot?" It was a landmark in all of their lives. It was also history in the making, something their future children would study in school. At the time, of course, they did not think of it that way.

Everybody else remembered being at school when the news came. It was a Friday afternoon. Why was Joanna at Woolworth's? Maybe she wasn't at Woolworth's. Maybe she has made the whole thing up. Why would she manufacture such a story? If it isn't true, why does she remember so clearly the hundred-year-old goldfish, the look on her mother's face, and the woman crying over her pie? Why does she remember not much enjoying her double Coke float, staring instead behind the counter at the milk shake machine, the glass case filled with half-eaten pies, and the yellowed photographs of a hamburger, an egg salad sandwich, and a chocolate parfait with whipped cream and two maraschino cherries on top? She does not remember if she and her mother were talking or silent, then or on the bus home later. She knows they were not crying. She would have remembered that.

Nineteen sixty-three was also the year Joanna first got glasses. She had been having trouble seeing the blackboard at school and they had discovered she was myopic. So maybe she had been to the eye doctor that day. But then wouldn't she remember stumbling around Woolworth's with her pupils still dilated from those horrible drops that took all day to wear off? Perhaps that would explain why she remembers feeling like she was going to throw up, fall down, or stop breathing altogether. Perhaps it was the eye drops that had made her feel that way. But if she'd had the drops that day, she wouldn't have even been able to see those pictures behind the counter. But maybe she was remembering them from another day, an ordinary day at Woolworth's when nothing special happened. Maybe she was remembering them from another day and sticking them on to *this* day, November 22, 1963. Some memories were like that: bits and pieces pulled from different places, different times, grafted one on to another so seamlessly that you could never know any more what had really happened and perhaps it didn't matter or perhaps you didn't want to know.

What if, by sheer coincidence, that had been the day she actually got her glasses? Wouldn't she then be able to remember seeing the whole world clearly for the first time in a long time?

Although she is not religious, Joanna has moved the Sunday School Bible around with her for all these years. She has always intended to read it straight through. She has just been waiting to find herself in the right frame of mind, a frame of mind, she figures, which should be simultaneously lofty, studious, and ready to be swept away.

The Bible sits now on a shelf in the living room with several other seldom-opened volumes. She dusts it along with *War and Peace, Gray's Anatomy,* and *Remembrance of Things Past* in a handsome three-volume boxed set. In fact the only time these books are ever opened is when she is dusting. Bored and distracted, sometimes she flips through them for a minute or two.

She discovers several passages underlined in her Bible, blue ballpoint obviously drawn with a ruler under verses in both the Old and New Testaments. She had marked verses 7 and 8 of the Fifty-first Psalm: *Purge me with hyssop, and I shall be clean;/wash me, and I shall be whiter than snow./ Fill me with joy and gladness;/let the bones which thou hast broken rejoice.*

She had not only underlined Ephesians 6, verse 8, but had also drawn a light bulb in red ink in the margin beside it: *Knowing that whatever good any one does, he will receive the same again from the Lord.*

She cannot remember when or why she might have marked these passages. She is not sure what hyssop is and she has never had any broken bones. She does not remember ever being completely convinced that doing good would necessarily be repaid in kind, by the Lord or anyone else. She cannot remember what great idea this verse might have ignited in her mind. Had she been temporarily possessed by the urge to do good works? Had she indeed done them? When had she stopped? Why? When, for that matter, had she stopped patting and kissing her Bible and put it up on the shelf like any other book? When had the Bible become one of these books she never looks at but cannot give away either?

61. Memory

JOANNA THINKS A lot about memory. She reads about it too, articles by experts who seem utterly certain that memory is a brain function. They talk about engram trails which are memory-traces, supposedly permanent changes in the brain which account for the existence of memory. Like the grooves perhaps on a record album which, when the correct apparatus (turntable, needle, amplifier, speakers) is applied, will produce music. Perhaps this could also account for those songs that get stuck in your head. Or perhaps engram trails are like those lacy silver slug trails on the sidewalk in the morning. Probably they are more intricate than that. A doctor cutting open a brain in search of memory might find a complex configuration like that left on tree trunks which have been inhabited by termites. Loops and lines, channels and rivers, intersecting, overlapping, diverging, converging, veering off, circling back, a map to the center of the universe or the meaning of life.

But what about those memories which occur in other parts of the body? The picture Joanna has of her mother may well reside in her head, but the rest of it (the anger, the bitterness, the longing, the fear) could be lodged anywhere. What about those memories which are a lump in your throat, a vacuum in your lungs, a knot in your stomach, a cramp in your shoulder, your hipbone, your heart? What is the geography of memory? What is the difference between geography and anatomy? What if the last map is the heart?

Memory moves past the body too. Memory is that vast surreal territory in which all perspective is lost, a kaleidoscopic shifting plain upon which a tree may be larger than a mountain and a cloud may swallow the sky. Memory is also a microscope, a telescope, a magnifying glass which trained on one spot too long will cause an eruption of flame, fury, joy, or desire. Examining the contents of her own memory, Joanna finds disorder verging on chaos. And yet memory, she suspects, may well be the only vessel in which this disorder can be contained.

If all language is life in translation, then all memory is a conjugation of the past. Like learning the verb *to be* in French. All pasts are compound and conditional. Also imperfect and subjunctive. All pasts are imperative.

Memory is neither cause nor effect. Memory is both cause and effect. Once the paperboy was delivering in a thunderstorm. Just as he put the newspaper in the door, there was an audible strike of lightning to the west. For a long time Samuel was convinced that the paperboy had

made it lightning. For a long time Joanna believed that you could not
remember what had never happened. That you could not forget what
you never knew. Now she is not so sure. Samuel still has trouble with
the difference between *because* and *why*.

All memory is revisionist. All language is apocryphal. All memory
is collective, the sum of all your selves. All language is learned and all
the stories you tell yourself are hazarding a guess.

The antonym of memory is oblivion.

The anodyne of memory is oblivion.

The antidote to oblivion is memory.

62. Sheep

DRIVING THROUGH THE countryside on a Sunday afternoon, they pass
a flock of sheep grazing in a green field. The sheep are white. Their
feet and faces are black. Samuel in the back seat sings his version of
the nursery rhyme he has learned at day care: *Blah, blah, black sheep,/
Have you any wool?/Yes sir, yes sir,/Three bags full*. He goes on to recite
"Little Bo Peep" and "Mary Had a Little Lamb." Joanna throws in
"The Lord Is My Shepherd" and Gordon hums a few bars of "Waltzing
Matilda." Sheep lore. Wisely, they do not mention sheep to the slaughter, wolf in sheep's clothing, or the discomfort of feeling sheepish when
caught in some foolishness or petty larceny which no self-respecting
sheep would ever deign to consider.

Giggling, Samuel says, "Sheep sure are interesting, aren't they? But
what is this stuff in the song about wool?"

Joanna explains that wool comes from sheep. She describes the whole
process as far as she knows it. Samuel is at first skeptical and then
delighted with the idea. He presses his face to the window and says
he'll keep watching for more sheep, red sheep, blue sheep, green sheep.
Maybe he'll see a purple one like the sweater his grandpa gave him last
Christmas.

Gordon starts to explain about dyeing. Samuel is horrified. "Dying?"
he shrieks. "You mean they're dead? You mean they have to kill them?"

Joanna reassures him that no, they do not. There is *dying* and then there is *dyeing*—with an *e*. Samuel says that when it comes to dying, he will do it with an *e*. He would much rather turn purple, green, blue, or orange than go into a hole in the ground before he gets to heaven. He is pretty clear about heaven. He knows that good people go there after they die. His grandma has gone there. Joanna is not especially clear about heaven or the odds of Esther having gone there. But she, like most parents, finds herself calling up the notion of heaven in her attempts to explain death to a four-year-old.

It is easier, she has discovered, to convince a small child that people (pets too, although they have their own special section of heaven) go to a happy new home in the sky after they die than it is to tell him they just disappear, stop, cease to exist, expire, end, end, end. Null and void. Annihilated. Erased. She has not mentioned the antithetic apparition of hell because Samuel has expressed no curiosity as to where bad people go after they die. It seems that discussions of the afterlife (or the lack thereof) are best handled in the same manner as the birds and the bees—tell the child only as much as he wants to know at the time. Do not offer too much information.

An imaginative child can conceive of heaven easily enough. Samuel likes to speculate as to its contents and conditions. In heaven, he says, dead people turn into angels and then they can have whatever they want. Heaven is like a giant department store filled with toys and treats, flowers and fruits, books and movies, gum. But there is no money in heaven. Everything is free. There is no such thing as bedtime or bath-time. There are no doctors, dentists, or barbers. Nobody in heaven ever gets cavities or fevers or upset stomachs and their hair does not grow. In heaven there are no monsters, no bugs, no thunderstorms, no night-mares, no tears, and no fear. Heaven is a little crowded but there is always somebody to play with. In heaven nobody ever gets yelled at or sent to their room. In heaven nobody gets mad and nobody ever makes mistakes.

But oblivion is such an abstraction that even an imaginative child cannot imagine it. Perhaps oblivion is hell.

Samuel would also like to know where he was before he was born.

When he looks at the old photographs of Joanna when she was a child, a baby, even younger than he is now, he asks, "But where was I?"

"You weren't born yet," she says.

"But where *was* I?" he persists. He wants to know if he was in the kitchen, the backyard, was he at Grandpa's house, was he at day care, was he sleeping in the other room? He cannot conceive of a world which existed before he did.

After their Sunday drive in the country, they go home and have supper. After supper, they curl up and watch a little TV. Gordon clicks maddeningly through all the channels two or three times, muttering, as he always does, about the fact that even with all these channels, there's nothing on worth watching. Joanna grabs the clicker and finally they settle on a program about guardian angels.

There is the story of a woman travelling with her young daughter through an uninhabited desert-like portion of the American country-side. There are no towns, no traffic, just an unending hot road through nothingness. The young daughter's appendix is about to burst. The car breaks down. The daughter is delirious. The mother is desperate. Suddenly an old blue pick-up truck materializes out of nowhere and pulls onto the shoulder behind them. An elderly couple gets out of the truck. While the old man fixes the car, the old woman calms the little girl and strokes her forehead until she falls asleep. Then they get back in their truck. The mother drives away. When she looks in her rearview mirror, the truck is gone. She gets her daughter to the hospital just in time and the doctor saves her life. On the wall in the waiting room where the mother sits, there is an old photograph of the very same couple who rescued them. Below the picture is a brass plaque which says the couple left all their money to the hospital when they died in 1958. It is now 1989. They have been dead for more than thirty years.

There are more stories about guardian angels. Samuel is confused and a little worried about the fact that these angels would seem to be ghosts. Joanna tries to explain by saying that they are magical helpers from heaven.

Samuel says, "From heaven? Maybe my grandma could be ours." Joanna's eyes fill up with tears.

In the morning at breakfast Samuel asks, "Did you dream about them?"

"Who?" asks Joanna. She is only half-listening while she scrambles the eggs and puts the bread in the toaster.

Gordon is just coming out of the shower. "Did we dream about who?" he asks.

"Those angels," Samuel says impatiently. "Did you dream about those garden angels?"

63. Bath

WHEN JOANNA WAS trying to get over Lewis, she spent a lot of time in the bathtub. Three or four times a day she would fill the tub with steaming hot water right up to the overflow. As the water flowed into and out of the tub all day long, she was glad her rent included utilities. She felt only marginally guilty at the prospect of her nice landlady getting the bill. She would strip quickly, avoiding the sight of herself naked in the full-length mirror on the back of the door. She did not feel attractive or desirable. She could not see her naked body without also seeing Lewis admiring it, caressing it, kissing it, licking it, fucking it with all his might.

The sight of her own unused thighs, untouched shoulders, utterly abandoned breasts might send her over the edge, hurtling down into a crevasse of despair, where she might remain forever, irrecoverable, un-recognizable, rent. All her life she had been led to believe that love, true love, was an end in itself, an unequivocal accomplishment after the attainment of which everything else would take care of itself. Now she might have to face the fact that their great love had been a pointless exercise in destruction.

Immersed to her chin in water so hot it nearly hurt, she felt calmer, cleaner, rosy, soothed. She imagined all the anger, the hatred, the hurt, and the heartbreak being lifted from her body by the hot water as if she were in a sauna sweating the dirt out of her pores, all the toxins and tensions being sucked out of her until she was dizzily reborn into the steam. Silently she chanted, *Lewis, I love you. Lewis, I do truly love you. Lewis, I still love you. But Lewis, can't you see how much I love you?* Eventually she realized that these incantations were not breaking the spell but fortifying and prolonging it. So then she started thinking, *Lewis, I don't love you. Lewis, I don't love you. Lewis, I don't love you any more.* And for the time she lay sunk in the water at least, it might well have been true.

If she had been allowed to talk to Lewis, she would have told him this. But she was not allowed to talk to Lewis. The marriage counsellor Wanda was taking him to twice a week had decreed that in order to save his marriage he must sever all contact with Joanna—no meetings, no calls, no letters, no nothing. Before the counsellor said this, though, they were still talking on the phone sometimes. In fact, Lewis had insisted that Joanna should feel free to call him whenever she wanted to. He said he knew how hard this was for her. Usually these calls went on for a very long time until either Joanna slammed the receiver down in his stupid ear or else Wanda arrived home from work or else, if she'd been there all along, got fed up and started vacuuming or yelling in the background.

But usually they started out all right, these phone calls, with Joanna wanting to talk to Lewis not because she was upset but because she wanted to show him she wasn't upset. They talked calmly at first, reassuring each other, speaking in soft sad voices, a bit breathless but coolly articulate, reasonable, clement, politely philosophical. Then Lewis would start talking the new language he was learning from the counsellor. He would go on about how the worst part of it had been the lying. Depending on what level of maturity Joanna had managed to muster at that moment, she was or was not compelled to point out that Wanda might not see it that way, that from Wanda's perspective maybe the fucking or the falling in love was the worst part.

He would go on about how Wanda had been disempowered by not knowing the truth. Whenever Joanna heard this new psychological word, she thought of *disembowelled* instead. She pictured Wanda eviscerated, the ropes of her intestines dangling from her open but bloodless abdomen and there beside her was Lewis on his knees, trying to make amends, trying to save his marriage, trying to gather her guts into his hands and shove them back in. Meanwhile, the counsellor stood by with pompoms, cheering.

The truth, he told her, was empowering, enabling, ennobling. It was he alone, she thought nastily, who felt ennobled. Wanda might well be finding the truth unbearable.

Ultimately, he said, the truth was liberating. "Ah yes," Joanna replied sarcastically, "the truth shall set you free." He, no doubt, had been liberated from some large portion of guilt, also from having to feel like a bastard all the time. Wanda had likely been liberated too, from an elaborate sequence of romantic delusions about love, loyalty, and the sanctity of marriage. And she, Joanna, had been liberated from *him,* whether she liked it or not.

Now Lewis was saying, "I will never lie to her again. The lies were horrible. The next time it happens I will not lie. The next time it happens I will tell her the truth."

Joanna hung up. *The next time.* She went into the bathroom and turned on the taps. *It happens.* Over the sound of the water she could not hear the telephone ringing. *The lies.* She stripped and sank into the water. *The truth.*

One evening she went so far as to fill the darkened bathroom with candles and classical music. She thought the ceremony would help but in fact it only gave her the creeps, as if she were a human sacrifice, a vestal virgin spread naked against the white porcelain in the flickering candlelight with the symphony swelling moodily towards its inevitable irrevocable climax: a heart eviscerated still throbbing, still dripping, perhaps her intestines too.

Occasionally she indulged herself in a bottle of expensive blue bubble bath. She even tried aromatherapy, adding to the bathwater a thick orange liquid which promised to work psychological wonders. The smell of oranges was so strong in the steamy little room that she was nauseated.

Usually she just squirted a bit of dish soap into the running water to make bubbles. This was what they'd always used at home, all three of them, Esther, Clarence, and Joanna, regularly cleansed with Sunlight.

Esther said it was all the same. Esther said they just put perfume in the bubble bath and charged twice as much. For years, they each bathed once a week. They did not have a shower because there were two cupboards and a window on the wall behind the bathtub. Joanna had hers on Sunday night. She looked forward to it. She liked it, playing, splashing, singing, except for the hair washing which was torture.

There was even a photograph in the album of Joanna in the bathtub when she was five. Her dark hair is curly and damp, her shoulders are thin, there is a rubber duck in the water and His and Hers towels hanging from the rack. She is grinning and holding a large snowball in her outstretched hands. Clarence had brought it in for her from outside where he was shovelling snow in the dark while Esther did the dishes in the warm kitchen with the radio on. After the picture was taken, Joanna held the snowball in her hands until it disappeared.

Later, when Joanna began to insist upon bathing and washing her hair every day, Esther complained that it was expensive and bad for her skin. Joanna argued that her hair only looked good when it was freshly washed. She did not mention that she was afraid she smelled. There was a girl at school who smelled. Like fish, the boys said, like she had a rotten fish between her legs. "What's for dinner?" the boys taunted when she walked past. "Fish, fish, we want fish."

Perhaps because Joanna had never acquired the habit of showering when she was young, she never did come to enjoy it. A shower first thing in the morning was too abrupt, too invasive, too violent. The spiky water took her breath away. The feel of it pummelling her sleepy shoulders made her want to sink to her knees and weep. It always made her remember a drunken university party during which an unhappy young woman had tried to drown herself in the shower on the fifth floor of the women's dorm. They were all laughing as they fished her out and fixed her another drink.

So while Joanna tried to get over Lewis, she soaked and soaked and soaked. But just as Esther had warned, all that water was bad for her skin which itched and flaked, especially on her shins which she scratched in her sleep till they bled. Especially in the middle of her back which she could not reach except with a plastic ruler that left long red scratches which, under another circumstance, could have been made by fingernails. As she scratched compulsively, she contemplated how your elasticity decreases with age. She was nearly thirty. It took much longer now to snap back. From hangovers, broken bones, colds, and the flu. Also emotional upset, broken hearts, and dry skin.

64. Cottage

GORDON AND JOANNA are spending the August long weekend at the cottage of another couple, Allan and Barb Bousquette. It was an un-expected invitation which Gordon had accepted eagerly—they needed a break but couldn't afford to go anywhere exotic. They are driving out in Allan's car Saturday afternoon, returning early Monday. Joanna is nervous about spending the whole weekend with people they hardly know. Gordon knows Allan from work. Allan is the sales rep for the company. Joanna has met them previously only at parties. In fact, it was at a party at Allan and Barb's house where she and Gordon first met two months before. Allan and Barb are a notoriously sociable pair who are always giving and going to parties, having people over for brunch or dinner, once an all-night video party featuring the films of Wim Wenders. They are always organizing evenings out for everyone. They pride themselves on having so many friends that their social cal-endar is booked solid for the next three months. Joanna suspects that the root of this convivial frenzy lies not so much in the fact that they are genuinely gregarious but, rather, in that they do not want to be alone together. They have no children or pets.

Joanna, who is not the outdoorsy type, hasn't been to a cottage for years, maybe only once or twice since that time in high school when she went to Stanley Evans' parents' cottage on Buck Lake with Thomas Hunt and his penis went soft in her hand. Back then, back there, such summer places were not called *cottages* at all. Instead, people said they were going to *camp,* no matter how lavish or expensive the place might actually be.

Allan and Barb's cottage is on Mud Lake, a good 1500 kilometres from Buck Lake, but it is just the same. There is the same musty odour when they first enter, the same dilapidated couch with rough upholstery the colour of dried blood, the same battered pots and pans, mismatched dishes, tarnished cutlery, the same braided rug in the main room, the same selection of board games (Monopoly, Clue, and Scrabble), and the same calibre of reading material (romance novels, murder mysteries, fly-fishing magazines, and last winter's *Sears Catalogue*). In the night, Joanna suspects, the mattress will be lumpy, the threadbare sheets will be clammy, and there will be sand at the bottom of the bed. There will be buzzing herds of homicidal mosquitoes and the scritching sounds of small animals in the ceiling.

These suspicions prove correct. As do her suspicions about the unhappy marriage of their hosts. All through the preparation of the Saturday night meal (barbecued hamburgers, potato salad with too much mayonnaise, a listless bowl of lettuce, tomatoes, and bean sprouts with bottled dressing), Barb directs herself exclusively to Joanna while Allan takes Gordon for a long stroll by the water and then, after lighting the barbecue, engages him in a rousing game of Scrabble laced with liberal amounts of Canadian Club. At dinner outside on the picnic table, Allan and Barb speak to each other only when necessary (pass the salt, the burgers, the buns). Afterwards, over coffee and more whisky, they get really relaxed, they open right up and start sniping, but still without addressing each other directly.

"Isn't he charming, scratching his balls like that?" says Barb.

"Isn't she pleasant with a mouth like that and those ugly yellow teeth?" says Allan.

"He never was much for manners."

"She never was much to look at."

"He never could get it up."

"She never did turn me on."

It seems that the buffer zone which Gordon and Joanna were supposed to create has, through no fault of their own, sprung a leak, several leaks, been punctured repeatedly, shot full of holes, like the ozone layer now, perforated and dribbling lethal ultraviolet rays indiscriminately over everything in sight. The way Allan and Barb look at each other

—or rather, the way they refuse to look at each other—makes Joanna's skin crawl. She hugs herself against their relentless vituperation.

Soon they abandon the coffeepot and bring the bottle of Canadian Club to the table. Both Joanna and Gordon drink too much whisky (what else can they do?) and then they go to bed early. They can hear Allan and Barb still going at it in the living room. The argument, if that's what it is, does not appear to be about anything in particular. Rather it is an unfocused ebullition of pure hatred, like projectile vomiting with words. What Joanna and Gordon can hear is a diffuse spewing of bad language, juvenile name-calling: "Whore cunt bastard prick motherfucker asshole cocksucker slut pig fuck off fuck you go fuck yourself nobody else ever will." Joanna remembers looking bad words up in the dictionary nearly twenty years ago with Penny and Pamela, snickering and swearing gleefully at each other. Joanna remembers that time at the other cottage, she and Thomas Hunt primly playing cribbage while Stanley and Louisa made out noisily in the bedroom, Stanley moaning, Louisa's shrill voice steadily rising until at the ultimate moment she hollered, "Fuck me, fuck me!" and Thomas Hunt blushed furiously while pegging twenty-nine.

When Joanna lost her virginity a year after that, she was very excited but she did not moan or yell bad words. She gave herself, as they say, quietly, to a young man named Michael Hill, a fellow university freshman. The whole thing was her idea. Michael would have been just as happy to stick to the heavy petting they had been perfecting for the previous three months but Joanna said she wanted to "do it." Michael said he was flattered to be "the one." He kindly put a green bath towel beneath her in case there was blood. They were in his tiny furnished basement room. The bathroom was across the hall.

It hurt but not too much. There was only a little blood. She didn't have an orgasm but then she hadn't expected to. She was not so much disappointed as relieved to have it over with. Afterwards they read in bed together and then they went out for Chinese food. They continued to date and sleep together for another six months, at which time Joanna broke it off because Michael was too serious, always phoning and following her around. He was hurt, of course, but he took it rather well.

He took it like a man. At least this is how her memory tells her the
story now. In fact, it might well have been messy, painful, and time-
consuming for all concerned.

Now in the bedroom she cuddles in closer to Gordon. Allan and
Barb are silent. In the middle of the night Joanna is awakened by the
sound of them making love with exuberance—as if the foul language
they had smeared each other with had been a form of linguistic foreplay,
a set of terms of endearment which had roused them to new heights of
passion.

Gordon and Joanna are at that blissful stage of their relationship
where she is one hundred per cent sure that they will *never* fight. They
are not living together yet, but are planning to. Not planning to exactly, but expecting to, cohabitation being the next logical step. For
the first month Joanna was always warning Gordon that she wanted to
go slowly. But now she is not so afraid and the future looks kind or,
anyway, she can look at it kindly. Love not being completely blind
(despite all rumours to the contrary), Joanna is realistic enough to fore-
see that they are bound to disagree eventually. She imagines an amiable,
rather amusing discussion as to who left the cap off the toothpaste tube,
after which they will make love and then laugh.

When they do have their first fight, a surprisingly short time later,
it is also surprisingly vehement, not the least bit amusing, a complete
blow-out over the fact that Gordon has arrived for dinner two hours
late. The crab quiche is tough, the salad has gone limp, and Joanna
has already drunk most of the expensive white wine. Even as she is
shrieking at him, Joanna remembers Allan and Barb at the cottage and
is stunned by despair at the thought that they too had probably once
imagined they would never fight. Suddenly she knows for a fact that everyone thinks that. This is a revelation she would rather not have had.

Gordon, perfectly reasonable, is asking, "Why are you getting hysterical over nothing?"

Joanna is yelling, "I am not hysterical, you bastard!" rushing at him
with her fists up, pounding wildly on his chest and wailing, "Bastard,
prick, you bastard, asshole, prick!"

Finally Gordon loses his patience with her. "It was an accident!" he cries. "A mistake! I'm sorry! I've said I was sorry! What more do you want from me? Blood?"

"Yes," Joanna says weakly. "Yes," Joanna whimpers. "Yes."

Afterwards they do make love but then they aren't laughing later. Later Gordon is snoring (since when did he start snoring?) and Joanna is lying awake beside him, replaying the stupid argument over and over and over in her head. Finally she puts the pillow over her head, trying to block out the disgusting noises coming from Gordon's mouth and nose (burbles, snorts, snuffles, and wet gurgles). Trying to shut up the still-angry voices inside her own head. No luck. She puts the pillow over his head instead and prays that he will suffocate or choke to death on his own saliva.

65. Swift

JOANNA HAS NEVER seen a swift. At least, not to her knowledge. She knows only the basics of birds: sparrows, starlings, sea gulls, crows. Canada geese, of course, when they fly north or south in the V. Two raucous blue jays who spend a lot of time in the big tree out front and sometimes the sound they make is like a squeaky old clothesline. Once she and Samuel saw a cardinal in the backyard. In Branding Park near her parents' house there used to be ravens, and after seeing Alfred Hitchcock's movie *The Birds*, she was afraid to walk through the park for fear of being attacked. Clarence says the ravens are gone now, he hasn't seen one for years.

Joanna wouldn't know a swift if she fell over one. Or if one flew right into her face. As if her face were like the picture window of her parents' house which birds flew into often: a thump, a few feathers stuck to the glass, a plump dead body still warm in the flower bed, so that Esther would go outside with her rubber gloves on and retrieve it, wrap it in toilet paper, and drop it into the garbage can out back. Birds, she said, were covered with germs. You must never touch them with your bare hands. Birds (beautiful, graceful, coasting on air currents) were, like many things, not to be trusted, not what they seemed, riddled with microbes of danger, invisible, deadly, unclean.

When Joanna hears the word "swift" she does not think of birds. She thinks of other words which echo in her head: *Savage. Ravage. Relentless. Revenge.*

She thinks of a line which may or may not be from a poem she read somewhere once: *Swift and savage, soothe the beast.* She imagines this line to be about love. It could be from a song. Swift, savage, stolen kisses, swollen hearts, swords, knives, mortal danger, sudden death. She thinks of that old proverb: The race is not to the swift, nor the battle to the strong.

66. Blue

THE COLOUR OF all safety and sleep, sinking down into soft blankets, praying for wisdom, strength, and peace of mind, praying for a dream filled with oceans and sky, no horizons, no worries, no fear, waking up with your thumb in your mouth as if you are a child again and your mother is waiting just around the corner with clean clothes, a hot breakfast, and a hug, humming.

The colour of all sadness and lost love which the old bluesmen have let loose from their saxophones, and you've got to live the blues to sing them but you are not musically inclined, you cannot even carry a tune, and you wonder if you could, where would you carry it to, and so you try keeping your own blue counsel until you feel yourself so full of it that you are surprised upon looking into the mirror to find your face still white. Perhaps you have been wallowing not in a tub of the blues but of bluing, and now you're simply whiter than white and you still cannot carry a tune.

The colour of the baby your mother had years before she had you, a blue baby born dead, a phenomenon which mystified you as a child and which, now that you are pregnant yourself, you worry about with a passion. You are also worrying about each aspirin you've taken, each glass of wine you've sipped, each cup of coffee you've gulped, each nutritious and delicious meal you've skipped, and every mean and nasty thought you've ever had for which now you may be punished. You consider the possibility of a baby with the blues so bad it couldn't breathe. You wonder exactly what shade of blue that dead baby was: indigo, navy, royal blue, slate, midnight blue, turquoise, powder blue. Baby blue is for boys but you don't know if it was a boy or a girl and your mother is dead now too, so you can never ask her and you can never ask your father either because he might not remember.

The colour of all safety and all sadness. Why should it be surprising that blue is the colour of both? Safety and sadness. Abandonment and letting go. Abandoning yourself to the luxury of safety, letting go of fear. Abandoning yourself to the indulgence of sadness, letting go of happiness or its possibility. Either way you are quiet and full. Full of yourself perhaps, but full nonetheless. Your baby takes a long time being born. You imagine that he is hanging on to your womb with both little hands, pulling you inside out. You wonder why he does not want to let go. Your baby is pink and noisy, perfect and pink.

67. Hungry

THE BABY IS crying. The baby is hungry. The baby is eating. The baby is full. The baby is crying. The baby has gas. The baby is crying. The baby is hungry. The baby is eating. The baby is full. The baby is crying. The baby has a dirty diaper. The baby is crying. The mommy is crying. The baby is hungry again.

The mommy is losing her mind. The baby is always hungry. The baby is always attached to her breast. The mommy feels sweaty and weak and bored. Her arms go numb. The baby is not getting enough milk. The mommy is not getting enough sleep. The daddy is useless because he has no milk in his breasts. The mommy wonders why men have nipples anyway. Men's nipples are good for nothing.

The mommy feels guilty for hating the daddy. The mommy feels guilty because she does not love breast-feeding the way the book says she should. She reads this book while she feeds him. The mommy feels guilty because she does not have enough milk. The book says all normal mothers have more than enough milk. The mommy knows she is a failure. The book tells the happy story of a woman who breast-fed her son until he was eleven years old. This baby is only six weeks.

The mommy and the baby go to the doctor. The baby cries on the cold silver scale. The doctor says, This baby is not gaining enough weight. The mommy cries. The doctor says, Don't cry, we'll just switch to bottle-feeding. The mommy says, I'm a failure. The doctor says, Who says? The mommy tells him about the book. The doctor says, Stop reading that damn book. The mommy says she knows a woman who has so much milk she can squirt it clear across the room. This woman says bottle babies are sickly. This woman's baby is fat. The doctor says, You women do each other no favours with all this advice. We're not fatting a calf here. The doctor says, Your baby is wonderful and so are you. You are made for each other.

At home the baby is crying. The baby is hungry. The mommy heats the bottle. The daddy feeds the baby. The mommy has a bubble bath. Then everybody has a nap. The whole family survives.

68. Priest

THE MOST DISAPPOINTING thing about being a Protestant was that there were no priests. Having never been inside a Catholic church in her life, Joanna wasn't sure where her picture of priests had come from, but there was in her mind the indelible image of an old tall man with a long white beard in a black flowing robe moving his arms gracefully up and down with a golden bell in one hand and smoking incense in the other, while he chanted solemnly over the heads of the congregation in a foreign language which must be one of those *tongues* religious visionaries were said to sometimes speak in. She had once seen a gospel revival meeting on TV. Although the congregation in her mind was all white people, conservatively dressed with their heads carefully covered in a regular church (as opposed to the TV congregation which was all Negroes, clothed in bright and happy colours with their kinky heads bare in a tent the size of Barnum and Bailey's Big Top), in her imagination they too are whipped into a frenzy by the power and the glory of this old tall priest. They are leaping and weeping and wailing and swooning, crying out, "Hallelujah, hallelujah! Praise be to the Lord! Lordy, Lordy, Amen!" Their eyes are closed, their heads flung back, their faces lifted to the beautiful heavens.

It was impossible, Joanna discovered, to fall into a religious trance in the presence of Mrs. Ingram, her Sunday School teacher. Mrs. Ingram looked like any other teacher in her navy blue dress with her short curly hair held captive with a net and many bobby pins while her gold-rimmed spectacles slid perpetually down her shiny nose. In a windowless room in the church basement, Mrs. Ingram showed them how to make paper lilies at Easter, paper stars at Christmas, and many paper haloes all year round. She had them playing seasonally appropriate religious games: How many other words of four letters or more can you find inside the word CHRISTMAS?

Joanna nearly won this one. She found twelve words in the allotted ten minutes: *Christ, cast, mast, mass, match, march, miss, mist, this, thirst, sits, rich.* But Debbie Martin, who always said she was smarter than Joanna anyway, won the prize with thirteen words including *smart* which Joanna had missed. The prize was a shiny coloured picture of the Star of Bethlehem.

The next Sunday Joanna did win, finding ten words in MESSIAH: *mess, mass, miss, hiss, mash, mesh, sash, same, ashes, shame.* The prize was a slim illustrated book called *Heroes of the Bible.* It began naturally enough with a coloured drawing of Adam in the Garden of Eden, a lion fast asleep with its head in his naked lap, a fawn and a duck at his feet, a giraffe, an elephant, a horse, and a flock of bluebirds drawing near to his gently outstretched hand. In the accompanying story, there was no mention of Eve, apples, serpents, or later indiscretions.

Mrs. Ingram talked a lot about food which, she said, was just one of the many things they must thank God for in this country. (Joanna already knew that God in other countries was not nearly so generous.) She had them make lists and draw pictures of everything they were going to eat for Christmas dinner. They spent three whole classes working on these pictures and soon the room was ringed with drawings of larger-than-life turkey legs that looked like wooden clubs. Each leg was surrounded by coloured blobs meant to represent mashed potatoes (white blob), turnips (orange blob), dressing (brown blob), and cranberry sauce (red blob). Gravy was a brown puddle on the side.

Mrs. Ingram praised the Lord for these bountiful feasts as well as for the pictures themselves, and told them that, just as food was necessary nourishment for their growing bodies, so Sunday School was necessary nourishment for their precious innocent souls in bud.

At Christmastime, Mrs. Ingram began every class with her favourite carol, leading their quivering soprano voices through each verse at least once: *Away in a manger,/No crib for a bed,/The little Lord Jesus/Laid down His sweet head . . . /The cattle are lowing,/The Baby awakes,/But little Lord Jesus/No crying He makes.*

Joanna wondered what exactly lowing involved. She imagined a calm herd of brown-and-white cows with their front knees bent and their big heads lowered, mooing sweetly to Baby Jesus in His manger.

The rest of the year Mrs. Ingram stuck mostly to her two all-purpose favourites: *God sees the little sparrow fall,/It meets His tender view;/If God so loves the little birds,/I know He loves me too.* And: *Gentle Jesus, meek and mild,/Look upon a little child;/Pity my simplicity,/Suffer me to come to Thee.*

Joanna wondered about all the emphasis on suffering: should she be suffering even more than she already did over toothaches, tummyaches, her ugly hair, and the way Esther made her sit at the kitchen table and eat a whole bowl of vegetable soup which she hated and she thought she'd throw up but she didn't. What kind of suffering did Jesus have in mind? What more did He want from her?

Mrs. Ingram was not the kind of person of whom she could ask these questions. She was a kind motherly soul who was always polishing her pitch pipe and pushing her spectacles back up the bridge of her nose. Joanna could not imagine Mrs. Ingram ever being swept away by religious fervour, flinging herself on the floor, wrapping her freckled arms

around the ankles of Jesus, washing away the blood from the nail holes
in his feet with her ecstatic copious tears. Joanna could not imagine
Mrs. Ingram allowing herself to become over-stimulated by anyone or
anything. If The Lord Jesus Himself had appeared before them right
now, Mrs. Ingram would probably have set Him to drawing food and
cutting out paper haloes.

Each week Mrs. Ingram herded her Sunday School charges up from
the basement to be present for the last part of the regular service. It
was also impossible, Joanna discovered, to imagine anyone being
whipped into a divine frenzy in the presence of Reverend Charles Doak.
Reverend Doak was a short nervous man with a short nervous wife and
a retarded daughter named Doris. Usually Doris did not put in an
appearance but sat quietly in the choir loft at the back. Joanna never
understood why this small wooden balcony above the main room was
called *the choir loft* anyway. The choir in their slippery-looking blue
gowns sang up front behind the altar, carefully arranged in rows with
all the short people at the front and the tall ones at the back. They
were mostly older women who sang with their eyes closed. Except for
Mrs. Bronson who kept her eyes and her mouth open as wide as they
would go so that her warbling voice was always louder (and more irritating) than the rest. Joanna was embarrassed for her but Mrs. Ingram
said she had been blessed.

In addition to keeping Doris out of sight, the loft was also used to
store the old hymn books. One Sunday morning Doris let out a yodel
right in the middle of "Onward Christian Soldiers" and began flinging
the hymn books down upon the worshipful heads of the congregation.
Joanna was so embarrassed she thought she would die. Mrs. Ingram
said Doris was a special child who would never suffer like the rest of
them. Doris was in, but not *of,* this world. She too was blessed.

The next Saturday Joanna saw Reverend and Mrs. Doak and Doris
at the A&W Drive-In. Joanna and her parents had been shopping all
afternoon at Simpsons-Sears. They did this every Saturday afternoon.

While Esther looked at every single thing in the entire store and
finally bought two or three small items (another set of plastic placemats,
a pair of orange rubber gloves, or some clip-on earrings—she didn't

believe in pierced ears), Clarence stood around with his arms folded and his hat on.

Joanna stuck to the toy department where she looked through all the Barbie outfits and tried to talk her mother into buying her one. She wanted the bride outfit called *Wedding Day* the most: the white wedding gown had real satin and netting and it came with gloves, a bridal bouquet, white high heels, and a blue garter. It cost twice as much as the others. Joanna was willing to settle for *Miss Astronaut* with silver spacesuit, white helmet, and tiny American flag on a stick, or *Riding in the Park* with yellow jodhpurs, brown tweed jacket, black riding boots, hat and crop, or even for *Suburban Shopper*, a full-skirted blue-and-white dress with a cartwheel straw hat and a fruit-filled tote bag.

After shopping, they went to the A&W Drive-In for hamburgers and root beer. Clarence had a big two-patty Papa Burger, Esther had a Mama Burger with cheese, and Joanna had a Baby Burger, just plain, nothing on it. They had french fries all around and an appropriately sized mug of root beer each.

Just as the carhop hooked their tray of food to the rolled-down window, Joanna spotted Reverend and Mrs. Doak and Doris in the car right across from them. Joanna could see Reverend Doak trying to get his mouth around a jumbo three-patty Grandpa Burger. He was talking and laughing and eating like a pig. The ketchup and mustard dribbled down his chin. He washed it all down with a long gulp of root beer which left a foamy moustache on his upper lip. He wiped his face with a crumpled serviette, then blew his nose in it and jammed it into the empty root beer mug. Joanna was so disgusted she gagged. She was sure that no self-respecting God-fearing *real* priest would ever be caught dead stuffing his face like that at the A&W Drive-In on a Saturday afternoon. A *real* priest would be in his church where he belonged, making notes for his Sunday sermon, choosing the hymns, polishing the pews, praising the Lord privately and perpetually. A *real* priest would never be caught dead slurping up sugary root beer and wolfing down three patties of greasy dead meat in public. A *real* priest, if he ate anything at all, would be satisfied with a Communion wafer and a dainty glass of sweet Communion wine, the Blood and the Body of Christ being all the nourishment his body needed because his soul was so splendidly full.

Reverend Doak flicked on his headlights to signal the carhop. Joanna sank down in the back seat and tried to eat her Baby Burger without looking at it. As the Doaks drove away in their battered blue station wagon, Esther from the front seat said, "Wasn't that Reverend Doak across the way?" and Joanna said, "No. No, I don't think so."

69. Ocean

"HIS EGO," ESTHER often said, "is the size of the Atlantic Ocean." She was referring to any man who annoyed her, usually some famous personality on TV.

"His ego," Joanna said aloud into the empty room, "is the size of the Atlantic Ocean." She was referring to Lewis who had recently informed Joanna that if he left Wanda she would die. He was convinced that Wanda could not live, quite literally *could not live,* without him. He was also convinced that staying with her for this reason was the honourable, decent, and kind thing to do. How could she ever admit that she too thought she could not live without Lewis, that she too was afraid she would die, quite literally *die,* without him?

She'd had a dream once of swimming alone in the ocean, and though she couldn't swim at all in her waking life, in the dream she was an aquatic acrobat, all of her muscles gone supple and weightless in the warm salt water. She could hold her breath for hours on end and the mountains of the ocean floor were clear below her feet which the laughing fish were licking lightly. As she made her graceful way through the never-ending waves, a flock of bluebirds flew above her singing raucously and applauding with the tips of their wings.

She had to admit that sometimes she thought loving and being loved by an ego the size of an ocean wouldn't be so bad. Maybe it would be like lying in a warm bath for the rest of your life. Surrounded and buoyed up by it, enfolded within it, warm and weightless, you would never need to do anything ever again but lie still and be loved, swept along and saved forever by the sheer inexhaustible size of it.

Lewis's skin after they made love was salty and she liked to lick the sweat from his chest and his thighs. When he held her face and kissed her with his hands over her ears, the sound was like that magical mysterious ocean trapped inside of all land-locked seashells.

70. Head

"YOU'RE SOFT IN the head, woman," Henry said. "But hard, oh so hard, in the heart." It was April. They were getting ready for bed.

They had agreed to break up. Henry had rented a room in a sleazy downtown hotel until he could find a place of his own. In the room, he told her, there was a sink, a dresser with no handles, a single bed with an iron frame and an army blanket. "It's perfect," he said and she could not tell whether he was joking or not.

"You're soft in the head, woman, but hard, oh so hard, in the heart," Henry said. "You're heartless," he murmured. "Just plain heartless," he whispered as he slipped his hand between her wet thighs. Heartless, hapless, helpless, hopeless.

"Did you know that shrimps have their hearts in their heads?" Joanna said, spreading her legs and guiding his fingers inside. A convenient arrangement, she thought, one which human beings might do well to emulate, thereby eliminating those recurring dilemmas as to which you should follow, your heart or your head.

"We should be so lucky," Henry said.

Soft head, hard heart. This was like Clarence always saying, "Cold hands, warm heart." Maybe they were both right. Could her heart be both warm and hard, like a fist, clenched, sweaty, and strong?

But maybe they were both wrong. Maybe they were getting the pieces of her all mixed up. Cold hands, warm heart. Warm hands, cold heart. Soft head, hard heart. Hard head, soft heart. No head. No heart. Only hands, holding on to Henry's back as they came together.

IT IS FOUR days after Christmas. Clarence is in the living room watching the six o'clock news. Gordon and Samuel are outside shovelling the driveway. Joanna is in the kitchen making supper.

Clarence, in the living room, is supposed to be watching the six o'clock news but he is nodding off intermittently, his head falling slowly backwards until it touches the wall and then he snaps up straight again, awake for two minutes, until his chin drops slowly forward to rest upon his chest. His whole body is sagging into the corner of the couch. His hands are dangling like mittens between his legs. Occasionally he gurgles and snorts.

Gordon and Samuel, outside in the driveway, are supposed to be shovelling but mostly they are playing, throwing snow at each other, laughing, rosy-cheeked. Samuel leaps to the top of the biggest snowbank and proclaims himself king of the castle. Gordon as his loyal subject kneels in the deep snow and salutes him with the Mickey Mouse shovel.

Joanna, in the kitchen, is supposed to be making supper but she is clutching the warm stove with one hand and her full wineglass with the other while the radio blares Top 40 hits, a little off the station so all the sibilant lyrics are laced with static. Between sips of wine and an occasional peek at the chicken in the oven, she is gritting her teeth and glaring at the table which is covered with books and papers and Samuel's action figures. She knows that if she asked her father to come and set the table, he would. But she is too angry to ask and he never gets the cutlery right anyway.

She can hardly bear to look at him slumped there on the couch. The litter of Christmas-just-past is migrating all over the room. The festooned fir tree in the corner already looks junky and dry. In the night she can hear the needles hitting the floor. The TV news announcer has a green tinsel garland behind him which appears to be growing out of his head. She cannot bear to see her father's eyes rolling back as he nods off again and his mouth goes slack. He is probably drooling. All day long, it seems now, he just sits. Waiting, mostly, it seems, for the next meal. At home she knows that he stretches breakfast preparations, consumption, and clean-up until nearly lunchtime. Then he stretches lunch until late afternoon and then it's time to start supper. Here, he sits. He sleeps. He sits some more. He doesn't even do crossword puzzles or cryptograms any more. The puzzle book she put in his Christmas stocking lies unopened on the coffee table beneath a week's worth of newspapers. As it turns out, he will leave it behind when he goes home in a week.

She knows that at home he manages to look after himself well enough. He shops, he cooks, he cleans, he does the laundry. Often he tells her about these quotidian manoeuvres in detail when he telephones on Sundays, calling long-distance to tell her he made pork chops for supper last night, he vacuumed yesterday, he washed clothes on Thursday, he even ironed a shirt. Here he seems to fall helpless the minute he walks through the door. He cannot remember how to work the coffeemaker, the washing machine, or the VCR. He will not even walk to the corner store for milk. He will do without until someone else goes to get it. He does not like to mention that there is no milk. He does not want to be a bother. He tries to help out by doing the dishes after supper but he can never remember where the pots and pans go so he leaves them spread all over the counter for Joanna to put away. When she tries to assure him that it doesn't really matter where they go, just fit them into the bottom cupboard any old which way, he says, "Your mother had a special place for everything." He will not wash the metal vegetable steamer because one time when he washed it at home, one of the silver leaves fell off and Esther yelled at him. Now he leaves it on the counter, bits of broccoli, spinach, or cauliflower all dried out and stuck in the little holes. It takes him an hour to finish the dishes and he never wipes off the stove.

While his world folds in ever more closely around him, he especially likes to watch the weather channel. What is this delight he seems to take in tornadoes, hurricanes, blizzards, and floods? Why does he smile so intently at the wet women crying into the reporter's microphone that they have lost everything, everything, everything? When he is not watching the weather on TV, he is watching it from the window and relaying his observations back over his shoulder to her.

"It's clearing up a bit."

"Looks like more snow."

"Boy, that wind is really bad."

"Boy, it'll be a cold one tonight."

She wants to say, Who cares?

She says, "Oh, that's nice, it's clearing up."

She wants to say, What difference does it make?

She says, "Oh dear, we sure don't need any more snow, do we?"

She wants to say, I don't give a shit!

She says, "Oh?"

Everything he says makes her mad. She wants to feel sorry for him. She wants to feel sympathetic and patient but instead she feels angry and then she feels guilty for that. Which only makes her madder. She knows that she is mad at him for getting old, aging not the issue so much as the way he is doing it. She wants him to be another kind of old person. She wants him to be like the old people in TV commercials for life insurance, Geritol, and new improved denture cream. They are tanned and cheerful, confident and energetic. They are golfing, sailing, bike riding, swimming. They might take up sky-diving some day soon. They are fiercely alive, they are not waiting for anything, they are not afraid of death, and they don't give two hoots about the weather unless it interferes with their recreation. She wants him to be like the old artists she has met. They are charming and eccentric. They wear bandannas and blue jeans, cowboy boots and Indian cotton shirts, a single gold earring and a ring on every finger. They have long grey ponytails. They are busy, opinionated, vigorous, and often lecherous. They are determined to live forever and if they cannot manage that, they will go out painting, dancing, dreaming, or drinking.

She does not want her father to be this lonely tired old man who watches TV all day (*loud* because he will not admit that his hearing is going), who talks only about the weather, the housework, and his friends who are dying, who wears polyester bell-bottoms and cheap plaid shirts, felt slippers and slip-on rubbers. He does not read. He has no hobbies. He is not interested in much of anything any more.

Joanna knows she is being unreasonable. What does she expect him to do at this late date? Adopt a liberal attitude, study gourmet cooking, cultivate an interest in the arts, perhaps take up watercolours, learn to play the clarinet, write a book of poetry? He never did any of these things when he was young. Why should he start now?

She turns down the radio and hears him in the living room, stirring and snorting. She hears his felt slippers shuffling on the hardwood floor. He comes into the kitchen chuckling over a news item he's just heard: a man was stabbed last night in a submarine shop on the other side of the city, stabbed six times by his wife, critically wounded but still alive. They said he had been beating his wife for years. Clarence laughs. "Poor guy! Imagine being stabbed by a woman! How embarrassing! He'll never be able to hold his head up in this town again." Joanna thinks but does not say that it's too bad his wife hadn't cut his head right off, also his balls. Clarence looks at her, still laughing, wanting her to laugh with him. But she will not laugh if it kills her. It might.

He sits down at his usual place at the table, folds his hands in his lap, and looks out the window. He says, "Boy, it'll be a cold one tonight." He does not seem to notice that the table is covered with books and papers and Samuel's action figures. Joanna clears the table, just barely resisting the impulse to sweep it all up with her arm and send it crashing to the floor. She yanks the silverware drawer open so hard it nearly falls out. She tosses the plastic placemats onto the table. She begins to slap the plates down in that way all angry women do. He does not seem to notice. He is picking at the foam rubber backing of his placemat which has cheerful pictures of fruit on it: grapes, straw- berries, apples, oranges, watermelon, and a big pineapple in the center. Oblivious to her anger, he watches the window of the stove as if it were a television, the way people watch their clothes in the dryer at the laundromat. Perhaps he still thinks all women are like this: furious. Perhaps they are. Inside the stove the light is on and the chicken is sizzling and sputtering grease.

Gordon and Samuel come thumping in the back door, slapping the snow off each other, laughing and teasing, dropping their jackets and boots in a pile in the porch.

"What's for supper?" Gordon asks, innocently enough.

"Chicken," Joanna says.

"Again?" Gordon says. Joanna glares at him and he says, "Oh good, I love chicken."

"Oh oh, grumpy," Samuel whispers to his father and goes to sit on his grandpa's knee. She can feel them all looking at her back as she takes the chicken out of the oven. She accidentally slams the door.

Gordon gets Samuel settled at the table and then dishes out the potatoes and the peas. Joanna piles the chicken pieces on a platter of pink carnival glass which had been Esther's once and which Clarence had mailed to Joanna in a big box of Styrofoam a few months after Esther died. He had taped a note to the platter: *Maybe you can use this. I sure never will.*

Clarence has been here for nine days now. Joanna has come to the point in the visit where she has given up trying to impress him with her culinary skills. (This impasse arrives earlier and earlier each visit.) Last night they ordered Chinese food, pizza the night before, and the night before that she made sausages which she knows he doesn't like. Tonight, in an attempt to both apologize and appease her own guilt, she has made chicken just like Esther used to make. It is an old family recipe which Esther copied out carefully on a little card for Joanna when she moved away from home.

Joanna has taped the recipe card to a page in her own recipe book. Below it she has taped a black-and-white photograph of herself and her mother sitting at a picnic table in the pines. In the margin it says: *August 1957.* They are sharing a bottle of pop and smiling at Clarence behind the camera. They are sitting in the shade but behind them the sun is so bright it has washed the grass white. In the background in the bushes is a tilted wooden signpost with an arrow which says MEN. On the table is the big wicker picnic basket filled with this very chicken, prepared by Esther the night before, carefully wrapped in tinfoil and kept in the fridge overnight. As soon as Clarence has finished fussing with the camera, Esther will open the basket and set out the special picnic plates which are red plastic, divided into sections with a round one at the top for the matching red picnic cups.

Once every summer, towards the end of August, just before the Labour Day weekend, they drove an hour and a half to get to this park and have their annual family picnic. Every year they had this same chicken, cold and tender, delicious with pickles, carrot sticks, green olives, and white bread. Every year Clarence took a picture of Esther and Joanna just before they began to eat. Joanna has especially fond memories of these family picnics, preserved in the photo album now, Joanna a little taller, Esther a little older, year by year, except for the one year when the park had been invaded by swarms of horseflies and they had to eat their chicken in the car.

After Esther died, Clarence sent Joanna the old picnic basket, still filled with the red plastic plates and cups, mismatched and tarnished cutlery, turquoise plastic salt and pepper shakers. Samuel uses the plastic cups now and the plates come in handy for birthday parties. The picnic basket sits in Joanna's studio filled with old brushes and dried-up tubes of paint and glue.

Clarence takes a drumstick and a wing and digs in. "Boy, this is really good," he says with his mouth full. "I've never had anything like this before." Joanna reminds him that it is Esther's recipe, she used to make it all the time, always complaining about how it dirtied up the oven, spitting all over the place like that, but Clarence says he can't remember. When she tells him about the picnics, the basket, the horseflies, the plates, he says, "Oh well, if you say so, maybe you're right."

"Oh never mind!" Joanna snaps. She grabs the salt shaker away from Samuel who says, "I was just looking at it. You don't have to be mad at *me*."

Joanna is so busy hating herself for being such a grouch that she is not listening any more and does not notice when or how Gordon and Clarence have got to talking about the war. Clarence is telling the story of how one winter there was no food and it was so cold and there had been many casualties and he hadn't heard for weeks from his older brother Evan who was in another regiment and he was so worried but nobody knew anything and guess who showed up in the middle of the night, driving a General's jeep no less: Evan bringing blankets, a whole fresh chicken, and a half-empty bottle of rum. "I was so glad to see him I just started to cry," Clarence says and begins to weep softly right at the table.

He pulls a dirty handkerchief out of his pants pocket and blows his nose. "I'm sorry," he says. "I'm old, I'm sorry, I can't help it. I never used to feel like crying but now sometimes I do."

Gordon and Joanna look politely down at their plates while he pulls himself together. Even Samuel seems to realize that he should be quiet and eat, or at least pretend to. Joanna has never in her life seen her father cry.

Unless you count the time at Esther's funeral when his eyes were full but he would not let them run over. When Joanna patted him, he smiled. She did not cry at her mother's funeral either. She wanted to, especially when they dropped the dirt on the casket in the hole. But she was afraid that if she started, Clarence would too, and then neither of them would know how to stop or what to do next. She imagined then that the other people at the funeral were admiring her strength. Now she worries that they were thinking she was cold and hard-hearted.

"It's all right," she says now. "It's all right." But she cannot look her father in the eye.

Later she goes to bed early, exhausted by her own anger, her guilt, and the unnerving evidence that her father has feelings every bit as profound and painful as her own. Samuel is sleeping, Gordon and Clarence are watching the hockey game. Joanna falls asleep to the sound of the hockey commentator's voice rising and falling play by play. Gordon and Clarence are mostly silent but occasionally they groan or cheer softly, clapping their hands or slapping their knees. She falls asleep quickly but does not sleep soundly, the night behind her eyelids inscrutably spattered with restless discoloured dreams. She does not dream about the war, the stove, the horseflies, or the picnic.

72. Long

JOANNA LONGED FOR piano lessons. Every other child she knew took lessons of some sort: piano, accordion, violin, ballet, tap dancing, or Ukrainian. Most of these children hated their lessons. But Joanna, lessonless, longed for them. Penny and Pamela, who had to take piano lessons and hated them, longed instead for a pony. Joanna had been on the back of a shaggy Shetland pony once and both its height and breadth had terrified her. They were at the farm of her father's friend, Mr. Hartley, who was saying how his old mare Maisie would kick him to death if she ever got the chance. Then they made Joanna sit on the pony so they could take her picture. The pony twitched his tail so it slapped Joanna across the back of the head, and then he pooped, a smelly steaming mass plopping wetly to the ground. They made her sit on the pony until she cried.

Horses were like flowers, she figured, pretty but not to be trusted. Left to their own devices, they were just as likely to turn on you. In their house, flowers appeared only after an argument, their presentation, it seemed, most often prompted by guilt. Then Esther would either throw them out, still in the box, with the comment that she had plenty of her own flowers growing outside, *better* flowers, cheaper too. Or else she would snort at them while setting them in a vase on the kitchen table where she glared at them periodically until they drooped and dropped their petals all over the place.

It was not a pony but a piano that Joanna longed for. A sturdy upright piano: burnished wood, shining black-and-white keys, three bright gold pedals below. A plushly upholstered bench before it, the kind where the lid came right off and inside there would be piles of sheet music: sounds set down in a mystical language of lines and black dots. Joanna figured that if she just looked at this new alphabet long enough, she would be able to break the code, the way Clarence did the cryptogram in the paper every night after supper. He looked and looked at the letters until FHBVS ZHCDZ HCAL RNAVSI FNSDCVZZ RWVSV AHCI ZHJBVS KHZW KJLQSHZW became DIVER SINKS INTO WATERY DARKNESS WHERE TINY SILVER FISH FLOURISH. If she looked and looked long enough at the sheet music in the piano bench, perhaps the melody would similarly materialize.

Later it will be while seated on Penny and Pamela's piano bench that Joanna drinks wine for the first time, a sickening sweet red. She will always remember the name, Castelvetro, and the voluptuous look of the red liquid in the green bottle. She will not remember, however, how they got the wine, where Penny and Pamela's parents were, what music might indeed have materialized once they'd polished off the whole bottle between them.

Now Esther said, "Piano lessons cost money. Pianos cost even more. Besides, where would we put it? The front room is too small. Just look."

Joanna looked. Into the long narrow room crowded with armchairs, plant stands, a console TV, and a china cabinet which was Esther's pride and joy. She could spend all day just cleaning and rearranging its contents, squirting Windex all over its glass doors and shelves. There was the couch with Clarence stretched out on it, his long legs hanging over the arm, his bare feet dangling, bony and white. They made her think of a chicken before it was cooked.

Joanna tried to put pianos out of her mind. She decided that she wanted a set of *Encyclopaedia Britannica* instead.

Esther said, "If it's not one thing, it's another. Encyclopedias cost money." When the well-scrubbed salesman came around she wouldn't even let him get a foot in the door. Joanna sadly watched him walking away and thought he was probably the smartest man in the world, privy to all secret knowledge, science, history, and the meaning of life, and she would probably never see him again.

As it happened, not long afterwards, Safeway started selling the *Funk and Wagnalls Encyclopedia*, one volume per week, only ninety-nine cents each with purchase. They collected the set, one volume per week, and Esther cleared a place for them on the bottom shelf of the bookcase beside the big dictionary and the Bible Joanna had got for perfect attendance in Sunday School three years before. The other four shelves didn't have books on them, but knick-knacks: china horses, flowers and frogs, four Dalmatian puppies tied to their mother with little gold chains around their necks. Each ornament was set on a frilly starched doily which Esther had made herself by a mysterious process called *tatting*. Eventually these were all replaced with plastic doilies. Plastic was all the rage then and Esther took to it like a bee to honey. Plastic was a revelation: it never wore out, it never got old, and when it got dirty, you could just wipe it off with the dishcloth. Esther happily bought plastic doilies, plastic flowers, plastic placemats, plastic lamp-shades, a plastic Hallowe'en pumpkin, plastic mistletoe, and a plastic Christmas wreath for the front door.

The Funk and Wagnalls books looked all right: burgundy bindings with gold letters stamped on each spine. But they were disappointing: too small, the pages not shiny enough, and the illustrations were all in black and white. Joanna seldom looked at them. A set of encyclopedias bought one book at a time in a grocery store, of all places, was not likely to be much good anyway.

Clarence tried to console her. "Why the long face? Stop always wanting what you don't have," he said. "Make the most of what you've got. There's no time like the present. Life is too short."

From Joanna's twelve-year-old perspective, he was beginning to sound stupid or sadly mistaken, the unpleasant present was looking as if it would go on forever, and life loomed before her unbearably long. The future would probably never arrive.

Joanna figured she might well live for another sixty years. That would mean another twenty-one thousand and nine hundred days. Another five hundred and twenty-five thousand six hundred hours to get through, another thirty-one million five hundred and thirty-six thousand minutes, another one trillion eight hundred and ninety-two million one hundred and sixty thousand suffering seconds.

These depressing ruminations usually preoccupied her on Sunday, during that gaping wasteland between lunch and supper when there was nothing but sports on TV, her homework was done, and the phone never rang. It was the seriousness of Sunday, the longest day of the week, which inevitably overwhelmed her, the way it was always just dripping and dripping and draining away.

She realized she hadn't figured in leap years, which were even longer.

Esther said, "Stop wishing your life away. Once you hit twenty-one, the years will just get shorter and shorter and before you know it, you'll be dead."

Much to Joanna's grudging surprise, she was right. Time too, like horses and flowers, proved to be untrustworthy. It could be counted on to pass, yes, but never at the same rate, one hour plodding by too slowly as you checked the clock every five minutes, the next one flitting by so fast that you suspected it was probably faster than the speed of light, or maybe it had never happened at all. There was always too much of it. There was never enough of it. A week or a month which seemed interminable in the living, in memory turned out to have been the same length as any other, if not shorter. Time, it seemed, was just as likely to be a figment of your own imagination or, even worse, a figment of somebody else's.

Later, with Gordon beside her in bed and Samuel snug in his bassinet, Joanna will lie awake for hours praying that she will live forever, or at least, long enough. She will realize that there are times in your life when you don't know whether to regret or be grateful for time's passing. You are aging certainly and that is perhaps regrettable but there is also the self-congratulatory sense of having made it through another year (another month, week, day, another hour even). There is always the remote possibility that some day you will turn out to be not only older but wiser too.

"Time is of the essence," Esther often said. Yes, Joanna had to agree, the statement having the indisputable ring of truth, of secret knowledge, arcane wisdom. But *what,* Joanna will always wonder, the essence of what?

73. Religion

ESTHER WAS UNDECIDED about God. It was hard to tell what she thought of Him from one day to the next.

Joanna was sent to Sunday School every week. While Clarence stayed in bed, Esther made Joanna's breakfast and then helped her get dressed. Joanna wore a short two-piece grey suit, black patent leather shoes, white ankle socks, and a white lacy thing more like a doily than a real hat bobbypinned to her dark curly hair. Even though Joanna knows she couldn't have worn this same suit every week for all those years, she will always remember herself going off alone to Moseby United Church in this outfit.

In the photo album there is a picture of her wearing the suit, holding a pair of white gloves in one hand. It says: *READY FOR SUNDAY SCHOOL, EASTER 1960.* Behind her are the grey drapes patterned with floppy red flowers, also the TV set. On top of it there is a bouquet of yellow and red plastic roses on a white plastic doily and another photograph, of Joanna when she had the mumps the year before, propped up in bed in her red flannelette nightie with her glands bulging, surrounded by stuffed animals.

The Sunday School photograph is the last one in the album. The later photographs were kept in a shoe box all jumbled together, some of them still in the original developer's envelopes. It had always been Clarence's job to keep the album up to date. For years he was meticulous and then, for no apparent reason, he stopped. As if Joanna's life, or at least his belief in his own ability to keep it in order, had ended right after Sunday School, Easter 1960, when she was almost six.

Once Joanna was on her way to Moseby United Church, Esther went back to bed. By the time Joanna got home, her parents were just coming around, sipping their coffee at the kitchen table in their pyjamas, smelling of sleep, with their hair all messed up, their eyes soft and blurry. They were very kind to each other those late Sunday mornings, refilling each other's coffee cups, sharing yesterday's newspaper, Esther sectioning up pink grapefruit halves with her special grapefruit knife, Esther laughing merrily when the juice squirted across the room, hitting the window or Clarence's chin. Esther trailing her hand across Clarence's shoulder as she got up to butter the toast.

Joanna thought it wasn't fair. She wanted to stay in bed too and then lounge around in her pyjamas until noon. Although she hated the sour grapefruit which always made her eyes water, she wanted to be offered one anyway. She wanted to heap on the sugar with the special serrated spoon. But by the time she got home from Sunday School, the grapefruit halves sat gutted on the counter like broken baseballs or coconut shells. Why was she the only one who had to go?

Esther said she had to go because she was a child and all children need religious instruction. Sunday school, Esther said, would teach her the necessary moral values. Joanna at nine and three-quarters wasn't

worried yet about her values, moral or otherwise. She thought *value* was
something you got for your money when you found plastic placemats
on sale half-price at Simpsons-Sears.

moral *adj.* 1. relating to or capable of making the distinction between
right and wrong, or good and evil. 2. in accordance with the principles
of right and wrong. 3. of a good character; sometimes, specif., virtuous
in sexual conduct.

Sunday School, Esther said, would save Joanna's mortal soul. Joanna
hadn't yet given her soul much thought.

mortal *adj.* 1. destined to die eventually. 2. of man as a being subject
to death. 3. of this world. 4. of death. 5. fatal; deadly. 6. of war, fought
to the death. 7. unappeasable. 8. intense pain, fear, grief, etc. 9. *Theology:* a sin causing eternal damnation and death of the soul; distinguished from VENIAL.

Joanna never could keep the two words straight in her mind, *moral* and
mortal, but clearly they were connected: to each other and to Sunday
School with all its talk about God, death, and goodness, with all those
unlikely parables about Jesus and His miracles, each with a moral you
were supposed to figure out for yourself and then live by. Either way,
moral or mortal, Joanna wanted to stay home Sunday mornings and
sleep in.

Esther told Clarence (Joanna was eavesdropping again) that she was
undecided about God herself but she wanted Joanna to make up her
own mind. Besides, what if she was wrong? What if there really was a
God, an all-seeing all-knowing all-punishing God? It seemed wiser,
Esther said, to hedge their bets. Besides, Sunday was the only morning
they got to sleep in.

The summer Joanna was ten she went one afternoon with Penny and
Pamela to their friend Maria's house. Maria lived with many brothers
and sisters in a three-storey brick house two blocks over. Maria's older
brother, Bernard, who was going to be a minister, was holding a Bible

Study group that summer every Tuesday afternoon in their big shady overgrown backyard. There were eight or ten other children there and they sat around two wooden picnic tables while Bernard read to them from the Bible in a glorious soul-stirring voice. Soul-stirring, yes: now Joanna was starting to think about her soul because someone had finally touched it. Bernard. Bernard with his deep brown eyes and thrilling pouty mouth. All summer she had been secretly wishing she was Catholic so she could become a nun. She saw now that she would have to revise this desire because the conditions of nunhood (as she understood them) would make it difficult to pursue her love for Bernard. Her desire for divinity was quickly superseded by her desire for Bernard.

After the reading, Bernard gave each of them a small green-covered booklet which said: CONSECUTIVE DAILY BIBLE READING (A PLAN FOR READING THE ENTIRE BIBLE IN ONE YEAR). Then Maria and Bernard's mother came outside in her apron with lemonade and chocolate chip cookies for everyone. Joanna was converted, Joanna was saved, Joanna would give her whole life over to God, Jesus, Bernard, and his mother.

She flew home on the path of righteousness with the precious pamphlet in her hand. Esther, when she saw it, flew into a rage. (Esther was unpredictable those days, would fly into a rage over the least little thing, would fly, as Clarence put it, right off the handle over dirty socks left on the bedroom floor; over a quart of milk left on the counter, gone sour and smelly in the heat; over the fancy casserole she'd slaved over all afternoon and nobody even said how delicious it was; over cracker crumbs and popcorn in the chesterfield, wet towels in the bathroom, fingerprints on the furniture, and dirt. Dirt, dirt, dirt, nothing but disgusting dirt everywhere she looked. Clarence said it was a "woman's thing." What he meant was menopause but Joanna thought he was referring to Esther's obsession with cleanliness.) Esther tossed the Bible reading pamphlet on top of the pile of last week's newspapers all bundled and tied to go out with the garbage. She forbade Joanna to go to Maria's ever again.

"Tricks," she said scornfully. "It's all tricks, a bunch of mumbo-jumbo! What a load of rigmarole!" Esther liked this word. She gave it an extra syllable—"rig-*a*-marole"—in a disgusted voice. "These peo-ple," she said, "are no better than those damn Jehovah's Witnesses selling their religion door-to-door." Joanna had no doubt as to how Esther felt about *them*. Many times she had crouched in the kitchen below window-level while the Jehovah's Witnesses pounded at the back door in religious fervour, looking for lost souls, and Esther whispered, "Be quiet! Don't answer it!" Joanna stood there as if trapped in a game of statues and the mounting tension tickled inside her till she thought she'd laugh or scream her head off.

"Tricks," Esther said and the subject was closed.

She also said this about those Mexican jumping beans advertised in the back pages of Joanna's comic books. And about those little grow-your-own-seahorses you could send away for: *Just add water and they will come to life before your very eyes! Living seahorses! They will provide you with hours and hours of entertainment and joy!*

"Tricks," Esther said, about those beauty aids advertised in the back pages of her women's magazines: *Remove unwanted hair forever in just five minutes! Erase ugly age spots with Going, Going, Gone Fade-Out Cream! Look slimmer instantly with our new Tummy Trimmer! Increase your bustline without exercising, surgery, or pain!*

"It's all tricks," Esther said.

After supper that night, Joanna secretly rescued the Bible reading pamphlet from the garbage pile and took it to bed with her. She read it under the covers with a flashlight. The only other time she'd dared do this was last winter when she was reading *The Incredible Journey* by Sheila Burnford, the heart-warming, tear-jerking story of Bodger, the old bull terrier, Luath, the young golden Lab, and Tao, the Siamese cat, trekking two hundred and fifty treacherous miles through the wilds of Northern Ontario to get back home. She got caught in the act then, reading and weeping with the blankets like a tent over her head, the wavering flashlight trained on all that fine print held two inches from her sniffling nose. It was probably the sniffling that gave her away.

"You'll go blind!" Esther cried as she plucked blankets, flashlight, and book from Joanna all at once. The book was temporarily banished, as if it were some evil influence, something dirty and dangerous like those magazines Clarence kept hidden and which Esther didn't know Joanna had already found: all those naked long-limbed women with their big brown nipples and the sun shining on their bums. These women filled Joanna with desire: a desire to touch them, to be touched by them, to touch herself between her legs, a desire to feel the warm sun on her bare-naked bum.

The first required Bible reading (January 1: Morning) was Matthew 1. She consulted her Sunday School Bible. Matthew 1, she discovered, began with the genealogy of Jesus Christ, a long list of unwieldy unlikely names:

Abraham was the father of Isaac, and Isaac the father of Jacob, and Jacob the father of Judah and his brothers, and Judah the father of Perez and Zerah by Tamar, and Perez the father of Hezron, and Hezron the father of Ram, and Ram the father of Amminadab, and Amminadab the father of Nahshon, and Nahshon the father of Salmon, and Salmon the father of Boaz by Rahab, and Boaz the father of Obed by Ruth, and Obed the father of Jesse, and Jesse the father of David the king.

There was more. Joanna felt hysterical and flipped to the final reading, December 31, Malachi 4, which said, among other things:

For behold, the day comes, burning like an oven, when all the arrogant and all evildoers will be stubble; the day that comes shall burn them up, says the Lord of hosts, so that it will leave them neither root nor branch. But for you who fear my name the sun of righteousness shall rise, with healing in its wings. You shall go forth leaping like calves from the stall. And you shall tread down the wicked, for they will be ashes under the soles of your feet, on the day when I act, says the Lord of hosts.

In the middle of the night, Joanna put the pamphlet back on the pile and it went out with the papers in the morning.

She forgot about Bernard easily enough. She was still young, her desires were elastic, she was fickle and still largely unformed.

One Sunday morning later that year Esther said, "Do you want to go to Sunday School today?"

Joanna said, "No," and the subject was closed.

Neither Henry nor Lewis believed in God. They both liked to make disparaging remarks and bad jokes about Him. Henry's favourite was the one about the drunkard who boarded a bus and staggered to an empty seat beside a nun. The nun, mortified by his inebriated condition, said, "You, young man, are going straight to Hell!" The drunkard lurched to his feet and stumbled towards the door, yelling, "Driver, driver, let me off! I'm on the wrong bus!"

Lewis said he'd given up on God when he was eight. He'd been praying that year every night since October for a bicycle at Christmas, a red bicycle, of course, a CCM. He saw it in the window of Mattson's Hardware downtown. He and every other kid he knew was praying for that bicycle, praying to God and Santa Claus both, the two invisible deities they believed to be watching over them, making their lists and checking them twice, just to be sure who was naughty or nice. There were plenty of presents under Lewis's tree that Christmas morning but no red bicycle in sight. He checked the basement, the garage, and the backyard. Nothing. It was a sentimental trite little story which Lewis could make some fun of now but at the time it was enough to destroy his belief in God and Santa Claus both, those two white-bearded old angels who were, it was now revealed, mere figments of the collective imagination.

Lewis admitted that he had prayed for the odd thing since (for a safe airplane flight to Europe once because he was afraid of flying, for a lucrative commission from a local art aficionado, even for a painless solution to his situation with Joanna and Wanda) because, though he no longer really believed in God, praying was a knee-jerk reaction in times of fear and emotional distress. Besides, it couldn't hurt, you never know. But his prayers had gone largely unanswered. Or if they were answered, the answer was most often no. God, he figured, must be out of the office, gone for lunch, gone away for the weekend, or whooping it up on a cruise ship somewhere in the Caribbean.

On a more serious note, Lewis said that with the world in such a perpetual mess, how could any rational person still convince himself that there was someone in charge?

Henry and Lewis were both (as Joanna sometimes thought later, when she was trying to sort through the romantic disasters of her life thus far) *godless* men. Perhaps that was part of the problem. Maybe they were doomed by their disbelief and she, too, by being an accessory to their atheism.

Not that Joanna had got religion or anything. She did sometimes wish she was religious because maybe then she would have some guidelines to go by. Maybe then, when she found herself facing some prickly moral emergency, she'd be able to determine the appropriate rules and regulations and thus act accordingly without confusion or ethical compromise. If only she were imbued with a stalwart sense of divine conviction—if only she were, so to speak, divinely convicted—maybe then she could know, for once and for all, the difference between right and wrong. But she, like her mother, was still undecided about God and she too figured it was wiser to hedge her bets. Although she now attended church only under duress (that is, for weddings and funerals), she did still refer to Him in all His glory with a capital letter in a tone of voice which could be interpreted as reverential or, at the very least, respectful. She was certainly not above making deals with God when necessary: *God, please let me get this grant. If I get this grant, I promise I will never be greedy again . . . God, please don't let me have gonorrhea (syphilis, herpes, or AIDS). If I don't have a sexually transmitted disease this time, I promise I will never have sex again . . . God, please give me strength. If You will get me through this one, I promise I will never whine or complain ever again.*

Occasionally letting out a string of curses which featured all His various names in vain, colourfully modified by a series of good old Anglo-Saxon expletives, she would not have been completely surprised to find herself struck down by a lightning bolt vigorously hurled out of heaven by a divinely indignant and muscular arm.

If Joanna is still undecided about God, she is, however, pretty sure about punishment. Gordon likes to tease her about her Calvinist streak which, he says, is a mile wide and twice as long. Gordon, like Henry and Lewis, doesn't believe in God either and is remarkably untroubled by the whole concept of religion. Joanna doesn't know much about Calvin or his theological doctrines but she does know that she lives in a perpetual state of expecting punishment. If she spots a police car cruising the block, she imagines with a jolt that they are coming to arrest her for some major crime she has committed but conveniently forgotten. The story of the ten plagues of Egypt strikes her as likelier than Cinderella, Snow White, and all other more modern permutations of *happily ever after*.

She feels guilty. Guilty as sin. But she's not sure for what. She knows she is no longer an innocent. A truly innocent person would not be so suspicious and frightened when the phone rings in the middle of the night (or the middle of the afternoon, for that matter), and when she answers it, there is silence, sometimes the sound of a breath drawn in sharply or let out slowly, then an ominous click in her ear. A truly innocent person on such an occasion would simply say, "Must have been a wrong number," and go unperturbed back to bed, back to washing the kitchen floor and humming, back to a nutritious family supper with Cheery Cherry Cheesecake for dessert. A truly innocent person would not spend the rest of the day or night looking over her shoulder, trying to figure out who it had been, how much they knew, or what they were trying to find out.

Sometimes she would like to go and turn herself in. She would like to throw herself on the mercy of the courts: *mea culpa, mea culpa!* As if mercy were constructed like those black iron fences around churches and mansions, the ones with the uprights pointed like spears upon which the guilty will be unceremoniously but bloodily impaled. She would beg for forgiveness, amnesty, an official pardon, all of which would be withheld.

But she's not sure where she should go to confess. To church? For the sin of having fucked a married man, not once, not twice, but probably two hundred times, once seven times in a single day. To the police station? For the crimes of having stolen that pair of black lace panties when she was twelve, having forgotten to renew her licence plates, having imagined murder more than once. To city hall? For three unpaid parking tickets, property taxes again in arrears, the house needing a paint job, and several varieties of noxious weeds flourishing in the backyard. To the Children's Aid Society? For having given Samuel Kraft Dinner for lunch three days in a row, having once slapped him when he stuck his tongue out at her, having imagined how easy it would be to suffocate him when he was three weeks old, for having occasionally envied childless couples, for having many times wished he would go away and leave her alone, for having even gone so far as to say it out loud.

She suspects she will be punished not only for her transgressions, but for her pleasures as well. There are few enough things in life which offer pure pleasure, or there are few enough times in life when you can afford to take pure pleasure in anything. She remembers Esther often joking, "Everything I like is illegal, immoral, or fattening," as she polished off a butter tart, a piece of cherry cheesecake, or a jumbo Dairy Queen banana split.

She also remembers Esther often saying, "Don't get your hopes up, don't ever get your hopes up too high." Esther, having no apparent faith in happiness herself, could seldom bring herself to share in anyone else's. She felt compelled, it seemed, to warn them of its pitfalls, obligated to remind them of its untrustworthy transience and the need to keep their feet firmly planted on the ground. For a long time Joanna thought this was a mean streak peculiar to her mother.

Now she knows that many people share this trait. They cannot take pleasure in another person's triumphs, big or small. Instead they are sarcastic, resentful, and envious, as if there were only so much happiness available in the world and the fact that someone else now has a share must mean there will be less for them. It is not necessarily your enemies who will react this way. Just as often it is your friends, those very same friends who have listened sympathetically to your problems day after day in a small café over endless over-stimulating cups of cappuccino, night after night on the telephone, that invisible umbilical cord from one dark kitchen to another. Now that you're finally happy, they don't know what to do with you. Sometimes they cannot even look at you any more because they do not want to see that you have changed, that you have indeed become the person you meant to be before you got sidetracked—because if you have changed, then maybe they should too.

There is always someone, it seems, ready to remind you that hopes are mere delusions or tricks which, once drummed up, are bound to be disappointed, dashed, or found to be foolish in the face of real life. If pride goeth before a fall, then so might hopes and pleasure. Either way, Joanna is uneasy in her happiness. It strikes her as something for which you must pay and pay, and then some.

Sitting alone (Samuel having been safely deposited at the day care) one sunny October afternoon in a trendy downtown restaurant sipping cappuccino and munching on a toasted bagel with cream cheese, Joanna realizes that even now she wouldn't be greatly surprised to find herself struck down right here for no particular reason, struck down in the prime of her life just for the hell of it. Perhaps punishment does not incorporate a statute of limitations. Perhaps punishment, like wage increases, can be administered retroactively for something she thought she'd gotten away with years ago. For something like that fantasy she had one day walking downtown to this very same restaurant six months after Lewis had dumped her. She had imagined their mutual acquaintance, Mark Halliday, rushing up to her on the street, saying, "Have you heard the news?" obviously bursting with the hope that she hadn't so he could be the one to tell her, because although he had no proof of their affair, he had his suspicions. When Joanna answered innocently, "No, what?" Mark would say, "There's been a terrible car accident. Wanda has been killed. Lewis is in the hospital in critical condition asking for you." This was not an active fantasy, not a scene premeditated or constructed carefully over time. It had come to her that day like a waking dream, fully formed, precisely detailed, and deeply satisfying.

Now, five years later, it would not surprise her to find that God has just got wind of this blasphemy. He is, of course, extremely busy with world affairs, wars, famines, the environment, and so is likely to be behind in cleaning up the backlog of the many adulterous affairs committed by good-looking upwardly mobile fairly young men and women in this relatively stable corner of the world. It would not surprise her to discover that she is about to die a disgustingly flashy death right in the middle of this trendy restaurant, filled as it is in the afternoon with self-employed unusually dressed artists, musicians, and writers. The woman at the next table is writing a long letter on pink fluorescent paper. Farther over another woman is telling her whole life story to a total stranger with a Russian accent. Near the door another woman with striking red hair and charming freckles is having lunch with three handsome men while her puppy is tied to the parking meter out front and everyone who walks by stops to pat it and coo doggy-talk into its floppy black ears. The red-haired woman grins proudly. Joanna supposes that she too looks ordinary enough sitting here sipping her cappuccino. Boy, will they ever be surprised when that lightning bolt strikes.

Sometimes in the morning after Gordon has gone to work and she is doing the breakfast dishes—the sun is flitting through the window and into the soap suds; Samuel, still in his pyjamas, is trying to feed the rest of his soggy cereal to his teddy bear—sometimes then her happiness hits her like a hammer. She realizes that somewhere along the line she has taught herself (or been taught) to trust pain, suffering, anguish, catastrophe, sadness, and all types of tragedy, trial, and tribulation. Such difficulties are something you can count on, something you can master or, at least, make your way through. But you can't really do anything with happiness except enjoy it and hope it will last forever. Even now Joanna is reluctant to put her faith in happiness for fear of jinxing it. She feels burdened by the prospect of its potential loss and the pressure put upon her (or upon God or the untrustworthy fates) to prolong and protect it.

She finds herself praying a lot more than she used to. Her prayers now are about warding off loss. She is no longer dealing with God for gain. She is no longer worried about how to get *more* but how to keep from losing all that she has got.

Much as she doesn't trust her own happiness, she also feels guilty when she isn't happy. She prays, *God, please forgive me for being unhappy,* as if unhappiness were a personality defect she knows better than to indulge but sometimes she has relapses. She knows she has a great deal to be thankful for. She knows there are a great many people far worse off than she is. So what right does she have to be unhappy, even a tiny bit? Where can she go to confess these recurring crimes of discontent, hubris, self-satisfaction, and greed? What if the punishment for not being happy with what you've got is to lose everything? What if God is like those frustrated mothers in the A&P who bend down and hiss at their cranky children, "You stop that right now or I'll give you something to cry about!"?

She finds herself praying a lot more than she used to. She finds herself chanting silently, *Please God, please God, please.* It is an unfinished, perhaps ineffectual, plea, she realizes, for paradise.

74. Whisky

As a young child, Joanna associated the smell of whisky with her father's good-night kisses, her father leaning gently over her, her father's eyes gone soft and shiny, her father's lips moist on her cheek. When he was getting a lot of overtime at the mill and money was good, Clarence sometimes splurged and bought himself a bottle of Seagram's Crown Royal instead of the regular "rotgut rye," as he called it. The Crown Royal came in a velvety purple bag with gold lettering and a golden drawstring. Joanna was given these bags to keep her marbles and other small treasures in. The smell of whisky on her father's breath always made her hope that he'd splurged again and she would be getting another bag for her collection. For a time the smell of whisky made Joanna feel safe and loved and hopeful.

But soon enough she noticed that while her father's eyes were going soft and shiny over his third glass of whisky, her mother's were going cold and hard. Esther did not approve of alcohol in any form or quantity. Esther said she had watched her father drink himself to death and she did not intend to witness such degeneracy again. Joanna could not imagine how a person went about drinking themselves to death. Was it something like drowning from the inside out, your body filling up with whisky over the years until finally you suffocated and it went bubbling up your nose the way Coca-Cola did if you drank it too fast? "He was a man stuck in a bottle," Esther once said of her father and Joanna imagined him like one of those ships in a bottle you could buy downtown.

Joanna began to see the tension rising in her mother every time her father opened the cupboard over the fridge where the liquor was kept. She began to feel it herself, a knot in her stomach at the sound of her father dropping more ice cubes into his glass. She wished he would stop. She wished her mother would stop him. She did not understand why her mother, who had no problem expressing her disapproval about other things, could not seem to bring herself to say anything directly about this. Instead she would bring up her own father again. Or she would just go silent and tense. Joanna too got to the point where she could not look at her father when he had a drink in his hand. She too had the sense that something terrible was going to come of it. But nothing ever did. Clarence did not get cirrhosis of the liver. He did not lose his job. He did not end up dead or in jail for drunk driving. He did not get miserable and mean. He did not beat them in a drunken rage. When Clarence drank, he just got quieter and quieter, usually sitting in front of the TV watching hockey or football with his glass on the floor beside him. He seemed with each drink to travel further and further into himself until Joanna felt that no one could reach him at all. He drank until he became invisible and then he went to bed.

When Clarence comes to visit now, Gordon, who seldom drinks, buys a bottle of Crown Royal so they can have a drink or two together in the evenings. "Just to keep him company," Gordon explains. "I don't like to think of him drinking alone."

Joanna is angry but she's not sure at what or who or when it began. She says he probably does it all the time at home.

Gordon says, "Then he shouldn't have to do it here." The smell of whisky or sympathy is pungent on his breath.

75. Child

child *n.* 1. a baby; infant. 2. a fetus. 3. a boy or girl before puberty. 4. an offspring; son or daughter. 5. a descendant. 6. a person like a child in character, manners, interests, etc.; a person regarded as immature. 7. a person regarded as a product of a specific time or place [a *child* of the future]. 8. a product; something that springs from a specific source [a *child* of the imagination]. *See also* CHILDBEARING, CHILD-BED, CHILDBIRTH, CHILDHOOD, CHILDISH, CHILDLIKE, CHILD'S PLAY.

76. Bitter

"YOUR MOTHER," CLARENCE says suddenly during one of their Sunday morning phone calls, "your mother was a bitter woman." Esther has been dead for seven years.

Joanna says, "What?" They have been talking about gardening. The garden was Esther's domain, filled with flowers only, no vegetables, a few strawberries and a small rhubarb patch in the back corner. The annual spring trip to the nursery for bedding plants was a sacred ritual, a pilgrimage. She planted carefully so there were abundant blooms all summer long. She cultivated and weeded so meticulously you'd have thought the soil had been vacuumed. She was also partial to lawn ornaments.

In those days neither Clarence nor Joanna was much interested in Esther's garden. They helped her only grudgingly when pressed. They rolled their eyes at each other while she ranted on about the neighbours' damn cats digging up her precious plants. They laughed behind her back as she tried one thing after another to keep the cats away, spreading mothballs or hot chili pepper flakes all over the dirt.

Since Esther's death though, Clarence has taken on the garden with enthusiasm. He brags about the size of his gladioli, the number of blooms on the rosebushes, the abundant beauty of the window boxes out front. He sends photographs of the begonias, the hydrangea, the yellow tea roses, and the honeysuckle hedge. He complains about the sabotage of slugs, cutworms, birds, the neighbours' damn cats, and the weather (which is always too hot, too cold, too wet, too dry). He mutters unkindly about Mother Nature. He has even added a few new lawn ornaments to the menagerie: a blue jay on a metal spike, two dwarves, and a white cat. "Remember that cat you had?" he asks. "That cat that got hit by a car?"

Joanna is glad he has kept up the garden, partly because it keeps him occupied and partly because, through the revisionist vagaries of memory, it has become a fond and comforting piece of her past despite the fact that at the time she wasn't interested. She is happy enough that it never seems to have occurred to Clarence that he could have just let Esther's garden go wild.

But she cannot tell in exactly what spirit he has entered into this horticultural activity. Does he do it perhaps to appease his own guilt? Guilt for not having helped Esther more when he could have. Guilt for not having shared or encouraged her pride in those flowers she so lovingly fussed over all summer long. Guilt for having only grunted when she pointed to the dahlias, the geraniums, the purple phlox, the peonies so heavy with blooms that they drooped nearly down to the ground, when she pointed and cried, "Look, aren't they beautiful? Aren't they just gorgeous? Look, look!" Or could he have embraced gardening now just to show her he could do it if he wanted to? Or is he hoping, better late than never, to finally make her happy? Does he believe that she is up there in heaven smiling benevolently down upon him as he babies the begonias, fertilizes the bleeding hearts, and prunes the rosebushes perfectly? Does he believe in heaven? Does he believe she has gone there?

Now on the phone Joanna says, "What?" and Clarence says it again: "Your mother was a bitter unhappy woman."

He says it clearly and firmly. Either this notion is something that

has just come to him or else it is something he has known all along
and has only now found the courage to say out loud.

Joanna says, in a question, "Yes?" She is hoping he will elaborate.

He does, but not much. He says that Esther used to be happy, she
used to be a lot of fun. He says, "I don't know what happened. I don't
know when it started, the bitterness. I don't even know what she was
so bitter about. For years I tried to figure her out. I guess I never will
now. I guess you don't remember how she was when she was happy."

Joanna says, "No, I don't."

"I wish you could," Clarence says. "I wish you could think of her
that way. Not bitter. But bittersweet." Then he goes back to talking
about the garden.

Joanna pretends to listen but really she is thinking that it is not
like Clarence to wax poetic. She is thinking about *bittersweet,* the only
kind of chocolate she ever craved as a child, a big block of it for baking
that Esther thought she kept well-hidden in the fridge but sometimes
Joanna sneaked it out and broke off a chunk, sucked it so quietly that
nobody noticed. *Bittersweet,* also a plant she now knows, another name
for garden nightshade, a poisonous plant with purple star-shaped flowers and bitter scarlet berries, a plant symbolic, like many, of truth.

No, she does not remember her mother when she was happy. Often
she wonders why all her memories of Esther are still so unpleasant.
Shouldn't time by now have softened her brain (or her heart or whatever
part of the human anatomy it is that memory actually inhabits) and
worked its reputed wound-healing magic? Shouldn't she by now be
able to romanticize her mother a bit so that Esther too, like all the
other dead people she knows, could be purified by passing on, her faults
having fallen away like dead leaves and been replaced by a new growth
of virtues, tenderness, and charming nostalgic anecdotes?

Joanna worries that she too is becoming bitter. Why is she still
nursing her unhappy memories? Why does she still remember in vivid
detail those Thursday nights when Esther made her sit at the table
with lumps of casserole and jellied salad stuck in her throat until bedtime? Why does she still get mad when she thinks of the first time a
boy (what was his name?) tried to feel her up and she was so outraged
and frightened and thrilled that she confided in Esther but Esther said,

"I don't want to hear about it," and walked out of the room? She can still hear Esther's voice telling her that she was lazy, sloppy, cheeky, silly, foolish, irresponsible, ungrateful, too thin, too smart, too deep, too honest, too trusting for her own damn good. There must have been times when Esther praised her. Why can't she remember any of them now? She does remember her mother often saying, whenever Joanna had a new blouse or dress or hairdo, "Well, anything looks good on a model." But she said it so often and so sarcastically, that Joanna soon realized this too was another reminder that she was not supposed to think well of herself. Esther did not believe in getting too big for your britches. Esther believed in comeuppance.

There must have been good times too. There must be sweet memories in there somewhere. There must have been a time when Esther held her, comforted her, brushed her hair, rubbed her back. Surely when she was a baby her mother must have touched her, sung to her, cuddled her, and loved her just as other mothers do. But neither her memory nor her imagination will stretch that far.

Joanna realizes that this is the first time her father has said one remotely unkind word about her mother since she died. In fact, Joanna realizes in retrospect, he has not said much about her at all. Joanna does not mention her very often either. It is as if they are both afraid of starting a conversation they don't want to have, a conversation they will never be able to finish. It is as if they are both hiding something, some secret knowledge about Esther that would change everything they ever thought they knew about her when she was alive.

Once, shortly after Esther's death, Clarence asked on the phone, "Where does the garden hose go in the winter?" This was like Samuel asking, "Where do the butterflies go in the winter? And the ants? Where do the ants go when it snows?"

To Clarence, Joanna said impatiently, "How am I supposed to know? I haven't lived in your house for nearly seven years."

"But your mother," Clarence said, "your mother had a special place for everything."

"It doesn't matter now," Joanna said. "Put it wherever you want." By his silence she knew she had hurt him.

Another time on the phone Clarence said, "Since your mother left,

I haven't been able to find the roasting pan." As if Esther had run off with another man and taken the roasting pan with her.

Sometimes, when he had figured out how to cook a new dish, iron a shirt, or wash the living-room drapes, he said, "I did it! Your mother sure would be surprised."

He has never said anything about missing her. The closest he has come to this was in a letter written on the third anniversary of Esther's death in which he said, *It is three years today since your mother died and I hope things get better soon. I'm going out to the cemetery after lunch.* He goes to the cemetery often and takes good care of the peonies and geraniums he has planted at her headstone. He complains that the groundskeepers are lazy and sloppy. If he didn't look after her grave himself, he says, the whole thing would be overgrown with dandelions and ragweed. He says this with such resentment that Joanna feels guilty for not being there to help him. When she suggested once in passing that he might consider selling the house and finding a place here near them, he said, "But what about the grave? Who would look after the grave?"

Now, just as they are hanging up, Clarence says, "It wasn't your fault, you know, her being so bitter. I don't know what it was but I know it wasn't your fault."

As she puts the receiver down gently, Joanna realizes that for all of her life she has thought it was.

When she went back home for the funeral, the job of going through her mother's things had fallen, naturally enough, to her. She realizes now that she had been hoping to find something that would explain her mother's bitterness, something that would let her, Joanna, off the hook. But there were no secrets, at least none that she could unearth. There were no love letters, no secret scandalous diaries, no photographs of mysterious men. The letters she did find were the ones she herself had written to her parents since she left home. She could not bear to read them and so she threw them out. The photographs she did find were those which Esther had taken of her flowers over the years. What she thought at first were diaries were in fact lists of the flowers Esther had planted each year, annotated with fertilizing schedules and occasional comments on successes, failures, and the weather. These were all in a small box in the cedar chest in her parents' bedroom. In this fragrant polished chest she also found a whole set of yellow towels, unopened, a box of twelve tiny cocktail forks with coloured plastic handles, a white linen tablecloth stained in several places, a padded push-up bra with rusted underwires, and a blue douche bag.

There were no skeletons in the closet either. Only dozens of the polyester pantsuits which Esther had favoured in her later years, many sleeveless shiny blouses in various floral patterns, a green velour housecoat she had never worn, and one floor-length black skirt which she wore to weddings and the annual paper mill party. In the bottom of the closet there were plastic boxes filled with scarves, hats, and purses.

It would seem there had been no central act, no pivotal event, no murder, no mayhem, no mystery. Perhaps it had been merely the ineffable sadness of daily life that had made her mother so bitter and angry. It would seem there was no one to blame after all.

Just as she had never known why her mother was always so angry, now she will never know why she was so bitter either, and she has not craved a chunk of that bittersweet baking chocolate since her mother left.

77. Hammer

WHEN CLARENCE WAS renovating the house, it was filled all summer with the sounds of hammers and saws. Joanna tried with all her might to keep her eyes from blinking shut at every hammer blow. She asked Esther why the noise made her eyes close and Esther said it was just a reflex, like when Dr. Graham tapped her kneecap with his little silver hammer and her leg jerked up all by itself. (And, Joanna will think much later, like every time she sees Lewis on the street or hears his voice on the phone and her heart jumps up.)

When occasionally Joanna managed to master the reflex and hold her eyes still against the hammer blow, they filled then with tears like Esther's always did chopping onions. They filled with stinging swimming tears as if someone had called her a bad name or slapped her hard across the face.

Which had only happened once so far, that time in the car when Clarence said she was a bad girl for sticking her tongue out at him when he said they couldn't stop for ice cream and then she said he was stupid poop and his hand from the steering wheel flashed across and slapped her. While she howled with outrage, he stared at her as if he'd never seen her before, stared at his hand too and then wiped the back of it across his mouth, stopped for the red light, turned on the radio to listen to the news.

They were all in the front seat, Joanna in the middle, her mother on the other side saying nothing, looking out the window, a muscle twitching in her jaw. Joanna could feel her own heart throbbing in her throat, pounding in her left ear.

Later in school she will learn about the working parts of the ear, all of them confusing. The canals which could not be like the ones that boats went through. The drum which could not be like the one in the marching band in the Santa Claus parade. The anvil which could not be like the iron block they made horseshoes on in *Black Beauty*. The stirrups which could not be like the ones they put their feet in when riding Black Beauty. The hammer which could not be like the one her father used but which could maybe explain the occasional pounding in her head.

78. Thirsty

IN THE DREAM Joanna is saying, "You have always been unhappy. The more you talk about being unhappy, the more unhappy you get. Maybe you'll never be happy. Maybe you've lost your happiness plug." She is sitting at a table, and after she says this in a calm quiet voice she drinks a large glass of cold water. She drains the glass and puts it down on the table. It is a trick glass. When she looks at it, it is full of water again. She drains it and puts it down. It fills up again. She drains it and puts it down. It fills up again. She feels hot and panicky. Both the glass and her thirst are bottomless. It is a liquid version of the myth of Sisyphus.

She awakens so thirsty that her throat hurts. She cannot remember who she was talking to in the dream. She does remember that this notion of the happiness plug came from a self-help book she'd read once, probably when she was trying to get over Lewis. The book said that some people have indeed lost their ability to be happy, as if they were like the Dutch dikes come unplugged, having popped the cork that held them together, and so all happiness, satisfaction, and contentment which they might have been harbouring just leaked away. This book said that being happy was largely a matter of *deciding* to be happy.

She gets out of bed without waking Gordon and pours herself a glass of cold water in the kitchen. She pads around the dark house in her bare feet sipping the water. Each room at this hour seems to have drawn into itself, perfectly quiet and self-contained. Tiptoeing into the living room, she would not be surprised to find it empty or all the furniture covered in white sheets as if vacated years ago. Through the blinds, the streetlight casts pinkish stripes across the hardwood floor. A car passes like a barge. A light goes on in an apartment on the top floor of a building three blocks over. It is early December. There is no snow yet. In three weeks Clarence will be here for Christmas. Smoke rises from the chimney of the house across the street. A train whistles. A dog barks once. The night is not ominous.

She puts the empty glass down on the coffee table. Nothing happens. She goes back to bed. Just as she is getting back to sleep, Samuel calls out for a glass of water. When she takes it in to him, he says, "I'm thirsty. I'm so thirsty I feel like I'm going to faint."

She wonders if dreams can be a contagion. Do they move from room to room, turning sideways like cartoon ghosts and slipping through walls? Do they possibly go from house to house so that even now all her neighbours are waking up thirsty and running large glasses of very cold water? Perhaps dreaming is like yawning, the way you just can't help yourself if another person yawns, even if you're not tired. Perhaps dreaming is like sadness, the way it dribbles off the sad person and oozes through the whole room, until even the happy people are left feeling ragged and eroded, smiling precariously.

Later in the day, while pouring herself a large glass of cold water she remembers the dream again. This time she sees a fur coat, a green café table, a woman's bowed head, a folded newspaper. She is saying, or the other woman is saying, "I'm always so thirsty, why am I always so thirsty? It's as if I can never be sure I've had enough."

79. City

JOANNA ALWAYS HEARD Toronto referred to as "that evil city." This descriptive phrase was seldom actually uttered aloud. Rather, it was implied by her parents' tone of voice, tacked on in judgemental parentheses whenever the name of the city came up in the news or casual conversation. Neither Clarence nor Esther had ever actually been to Toronto. Except for Clarence passing through on his way home from the war, spending a weekend in Toronto courtesy of the Canadian Army. It was in Toronto that he'd had the steak and couldn't finish it because his stomach had shrunk. Other than that, he did not have much recollection of the place except that it had rained. It was a wonder that it had been ordinary rain and not the fire and brimstone which had poured down upon Sodom and Gomorrah.

Clarence and Esther disliked Toronto in the way that people dislike books they've never read, movies they've never seen, foods they've never tasted, and people they've never met. Perhaps their dislike of big cities in general stemmed from some innate misanthropic mistrust of people in large groups. They just naturally assumed that so many people amassed in one place was bound to lead to trouble. Big trouble. Murder, mayhem, and communicable disease on an epidemic scale.

Toronto, according to Esther and Clarence, was dirty, noisy, smelly, and dangerous. So, no doubt, were each and every one of its inhabitants. Except for Esther's sister Florence who, the implication was, did not know any better or was being held there against her will. Children born and raised in Toronto were destined to fall into lives of crime and dissipation at a very early age. If they did not become criminals themselves, they were bound to become the victims of crime.

Joanna could not imagine going to Toronto or wanting to. She was mystified when Penny and Pamela spoke of it as a glamorous, exciting place filled with beautiful women, handsome men, expensive cars, huge mansions, and exotic animals (lions, tigers, elephants, and swans) who lived at the Toronto zoo. They said there was a castle too. They got their information from their cousin Doreen who had moved there after high school and lived now with her husband, Donny, and their four-year-old daughter, Mary Jane, on the twenty-first floor of a high-rise apartment building. Joanna had never been inside an apartment building of any height and could not imagine what it was like to live that far from the ground. When she asked where Mary Jane played, they said, "On the balcony, silly." Joanna was not sure what a balcony was. They drew her a picture of a shelf sticking out of the side of a tall building. Around it they drew vertical bars. When she worried that Mary Jane would fall off, they said, "Of course not. Look at the bars, silly." She looked at the bars. The balcony looked like a little jail in the air. That night she prayed that she would never have to go to Toronto.

For years she never did. For years whenever she thought of Toronto what came to mind was a string of stereotypical images: buildings so tall you could not see the tops of them, homeless people sleeping in doorways or boxes under bridges, zooming taxis, sirens in the night, pawnshops, strip joints, skinheads, motorcycle gangs, no trees, no gardens, no sanctuary anywhere. Over the years she knew a few people who moved to Toronto and were never heard from again. Henry was one of them.

Later she will have occasion to go there and she will like it. She will stay for three nights alone on the twelfth floor of a fancy hotel on Bloor Street. Everything about her hotel room is soft: the colours, the carpet, the bedsheets, the toilet paper. She happily spends a lot of money to do, see, and buy things she cannot get at home. She goes to an elegant reception in an even fancier hotel. As she nibbles hors d'oeuvres and sips champagne by the window, she watches black and white limousines passing down the busy street like cruise ships, bearing royalty, rock stars, and mysterious multi-millionaires behind their tinted windows. She knows she is supposed to either ignore them or be appalled by their decadence. But in fact she is impressed.

She attends an artists' conference by day and curls up in her pastel hotel room at night, feeling safe and sound above the busy street. She calls home each night and Gordon and Samuel are missing her very much. She checks once to see if Henry is listed in the phone book but he is not. He has well and truly vanished. Her relatives who might possibly live here cannot be reached either: poor Aunt Florence died years ago and she does not know her cousins' married names.

Standing in her darkened room she can see straight into the apartments of the high-rise across the street. In one apartment she can see two people, a man and a woman, who appear to be upside-down, walking on the ceiling as they move from room to room. She feels for a minute as if she is in a science fiction movie. Then she remembers that she is in Toronto. Where, it would seem, anything is possible. Perhaps they do it with mirrors. But why?

Nevertheless she feels energized by this and other absurdities as the whole city teems around her like a massive kinetic collage animated by a perpetual motion machine.

She travels home by train. The ceiling is painted to look like the sky, pale blue with fluffy summer clouds. Outside the train windows, the fields are snow-covered and the morning sky is grey. The trees without leaves in the distance look black as if they've been burnt in a forest fire. The men seated directly behind Joanna are discussing animal husbandry: slow sperm, fresher semen, cows who are all calved out. She has had enough of absurdity. She wants to go home. By eleven o'clock the businessmen in front and to the left have put away their briefcases, calculators, and cellular phones and are drinking rum and Coke greedily. The porter can hardly bring them fast enough. Joanna reads *Madame Bovary* and drinks bad coffee out of a leaky cardboard cup.

Samuel and Gordon are waiting at the station when she arrives. Samuel says, "I missed you. What did you buy me?"

That night she calls Clarence to assure him that she has been to Toronto and survived. Clarence says, "How was the weather?"

Joanna says, "Fine." In truth she cannot much remember the weather.

Clarence says, "Well, at least it didn't rain. That's something."

80. Square

JOANNA SITS IN front of a large white piece of illustration board on her drafting table. To the left is a pile of tissue paper in all colours of the rainbow and then some. To the right are a pair of sharp scissors, a pot of glue, and several sheets of Letraset numbers in various sizes. She is about to begin a new collage. She is tired of making meaning, telling stories, trying to transform complex abstract concepts into concrete visual acts of embodiment. Every picture tells a story. So they say. What she wants to make now is a picture that does not: a picture that is pleasing to the eye and nothing else. She aspires to the graceful symmetry of squares, the sensible, dependable, irrefutable balance of four equal sides and four right angles. She is inspired by the orderliness of geometry, the cleanliness of numbers, the luxurious conclusiveness of mathematics.

Mostly she got the idea from Samuel who is learning how to count. He counts his fingers. He counts his toes. He counts his eyes. He counts his nose. He counts wooden blocks. He counts teddy bears. He counts cars. He counts trees. He counts food. His apple, his toast, his hot dog are cut into pieces so he can count them while he eats. One two three four, yes. One two three five, no.

He is also learning colours. The grass is green. The car is red. The driveway is black. The toilet is white. The balloon is yellow. The balloon is not blue. If this balloon is yellow, it cannot be blue.

Yes, no. Black, white. True, false. Right, wrong. Joanna admires the clarity of colours, the logic of numbers, and Samuel's innocent certainty that this morning's right answers will still hold true tomorrow afternoon.

Joanna is reminded of the fact that, although English and Art were her favourite subjects in high school, she often slid into her seat in Math class with relief. There she could believe that answers were not only possible but permanent: once you got the answer right, it would stay that way. It could not be changed by circumstance, experience, or emotional upheaval. You could have confidence in numbers, you could always count on them. Perhaps you could acquire blind faith through mathematics. Later she will learn that faith is one thing and what you put it in is quite another.

In the Math textbook all the right answers were given at the back just like a crossword puzzle book. There was also a set of mathematical tables taken from a source originally published in 1620. Joanna found it reassuring to know that almost three hundred and fifty years later, the square root of 79 was still 8.888 and 199 squared was still 39,601.

At the high school level anyway, mathematics would seem to involve a practical application of quite reasonable (although perhaps difficult) operations which then resulted in an answer. Even if getting to that answer involved an entire page or more of intricate calculations, and even if there might occasionally be more than one way to get there, still there *was* an answer. In making your way to that end, there was no danger of finding out along the way other things you didn't want to know. These answers did not involve power, betrayal, or an untimely loss of innocence. These answers would not change your life when you weren't looking.

She begins cutting perfect squares of different sizes from the large sheets of tissue paper. The colours are rich and deep. She measures carefully with a metal T-square and glues them to the illustration board. She covers the whole board with coloured squares. Then she lifts numbers from the sheet of Letraset and applies them at random on top of the squares. She thinks about the straight lines, the accurate angles, the luminous congenial colours. She thinks about purity and permanence. She lays more tissue paper over some of the numbers. She works on this piece all afternoon and by suppertime she is satisfied that she has circumnavigated her own compulsion to make meaning. She feels lighter (if not enlightened), clearer (if not translucid), calmer (if not downright serene).

That night in bed after she and Gordon have made love she makes the mistake of wondering how many times they've made love this

month, this year, last year, how many times since they met? How many
more times will they make love before they stop or die? She cannot do
the calculations in either direction, backwards or forwards, past or future. She recalls those interminable twelve-year-old Sundays during
which she tried to figure out how many more miserable seconds she
was likely to live. The numbers were slippery, astronomical, out of this
world.

Now, twenty years later, how many seconds does she have left? How
many of those past seconds has she wasted feeling sorry for herself?
How many more is she likely to waste? How many times has she told
Gordon that she loves him? How many times has she told *Samuel* that
she loves him? How many more chances to say it does she have left?
There are other numbers, less momentous perhaps but equally intimidating, equally incalculable: how many times has she told Samuel to
be careful, be quiet, be brave, eat your supper, wash your hands, brush
your teeth, go to sleep, stop crying, don't worry, everything will be all
right, don't worry, come here and I'll hug you?

The insomnia has hold of her now. How many minutes till morning?
How many times has she cooked supper, done the dishes, defrosted the
fridge, cleaned the toilet, washed the floors, scrubbed the bathtub,
cleaned the oven (not very many, not often enough)? If she were able
to divine these numbers, all of them, would they tell the story of her
life? For that matter, how many times has she had insomnia? How
many times has she yet to have it?

For how many minutes exactly had she been so erroneously convinced
of the comforting simplicity of numbers? How many times has she
gone to bed believing something to be true, only to wake up again
knowing, or at least suspicious, that it is not?

She gets up and goes to the living room, roams through the shelves
until she comes up with a book called *What Counts: The Complete Harper's
Index*. There would appear to be ample proof that numbers are anything
but simple:

Percentage of Pepsi drinkers who say they would switch to Coke if
it contained oat bran: 74.

Percentage of American men who say they would not have sex with Madonna if she asked: 60.

Average number of days a West German man goes without changing his underwear: 7.

Barbie's measurements if she were life-size: 39-23-33.

Melting point of Dippity-Do: 122°F.

Number of hands Saeed Al-Sayyaf, a Saudi Arabian executioner, has chopped off since he was hired in 1954: 60. Number of heads: 600.

On the bottom shelf at the back she finds her old Math textbook. Like the Sunday School Bible, it has been carted around for years. It has a blue-grey cover with silver lettering that says: *Functions, Relations, and Transformations*. She realizes that she has forgotten to figure in the fact that numbers too are subject to manipulation, negotiation, and change. That numbers like words are open to interpretation. That mathematics, like any other language, can be used to obscure and complicate just as well as to clarify and simplify.

She has forgotten that even while he is learning to count, Samuel is also learning more questions for which there are no answers in the back of the book. How many is zero? How long would it take to count to a zillion? Why do the numbers look the same in French but you say them differently? She has forgotten that his favourite funny counting game has more to do with love than numbers.

He says, "I love you."

She says, "I love you too."

He giggles and says, "I love you three."

She laughs and says, "I love you forty-seven."

He throws his arms around her neck and says, "I love you a zillion and one."

She has forgotten about the impossibility of squaring the circle. Even geometry presents insoluble problems. She has forgotten that if a square is a neat empty space, then you can put anything at all inside of it. She will have to rework the collage in the morning.

81. Butter

THERE WAS THE childhood game played with buttercups plucked from the overgrown end of the back lane, then held under the chin, and if it showed yellow on your skin, it meant that you liked butter. Joanna never wondered why everybody she tried it on turned out to really love butter, except on cloudy days when it was hard to tell. She loved butter, especially melted on hot popcorn, and so she supposed that everyone did. Penny and Pamela soon set her straight, explaining how the yellow under the chin was just a reflection from the flower and had nothing to do with butter at all.

Joanna still liked to gather buttercups anyway. She brought them home in bouquets to her mother who usually refrained from pointing out that they were nothing but straggly weeds.

Esther loved butter too. Although she complained bitterly about the ever-increasing price, she continued to buy it exclusively, regarding margarine with great disdain. This was in the days when margarine was called oleo and came in thick white unappetizing sticks with a packet of orange dye you had to mix in yourself. Joanna only knew this because Penny and Pamela's mother used margarine. Whenever Joanna had lunch at their house, Esther interrogated her afterwards and sniffed when she heard they were still using margarine. Joanna, out of loyalty to Esther, always agreed that it was nowhere near as tasty as butter, although she did enjoy helping mix in the dye.

During one of these lunches at the Nystroms', Joanna overheard Mrs. Nystrom talking on the phone in the hallway while she and the twins ate their margarine-laden baloney sandwiches in the kitchen. Mrs. Nystrom was gossiping cheerfully with a friend, nodding and making satisfied sounds of agreement while the person on the other end went on and on, obviously relating a complicated story about somebody they both knew and disliked. Finally Mrs. Nystrom cried out joyfully, "Oh, isn't that just like her? Butter wouldn't melt in her mouth!'' Although surely Mrs. Nystrom was talking about somebody else, Joanna thought of her mother, pictured her sitting even now at the blue kitchen table across the street with her arms crossed and her mouth clamped shut around a large chunk of butter which perched whole and unmelting on her cold tongue while her own daughter sat over here gorging herself on cheap tasteless oleo, already reaching for more.

For a long time Joanna too bought real butter only, even when she could not afford it, could barely afford the bread to put it on. The quality of margarine had been steadily improved and perfected over the years but still she would not buy it, was just as prideful as her mother had been about real butter only, lopping a block off the pound and placing it carefully in the handmade ceramic butter dish she had paid dearly for at a local pottery shop, rewrapping the remainder in its silver paper and storing it obediently in the labelled compartment in the fridge door.

It is not until after she is married to Gordon that she abandons butter and switches to margarine, the cheapest brand at that, a startling yellow in its thrifty turquoise tub. It is a matter of money and cholesterol. They are, like most people in their circumstances, newly and deeply involved in an intimate relationship with the mortgage company. They are also, like most people in their age group, becoming more health conscious. Because, as Gordon likes to say, they must now live long enough to pay off the damn mortgage.

Joanna supposes it is more or less neurotic to feel a thrill of guilt and rebellious satisfaction every time she plops a sixty-nine-cent tub of margarine into her shopping cart. In the fridge, she now keeps several rolls of film in the butter box. She imagines Esther rolling over in her tidy grave, still with that solid chunk of butter lodged in the back of her mouth, perhaps with a plate of shortbread cookies levitating above her outstretched scornful hands. Esther was proud of her shortbread, which she made only once a year, the week before Christmas, from an old family recipe, simply but seriously delicious. Esther could not bake or serve these cookies without commenting on the fact that it was the butter, real butter, a whole cup of real butter, that made them so delectable. They really did melt in your mouth.

Joanna does not mention her margarine mutiny to anyone. Until one Sunday morning on the phone when Clarence is telling her that he got groceries the day before. He often does this, describing in detail the items he bought, how much they cost, what time he went, and how long it took. Sometimes it takes him all afternoon and he seems pleased with this. He tells her of these shopping trips, she figures, to prove that he is managing well enough without Esther. But it makes her depressed to picture him just like the old men she sees in the grocery store here, clutching their carts with one hand and their list or a cane with the other, seriously studying shelf upon bewildering shelf of cereal, spaghetti sauce, toilet paper, or tea bags. She knows just by looking at these old men that they are widowers like Clarence, deserted by their dead wives, forced at this late date to learn the rudiments of domestic life, forced to feed themselves or starve, forced to eat alone every night facing a blank wall, a bad oil painting of green hills and blue water, or last year's calendar still turned to November, facing a single plate of dry pork chops, mushy peas, lumpy mashed potatoes, and canned pears for dessert.

This morning Clarence mentions that he stocked up on margarine because it was on sale. Joanna laughs and admits that she too has made the switch. Clarence says, "What would your mother think?" They chuckle together like conspirators, like children caught in the act, caught, so to speak, with their hands in the cookie jar, proud of their own audacity but surprised by it too.

"Of course I still buy butter for the Christmas shortbread," Joanna says, as if to lessen the blow of her betrayal.

"Well yes," Clarence says soberly. "Yes, you would have to do that."

82. Doctor

ESTHER SAID SHE'D never had a single symptom of any kind until she went to the doctor and he told her she had cancer. "I felt fine, just fine," she liked to say, darkly. "I was healthy as a horse until I went for a checkup and then the next thing you know I was on the table, cut open, and he was scooping out my insides." Until that fateful visit, Esther had prided herself on the fact that she had not been to a doctor since Joanna was born thirteen years before.

Joanna saw no reason to doubt her mother's version of the story. Esther had never seemed sick and she had certainly never complained. Secretly Joanna blamed her mother's hysterectomy on herself, on the fact that two weeks before, she had stolen a pair of black silk panties from Woolworth's. For two weeks she thought she'd got away with it. She never wore the panties but she liked to run them, cool and silky, through her fingers in her dark bedroom in the middle of the night. They made her feel excited, adult, and dangerous. Then Esther got cancer and Joanna threw the panties away, having cut them into tiny pieces and hidden them in an empty Kleenex box that was going out with the garbage in the morning.

Esther, who did not know about the panties, had no reason to blame Joanna. It seemed, by implication, that Esther considered it to be all the doctor's fault. Somehow, if she hadn't gone to see Dr. Pesetsky in the first place, then she wouldn't have been sick. Could it be, Joanna wondered, that if you didn't *know* you were sick, if nobody *told* you you were sick, then you weren't?

Ten years later, when Joanna was twenty-three, she found a lump in her left breast. It was a year since she had moved away from home. It was at the time when breast self-examination was the subject of a national education campaign and illustrated pamphlets on how to do it correctly were available everywhere. Joanna and all her friends were conscientiously examining themselves, carefully following the detailed steps in these diagrams, proud to be taking such good care of their bodies, their selves. Joanna was the only one who ever found anything.

At the feel of the lump that morning in the bathtub, she was seized with terror. The lump itself, upon detection, filled instantly with pain and within minutes her whole breast was aching and aflame. It seemed to be swelling, engorged with evil malignant cells. When her hands stopped shaking, she called Dr. Millan and made an appointment for early the next morning.

She passed the rest of the day in a fever of anxiety, tormenting herself with half-remembered stories of young women having their breasts sliced right off and then dying anyway. She'd seen Before-and-After photographs of these women in the pamphlets. In the Before pictures, black lines had been drawn around their perky-looking breasts to indicate where the incisions would be made. In the After pictures, there were only flat spaces and scars where their breasts had been. There were no faces in any of them. These photographs were like the cookbook diagrams of animals she had coloured as a child, all of them divided into carefully labelled sections, all of them headless and legless except the pig.

All night long her left breast ached, also her right breast, her stomach, and her thighs, as if the disease were running rampant through her body. All night long she dreamed of doctors and breasts, bloody breasts held up by grinning doctors like dripping trophies dangling from the ends of long knives.

In the morning she arrived early at Dr. Millan's office. Fidgeting around in the empty waiting room, shuffling through the pile of old magazines and dilapidated children's books, she found a volume called *The Bible Story*. It was the same book she'd read as a child in Dr. Pesetsky's waiting room (Dr. Pesetsky having taken over Dr. Graham's practice after his death). It must, she thought, be a permanent fixture in medical offices everywhere. It was a large hardcover book, lavishly illustrated and written especially for children. Actually it was the first of a series you could order by mailing in the perforated card inside the front cover. After each visit to Dr. Pesetsky's office, she had begged Esther to please, please, please send in the card but she wouldn't.

The receptionist called her name. Dr. Millan examined her thoroughly. He congratulated her for having discovered the lump herself. He said it was probably nothing, we'll just keep an eye on it, try not to worry, come back in a month, try not to worry yourself sick. He patted her hand and sent her on home.

That evening she called her mother and said, with little preamble, "I have a lump in my left breast."

"Did you call the doctor?" Esther asked.

"Yes, I've already been to see him."

"Good, good, now don't cry, crying won't help anything. What did the doctor say?"

Joanna told her.

"Well then, don't worry, I'm sure it's nothing, I'm sure the doctor is right."

"But I thought you didn't trust doctors," Joanna wailed. "I thought you said you were fine, just fine, until you went to the doctor and he told you that you had cancer. I thought you said you had no symptoms at all until he said you were sick. I thought you said it was all his fault."

"Well, of course I had symptoms. Why do you think I went to the doctor in the first place? Of course it wasn't his fault. He saved my life. I haven't been back to see him since, mind you, but then again I'm not sick." She also said they should not say anything to Clarence until they knew for sure. Just in case.

Esther, it seemed, was as ambivalent about doctors as she was about God. In both cases, it seemed wiser to hedge your bets. God might be real, right, and omnipotent after all. Doctors too.

For a month Joanna tried not to worry and kept her hands well away from her breasts. All her prayers were promises: *If you let me live, I will be a good person for the rest of my life. I will never again be selfish, greedy, quarrelsome, or cruel.* She wasn't sure if she was talking to God or Dr. Millan.

When she went back to Dr. Millan, he said the lump was gone. When she called her mother that evening, Esther said, "Good. He was right. Good for him." Joanna, for the time being, was saved and she never performed breast self-examination again.

When Esther died five years later, it was a heart attack, not cancer, that killed her. Clarence told Joanna that even Dr. Pesetsky was surprised. The doctor said he thought Esther was healthy as a horse, especially her heart which had never shown any signs of weakness. But then again, Dr. Pesetsky said, she hadn't been in for a checkup in God knows how long.

Joanna thought about horses and hearts. She pictured a horse's heart jammed into her mother's small chest, a huge horse's heart leaping and throbbing, heaving and pounding, finally bursting and breaking out free. She pictured her mother dead on the kitchen floor with a horse's heart twitching on the tile beside her. In fact, Esther had not died on the kitchen floor. She had died in the hospital later, hours later, after Clarence, just coming home from the corner store with a loaf of bread and a litre of milk, had found her on the floor and called the ambulance. She had died in the hospital hours later with Clarence beside her and neither horses nor hearts anywhere in sight.

83. Loud

ESTHER HAD RULES about makeup: no nail polish (especially not red which was for tramps), no mascara (especially not blue which was ridiculous because who in their right mind would want blue eyelashes), no lipstick (especially not that ghastly white which made perfectly normal young girls look like bloodless drug-addicted ghouls). She finally relented a little during Joanna's later years of high school and allowed her to wear clear nail polish, a little brown mascara, and pale pink lip gloss which you could hardly even see anyway, so what was the point? She still would not allow Joanna to get her ears pierced. Instead she had to wear those stupid clip-ons which were either so loose that they fell off and were lost forever in snowbanks, storm sewers, or the long summer grass—or so tight that her earlobes felt like they were being pinched in a vise and ached for hours afterwards.

What all these things, nail polish, pierced earrings, mascara, and lipstick, had in common, in Esther's estimation, was that they were loud.

loud *adj.* 1. garish, gaudy, flashy, tasteless, lurid, glaring, flaring, flashy, blinding; conspicuous, striking, flagrant, outstanding, outlandish, pronounced, obtrusive, extravagant, spectacular; ostentatious, showy, flaunting, snazzy, splashy, jazzy; tawdry, meretricious.

For a young girl (indeed for all females in general), the only thing worse than being dirty, in Esther's estimation, was being loud.

loud *adj.* 2. bold, brassy, brazen, vulgar, gross, crass, rough, earthy, ribald; uncouth, uncivilized, unrefined, ill-bred; wild-and-woolly, rough-and-ready, hooliganish; coarse, rude, gruff, crude, raw, boorish, loutish, rowdy.

By the time Joanna was old enough to do more or less whatever she liked (as long as she could override the sound of her mother's admonishing voice in her head), makeup had generally fallen into disfavour. She did get her ears pierced and began to accumulate a collection of colourful dangling earrings which she kept on a screen hung on her bedroom wall. Earrings were still all right but makeup had come to be regarded as a vain and shallow adornment practised only by silly, superficial, or insecure women who thought that plastering themselves with cosmetics made them more attractive to men. The use of makeup constituted an unenlightened form of participation in patriarchal society's conspiracy to keep women subordinate and powerless. Makeup was one of the prime forces in aiding and abetting women's conditioned inability to accept their own bodies as naturally beautiful and desirable. Such an obsession with one's physical appearance was generally considered to be clear-cut evidence of brainlessness, vacuity, and/or inauthenticity. It was a form of facial fraud which benefited no one except the makeup manufacturers, men who had become multi-millionaires in the process of promoting and exploiting women's insecurities. Women who wore makeup were foolish. Men who liked women who wore makeup were male chauvinists not worth having anyway. Women must strive to believe, as men always had, that they were perfect just the way they were.

Joanna was prepared to go along with these ideas but not to the extreme of forsaking her deodorant or her little pink razor for armpits and legs. She never did get over the sheer sensual pleasure of lathering her legs in the bathtub with musky-scented soap, drawing the razor carefully up from the ankle, gently around the knee, stroking her smooth skin with the fluffy towel afterwards, admiring the way they glowed brown in the summer, the way they slipped between clean sheets or under the very hairy legs of a very eager man. She never did get over how happy it made her to be told (by some such eager hairy man) that she had the smoothest skin in the world. She also never gave up mascara altogether either, because she knew it accentuated the impact of her pretty brown eyes. She was sometimes a little ashamed of these concessions to fashion and flattery, but never ashamed enough to give them up.

She occasionally wondered about the fate of a girl named Cecilia Wright she'd known in high school who proudly and frequently proclaimed that she got up an hour early every morning to put her makeup on. This information was usually dispensed in the girls' bathroom between classes. There was cigarette smoke rising like a blue veil from the toilet cubicles and a dozen girls ranged in front of the mirrors, leaning over the sinks to apply more mascara, more blusher, more lipstick, squinting and contorting their faces until they looked like a row of animated gargoyles, bemoaning pimples, freckles, and laugh lines, sucking in their cheeks to look like Twiggy, whose emaciated face was on the front of every fashion magazine. Cecilia Wright had a whole bag full of makeup which she generously shared around with those less fortunate. At home she had a makeup mirror, the professional kind with little round bulbs around the edges. She absolutely hated these fluorescent lights which made even her perfect complexion look pale and blotchy. She said that even after she got married she would still get up early to put on her makeup because no man in the world wants to wake up to the sight of a woman without her face on.

It is Saturday and Joanna is downtown doing errands, trudging up and down the slushy sidewalks with Samuel yanking on her arm. More wet snow is just starting to fall. They are slopping in and out of the bank which is jammed with end-of-the-month cheque-cashers, in and out of Zellers to buy him more socks, Batman underwear even though they cost twice as much as the plain white, another pair of mitts because he's lost the other ones again, in and out of the hardware store looking for a new kettle that doesn't whistle and doesn't cost an arm and a leg, in and out of the health food store for vitamins, sunflower seeds, seven-grain bread, and organic peanut butter. Samuel is still yanking and yacking on about all the things he wants for Christmas because there are decorations everywhere already even though it's only the middle of November and he hasn't even finished his Hallowe'en candy yet. Her other arm is aching with the weight of her purchases and her feet are wet and she almost has a headache which somehow feels worse than really having one and why should Gordon have the luxury of spending Saturday afternoon at home alone with classical music on the stereo, a fresh pot of coffee, and a fat hardcover novel, while she is doing all this errand shit, even though she offered to do it. She was just being polite and he was supposed to be polite too and say, "Oh no, dear, that's all right, you deserve a break, I'll do it." But he didn't. He said, "Okay, great," and headed for the couch, and now here she is, every few steps passing another mother whose arm is also being yanked off by another small chattering child and she would like to smile exasperated sympathy at one of these women but they're all looking down, at the slushy sidewalk, at their wet feet, at their tired trudging legs which would be better off dancing in silk pantyhose and red high heels. She passes a very handsome dark-haired young man in tight jeans and a black leather jacket and she would have spotted him a mile away because he is her type, just the type of man who can always make her heart twitch even though she is a perfectly happy wife and mother, she's not dead yet, she can still look, can't she? This young man walks right past as if she is invisible. There was a time, she's sure there was a time, when this handsome dark-haired young man would have looked straight into her eyes, his heart twitching too, other parts of his anatomy also shook up, and they would have gazed at each other with electrifying lust and walked away fantasizing about all the things they could have done to each other given half a chance, given half an hour, given another life-time. She catches sight of herself in the plate-glass window of Shoppers Drug Mart and she looks like all those other mothers she's been trying to smile at all afternoon, dowdy, harried, and defeated, her posture is bad, and if she's not really invisible, she might as well be. There have been times, many other times, when she hoped she did look like all those other mothers, times when she just wanted to be normal so that Samuel would not grow up scarred for life having had a mother who was an eccentric artist-type and not at all like June Cleaver with her pearls and perfect hairdo first thing in the morning, not to mention her melodious voice and her infinite patience. Yes, there have been times when she wanted to look like all those other mothers but this is not one of them.

She marches straight into Shoppers Drug Mart and walks right over to the lipstick counter and picks out three tubes from the hundreds on display. She wants the loudest brightest colours she can find: Cherries in the Snow, Wine with Everything, and Really Really Really Red.

She also buys a chocolate bar for Samuel, a newspaper, and the current issue of *Vogue* which is as thick as the phone book. She does not buy shampoo, mouthwash, or Gordon's favourite foot powder which are the things they really need.

When they get home Gordon has nodded off over his novel. The house is quiet and warm. Samuel, still chewing on his chocolate bar, goes into the living room to pester his father awake. Now that he no longer naps himself, he doesn't think anybody else should either.

Joanna puts away her purchases and then tries on one of the lipsticks, Cherries in the Snow, which is a rich deep pink. She goes into the bedroom and picks a fancy pair of earrings off the screen, a four-inch-long dangling pair which she bought on a day not unlike this one, a day when she wanted to be (or at least look like) somebody else, a day when she wanted to be brazen and loud, but she hasn't had the nerve to wear them yet. They are made of wooden beads in different colours and sizes strung in three strands, hot pink, blue, green, fluorescent yellow and orange, also a few pearly seashells. They brush her neck gently whenever she moves and the beads rattle softly like a new voice inside her head, like music, the blues, temptation, seduction, a saxophone. She puts on her pretty pink blouse.

She should be vacuuming, she should be starting supper, she should be washing the bathroom floor. She is sitting at the kitchen table with her lipstick on, fancy earrings, hot pink blouse, sipping a glass of white wine, and reading the new issue of *Vogue*. She is skimming the ads for makeup which will do magic, shoes that will change your life, and underwear that would turn on the dead. She is studying the beautiful models displaying their wares in front of motorcycles, fast cars, helicopters, and the French Riviera. These women look lovely in $350 T-shirts, $800 orange satin slingbacks, $1,600 silk jackets with matching $500 pants by Ralph Lauren, and $1,700 pink purses by Chanel.

Eventually Samuel and Gordon, who have been horsing around in the living room, peek their heads into the kitchen, intrigued no doubt by her silence.

Samuel says, "Oh, Mommy, you look beautiful! Kiss me!" He is not always this good at saying exactly the right thing. She kisses him on the cheek and he runs off to the bathroom to examine her lip prints on his skin.

Gordon says, "Well. Who are you supposed to be?" He is not always this good at saying exactly the wrong thing.

Joanna says, "I can't remember." She throws an old Steppenwolf tape into the cassette player, turns it up loud loud loud, and starts slamming around in the cupboards, starting the spaghetti sauce for supper, singing "Born to Be Wild" through gritted teeth.

Gordon, who is not so stupid after all, says, "Never mind that. We'll go out to eat."

Joanna says, "We'll never find a babysitter now."

"Yes we will." He phones a dozen people in fifteen minutes and finally Jennie Holmes from down the street says she'll be over at 7:15.

They go to their favourite place downtown, the Long Street Diner, which is not on Long Street and not a diner either. It is a small trendy upscale place, lushly decorated with hanging plants, potted trees, wicker furniture painted in glossy primary colours. The dishes are chunky authentic Mexican pieces, hand-painted. The cutlery has matching ceramic handles. The napkins are one hundred per cent cotton printed in various colourful native North American motifs, folded accordion style and placed in the crystal wineglasses with an aesthetic flourish. On the plain white walls there are paintings by local artists offered for sale and changed every two months. The regular clientele is composed largely of young downtown professionals and artistic types. In the summer, add to these a number of wealthy American tourists whose yachts are parked in the marina at the foot of the street. The Diner is consistently crowded, and at the height of the season people will wait for an hour or more to get a table. Visiting celebrities always eat at The Diner, so there is the added allure of spotting someone famous over your Salad Niçoise. Once Joanna saw Henry Winkler having a snack of jumbo shrimp and champagne while his chauffeur leaned against the idling white limo out front. There was an unconfirmed rumour that Joanne Woodward had eaten there last summer. The rumour was occasionally expanded to include Paul Newman.

Although Joanna has been here a hundred times or more, tonight she feels festive and celebratory because of the lipstick and the flashy earrings. She feels like a tourist on vacation from her real life. She feels that anything could happen and she feels ready. Three different people (other regulars, they all know each other) tell her she looks fabulous. They say, "Did you get your hair cut?" "Did you get new glasses?" "Have you lost weight?" Only one person asks where Samuel is and she has to stop a minute and think. Is this all it takes then to feel free again? A six-dollar tube of lipstick? She should have tried it years ago. How simple. How pathetic.

The taste of the lipstick makes her think of Esther who always wore an orange-red shade and when she kissed Joanna good night the taste lingered as she drifted off to sleep. Esther was always complaining that she couldn't keep her lipstick on, that she chewed it all off in half an hour and then had to reapply. She was always looking for a mirror until finally she bought a compact to keep in her purse.

Joanna discovers that she has the same problem. During the course of their meal, she has to go to the washroom four times to put on more lipstick. Gordon smiles patiently and orders more wine. He refrains from saying any more stupid things.

At the table, Joanna spends most of her time staring at a young woman at the next table whose dramatic red lipstick remains intact through three glasses of white wine, a bowl of creole peanut soup, a garden-fresh green salad, a huge plate of Fettuccine Alfredo, a slab of chocolate cheesecake, two cups of coffee, and six cigarettes. While consuming this feast, the young woman is also smiling uncontrollably at her date and talking the whole time. Once she even leans across the table and kisses him. Joanna is mesmerized. The woman's lips have never once stopped moving and yet, after such a spree of prolonged and varied oral gratification, her lipstick is still perfect. Not only that, but she's thin. Joanna also notices that while her own white coffee cup has lipstick and dribbles all over one side, the other woman's cup is still clean. There must be a trick to this stuff that she is not privy to. How do you find out these things, where do you learn them? Joanna wants to go over and ask the woman how she does this but Gordon sensibly talks her out of it.

On the way home they stop at the all-night drugstore so she can buy a compact. In the car she tells Gordon about the tube of lipstick Clarence brought home from the war. A plain black tube, a dull orange colour which tasted like pencil lead and cardboard, not at all like North American lipstick. Her father kept the lipstick in a wooden box with his dog tags and a pile of tattered French francs. Gordon says maybe it belonged to that buxom dark-haired woman in the old photograph.

No, Joanna says, she has always understood that he got it from the body of a dead woman, a dead Czechoslovakian woman. Gordon says this does not sound likely. No, Joanna says, it doesn't but that's what she remembers being told. Gordon says that even if it was true, it's not the sort of thing you would tell a little girl, that in the war her father took a tube of orange lipstick from the body of a dead woman. No, Joanna says, but that's what she remembers. Gordon asks what became of the lipstick. Joanna says she can't remember.

Gordon takes the babysitter home. Joanna checks on Samuel who is sound asleep. She puts the Steppenwolf tape back on. She takes off her earrings and all of her clothes. She redoes her lipstick and waits naked in the bed for Gordon to return.

He is pleasantly surprised but keeps fussing about the music as he undresses. He wants to turn it down, he's afraid it's going to wake Samuel. No, Joanna says, she wants it on, she wants it loud, he won't wake up, he can sleep through anything these days, he won't wake up, he won't, he won't.

Already her nipples are tingling, her hips are rising, the insides of her thighs are wet. She wants to moan when he enters her. She wants to howl when she comes. She wants to come six times in a row, howling louder every time. She wants to forget herself and everyone else she's ever been. She wants to lose track of reality and make sounds she's never heard before.

Take it easy, Gordon says, he'll hear you, he'll hear you, shit, the *neighbours* will hear you! He won't, he won't, she cries, they won't, they won't, I don't care! Take it easy, Gordon says and tries to kiss her to shut her up and for a good five minutes she hates him with all her heart, grinding harder against him because she hates him, moaning louder because she hates him and they will probably never make love in Patterson Park again.

In the pause between "Hey Lawdy Mama" and "Magic Carpet Ride," there comes the sound of Samuel sobbing in his bedroom. Gordon leaps off her and goes down the hall. Joanna is left lying flat on her back in the middle of the damp rumpled bed. Her hips are still twitching, like the limbs of an animal still twitching after it's been shot between the eyes. At least, she imagines they must twitch for a few minutes, she's never seen such a thing, but she imagines they must twitch and twist for a while like chickens with their heads cut off, the life not draining out of them slowly and with grace but jerkily, angrily, mean, convulsively dancing but silent. There is lipstick smeared across the pillowcase and the tape howls foolishly into the dark.

84. Thief

WHEN JOANNA WAS twelve years old, she stole a pair of earrings from Peoples Credit Jewellers on Sheppard Street downtown. They were two tiny silver peace signs and they were clip-ons because Esther didn't believe in pierced ears.

Joanna had walked all the way downtown that Saturday afternoon with Penny and Pamela. They often did this in the warm weather, especially when they could sneak away from Penny and Pamela's little brother Billy, who was just a pest, always wanting to tag along and bug them.

Once downtown, the girls went first to the record store, Jerome's, where they flipped through the 45's and studied the weekly Top Ten posted on the wall. If they had enough money they bought one: "Summer in the City," "I Am a Rock," "Nineteenth Nervous Breakdown," "Wild Thing."

They went across the street to the new clothing boutique called Threads, where they breathed deeply of the incense-rich air and caressed the colourful geometrically patterned blouses and the psychedelic miniskirts with matching beaded headbands. Although they sometimes tried things on, Joanna had no hope of ever dressing this way in real life because Esther, she knew, would have a fit. Joanna had not yet seriously considered the possibility of ignoring her mother and doing whatever she wanted. Esther was too good at making her life miserable. Joanna was still too eager to please, too desperate to keep the peace. Besides, as she pirouetted in front of the change room mirror in this finery, she knew she'd never have the guts to go around like that in public anyway.

With the scent of patchouli still clinging to their hair, they went next door to Peoples Credit Jewellers. They glanced through the costume jewellery displayed at the front of the store and then made their way to the back which was devoted to the display and dispensing of fine china, real silverware, and genuine Bohemian crystal. In the middle of all this was the Bridal Registry.

The Bridal Registry was set up on a round table covered with a white linen cloth. Each of the eight place settings was different, marked with a little white card giving the bride-to-be's name and listing the china, crystal, and silverware patterns she had chosen. The idea was that all prospective wedding guests would thus be able to buy a present the bride really wanted and not some dumb thing she would return right after the honeymoon. These elegant table settings, complete with matching linen napkins, were just like the pictures Joanna had cut out and pasted into her scrapbook. These were dream dishes, dream tables, and Joanna imagined them being presided over by a beautiful young woman in a frothy wedding gown and long white gloves. Around the table she would go, gracefully ladling perfect rich food on to the glowing plates of a handsome dark-suited man and two lovely children in white linen bibs and lacy bonnets. Before she poured the wine, she would remove her gloves and flick a perfectly manicured fingernail against the crystal glasses to make them sing. (The children, of course, had bubbly milk in theirs.) When she came to her own place, she paused and held the plate up to her face and admired her own reflection on its shiny surface. They said grace and then the sound of the silverware on the china was like music to their ears.

The girls argued amiably over which patterns they would pick when their turns at bridehood came. Joanna was pretty sure she would have something by Royal Albert because it was the best and also the most expensive. At home they were still eating off those brown-and-white plaid plates which made her miserable just to think of them.

On the way out of the store, she plucked the peace-sign earrings off the counter and put them in her pocket.

Two blocks down the street she produced them with a magician's flourish and showed them around like a prize. Penny and Pamela were bug-eyed and thrilled.

She wore the earrings every day for a week, hiding them in her pencil case at home and then clipping them on in the girls' bathroom after she got to school. When the bell rang at the end of the day, she slipped them off and into the pencil case again. She figured she had finally pulled one over on Esther. Finally she was daring and dangerous, one of those exciting and alluring girls living on the edge of trouble. The next thing you knew she might be wearing midnight blue mascara, a micro-mini, lime-green fishnet stockings, and a peace sign on a leather choker at her throat. The next thing you knew she might go wild and get her ears pierced. The next thing you knew she might try ironing her ugly curly hair.

The next Monday afternoon when Joanna got home from school, Esther was sitting at the kitchen table with a pile of papers in her hand. Joanna deposited her schoolbooks on the other end of the table and said brightly, warily, "Hi, Mom!" At this time of the day Esther should have been in the living room ironing and watching "Another World."

Esther flung the papers at her. They fluttered down all over the floor, many sheets of parchment notepaper with a lacy gold design at the top. They were, Joanna realized with a jolt, a kind of diary she had been keeping, carefully hidden in a box behind the books on her middle shelf.

These pages were a series of letters she had been writing to her dead cat, Daisy, who had been killed by a car six months before. As the speeding driver zoomed away, Joanna, who had seen the whole thing from the picture window, ran into the street and held Daisy's bloody body in her arms. She laid her head against the matted fur that had been white and the cat's warm blood smeared all over her. Even after Clarence had disposed of the body (what did he do with it?), she could not, would not, stop crying. Finally, after she had refused to eat her supper and was still sitting on the front step crying in the twilight, Esther lost all patience and said, "Oh stop it! She was only a cat. Don't be such a baby!"

Joanna vowed that she would never cry in front of her mother ever again and she would never tell her anything either, she would never be nice to her, she would never trust her, talk to her, or love her. Daisy, she decided, was the only living creature on the face of the whole stupid earth who had ever loved and understood her. That night she began writing her diary to Daisy. She told Daisy everything. She told Daisy about the stolen earrings.

"How could you do this to me?" she cried now as she tried to gather the pages up off the floor.

Esther said, "Now you'll have to face the music. You will take those earrings back to the store and you will apologize. You'd better hope you don't end up in jail. You are grounded for a month."

In bed later that night, Joanna could hear her parents talking in the living room, Clarence not saying much, Esther going on and on, getting herself more and more worked up, until suddenly Joanna's bedroom door was flung open and there stood Esther framed in the yellow light

from the kitchen. "You are a liar and a thief!" she cried. "How could
you do this to me?"

A month later Joanna stole a pair of black silk panties from Woolworth's. Two weeks later Esther had to go into the hospital for a hysterectomy. Joanna could imagine her mother floundering up through
the anaesthetic in the recovery room, whispering, "How could you do
this to me?" She could imagine her mother dying on the operating
table and as they covered her face with a sheet, she, Joanna, was crying
and whispering, "How could you do this to me?" She got rid of the
panties and was not caught. She did not steal anything ever again.

85. Lion

IN *HEROES OF THE BIBLE*, which Joanna won at Sunday School, there
was the very short story of Daniel who was put into a den of lions
because every day he worshipped God and this was against the law.
But God sent his angel to close the lions' mouths. Because he believed
in God, Daniel was not harmed. In the picture there is Daniel on his
knees, face uplifted to the Lord, hands folded, black beard curled up at
the end like an elf's shoe. There is a lion on either side of him, one
frowning slightly in its sleep, the other smiling coyly.

In *Aesop's Fables* there were at least two stories about lions. First there
was the one about the mouse and the lion, in which the unsuspecting
mouse runs across the sleeping lion's nose. The lion grabs the little
mouse in his big dangerous paw but the mouse convinces the lion to
spare her, promising that some day she will repay him. The lion is
skeptical but agrees and lets the little mouse go free. Sometime later
this same lion is caught in a hunter's net. This same mouse hears his
cries and runs to his rescue, gnawing through the ropes of the net and
setting him free. The moral of this story was: *Little friends may prove to
be great friends*.

There was also the story of Androcles and the lion in which Androcles, a mistreated slave, escapes from his cruel master, but as he is
running away he stops to remove a thorn from the paw of a lion.

Sometime later Androcles is caught and sent into an arena before the
emperor. He is to be thrown to the lions. As it turns out, the lion who
charges into the arena is the same lion and, to the amazement of all
assembled in the arena, it greets Androcles joyously. The moral of this
story was: *A noble soul never forgets a kindness.*

Joanna wondered if it was the same lion both times. Joanna wondered
if there was a moral to every story. She was still attending Sunday
School every week where, Esther said, she would be taught the necessary
moral values. Were morals something to be found in stories, secrets to
be discovered a bit at a time, story by story, and then assembled like
the pieces of a jigsaw puzzle so in the end you had a clear view of the
whole picture? Were morals hidden in *all* stories or only in the ones
she read in *Heroes of the Bible* and *Aesop's Fables?* The fables were easy
because they gave you the answer at the end. What about all the other
stories? How could you ever know for sure what you were supposed to
be getting out of them? How could you ever know for sure when you
were right?

86. Joy

IN THE DREAM Joanna is reading a letter from Lewis. In real life she
has, in fact, just received a letter from Lewis. It's not a letter really,
just a note jotted on the bottom of an invitation to the opening of his
new show in two weeks. The note says, *Hope you are well and happy now.
I am happy enough.*

In real life Joanna is furious. Except for the deceptively simple words
now and *enough,* this offhand sentiment might as well have been written
by or sent to a total stranger, somebody met once or twice in passing,
at a party, at an art show, on the crosstown bus. In real life Joanna
wants to call him and ask, "Happy enough for what?" In real life she
will not call him and she will not go to his show.

It has been five years since they last slept together. Samuel has just
had his second birthday. Gordon is working hard and wallpapering the
bedroom in his spare time. Joanna is working hard too, on a collage

called *Landscape With Figures* which involves many Chinese pictographs superimposed upon a mountainside, a small forest, a still lake, a cloudy threatening sky. On the lake there is a dock and on the dock she has drawn the Chinese characters for *man, woman, child,* and *dog.*

Lewis has never sent her an invitation to anything before. Why start now? Perhaps he thinks enough time has passed to render their romance a distant, maybe even fond, memory, a nostalgically innocuous aberration, harmless (harmless enough), purged at long last of all reverberation, recrimination, and vestigial power, as if the pain it had engendered was a dairy product with the expiry date stamped on the bottom. Perhaps he imagines there has been an annulment. Perhaps he thinks they can be just friends. Perhaps he thinks the coast is clear, as if they have now safely passed the requisite statute of limitations.

When Joanna first heard this phrase twenty years ago, it was in a conversation her parents were having about a scandalous tangled criminal trial which had rocked the whole community. Joanna cannot remember the details of the case but she does remember that Clarence and Esther discussed it over supper every night for weeks and this phrase was often repeated: "statute of limitations." At first Joanna thought they were saying "*statue* of limitations," which made her think of photographs she'd seen of classical statues, naked marble men and women with various parts of their bodies knocked off, arms, feet, sometimes their heads.

Now in the dream Joanna is reading the letter from Lewis in a very large room filled with paintings. There is no furniture. Joanna is sitting on the hardwood floor and every inch of wall space is covered with Lewis's paintings. They are not, she recognizes in the dream, paintings he has done yet in real life. They are paintings he will do in the future, paintings for which he will become famous (famous enough). In this large room there is one large window out of which Joanna can see one large tree with the sun shining yellow through its dark green leaves. On the trunk of the tree there is a carving of the Chinese character for *east,* which is, she remembers in the dream, a combination of the characters for *tree* and *sun,* the east being that place where the sun can be seen shining through the trees. Joanna is delighted to see that this tree is labelled. She thinks in the dream that this is how it should be in real life: everything labelled clearly to avoid confusion and misunderstanding, the way it is in her collage.

In the letter in the dream Lewis says that he is happy now (happy enough). He writes to say that he has everything he deserves, if not everything he has hoped for. In the dream Joanna is a very mature and understanding woman. She reflects that Lewis is rather young to have settled for less than he had dreamed of. In the letter he says that he has stopped searching for happiness and is now looking for the meaning of life instead. He says that he is learning how to repair small motors in his spare time and he is never bored. At the bottom of the letter there is a single word in large black letters. The word is ENTRANCE.

As Joanna puzzles over the significance of this word, its Roman letters begin to swirl like whirlpools or doves and it is transformed into a string of Chinese pictographs which Joanna struggles to decipher even as she feels herself beginning to wake up. The only character she recognizes is the one for *happy* which, she remembers from her research in real life, is a combination of the signs for *wife* and *child*.

It is the kind of dream where the slide from sleeping to waking is virtually seamless and she is not sure whether she has made this identification in the dream or in real life. Either way her eyes are open and it is morning. She feels briefly guilty for having dreamt about Lewis while sleeping in bed beside Gordon but at least it wasn't a sex dream. While waiting for the alarm to go off, she is just as mature and understanding as she was in the dream, and she thinks that she would like to tell Lewis that there is more to happiness than learning small-motor repair and never being bored. There is more to the meaning of life than looking for it. She hears Samuel down the hall stirring in his crib, talking to himself, and then calling out to her. She would like to tell Lewis that there is such a thing as joy, which he has neglected to mention.

There are avenues in life, she is now convinced, which cannot be entered or navigated without joy.

entrance *vt.* 1. to captivate and delight; put into a trance. 2. to fill with rapture or joy; enchant; enrapture.

She would like to remind Lewis that when she told him about the statue of limitations, he nodded and said, "Yes, we're all like that, whole chunks of ourselves lopped off. These are our limitations." He was more depressed than usual that day. He went on to wonder why so many of our limitations are actually self-imposed, as we tremble at the brink of utter despair or absolute joy but then we pull back just in time. "We are as afraid of one as of the other," he said gloomily. When he was this depressed, he tended to make pompous pronouncements on the nature of life as we know it. "Joy and despair, the dragons of extremity," he mused. "All things in moderation. We are afraid to enter our own extremes."

entrance *n.* 1. the action or point of entering. 2. a means of entering; door, gate, passage, etc. 3. opportunity, permission, or right to enter; admission.

She would like to call Lewis and tell him that she has finally found the entrance to her own real life. She would like to tell him that she does not love him any more and she does not want to be his friend either. In real life she will pluck up her courage and do nothing. As if her courage were a silky slip that has slid down from her waist when she wasn't looking and lies now in a slinky puddle at her feet. As if she need only reach down swiftly and hook it up on one finger before anybody notices. As if doing nothing were the hardest thing of all.

In real life, as the day unfolds, the dream will disappear, the Chinese characters will disengage and disperse like whirlpools and doves. In real life the dream will eventually evaporate as all dreams do, but with any luck the joy will not. In real life there will be another dream in which the statue of limitations will grow back its arms and feet, also its head, especially its head.

87. Bed

JOANNA'S CHILDHOOD BED looked like an ordinary bed but it was not. It was hinged on the backside so that it opened like a piano bench, the mattress part lifting up to reveal a storage space in which there were extra blankets, board games, old stuffed toys, a lace tablecloth stained but too expensive to throw away, a black velvet pillow with Niagara Falls painted on it, and a large needlepoint picture of poppies which Esther had started when she was pregnant but never finished. It was also where the Christmas presents were hidden until Joanna grew big enough to open the bed herself. There was just enough room between the bottom of the bed and the floor for the cookbook drawer.

Trying to fall asleep at night, Joanna liked to picture all these things stored beneath her. The sense of their weight tucked away neatly under the mattress sometimes made her feel safe and securely attached to the floor. Sometimes she wished she could sleep inside the bed instead of on top of it.

Joanna was an uneasy sleeper, afraid of the dark and all it was likely to conceal or contain, coming instantly alert not only to things that went bump in the night, but also to anything that hummed, rattled, creaked, or possibly groaned. She would lie awake rigid and sweating, alternately hot and cold, trembling, unable to cover her head or close her eyes for fear that even these minuscule movements would give her away. Partly too she wanted to see whatever it was before it got her. The bedroom in the dark was filled with the sound of breathing, coming closer and closer, growing hotter and hotter, until she could hear the blood in her head like the ocean in a seashell. Until she would have screamed if she hadn't been paralysed. Until she realized that the breathing she could hear was her own.

Esther was impatient with such foolishness. "You're imagining things," she said after yet another night of terror. "There's absolutely nothing to be afraid of." Even as a young child Joanna recognized this statement as patently untrue, a lie akin to "Don't worry, this won't hurt a bit," uttered by the doctor wielding his hypodermic needle or the dentist revving up his drill. Esther said, "Don't be such a baby."

Clarence was more sympathetic. It was always Clarence who came to her when she called out in the night. Esther would not allow her to crawl into their bed for comfort (in fact, Joanna would have been too scared to creep through the kitchen to get to their bedroom anyway). So Clarence came to her room and lay down gingerly beside her on the very edge of the narrow bed. "It's all right," he said softly. "It's all right, I'm here now," and he stayed there, lying flat on his back, perfectly still, until she fell back to sleep.

One night there was a sound so loud that Joanna leapt out of her bed, ran through the kitchen, and landed headfirst gasping between Esther and Clarence. To her surprise they were sitting straight up in their bed, wide-eyed and confused. This was nobody's imagination. They all got up and went into the living room to look out the front window. There were lights on all up and down the street, their sleepy neighbours in their pyjamas peering into the darkness. But there was nothing to see, no evidence of a thunderstorm, an explosion, an earthquake, a plane crash, a bomb, or a full-scale nuclear war. They could not explain it. They went back to their beds shaking their heads, Esther to her own room, Joanna and Clarence to hers, where this time he lay down beside her and stayed until morning.

At breakfast on the radio the announcer said it had been a sonic boom. They were all relieved, Joanna mostly because this time Esther could not possibly say she was making it up. She had no idea, however, what a sonic boom actually was. Clarence explained that an airplane had broken the sound barrier. Joanna did not understand. Clarence said he was not all that clear on it either but on the radio they said it had something to do with a plane flying faster than the speed of sound. This caused high-pressure shock waves to hit the ground and that was what made the boom.

Esther said, "It doesn't really matter. At least now we know what it was."

But Joanna was not satisfied. It was too hard to imagine. In the first place, she had never thought of sound as a *thing,* as something moving at a certain speed like a car. She had never thought of sound as having waves like a lake. She had never thought of sound as having a barrier like those yellow wooden barriers they put up when they worked on the street. How could sound, which was invisible and everywhere all around them all the time (even or especially in the dark) be like any or all of these things?

Joanna had heard of opera singers who could break glasses when they hit the high notes. Could the sonic boom be like that? What then had happened to the people in the plane? What about the pilot? Were they all dead now, or gone deaf, or just gone? What about the shock waves? Where did they hit the ground? Did they leave a hole where they hit, a big hole shooting flames like a volcano? Did they go right through and come out the other side like bullets? What if they'd hit somebody's house? Were those people dead now too?

Esther said, "Don't worry about it any more. Nothing happened. We're all still here safe and sound." What kind of sound was this then, Joanna wondered, that meant you were safe? What speed did it travel at? When would it get here? How would she know? She had always imagined that safety would be soundless like a blanket, snow, or a small yellow flower blooming in the sun.

88. Heavy

JOANNA GENUINELY ENJOYS being pregnant. Having gained nearly forty pounds, she truly is heavy with child.

heavy *adj.* 1. weighty; hard to lift or move because of great weight. 2. larger or more intense than usual. 3. of weighty importance; grave; serious; solemn; profound.

She likes to think of herself this way. She enjoys her blooming belly. She pats it often as if it were a large cat on her lap. She lies flat on her back in bed at night and admires the mound it makes in the blankets. She loves it when the baby kicks or rolls over so that her whole belly goes lopsided left or right. She is always grabbing Gordon's hands and placing them upon her. She loves to imagine those pockets inside her filling up with the heavy weight of the baby, her muscles stretching to accommodate him, her blood flowing warmer and thicker through him.

It is only towards the end that she comes to resent having to manoeuvre her belly around whenever she stands up, sits down, or needs to roll over in bed. It is only towards the end that she begins to feel like a whale, an elephant, a hippopotamus, or a Mack truck.

heavy *adj.* 4. hard to endure; oppressive; distressing; troublesome; burdensome. 5. strained, dull, or tedious. 6. coarse; thick; lacking grace or elegance. 7. clumsy; awkward; unwieldy. *See also* HEAVY-DUTY, HEAVYFOOTED, HEAVY-HANDED, HEAVY-HEARTED, HEAVYWEIGHT.

She gets used to the fact that people she hardly knows will reach out and touch her belly by way of greeting when they meet her on the street. Perhaps they too are pleased by how hard it is. She had never touched a pregnant belly before she touched her own. She is happy to discover that it is not puffy like fat, not spongy like a swelling, but solid, hard, and tight. Once a total stranger in the grocery store, an elderly woman in a jogging suit, patted her belly in front of a bin of apples and commended her for eating right. No one would ever presume to do this to a non-pregnant woman. With a non-pregnant woman they would just shake hands.

She also gets used to all the examinations at Dr. Millan's office. Sometimes he has an intern doing practical training with him and Joanna generously lets the intern examine her too. She says that by the time this baby is born, she'll spread her legs to anyone who wants to have a look.

She is aroused all the time now. Between her legs she is always wet and tender, engorged. Gordon at first is nervous about making love. He is afraid he'll hurt the baby. But she convinces him, she insists, every night she insists. Often during the day she masturbates, in the bathtub, in the bedroom, once in the kitchen with the blinds closed. She is never satisfied. This is one of the many things they do not mention in prenatal class. She does not know any of the other expectant mothers well enough to ask them if they are horny all the time too.

In the class, she receives detailed chronological information about the physical changes she will go through week by burgeoning week.

The prenatal teacher, Mrs. Irene Harper, herself an RN and mother of six, warns the expectant mothers that their raging hormones will wreak havoc with their emotions, producing unpredictable, sometimes violent, mood swings. Joanna is gently prepared for the fact that the hitherto trivial frustrations of daily life (a broken vacuum cleaner, a dead car battery, an unkind word from an unhappy waitress, even a broken fingernail for that matter) will now reduce her repeatedly to tears. She is informed with insouciant good humour that, during the course of her pregnancy, especially in the last trimester, she will be frequently overwhelmed with sheer terror at the prospect of the course she has so naïvely embarked upon. This fear of impending motherhood may occasion a full-scale bout of existential despair and an unnatural preoccupation with the meaninglessness of life as we know it. Mrs. Harper assures the class that this is just a phase which will pass quickly enough. She says that on the fourth day after giving birth all new mothers cry, usually for the whole day. With any luck, this crying jag will not blossom into an all-out case of post-partum depression.

Mrs. Harper does not mention what pregnancy does to the brain. Joanna is unprepared for how stupid she is. She cannot read a simple story without losing track of the characters and the plot. Words apparently strung together quite logically across the page make no sense at all any more. She must reread everything three or four times, even recipes, her horoscope, letters from Clarence, the phone bill. The only books she can concentrate on now are about pregnancy, childbirth, and breast-feeding.

She is also unprepared for the way her brain sometimes hooks on to something and will not let go. She can become utterly obsessed with the least little thing. It is as if, on the brink of motherhood, she cannot take anything for granted any more. The look of the rain on the windowpane. The sound of a dog barking mournfully in the distance. The look of her own fingers clenched around a coffee cup, a frying pan, a tear-filled Kleenex. The cool pillow under her head in the night, the sound and the feel of her own heart pulsing in her left ear. Perhaps this is where the old wives' tales come from: expectant mothers obsessing about giraffes, ducks, elephants, passing these obsessions through the placenta along with the other essential nutrients, and then giving birth to babies with long necks, webbed toes, floppy ears.

The baby is due in a week. She has a twinge. She grits her teeth. Gordon asks, "What's the matter?" The cramp passes.

"Nothing," she says, "it was nothing." She sits for half an hour staring out the window and thinking about the question.

Matter, matter, what's the matter, it doesn't matter, it matters, it does matter, it does, it just does, yes, it matters, it all matters.

Matter can be neither created nor destroyed. Matter, matter, oh dear, what can the matter be?

The weight of the matter. The truth of the matter. The heart of the matter. In her heart of hearts she cannot imagine herself as a mother. Beyond a soft romantic picture (the kind they take with Vaseline on the lens) of herself thin again and beaming down at a pink or blue bundle in her arms, she does not know what will happen next.

The baby, if that's what's in there, is due in a week. It is impossible to imagine. Perhaps she will be pregnant forever. Perhaps she's not really pregnant at all. Perhaps the doctor will give her big belly a good hard squeeze and pus will spurt out, pus and blood and other subcutaneous somatic matter.

Her head is heavy with enormous thoughts. Her blood is thick with oxygen and obsessions. Her belly is heavy with another being's body parts: arms, legs, skull, ribs, toes, fingernails, heart. Heart of her heart. Heart of his heart. Heart of your heart. Heart of my heart. Here is the heart of the matter.

heart *n.* 1. the hollow, muscular organ in vertebrate animals that receives blood through the veins and pumps it through the arteries by rhythmic contraction and dilatation. 2. the central, vital, or essential part; real meaning; core. 3. the source or seat of emotions, personality, etc., specif., *a)* inmost thoughts and secret feelings; consciousness; the soul, *b)* the source of emotions: contrasted with HEAD, the source of intellect and reason, *c)* one's emotional disposition or temperament, *d)* any of various humane feelings, such as sympathy, devotion, love, kindness, compassion, etc., *e)* courage, spirit, energy, enthusiasm, or ardour.

See also HEARTACHE, HEARTBEAT, HEARTBREAK, HEART-
BURN, HEARTSICK, HEARTSORE, HEARTSTRINGS.

89. Tobacco

JOANNA, PENNY, AND Pamela smoked menthol cigarettes in the dugout
of the baseball diamond at Branding Park. They smoked a brand called
Alpine with green and white mountains on the paper package. Even in
the winter they went there after school and huddled together, striking
a dozen matches to light one cigarette, passing it around, complaining
that someone was putting a heater on it, smoking right down to the
filter, so sometimes their mittens got singed. When it rained, Joanna
sometimes smoked at home in the bathroom, blowing the smoke out
the open screen window, imagining that her mother would never know.

By the time she got to university she was smoking openly at home.
Her mother, as it turned out, had of course known all along. Joanna
couldn't figure out why Esther, who had no trouble expressing her
disapproval about all manner of other questionable, possibly immoral
behaviours, had said nothing.

"There are a lot worse things you could be doing," Esther said by
way of explanation. Joanna supposed she meant drinking, doing drugs,
and having sex.

"At least you're not pregnant. At least you're not in jail," Esther
said. As if allowing yourself one bad habit would render you immune
to acquiring others.

"It's your life," Esther said. "You can do what you want, you're an
adult now." Which Joanna did not believe for one minute.

That year she and Clarence made a New Year's resolution pact to
quit. She lasted for three days. Clarence never smoked again.

Joanna finally quits when she finds out she is pregnant. She has been
smoking steadily for fifteen years. As she lies in bed at night admiring
the mound of her belly under the blankets, she concentrates on either

the baby stretching in her womb or her lungs gratefully going pink again. She is filled now with virtue and self-love instead of tar and nicotine.

90. Baby

JOANNA, LIKE MOST people, has no recollection of her own birth. All she knows for sure is the precise time of her arrival: 9:50 A.M. Esther, like most mothers of the time, had no recollection of the birth either. She was out cold. She was fond, however, of mentioning that three months later Hurricane Hazel hit Toronto (that evil city), killing eighty-three people and causing extensive property damage.

Later Joanna will learn that several other memorable events took place in 1954 besides Hurricane Hazel and her own birth.

In India three hundred and forty pilgrims were killed in a stampede while bathing in the Ganges River.

The United States set off its second H-bomb in the Marshall Islands in the Pacific Ocean between the Philippines and Hawaii. To the scientists' surprise, this bomb was six or seven hundred times as powerful as that which destroyed Hiroshima.

Also in the United States, President Eisenhower signed the Communist Control Act outlawing the Communist Party, the Supreme Court voted unanimously for school integration, Elvis Presley made his first record, work began on the St. Lawrence Seaway, and ground was broken at Shippingport, Pennsylvania, for the world's first nuclear power plant.

Roger Bannister became the first person to break the four-minute mile with a run of three minutes and 59.4 seconds. Sixteen-year-old Marilyn Bell became the first person to swim across Lake Ontario. Bing Crosby and Danny Kaye starred in the movie *White Christmas*. Alex Colville completed his famous painting *Horse and Train*.

But Esther never mentioned any of these events. Consequently Joanna identified heavily with Hurricane Hazel and liked to quip in later years that everything since then had been all her fault. Years later still, she will realize this is not funny.

When Joanna became curious about her own existence as a baby, she liked to look at the photographs in the album. Although she knew these were indeed pictures of her, she also knew that in some mysterious way they were not. Since she could not remember having been a baby, she had a sense of her life being rolled up behind her like a rug as she grew older. On the first page there were four blurry black-and-white shots. Herself in her crib laughing. Herself propped against the arm of a large flowered chair. Herself staring bug-eyed at a teddy bear twice her size. Herself naked on her stomach looking stunned.

On the second page there were another four pictures, clearly in focus this time, Clarence apparently having mastered the new camera. Herself in a snowsuit in a sled in the snow. Herself on a blanket on the front room floor with a stuffed yellow dog she called Wyatt Earp. Herself on Esther's knee: they are both smiling, there are white lace doilies carefully arranged on the back and arms of the large chair, not flowered now, but some dark solid colour, perhaps reupholstered in burgundy or brown. Herself on Clarence's knee: he is wearing a grey suit, white shirt, dark tie, Esther beside him is bright-eyed in a sheer white blouse through which her brassiere is visible.

When Joanna was old enough to know the facts of life (more or less), she could not imagine that she had been conceived in the regular way. She'd never even seen her parents really kiss each other. She'd never heard them having sex. Penny and Pamela said they heard their parents doing it every Saturday night and it was just disgusting. They said they put their pillows over their heads and their fingers in their ears. What was even more disgusting, they said, was the way their parents acted the next morning at Sunday breakfast: as if nothing had happened. They acted just like normal parents again, drinking their coffee, eating their eggs, getting ready for church, and then actually sitting through the service, singing, praying, pious and purified, as if nothing dirty had happened at all.

Joanna had seen Clarence in his underwear once by accident and that was disgusting enough. She had also seen Esther's left breast once when her housecoat slipped open. It was just hanging there, flabby white flesh marbled with blue veins. The brown nipple was puckered and chapped-looking, much bigger than Joanna could have imagined, if she had ever been sick enough to imagine such a thing, that her mother had nipples that she might have sucked on when she was a baby (thank God Esther had not believed in breast-feeding), that her mother had nipples that her father might have licked and kissed and sucked on in the disgusting depths of passion. The nipple was the size of one of those cork coasters Esther was forever slipping under drinks on the coffee table.

Samuel is a week overdue. Joanna waits impatiently, although she does not know that it is Samuel she is waiting for. She waits and worries. She is afraid about it in all the ordinary ways. She has never held a newborn baby. She is afraid she will do it all wrong, afraid she will hurt him (she and Gordon have always referred to the unborn baby as "him," which turns out to be true). She is afraid she will drop him, the way Esther said her distant cousin Jimmy was retarded not because he'd been born that way, but because his stupid clumsy mother had dropped him on his head.

She is also afraid that she will look so awkward when she holds her baby that everyone will know she doesn't know what she's doing and then they won't let her keep him.

She is afraid he won't like her. She is afraid he won't like her holding him. She is afraid he will cry in her arms. She is afraid she has no maternal instinct whatsoever. She is afraid that she will not be a good mother.

When the labour pains finally start, she feels, despite the many weeks of prenatal classes, completely unprepared. What if she cannot remember all the stages of labour? What if she does the wrong breathing at the wrong times? What if she cannot give birth at all? What if she is going to be pregnant forever?

She can hardly believe that this big belly is about to translate itself into a baby. She cannot imagine all the ways in which she too is about to be transformed. Afterwards she will think that it was probably just as well.

When Dr. Millan places the bloody, wet, crying baby on her chest (after twenty-four hours of labour, eleven of them in the delivery room), Joanna is speechless, besieged with tenderness and panic. It will prove to be untrue what everyone says about not being able to remember the pain of giving birth afterwards. She remembers, oh yes, she does remember. What she does not, cannot, will never be able to remember, is exactly how she feels at that moment of first cradling between her sore breasts his small head, soft and hard at the same time, covered with thick black hair.

Although it is hard, as a new mother, to believe that major world events are still occurring, indeed they are. She sees them on the TV news and reads about them in the newspaper.

In Red Deer, Alberta, Jim Keegstra, former teacher and mayor of Eckville, is convicted of wilfully promoting hatred against Jews.

A Japan Air Lines Boeing 747 slams into a mountain in Central Japan, killing five hundred and twenty people. It is the worst single-plane disaster in aviation history. Four passengers survive.

An earthquake measuring 8.1 on the Richter scale devastates Mexico City, killing up to 20,000 people, leaving another 30,000 homeless. On television Joanna watches over and over and over again the miraculous rescue of a baby girl who has been trapped in the rubble for seven days. The baby is seriously dehydrated but otherwise okay.

Ronald Reagan and Mikhail Gorbachev meet for three days in Geneva, the first American-Soviet summit since Jimmy Carter met Leonid Brezhnev in Vienna in 1979. Both countries vow to work for peace and the reduction of nuclear armaments.

The space shuttle *Challenger* explodes shortly after lift-off from Cape Kennedy, killing all seven astronauts aboard, including Christa McAuliffe, a schoolteacher from New Hampshire who was the first ordinary citizen chosen to go into space.

In response to the bombing of a disco in Germany and various other acts of terrorism, the U.S. bombs Libya. Eleven days later the world's worst nuclear accident occurs when a reactor blows up at Chernobyl power plant, near Kiev, U.S.S.R. Between these two incidents, the first test-tube baby is delivered from a surrogate mother at Mount Sinai Hospital in Cleveland, Ohio.

As the world goes through its historical convulsions, Joanna feeds the baby, burps the baby, changes the baby, bathes the baby, walks the baby, rocks the baby, talks to the baby, and often cries. Dr. Millan assures her that crying is a natural response to motherhood. He says her hormones are to blame and they will not return entirely to normal levels for a whole year.

The baby grows into himself by increments, living solely in the present tense. The world unfolds. History happens. Time passes. Slowly or suddenly. Through no fault of its own.

It occurs to Joanna (with her arms full of freshly washed diapers, her mouth full of clothespins, her head full of baby lore, out in the backyard in the sunshine, Samuel snoozing in the stroller in the shade) that there is no turning back now. Not that there ever was, not really. The possibility of retreat has always been an illusion, never a viable option. But it is only now that she truly understands that there is nowhere else to go but forward. The baby will grow. The world will unfold. History will happen. Time will continue to flow in one direction only. This revelation will produce within her alternate episodes of liberation and despair.

91. Moon

JOANNA, LIKE ALL young children, accepted nursery rhymes at face value. Her elastic imagination easily accommodated the stories of an old woman who lived in a shoe, a giant egg who fell off a wall, a pie full of blackbirds, and a cat who played the fiddle while the cow jumped over the moon. *The little dog laughed/To see such sport,/And the dish ran away with the spoon.* The rumours that said moon, in addition to being frequently jumped over by said cow, was made of green cheese and contained a man were no harder to reconcile than the idea that Santa Claus flew through the sky in a sled drawn by eight tiny reindeer and then came down the chimney to deliver her presents while she slept. There was no fireplace in their house. Their chimney led directly to the furnace. She did not consider this a problem any more than she questioned the notion that the Easter Bunny hopped from house to house delivering eggs when everybody knew it was chickens, not rabbits, that laid eggs. To Joanna these were not stories, rumours, or notions at all. These were facts.

It was only when the moon was visible during the day that she was confused. The moon was supposed to be shining at night. What was it doing out in the daytime looking so ghostly, flat, and pale, nearly see-through against the bright blue sky? Maybe it was lost, wandering around in the puffy white clouds, feeling frightened, sad, and small the way she imagined she would feel if she ever got lost in the woods. (She had never actually been in the woods herself, but it happened to children in fairy tales all the time.)

By the time Joanna reached adolescence, the moon, like many formerly frivolous things, had acquired several new disturbing dimensions.

"Quit your mooning around," Esther often said, so often in fact that Joanna began to imagine her own face as possessing the same white flat roundness as the moon: bland, vague, airless, reflecting all and sundry, rotating through no fault of its own, idle and dreaming, magical perhaps, but misunderstood.

Then she heard about the moon's power. She liked to gaze up at it through her bedroom window and imagine herself being slowly transformed by its milky light as it shed its mysterious pull down upon her upturned face. She'd heard that in some countries they believed the moon incited their women to orgies and so the women were not permitted to go gazing for long. When the moon was full, the German shepherd at the end of the block howled plaintively all night long. Joanna sympathized but never had the nerve to try it herself. She'd heard there were more crimes committed under the full moon, crimes of passion, no doubt, crimes of anguish and despair. Better to stay inside and admire the moon from afar.

She'd heard how the power of the moon and its monthly resurrection influenced the tides of the ocean and the menstrual cycles of women.

She'd never been to the ocean but she had started her period two years before. Although she hated it every time (the cramps, the pads, the chafing, the indignity of it all), still she liked to imagine that it was the moon pulling the blood out of her, growing her up like a seedling planted, according to horticultural superstition, under the waxing moon for the best results. She liked to imagine that it was the moon in her own belly, fertile and feminine, quietly changing everything from the inside out.

Having witnessed the American moon landing on TV might well have dispelled or at least diminished some of the romantic notions she had embroidered around the moon. But it did not. She had more faith in the moon than in the astronauts. She'd heard about the dark side of the moon, the moon as receptacle for everything wasted on earth: time and money squandered, promises broken, prayers unanswered, tears shed fruitlessly, dreams and desires forever unfulfilled. She'd heard about the moon as shelter for the dead and the unborn.

Later she will appreciate the irony of the astronauts (male) tramping around the surface of the moon (female), planting their flag, staking out their territory like dogs pissing on a tree, believing that they had claimed and conquered, having apparently not noticed the dead or the unborn or the billions of Fallopian tubes down below waving their fronds in time to the potent bloody rhythm of the moon.

Later she will learn more about the landscape of the moon. That in addition to the Seas of Tranquility, Serenity, and Fertility, the Bay of Rainbows, and the Lake of Dreams, there are also the Marshes of Disease, Decay, and Sleep, the Ocean of Storms, the Sea of Crises, and the Lake of Death, all of these watery fates discovered on a heavenly body found to be without air, without water, without life. In the south there is a small crater called Hell.

Later she will learn that even during a total eclipse of the moon, the boundary between dark and light is never clearly defined. Later she will learn that librations are irregularities in the moon's movement which cause its edges to be alternately visible and invisible. Libration. Liberation. Visible. Invisible. This knowledge may or may not prove useful. This knowledge, like all knowledge, may be remembered or forgotten when necessary. Later she will learn about lunacy in all its moon-fed splendour. Later she will imagine that the man in the moon was a woman all along.

92. Scissors

THE SUPPER DISHES have been cleared away. Joanna and Samuel are sitting at the kitchen table with their chairs pulled side by side. It is early evening, already dark, a windy night in late October. Hallowe'en is in the air. They have put the clocks back for the winter. Spring forward, fall back. Joanna has been unable to explain satisfactorily to Samuel where that extra hour comes from and where it will go again in the spring. He has an unreliable sense of time at the best of times and this peripatetic single hour is a metaphysical mystery which escapes him. What if you were *in* that hour, he wants to know, when it disappeared? Where would you go? How would you get back again? His concept of time as a place you can physically inhabit is unshakable. Joanna has to admit there is something to be said for this idea but does not encourage him to contemplate further the vagaries of the time-space continuum. He would have nightmares for sure.

The kitchen windows face the street and the blinds are still up. They can hear their neighbour calling her cat. She is an eccentric elderly woman who has named her cat after herself: Geraldine. Often after dark she can be seen in her nightgown in her driveway, calling her own name, coaxing, clucking, scolding, sometimes growing impatient and yelling, "Geraldine, you stupid bitch! You get home here right this minute!" Tonight it is still early enough, she is still feeling friendly, she is calling, "Geraldine, Geraldine, where have you been? Have you been to London to visit the Queen?" Samuel and Joanna giggle and roll their eyes.

On the table there are coloured markers, glue sticks, a thick pad of construction paper, and two pairs of scissors. Samuel has his own special scissors, green plastic over the metal, rounded tips for safety. So Joanna doesn't really have to say, "Keep those scissors away from your face!

You'll poke your eye out!" But she says it anyway just to hear the sound of her own voice amidst the chorus of other mothers' voices in her head, good mothers, model mothers, *real* mothers.

Gordon has gone to a meeting of the Historical Society which he has belonged to for several years. He would like Joanna to join too but she hates meetings. Theoretically she believes in the democratic process but in practice she finds it horribly inefficient. She simply cannot bear to sit in a stuffy room with ten or twenty other people taking an hour and a half to decide which refreshments should be served at the next public information session and then deciding to elect a refreshments committee to look into it first. She would rather stay home.

Tonight, in a wave of maternal selfishness, she is happy to have Samuel all to herself. They are going to make their own Hallowe'en decorations. While Samuel pulls sheets of paper from the thick pad, Joanna cannot help but admire the picture they make: picture-perfect mom doing crafts with her charming clever child. They are happy, they are good. More to the point: *she* is happy, *she* is good. She is a real mother after all. She imagines real mothers everywhere, those mothers she has seen in the park, those mothers who have all afternoon to push their children on the swings and actually enjoy it. They go home singing afterwards, home to their picture-perfect houses for a nutritious snack of carrot sticks, oat bran muffins, and homemade granola. These mothers who, all evening every evening, read stories, draw pictures, and make elaborate animals out of Play-Doh or (better yet) papier mâché. These mothers who do not believe in TV, synthetic fabric, or junk food of any kind. These mothers who are never impatient, irritable, bored, or too tired to play. These mothers whom she admires, envies, resents and is, more often than not, afraid to speak to for fear of being found wanting, wicked, negligent, selfish, incompetent, inadequate, inferior, and unfit, with a bag of Cheezies in one hand and a Teenage Mutant Ninja Turtle in the other.

Tonight she wants to be one of them. Tonight she *is* one of them. Or at least, tonight she could be mistaken for one of them. She is, after all, spending quality time with her child. Lucky child. Good mother. What are the qualities of time?

Samuel interrupts her thoughts. "I love paper, don't you?" he says. "Why yes," she says, "as a matter of fact, I do."

She remembers going to the art supply store as a teenager, wandering through the aisles filled with paper, pencils, sketchbooks, huge rolls of canvas, tiny tubes of paint. She got a knot in her stomach, a lump in her throat, not of tears, but of longing and excitement. She cruised the store with her head down, eyes averted, avoiding the salesclerk who seemed to be following her, who *was* following her. When the clerk finally cornered her near the drafting tables at the back, when the clerk finally asked, triumphant, too loudly, "May I help you?" Joanna could only mumble, "Just looking, thanks," and walk away. Guilty, guilty, caught in the act, as if she had been caught shoplifting, drinking, smoking, necking, or masturbating. As if she had been arrested while pursuing some illicit, illegal, immoral pleasure. Had she not been taught that all pleasure was suspect? When she came home with another set of oil pastels, another spiral-bound sketchpad, another pair of scissors, another art book (another book, God help her if she came home with another book), Esther was bound to say, "Why do you keep buying this stuff? How many sketchpads do you think you need? You've got enough books. Why did you buy another book? How much did it cost? Paper? More paper? What's wrong with the paper you've already got? What's wrong with you? What's wrong with you? What's wrong with you?"

Although Clarence worked at the mill and came home smelling of paper, he could not make sense of Joanna and her obsessions either.

Even now, she cannot help but wonder what her life would have been like if she'd had parents of a different sort altogether, parents who were well-educated, creative, sophisticated, and supportive of her artistic inclinations. She knows this is a contemptible (although not uncommon) blasphemy. But what if? What if she had actually had parents like Gordon's, parents who listened to Mozart, admired Picasso, understood Dali, read Camus in the original French, and went to museums in their spare time? She remembers wishing for a father who wore a suit every day, instead of only to funerals and weddings, to the doctor, to fly. A father with a briefcase. She remembers wishing for another mother sometimes too. But before she'd had time to redo Esther in detail, before she'd got past imagining a tall slender woman in a white silk dress reading a book in a large chair by a sunny window, she was bludgeoned by guilt and the fear that either Esther would die or she would die or maybe they would both die because of her ungrateful, traitorous betrayal.

What if she had known all along that the things she loved were indeed valuable, that the pursuit of them was as important as she thought it was, and that she too was valuable and important? What if she had had parents who believed in her? What if she had not had to spend most of her adult life struggling to believe in herself?

Even now, as a practising, fairly successful, professional artist, even now, when accosted in the art supply store by the over-eager salesclerk (May I help you? May I help you? May I help you?), she feels instantly guilty (*Mea culpa, mea culpa, mea culpa!*), as if she had been exposed as a pervert who loves paint, glue, canvas, paper. Especially paper. The look of it. The feel of it. The smell of it. The taste of it. Had she not repeatedly chewed up and swallowed parts of her Sunday School program as a child? Had she not once, in a hardware store on the edge of town, licked a huge blue block of salt meant for cows? Some day she might lose control and lick a forty-dollar sheet of handmade Japanese watercolour paper and then, for sure, they would have her taken away. Better that perhaps than the humiliation of having to explain yet again to the irreverent slack-jawed gum-chewing vacant-eyed clerk that she is just looking, thanks, just loves to look. When all else fails (all strength, hope, ideas, hope, love, hope), she just loves to look. How could she possibly explain the comfort to be drawn from a piece of blank paper, unsullied, unsuspecting, fragrant, expectant, and pure?

"Yes," she says again to Samuel. "I do love paper, I truly do. I'm glad you love it too."

She resists the prideful urge to point out to him how lucky he is to have a mother like her, a mother who loves paper and is not afraid any more to admit it, a mother who not only loves him but who also likes every little thing about him, a mother who loves him just the way he is, and if he wants to love the feel, the smell, even the taste of paper, she will not get mad at him or even laugh. She will just go along with him, loving paper too.

She would like to mention what a good memory this evening will make if only he takes the time to treasure it now. Then he will be able to carry it forward with him forever. *Please remember this*. As if she could possibly control the contents of his mind five, ten, fifteen, twenty years from now. As if she can control them now. As if she can ensure that he will never wish for another mother. Of course he will. Yes he will. And her heart will be temporarily broken or turned to stone. But that mother-hating phase is still in the future which they are moving towards, yes, but slowly, so slowly that it is still possible to forget how much pain they may inflict upon each other when they finally get there.

For now, Samuel still loves her. For now, he wants a pumpkin, a bat, a witch, a ghost, and a monster, a purple monster. Joanna starts cutting and singing "The Purple People Eater." Samuel wants to trade scissors. His are not sharp enough. Gently she reminds him that he will poke his eyes out.

The wind is rising. The branches of the large fir tree in front are waving. Samuel says, "It looks like the wind is singing too." He wonders what it would be like to be a tree. Joanna reminds him that when he was a year old, he was afraid of trees. Samuel does not believe her. He says he can't remember that, so how can it be true?

They debate the pros and cons of treeness. It would be good, they decide, to be outside all summer long. It would be fun to have birds in your branches. This, Samuel figures, would probably tickle. It would be great to be taller than the house, to never have to eat, sleep, or brush your teeth. It would be interesting, Samuel says, to be green.

But trees have troubles too. It would be awful to be outside in a thunderstorm, a windstorm, or a blizzard. All that snow on your branches would be heavy and cold. It would be disgusting to have every dog in the neighbourhood pee on your feet. And cats would climb up you with their claws out. It would be awful not to be able to talk, laugh, kiss, or hug. Joanna points out that some people are fond of hugging trees. Samuel says yes, but the trees can't hug back. Worst of all, a bad guy might come along and chop you down with an axe.

Samuel decides he would rather make a tree than all that Hallowe'en stuff. He wants a happy tree, a summer tree, with birds and flowers in its branches. Joanna sets aside the witch hat she has been working on and cuts out a thick brown trunk with roots like giant feet. To the top she glues large overlapping circles of emerald and lime green. To these green circles she glues many smaller circles in all colours: pink, blue, red, yellow, orange, purple, black. She continues gluing small circles until they hang down from the tree like strings of pearls or other equally precious stones.

Samuel is very pleased with his beautiful bejewelled paper tree. He says she looks beautiful too, when she's making trees.

An hour later she tucks him into bed. He has carefully placed the paper tree on the chair beside him, the chair which is pulled into place every night so he doesn't roll over and fall onto the floor. There are sirens in the distance, the sound whipped around on the wind so they cannot tell where they're coming from or going to. Joanna shivers. This sound always makes her feel frightened, acutely aware of the dangers which might befall anybody anywhere anytime. Her. But when the sirens have faded away, she feels relieved that this time they have passed her by, as if there were only so many catastrophes to go around and this is one more that hasn't happened to her.

Samuel is listening to the sirens too. He says maybe it's a fire truck, an ambulance, maybe it's a police car chasing down the bad guys. He says he would like to have the scissors on the chair too, the *real* scissors, the sharp scissors. He says, "Then if a bad guy comes after you, I will cut his heart out!"

Joanna knows she should remind him that such bloodthirsty fantasies are inappropriate, that murder and mayhem are generally unacceptable, that violence is altogether politically incorrect. A good mother would, a model mother would, a *real* mother would.

Instead she lies down beside him on the narrow bed.

Instead she rests her head next to his on the soft cool pillow.

Instead she whispers, "Please remember this," which of course makes no sense to Samuel at all.

93. Quiet

JOANNA WAS ALWAYS longing for peace and quiet. After school, on weekends and holidays, she spent as much time as she could in her bedroom with the door shut, reading and writing and sketching at the small white desk Clarence had made for her.

Esther and Clarence did not actively discourage her interest in art. Rather it was something they seemed to prefer not to notice or dwell on, as if acknowledging it might make it worse. They seemed to view her artistic inclination as just another phase she was going through, like that summer she'd been swept up by religious fervor and wished to become a nun although she was not Catholic. That had passed quickly enough. Perhaps this would too. After all she was only a teenager. Perhaps this was just another form of adolescent rebellion.

What seemed to bother Esther the most was Joanna's closed bedroom door. She took that expanse of varnished blond wood personally. Its very appearance seemed to fill her with resentment, anxiety, and intense curiosity. Whenever Joanna was safely ensconced on the other side of that door, sinking down gratefully into the precious peace and quiet, Esther could always find a reason to barge right in. She never knocked. Most often, when the door swung open, there was Esther with a cookbook in her hand, saying, "Now listen to this one, this sounds good." Then she would read aloud with such dramatic flourish she might have been reading illuminated scripture. She especially favoured those recipes which featured canned goods in innovative combinations. She was a great believer in canned goods and always kept a plentiful store on hand.

"Now doesn't that just sound delicious?" she would ask after reading it.

"Yes," Joanna would say.

"Well, I think I'll just try that tomorrow night."

"Yes."

"Your father will just love it."

"Yes." Joanna thought she would go crazy with anger.

"What are you doing in here, dear?"

Joanna *would* go crazy with anger. What did Esther think she was doing in here? Smoking? Drinking? Playing with herself or slitting her wrists?

"Oh nothing."

"Oh well then," Esther sniffed and sailed back into the kitchen to rummage in the cupboard for canned carrots, onions, pickled beets, and Campbell's tomato soup. She left Joanna's bedroom door half-open. Just to be on the safe side. She was not a great believer in privacy.

Towards the end of high school Esther and Clarence began to circle around this persistent and problematic issue of art. They were always mentioning how Ginny Lacosta from down the street had decided to become a pharmacist. Now *that* would be a good job: steady work, good pay, and interesting too. And had they already mentioned that Susan Shanks was applying to veterinary school? Which of course wasn't as good as being a *real* doctor, but still.

Joanna wondered how her parents knew all the plans of these girls who would become dermatologists, chartered accountants, florists, dentists, bank managers, nuclear physicists, advertising executives, and astronauts, yes, probably astronauts too. How did they know and why should she care?

Then Esther and Clarence changed tactics. They talked a lot about Pamela and her boyfriend Bob who worked at the paper mill with Clarence and they were going to get married three days after graduation and they were saving for a honeymoon in Hawaii. Penny had started her hope chest. Debbie Lipinski got a diamond ring for Christmas. Angela Dolcetti was engaged too but she was going to go to hairdressing school anyway and she'd work at her aunt's beauty parlour until she got pregnant.

By this time Joanna had a part-time job in Ladies Wear at Simpsons-Sears, two nights a week and all day Saturday. She would work there all summer too, this last summer between high school and university. She didn't really want to work all summer: she wanted to stay home and read and write and draw all day. Esther said she was just lazy. Joanna kept working at the store.

She could just imagine her mother running into other mothers at the store some Saturday afternoon, the bunch of them chatting merrily in their polyester pantsuits between tableware and towels, clogging up the aisle with their carts full of shampoo and bubble bath on sale half-price, woolly work socks for their husbands, white brassieres and briefs for their daughters, and plastic placemats for themselves. She could just imagine them gossiping joyfully about their marvellous daughters and the forthcoming brilliant rest of their lives. She could just imagine her mother dragging these other mothers over to have a look at her in Ladies Wear brushing lint off blazers, Esther proudly proclaiming that if she kept at it, she'd probably get promoted, she'd probably be head of the department by the end of the summer, and she got a staff discount now too.

When Joanna was well into university, enrolled in a general program, studying fine arts, literature, and philosophy, Clarence and Esther were vaguely pleased with her good grades but were not generally willing to discuss the details of her education in any depth. Neither of them had even finished high school.

Everything Joanna studied was falling into place. For whole weeks every idea she encountered was connected in an elaborate and infinite conjugation of knowledge. Perhaps the whole world could be conjugated inside this polymorphic synergy. Perhaps all knowledge was a feat of association. Sometimes she thought her head would explode with the sheer multifarious energy of ideas.

Sometimes, flushed and sparking with a new enthusiasm, she would blurt it all out without thinking. Usually her ecstatic outbursts occurred around suppertime, when she was just home from classes, Esther was in the kitchen in her apron, whipping up a tuna casserole, opening a can of peas, and Clarence was just coming home from the mill, dropping his lunch pail and boots at the back door, stripping off his dirty green work shirt, fixing himself a whisky and Coke in his undershirt. It was no longer Esther bursting into the bedroom reading recipes. Now it was Joanna bursting out of the bedroom reading aloud from Kant's *Critique of Judgement* or the *Code of Hammurabi*.

To which Esther would smile and nod nicely enough. But then she would seem to be seized by a rising bubble of panic which caused her to duck her head slightly, purse her lips tightly, and start slapping the brown plaid plates down upon the yellow placemats on the blue tabletop.

Clarence usually said nothing, just kept on rattling his newspaper, tinkling the ice in his drink, tapping his bare bony feet on the tile. Of course there was that one time when Joanna was gushing on at supper about the essay she'd just finished, "Pablo Picasso and Plato's Theory of Art," and Clarence choked on a mushroom cap. They were trying Esther's latest discovery, Chicken and Mushroom Pie. Gasping and gagging, he leapt up from the table and rushed for the bathroom with Esther right behind him, thumping his back until he brought the mushroom up again, still whole. He came back to the table with his eyes watering, wiping his mouth with a white handkerchief, still heaving a bit.

Esther, back at the table, said, "That Picasso, why can't he just draw like a normal person? These modern artists don't know how to draw so they just do it however they like. Maybe they all need glasses. Either that or they all need their heads examined."

Joanna said nothing. Clarence dug back into his dinner, wary now of the mushrooms, picking them out with his fork and placing them in a tidy pile on the side of his plate.

Surely this incident was just an accident, an unfortunate coincidence which should not be dwelled upon unduly.

Joanna came to spend a lot of time and energy feeling unappreciated and misunderstood, which alternately propelled her with anger and a secret belief in her own superiority, or paralysed her with anxiety and depression, as she dripped down into loneliness and paranoia. Sometimes it prompted her to think with despair that she would never be happy. Perhaps she'd never get the hang of it. Perhaps she didn't know the meaning of the word.

happy *adj.* 1. of a person favoured by circumstances; fortunate; successful; lucky. 2. showing or causing great pleasure, contentment, joy, etc.; pleased; glad; satisfied; joyous. 3. [*Slang*] mildly drunk, or irresponsibly quick to action, as if intoxicated. *See also* HAPPY-GO-

LUCKY, SLAP-HAPPY, TRIGGER HAPPY, HAPPY AS A PIG IN SHIT.

Sometimes she thought she was crazy. Sometimes she wished she was normal. Mostly she just wanted peace and quiet. She was working in her bedroom for hours, carefully noting ideas and quotes on blue-lined index cards which she then spread all over the floor. She pieced her essays together this way like puzzles. She worked hard and got straight A's in everything.

Joanna has been rereading these essays which she found in a box in the basement. She is impressed by how nimble her brain used to be, how clever she was, how serious, how smart, how sure of her own intelligence. She suspects that motherhood has softened her brain. She could not write these essays now. Rereading them, she can hardly even figure out what she was talking about. She imagines that if she heard the word "Plato" these days (and where do you suppose she might hear it? At the day care? In the park beside the monkey bars? In the grocery store while browsing through the dairy case?), she would think she was hearing a conversation about Play-Doh (how quickly it dries out if you don't put the lid on, how it gets ground into the rug and cannot ever be removed, how all the colours get mixed together and end up a mottled murky brown, how it, like many things, is always a big disappointment because it's not nearly as good in real life as on TV).

It is early Sunday afternoon. Joanna is working in her studio. Gordon is keeping an eye on Samuel, doing the laundry, defrosting the fridge, making grilled cheese sandwiches and chicken noodle soup for lunch. After lunch he and Samuel are going to bake chocolate chip cookies. This was all Gordon's idea. After breakfast he said, "You need some peace and quiet. Go and work, I can do the rest." Joanna is pleased and secretly proud of Gordon for beginning to disprove one of her theories about the difference between men and women.

Men, she has observed since Samuel was born, can only do one thing at a time. They graciously offer, for instance, to watch the children one evening while you go out for a drink with your friends. You are very grateful because you need a break. You dress up a little, put some makeup on even, and those new earrings you've been waiting for a special occasion to wear. You are humming as you leave. Husband and children wave happily as you back out of the driveway. You have a splendid time and are home by ten o'clock, just as you promised. Husband too has done exactly what he promised: he has looked after the children. He has not done the dinner dishes, put away the toys, taken out the garbage, swept the kitchen, wiped the toothpaste blobs out of the bathroom sink, or picked up the newspaper which is spread all over the house. He has certainly not cleaned the oven, baked banana bread, or put in a quick load of laundry. He has not even put away the milk. He is sitting in front of the TV watching the news and drinking a beer with his bare feet propped up on the coffee table. To get comfortable, he has had to wedge them around a pile of comic books, three dirty juice glasses, a soggy bowl of Froot Loops, and a blue teddy bear. He is pleased as punch. He says he does not understand what you're mad about as you fling your fancy earrings onto the windowsill and run the hot water into the sink as hard as it will go. You know you are being difficult. He is muttering about PMS. You know you are being childish and ungrateful. He says he does not understand. You wonder how such a sensitive and generally enlightened man can be so stupid. He says he is trying to please you but you are never satisfied. You know you are being just like your mother. He says he just does not understand women. This is the story of his life. What is the story of yours?

He does not understand that women are ambidextrous. No. He does not understand that women are *multi*-dextrous. He has never noticed that you can cook dinner, pour apple juice, feed the cat, drink coffee, talk on the phone to your best friend who is depressed and needs you, set the table, stop the crying over a bumped elbow, wipe up the spilled apple juice, break a red popsicle perfectly in half, and pay the paperboy all at the same time. He has never noticed that you are miraculous and without you he would die.

But Gordon is trying and Joanna is working. Or trying to. She is at her drafting table with the studio door open because, despite or due to all those years with Esther, she too has developed an aversion to closed doors. She cannot help but listen to the sounds of Gordon and Samuel in the basement, laughing over the laundry, then the two of them traipsing up the stairs and rummaging around the kitchen for lunch. Why do they have to be so noisy? Why are they always singing? She is happy that they are happy together but why can't they do it quietly?

She grits her teeth and peers at her new collage which is called *A Fashion Statement*. She has cut out a series of anatomical engravings from the nineteenth century, medical drawings of body parts (heads, hands, arms, legs, feet) and skeletons (skulls, spinal columns, rib cages, breast-bones, clavicles, femurs, scapulae). She has also clipped various articles of clothing from *Vogue* and other fancy fashion magazines. She has cut all of these illustrations into their individual parts. She is just starting the final assembly on a large black sheet of illustration board. She will do the accessories last, real earrings, a necklace, a small embroidered handkerchief tucked behind a rib bone. Gordon and Samuel are singing "Frère Jacques."

She grits her teeth harder and tries to concentrate. She will paste that pink silk jacket right beside that rib cage. Gordon stands in the doorway wanting to know how much fabric softener he's supposed to put in.

She will paste that bowler hat right beside that skull. Samuel needs some calamine lotion for his mosquito bites.

She will paste that lime-green velvet catsuit right beside that full-length front-view skeleton. Gordon can't find the cheese.

She will paste those paisley boxer shorts right between those two femurs. Samuel is in the doorway again, doing his Dracula imitation.

She will paste that ecru lace camisole right beside that breastbone. Gordon wants to know if she's hungry, will she have lunch with them too?

No.

No.

No.

She will paste that purple high heel right beside that ankle bone if it kills her. Why can't they just leave her alone?

Samuel comes to the doorway again, tiptoeing this time, whispering, telling her that he is going to be quiet and leave her alone now, forever and ever.

Which of course is not what she wants either.

94. Green

THE COLOUR OF the back step of your parents' house, a back step big enough for a tea party with all your dolls, a circus of stuffed animals, or a whole farm with a dozen plastic cows and thirteen white rabbits, a back step for long hot summer afternoons with a can of water and a fat paintbrush and you paint it for hours, the clear water making the faded green shiny just like new again, but you can never keep up with the sun, and by the time you are done painting one board the last one has gone dry again, drab, the way rocks sparkling in the streambed have turned back grey by the time you get them home in your hot little hands, so you give up painting and practise instead with your hula hoop which is also green around your skinny waist.

The colour of the back step of your parents' house, a back step big enough for sulking on through long adolescent August afternoons spent sitting on the verge of tears over *Doctor Zhivago* spread open on your lap, so full of snow and sadness that you feel closer to Lara trekking through the tundra for love than you do to anyone you have ever met in your real life and you are memorizing Zhivago's poems until you remember with disgust that your life is as stupid and meaningless as this back step in suburbia and you will never have anyone to recite poetry to anyway, so you lean your head against the green railing, but even weeping is not as romantic as it should be and your face is all covered with hot tears and green snot.

The colour of the tender new leaves on the mock orange bush in front of your kitchen window which you stare at every morning in May with the seven o'clock sun on them and every morning they are a bit bigger, a bit greener, and by June the white flowers will have bloomed, filling the kitchen with their lush sweet fragrance coming in through the screens on a leisurely breeze. Sometimes when you look at the green leaves, you are poured full of the pleasure and promise of spring, new life, new chances, hope, happiness, all of that. But other times you are overcome by a curdling green despair (green, the colour of envy, poison, monsters, death, and gangrene) so paralysing that you imagine you will never again be able to raise your body from this sturdy brown chair. Last night you planted a dozen oxalis bulbs around the base of the bush but you have no faith in them, those shrivelled brown blobs buried now in the warm black earth and your son is helping, darting around with his plastic watering can and the glossy seed catalogue, trying to imagine what they will look like. He is skeptical too, asking, "But how does it work?" When you say, "I'm not very good at this sort of thing, they'll probably never grow," he says, "Don't worry, Mommy, of course they'll grow. Look, they're magic, they're growing already!" You know this cannot possibly be true but still you get down on your hands and knees and peer fiercely at the wet black dirt, praying for green. By this morning, of course, he has forgotten all about them but you are still praying, silently, suddenly, unbearably brimming with stubborn green faith and tender green fear.

95. Salt

MUCH AS JOANNA cannot always make up her mind about God, she frequently believes in the story of Lot's wife. Belief, she figures, is like memory: selective, apocryphal, juggled and jury-rigged to meet the current circumstance. This could be perhaps construed as cynicism. She is no cynic but she knows that as far as the truth goes, there is no bottom line. Truth is not like the Gold Standard or Greenwich Mean Time: there is no absolute against which all else can be accurately measured. She has never held a gold bar in her hand. She has never been to Greenwich, nor even thought of going. And if she knew the truth, surely she would tell it.

She recalls the story of Lot's wife from Sunday School. The cities of Sodom and Gomorrah had become so wicked that God decided to destroy them. Lot lived in Sodom and did not want to leave. But when the fire and brimstone began to fall, he fled, along with his wife and their two daughters. Joanna imagines that brimstone must be something like lava. Despite being warned not to, Lot's wife turned to look back upon the burning cities. She was then turned into a pillar of salt.

salt *n.* 1. sodium chloride, NaCl, a white, crystalline mineral with a characteristic taste, found in seawater, natural beds, etc., and used for preserving and seasoning food. 2. a chemical compound derived from an acid by replacing hydrogen, wholly or partly, with a metallic element or an electropositive radical. 3. that which lends liveliness or piquancy to something; pungent humour or wit.

Joanna can understand Lot's wife. Most people think she was just being greedy, not wanting to lose her house, her barn, her animals, all the luxuries of life in the big city. But Joanna can understand the need to look back. How else to catch sight of the future without first making peace with the past? How else to be saved without knowing full well what you are being saved from?

Perhaps Lot's wife was just an ordinary woman, middle-aged, slightly overweight, greying hair trimmed and curled, an apron tied around her waist, a damp dishtowel draped over her shoulder. Perhaps she was simply loath to abandon all she had accumulated, unwilling to walk obediently away from her nice kitchen, her crockery, curtains, knick-knacks, and a pot of red geraniums in the window. Perhaps Lot's wife, like most people, was simply afraid of change.

Joanna feels sorry for Lot's wife, the poor woman gone all white and grainy for one simple mistake, the mistake perhaps that everyone makes, the mistake of nostalgia, the way memory will always make the best or the worst of it and knows no middle ground. The poor woman is not even known by her name, only remembered as Lot's wife, as if she had no mind, no dreams, no life of her own.

Most people know the story of Lot's wife but they are wrong to think it ended there, with that legendary pillar of salt. They don't know the story's epilogue which, generally speaking, was not discussed in Sunday School. After Lot got away and got settled in a cave with his two daughters, they proceeded to get him drunk on wine and sleep with him on consecutive nights. They did this because there were no other available men. Their time had come to reproduce. Their biological clocks were booming. They assumed that the task of continuing the human race had fallen squarely to them. They both became pregnant. The oldest daughter gave birth to Moab who became father of the Moabites. The younger daughter bore Benammi, father of the Ammonites. These daughters, like their mother but unlike their progeny, shall remain forever nameless.

Is this a reversal of the practice of changing the names to protect the innocent? In this case, have the names been eliminated in an attempt to protect the guilty? Are these three women, Lot's greedy or nostalgic wife and his incestuous or altruistic daughters, guilty or innocent? Are they nameless because their lives were too trivial to commemorate or because their crimes were too horrible to contemplate? This is like the photos in *True Detective* magazine where the eyes of the criminals and victims alike are blocked out by a solid black bar so you can never know who they really are, can barely even tell them apart, could not recognize them even if you met them on the street.

Perhaps Lot's wife was the original salt of the earth, that pillar having been dissolved in a warm rain and then leached silently into the fertile black soil. Or perhaps that pillar was a nasty reminder to all women, an obelisk to all their imaginary crimes and the punishments they have endured, to the fact that they are best known for who they have attached themselves to: daughter, wife, mother (preferably of sons who will go on to make a name for themselves), a memorial to all the nameless women recognized in retrospect only by the men who have come into or out of them. Perhaps the story of Lot's wife is another subtle way of rubbing salt into the wounds of women, all women, ordinary women everywhere.

96. Street

JOANNA AND SAMUEL are standing at the intersection of James and Lawrence Streets downtown. It is three o'clock on an icy pre-Christmas Saturday afternoon. They are standing on the northwest corner in front of the Bank of Montreal. On the southeast corner is the usual weekend market, pared down now to its winter incarnation: five or six stalls at irregular intervals along the sidewalk, the bundled-up vendors huddled behind tables of apples mostly, also homemade cider, bread, cheese, hand-knit sweaters, mittens, toques, and skating socks in all sizes. The vendors are frost-bitten but cheerful, bagging purchases and making change, their breath on the winter air like fleeting white clouds or those speech balloons which come out of comic-strip characters' mouths.

One block further east, Lawrence Street ends at the lake where the Bruce Island Ferry labours through the shifting open channel in the ice. Joanna and Samuel, in their winter coats with their hoods up, are holding hands and stamping their feet, waiting for the light to turn green, waiting to cross the street to Gordon who is standing with his hands deep in the pockets of his down-filled parka on the other side of the intersection in front of Canada Trust. They are all going to Morrison's for hot chocolate with marshmallows. They will share a huge plate of fresh-cut french fries and then Samuel will have a dish of vanilla ice cream for dessert. He likes ice cream best in the winter because, he says, it tastes the way snow looks.

The light changes. They walk across the street waving. Samuel strains away from Joanna's firm hand but she holds on tight. When they reach Gordon, he tugs his bare hands from his pockets and hugs Samuel to him. He kisses Joanna on both rosy cheeks and brushes back the stray curls which have sprung out of her hood. They turn and walk up James Street with Samuel between them, his left hand tucked warmly into Gordon's parka pocket, his right into Joanna's.

Coming sideways towards them down Lawrence Street are Lewis and Wanda. They look like any ordinary unhappy couple. When Lewis sees Joanna and her family, he deflates even further with a long sigh and grits his perfect teeth with, Joanna imagines, miserable envy and the full force of seven years' worth of regret.

The first thing that makes Joanna realize this is a dream is the fact that, despite the heavy Saturday traffic, the amiable crowds of Christmas shoppers with many excited children in tow, and the cluster of carollers assembled on the northeast corner of the intersection, this scene takes place in utter silence.

The second thing that makes Joanna realize this is a dream is the fact that, although she does not actually see Lewis and Wanda, she knows they are there. It is as though she is simultaneously in her body walking down that street and also a hovering entity having an out-of-body experience which enables her to observe the whole scene from above. She is both character in and omniscient narrator of this moment.

This dream becomes a recurring well-rehearsed waking fantasy from which Joanna invariably derives great comfort. She plays it out in her mind over and over again, slow motion, fast forward, rewind, pause, making minute climatic adjustments, tiny but crucial scene and costume changes. She puts this fantasy through an infinite number of precise permutations in the pursuit of its perfection.

It is clear and cold. It is snowing. It is snowing lightly. It is snowing heavily.

Carollers stand on the corner with their songbooks open. A Salvation Army soldier stands on the corner with a bell and a clear plastic bubble filling up with money. Santa Claus himself stands on the corner with a big sack of presents from which he pulls candy canes for all the wide-eyed children.

She has her hood up against the cold wind. She has her hood down and her hair blows beautifully in the wind. She has on a blue beret with matching scarf and mittens.

Gordon hugs Samuel. Gordon lifts Samuel off his delighted feet and holds him high in the air. Gordon lifts Samuel off his delighted feet and plops him square on his shoulders for a piggyback ride.

Gordon kisses her left cheek. Gordon kisses her right cheek, her forehead, her chin, her mittened hand. Gordon kisses her full on the mouth, tongue and all.

The street is crowded with shoppers and traffic. The street is empty with silence and expectation. The street is suddenly somewhere she has never been before.

97. King

JOANNA DID NOT understand why they had a Queen with no King. There was Philip, of course, but he was only a Prince. Most of what she knew about Princes came from fairy tales and fables: *The Frog Prince, The Prince and the Pauper, Prince Charming, Robin Hood: The Prince of Thieves*. Most of what she knew about Kings came from the story of King Edward VIII who had abdicated his throne after only eleven months to marry Mrs. Wallis Simpson, a fashionable American divorcée. This took place in 1936, eighteen years before Joanna was born. But over time and often told, this story had lost none of its love-conquers-all lustre. Compared to this true royal romance, the fabled escapades of Prince Charming and the others were soon enough revealed to be unrealistic and unsatisfying.

Even Esther (who might have been expected to consider the King an old fool and Mrs. Wallis Simpson a slut) was obscurely pleased by the story. Apparently it proved something which she had suspected all along, although it was never clear exactly what. Perhaps that love was stronger than power. Or perhaps (Joanna will think later, not kindly) that people, men especially, were stupid, divorcées were dangerous, and desire could destroy your life.

Esther was also pleased (more plainly) when people said she looked a lot like the Queen. It was Elizabeth II they meant, who had been crowned the year before Joanna was born. Joanna knew that Elizabeth was Edward VIII's niece but was completely confused by the complicated royal lineage and did not try to figure out how Elizabeth was descended (or ascended) from Elizabeth I, Queen Victoria, the several Georges, the many Edwards, the ancient Williams, Henrys, Charleses, and Harolds. The Queen Mother appeared frequently but she did not appear to have a name of her own and what had become of the Queen Father?

Later Joanna will be surprised to learn that Elizabeth, at the time of her coronation, was only twenty-seven years old. Other things had happened that year too. The Korean War ended, Joseph Stalin died, the Rosenbergs were executed, Mount Everest was conquered by Sir Edmund Hillary and Sherpa Tenzing Norgay, and John Fitzgerald Kennedy married Jacqueline Lee Bouvier.

However Elizabeth had ended up Queen and whatever had happened before or since, Esther was obviously flattered by the perceived resemblance. Joanna could not imagine why. Every year on Christmas Day they watched the Queen's Address on television while the turkey sizzled in the kitchen. She was a short pale woman with an old-fashioned hairdo that never changed. Her thin high voice droned on, a shrill tense warble of words which did not seem to change much from year to year either. She did have nice clothes. She looked tired. No wonder.

Every year after her little speech, Esther turned to Joanna and asked, "Do you remember the time you saw the Queen?"

Joanna said, "Yes." But in fact what she remembered was the crowd, the car, the tiny flag in her hand which she was waving madly while trying to see around the large woman in front of her. She was only five years old. The Queen had passed through their city that summer, having come to Canada to open the St. Lawrence Seaway. Joanna did not remember seeing the Queen's face at all, even though Esther ever since had insisted that she, Elizabeth, had looked right at them and smiled.

The former King Edward VIII, who had become Duke of Windsor the day after his abdication, died in his Paris home in 1972, ten days after a visit from his niece, the Queen. By this time he was seventy-seven years old and she was forty-six. Joanna was eighteen, in her final year of high school, and far too engrossed in her own stories of love and power to spare much thought to these fabled old figures living out their fates on the other side of the world. They were no more significant now to her life (or to modern life in general, it seemed) than King

Midas of the Golden Touch or the Red and White Queens of *Alice in Wonderland*. They were as ancient and irrelevant to her as the poem she had studied in English class earlier that spring: *"My name is Ozymandias, king of kings:/ Look on my works, ye Mighty, and despair!"/Nothing beside remains. Round the decay/Of that colossal wreck, boundless and bare/The lone and level sands stretch far away.*

98. Cheese

"SAY CHEESE!"

Clarence was taking a picture of Esther and Joanna. Actually he was taking a picture of his new car, a 1958 Ford Fairlane, four-door, two-tone brown and white. The film in the camera was black and white so the car will come out looking two-tone grey and white. Esther and Joanna are posing beside it. For some reason Clarence has driven to the parking lot of the paper mill for this photo session. He has parked in the far northwest corner which is deserted. Joanna is sitting on the shiny brown (grey) hood of the car. Esther is standing beside her on the driver's side, holding her in place, smiling. Esther did not think they needed a new car but her disapproval, his stubbornness, the previous month of debate and disagreement, are not in the picture.

"Say cheese!"

Esther took the next two photographs: Clarence and Joanna in the same pose outside the car, then Clarence sitting inside the car in the driver's seat, right hand on the steering wheel, left arm angled jauntily out the window. The top of his face is in black shadow. Behind him there is a dark blurry shape which may or may not be Joanna bouncing around in the back seat. They are all dressed up. They have come directly from the car lot. The paper mill is a large dirty complicated building in shades of grey behind them.

"Say cheese!"

Clarence took one more picture: the car empty in the parking lot, its grill like a wide smiling mouth, its double headlights like compound eyes. Even the licence plate number is clear: H91792.

Afterwards they got back into the car and went for a long drive in the country with all the windows open.

"Say cheese!"

Joanna was taking a picture of Henry and his friend Eddie from the band. They were all at a Sunday afternoon barbecue at Eddie's house. Actually Eddie did not live in a house. He lived in a converted garage behind a house. Actually they were not eating much although there were salads on the picnic table and burgers on the grill. Mostly they were drinking beer and horsing around. Henry and Eddie are posing in the middle of a very large mud puddle. They are both wearing mirrored sunglasses. Henry is holding his bass guitar. Eddie is holding an axe, a real axe, strumming the silver blade which rests on his right thigh. He is twisting his face out of shape and making heavy-metal guitar sounds. Henry is yelling, "An axe! It's an axe! Do you get it?"

Then Henry hands his guitar and his glasses to Eddie and throws himself facedown spread-eagled into the puddle.

"Say cheese!"

He comes up with his fists raised. Muddy water streams from his long beard, his forehead, his nose. Everyone is roaring and applauding and handing him more beer. There is no telling what Henry might do next.

"Say cheese!"

Joanna was trying to take a picture of Lewis. She had only one other picture of him, taken before they fell in love, taken when he was playing baseball in the park. In this picture he is a barely recognizable person in a white baseball cap, navy T-shirt and cutoffs, standing in left field squinting at the sky where presumably there is a baseball. Now she was trying to get a picture of him lying naked after sex, reading a magazine in her bed. But the floor creaks, he hears her coming and throws the sheet over his head.

"Say cheese!"

He refuses to be photographed, he says, in such a compromising position. She says what does he think she's going to do with it—blackmail him? Send it to the newspaper? Have it blown up and framed to hang over the couch? She only wanted the picture to look at privately after he had gone home to Wanda. They argued until she put the camera away.

Later he gave her an old passport photo in which he looked like a terrorist or someone being hunted by a terrorist. She wore it in a locket around her neck. Until one day he said what if she got in a car accident? What if the locket sprang open and the doctors and nurses saw the picture? She did not argue. She took off the locket, took out the picture, and dropped it in the bathroom garbage can. He was hurt.

Afterwards she regretted it and picked the picture out from among the dirty tissues, waxy Q-tips, and one semen-filled condom. She put it back in the locket but did not wear it. She kept it in her jewellery box but did not tell him.

"Say cheese!"

Gordon is taking a picture of Joanna and Samuel. Samuel is one day old. Joanna is exhausted, sore, sweaty, and her hair is a mess. She has just returned from the room where she has to have a sitz bath four times a day. She has just seen herself in a full-length mirror and wept. She does not want to have her picture taken. But Gordon has bought an expensive new camera and loaded it with fast film so he doesn't have to use the flash which might hurt the baby's eyes or scare the hell out of him. She arranges herself in the rumpled hospital bed. She holds Samuel in her hands and smiles down at him. He yawns. Her flabby belly and her big hard breasts are not in the picture. Neither are the small red forceps marks on Samuel's temples.

"Say cheese!"
  "Say cheese!"
  "Say cheese!"

Joanna takes many pictures of Samuel with the expensive new camera. In the first few months it seems that every day he does something new and notable. She even takes pictures of him when he's sleeping, the way he sprawls, curls, smiles, frowns, covers his little face with his little hands. It is as if she would like to take pictures of his dreams. She spends a fortune on film and processing. Often she takes sequences of photographs, four, five, or six shots of one movement. From frame to frame, the differences are minuscule: left arm up, right arm down, eyes open, eyes closed, mouth smiling, mouth frowning, mouth working up to a full-scale howl. Afterwards, in the photo album, these are like stills lifted from a never-ending film. She does not make the mistake of thinking that she will remember this. Instead she documents every detail of his development. She knows that these are things she will some day need to know.

"Say cheese!"

Joanna is taking a picture of Samuel on his first day of school. Gordon has already gone to work. Samuel is posing shyly in front of the house. He is wearing light grey pants and a red T-shirt. He is carrying a Teenage Mutant Ninja Turtles backpack. He has recently had his first professional haircut. His luxurious curls are now in an envelope in Joanna's studio. She has thought about using them in a collage but the idea seems somehow barbaric, cannibalistic. With his hair short and neatly combed, he looks like a real boy, sturdy, stalwart, and brave. He also looks too little to be going anywhere.

Afterwards Joanna will walk him the three blocks to the school and leave him there crying in the classroom with twenty other four- and five-year-olds also crying or wanting to.

Afterwards she will spend the morning on the front step drinking too much coffee, watching the clock, and worrying. She will get out the old photo album where there is a picture of her on her first day of school in 1959.

"Say cheese!"

Esther took this picture. Clarence had already gone to work. Joanna is posing shyly on the front step. She is wearing a flowered sleeveless short summer dress, white ankle socks, and black patent leather shoes which she loves because they have straps and gold buckles and they click on the concrete. She has a barrette in her hair and a small book in her right hand. As she looks at this photograph, her eyes automatically compensate for the fact that it is black and white. As she sees it, the book is red, the barrette is blue, the front step is green, and her dress is mostly pink.

She does not remember what happened next: the walk, the school, the classroom, the crying or not. She cannot imagine what Esther did afterwards. It would seem that the photographs you would most like to look at, five, ten, fifteen, twenty, now thirty years later, are those which no one thought to take at the time.

99. Blossom

GETTING OUT OF the yard in the morning to go to school and back into it at four o'clock when she came home meant Joanna had to run the delphinium gauntlet. They grew tall on either side of the front gate, their hooded blossoms purple, blue, and white, bobbing and humming with full-bodied bumblebees deep inside. The bees buzzed out fat and furious as Joanna ran past waving her arms and hollering and the white picket gate snapped shut behind her. She was never stung, not even once. Later she will learn that although Esther called them delphiniums, in fact these living beehives were really monkshoods.

Esther loved flowers of all kinds, no matter what they were called. There were begonias in pots on the front step, tiger lilies and baby's breath in beds along the side of the house, hollyhocks, dahlias, irises, chrysanthemums, peonies, phlox, and gladioli in the garden at the back. At one corner of the house there was a large bleeding heart. Penny and Pamela showed Joanna how to open one of the hearts to reveal the upright stamen so that it looked, they said, like a naked lady in the bathtub.

Each spring there was the ritual of the bedding plants to be performed. Clarence drove Esther to the nursery east of town where she spent hours browsing and choosing and browsing some more while he paced and Joanna waited, reading, in the car. They drove back home with the trunk open to make room for many wooden flats of small but sturdy plants: forget-me-nots, impatiens, marigolds, nasturtiums, bachelor's buttons, portulaca, petunias, snapdragons, and salvia. Which always made Joanna think of saliva (how gross) and Sally Delvecchio in her Grade Six class who always spat when she talked and so they called her "Sally Saliva" behind her back.

Esther put the plants into the well-prepared earth immediately, no matter how long it took, no matter how late it was, so that some years she was still down on her knees in the dirt as the dusk fell upon her.

Although Esther tended all her flowers with equal and ardent dedication, the roses were her special favourites. "I have to admit it," she often said, "I love the roses more than the rest." As if they were children and she were finally confessing to a shameful favouritism, loving one more than the others. Each year she added at least one new variety to the bed in front.

Thanks to her mother's insistent coaching, even Joanna knew their curious names by heart: Circus, Fashion, Mischief, Ballerina, Prosperity, Vanity, King's Ransom, Joseph's Coat, Blue Girl, Red Devil, Lavender Lassie. Some were named after famous people: Queen Elizabeth, Don Juan, Mister Lincoln, Maria Callas, and John F. Kennedy. Others were named after people she had never heard of: Constance Spry, Marjorie Fair, Adolph Horstmann, Wendy Cussons, Grandpa Dickson, and Just Joey. Joanna could only imagine who these people might have been and what they might have done to warrant having a rose named after them. Her mother, she suspected, would have given anything to be so honoured.

All summer long Esther babied them, fed them, fertilized them, and waged war against the aphids, leafhoppers, spider mites, thrips, black spot, cankers, mildew, rust, and root-knot nematodes which threatened them. She was always watering them, spraying them, deadheading or disbudding them, removing suckers and pruning precisely. In the fall she prepared them for winter by mounding soil and leaves around the crowns. Once they were safely tucked in, she let the snow pile up on top of them because, despite what you might think, it provided the best insulation. So she told Joanna every time they walked past them and she had to resist yet again the urge to clear the snow away even though she knew better. Joanna came to think of the wintering roses as little babies sleeping under the snow.

Esther knew the hardiness zones of the whole country the way other people knew the time zones. There was a coloured map in each of her gardening books, the country divided into nine zones according to climatic conditions. Esther often bemoaned the difficulty of living in Zone 2 (or 3, depending on which map she consulted). Due to very cold winters and a very short growing season, many of the flowers she longed to grow remained forever out of reach.

One April Sunday afternoon when Esther had her gardening books spread all over the kitchen table, Joanna suggested they try a plant she had spotted in the current seed catalogue. She was only looking over Esther's shoulder because she was bored. The flower was called Bird of Paradise, an exotic orange, blue, purple, and white blossom on the end of a three-foot straight stem. Esther pointed out that it would not grow in their zone. Joanna thought they could try it anyway, just for fun. Esther scoffed. Whether at the notion of paradise or fun or the naïvety of believing in the possibility of either, Joanna was not sure. Esther put the books and the catalogues back in the bottom of Clarence's closet and went on with preparing the roast beef for supper.

Looking through the pile of gardening books later (looking perhaps for some proof that living in Zone 2 was not as hopeless as it seemed), Joanna found a small slim volume called *The Language of Flowers*. It was a modern reissue of a book originally published in 1884 by a woman named Kate Greenaway. It contained many delicate drawings in pastel colours of cherubic children in straw hats and white tunics. These androgynous children were dancing and singing with flowers in their hair and hands. Some of them had wings. On other pages there were drawings of white-skinned women in bonnets and long dresses, also white. These women were portrayed in various limp poses beside a stream, at the seashore, by the garden gate. There were no men in this book, only women and children and many fine flowers.

Joanna could not imagine how her practical hard-hearted mother had come to own such a book. There was no inscription but perhaps it had been a gift. From whom? From Clarence? Not likely.

The text was an alphabetical list of flowers and what they symbolized, the messages they carried. Marigolds meant grief, nasturtiums meant patriotism, peonies meant bashfulness, and there was something called Love-lies-bleeding which meant *Hopeless, not heartless.* Esther's favourite, the rose, in general symbolized love. But there were variations within the theme. Particular types of roses carried particular messages. *Grace. Variety. Simplicity. Capricious beauty. Tranquillize my anxiety. Winter. Age. Pride. Pleasure and pain. Jealousy. War. Secrecy. Love is dangerous. War of Roses. Crown of Roses. Crown of Thorns. Death is preferable to loss of innocence.*

Later Joanna will come to appreciate the treachery of flowers, grown out of love, no doubt, yes, usually by women. But most often given by men out of a desire to exorcize guilt, to exercise power, to expedite attraction, to extol their virtues and insist upon themselves, to apologize for any indiscretion, major or minor, as if a dozen red roses (long-stemmed, hot-house, over-priced) could as well expunge an illicit affair as having forgotten to take out the garbage again. Flowers as extortion, exculpation, expectorant. For a time all flowers will strike her as funereal.

Later still she will plant and grow her own flowers at her own house with her own husband and child beside her. At first every time she kneels down in the dirt she will hear her mother's voice in her head, telling her that she is not a gardener, she is doing it all wrong, she is a fool to think she can grow those flowers even here in Zone 5. Just who does she think she is?

But soon enough the flowers do grow. Their brilliant blossoms fill the beds and the boxes at the kitchen window. Sitting inside at the kitchen table early in the morning, she watches the flowers in the window boxes as if they were fish in an aquarium or flames in a fire-place. Esther always said she would be a late bloomer, meaning her small breasts, her slim hips, her fear that she would always look like a boy.

At last she can appreciate these blossoms for what they are: pretty, fragrant, voiceless gifts. At last she can extract the excellent comfort to be found in their beauty, which is mindless, indifferent, stubborn, and still.

100. Afraid

IT IS ONE of those days when Joanna finds herself repeatedly moved to the sharp verge of hot tears. A radio news story about a crippled woman in a car accident dragged from the wreckage to safety by her Labrador retriever, Blue, sets her eyes stinging. She is waiting for the major winter storm which has allegedly been on its way for two days. Toronto (that evil city) has come to a snowbound standstill. The highways to and from are closed. Tractor-trailers are jack-knifing all over the place, spilling citrus fruit, TV sets, and half-dead chickens into the snow. People are abandoning their cars on the roadsides. What do they do next? Where do they go? Do they just strike out on foot into the blizzard like a scene from *Doctor Zhivago*? Where do they end up? You never get to hear the end of these adventure stories. It's like hearing sirens raging through the city in the middle of the night and then you never hear what happened or to whom, unless they died. Anything less than death is left to your aggravated imagination.

Now the radio announcer's voice thrills with the prospect of bad weather. Joanna too is energized by the possibility of being snowed in. Perhaps this is the true mark of a Canadian: that only a good old-fashioned blizzard, with freezing rain, gale-force winds, and three feet of snow, can really get your adrenaline going. Perhaps it is bad weather that keeps the country together. Clarence is bound to call later—he will have seen their storm on the weather channel. He will be calling to see if they're all right.

Joanna is searching for the candles in case the power goes off. Samuel is curled up on the couch with the Walkman on. He looks rapt and angelic, transported.

Everything is closing early in anticipation of the storm. Gordon will be home soon. Joanna remembers early school closures when she was a child, the excitement of being home in the middle of a weekday afternoon, and sometimes Esther let her put on her pyjamas and then made her a big bowl of buttered popcorn while Joanna knelt at the picture window and watched the weather like a movie. Once when Clarence got off work early, he stopped for chocolate milk shakes on his way home. Apparently the Dairy Queen intended to weather the storm. They sucked on their shakes while the snow piled up in the street. When the power went off just at suppertime, Esther got out the candles and Joanna and her father stood on the front step peering through the snow to see how far the blackout stretched. People skimmed by on Skidoos, waving. Then they had baloney sandwiches, potato chips, and carrot sticks by candlelight. When the lights came back on, they were all deflated somehow and the party just leaked away. Esther did the dishes, Clarence did the cryptogram, and Joanna did her homework.

Suddenly, in the midst of this memory, she misses her mother intensely. Her throat is swollen and tender with unshed tears.

The snow is finally starting. Samuel abandons the Walkman and peers out the kitchen window. The flakes are falling straight down, slowly, like weightless white coins. "How deep will it get? How long will it last?" he asks. "Will it cover the windows, the whole house, the world?"

He wants to go outside and stand in it. He wants to build a snowman, a castle, a fort. Joanna likes snow too, but as she helps him pull on his snow pants and zip up his parka, she thinks about having to shovel out tomorrow and she groans. Perhaps this is a true sign of having become a grown-up: she now sees snow as another chore instead of as an adventure, a treasure, a gift from the sky.

Samuel is out the door ahead of her. The snow falls into the porch. The whole neighbourhood is muffled, breathless, still. All the windows are yellow squares in the sturdy warm houses in the early winter twilight. Joanna is on the verge of tears again, at the sight of Samuel's face turned up to the sky, his mouth open, catching snowflakes on his tongue. He sees her stricken face and asks, "What's the matter, Mommy? Are you scared? Don't you like the snow?"

She says, "Of course I do, I love it, I'm not scared at all," laughing, lying, and the snowflakes fall into her mouth.

Joanna is an optimist, generally hopeful about the future, despite all evidence to the contrary. Often it is this stubborn optimism which sends her to the shimmering brink of tears. Some days she is propelled by a sense that any minute now everything will be all right. Some days she is scared to death.

The splendid terrors of daily life are like the power of gravity: invisible and inevitable, infinitely more dangerous than other more apparent enemies. Also reliable, dependable, and undeniable.

gravity *n.* 1. the state or condition of being grave; esp. *a)* dignity or sedateness of conduct or demeanour; earnestness, *b)* ominous quality; danger or threat, *c)* seriousness of a situation. 2. weight; heaviness; authority. 3. terrestrial gravitation; force that tends to draw all bodies in the earth's sphere toward the center of the earth.

Only a fool would presume to be fearless, weightless, free. There are many things in life worth being afraid of. The trick lies in knowing what they are. There are fears you will grow out of and fears you will grow into. No matter what kind of life you are living, there is the dialectic of faith and fear which will turn you inside out eventually and then you will know how to begin.

Gordon's car creeps round the corner. Samuel stands at the end of the driveway, waving his father home. Joanna waves too but she might as well be teetering on the edge of a crater on the moon, on the shores of the Sea of Tranquility perhaps, which even now is filling up with snow.

Acknowledgments

The Kent-Rosanoff Word Association Test originally appeared in their article, "A study of association in insanity," in *American Journal of Insanity* (1910).

Grateful acknowledgment is made for permission to reprint the following copyrighted works:

Definitions in 83. LOUD from *The Synonym Finder* by J. I. Rodale. Reprinted by permission of Warner Books, New York.

Two cryptograms from *Dell Crossword Yearbook,* Winter 1991. © 1991 by Dell Magazines, Inc. Used by permission of Dell Crossword Yearbook. All rights reserved.

Excerpt from *Mastering Effective English,* Tressler-Lewis, Third Edition, 1961. Used by permission.

Selection from *501 French Verbs* by Christopher Kendris, Third Edition. Copyright © 1990 by Barron's Educational Series, Inc. Reprinted by permission of Barron's Educational Series, Inc., Hauppauge, New York.

Selections from *What Counts: The Complete Harper's Index* by Harper's Magazine. Copyright © 1988 by Harper's Magazine. Reprinted by permission of Henry Holt and Company, Inc.

Excerpt from "One Hundred Ways To Save Our Environment" by Harvey Schachter in *The Kingston Whig-Standard*. By permission of The Kingston Whig-Standard.

Selections in 99. BLOSSOM from *Kate Greenaway's Language of Flowers*, Avenel Books, Barre Publishing, New York.

Historical information was verified in *The 20th Century: The Pictorial History* (Hamlyn Publishing Group, London, 1990) and *Timelines* by Paul Dickson (Addison-Wesley, 1990).

9. MOUNTAIN appeared in different form as a story called "Still Life With Lover" in *paragraph*, Volume 13, Number 1, 1991. Six other chapters have been previously published as excerpts in slightly different form: 14. HAND in *Quarry*, Volume 41, Number 3, Summer 1992; 16. FRUIT in *The Moosehead Anthology*, Number 13, 1992; 30. WINDOW in *What!*, Numbers 31 & 32, Fall 1992; 45. TROUBLE in *Prairie Fire*, Volume 13, Number 2, Summer 1992; 60. BIBLE and 95. SALT in *Quarry*, Volume 42, Number 3, Fall 1993.

I would like to thank the Ontario Arts Council for their generous financial support. For the many other forms of support given during the writing of this book, I would also like to thank Carla Douglas and Jim Kane, Bella Pomer, Colleen Dempsey, John Metcalf, Michael Carbert, Nora Gold, and Walter Cipin of Wayfarer Books. I am especially thankful to George Schoemperlen, my father, and Alexander, my son, for their patient and sustaining love.